"I'm here to care for my sister's babies.

"I already love them. I did from the moment I learned they were coming."

"I can take care of them. I want you to leave," he said.

"Nathan, be reasonable. You need help."

He faced Maisie with his arms crossed over his chest. The moon came out from behind the clouds, bathing his face in its cold light. "It can't be you."

"Why not?"

"Because every time I look at you, I see Annie. I don't want you here."

The bitterness in his clipped words left Maisie speechless. He walked away into the darkness.

"But they're all I have left of her," she whispered as a deep ache filled her chest. "Please don't make me leave them."

She felt Charlie lick her fingers. He whined as if he knew she had been hurt by Nathan's words. She dropped down to hold the big dog close and draw some comfort against the new grief she felt.

How could she change Nathan's mind?

After thirty-five years as a nurse, **Patricia Davids** hung up her stethoscope to become a full-time writer. She enjoys spending her free time visiting her grandchildren, doing some long-overdue yard work and traveling to research her story locations. She resides in Wichita, Kansas. Pat always enjoys hearing from her readers. You can visit her online at patriciadavids.com.

Growing up on a farm, **Jocelyn McClay** enjoyed livestock and pursued a degree in agriculture. She met her husband while weight lifting in a small town—he "spotted" her. After thirty years in business management, they moved to an acreage in southeastern Missouri to be closer to family when their eldest of three daughters made them grandparents. When not writing, she keeps busy hiking, bike riding, gardening, knitting and substitute teaching.

USA TODAY Bestselling Author

PATRICIA DAVIDS

&

JOCELYN McCLAY

An Unexpected Amish Family

2 Uplifting Stories

An Amish Mother for His Twins and
Their Surprise Amish Marriage

LOVE INSPIRED

INSPIRATIONAL ROMANCE

LOVE INSPIRED®

INSPIRATIONAL ROMANCE

Recycling programs for this product may not exist in your area.

ISBN-13: 978-1-335-46066-0

An Unexpected Amish Family

Copyright © 2022 by Harlequin Enterprises ULC

An Amish Mother for His Twins
First published in 2021. This edition published in 2022.
Copyright © 2021 by Patricia MacDonald

Their Surprise Amish Marriage
First published in 2021. This edition published in 2022.
Copyright © 2021 by Jocelyn Ord

For questions and comments about the quality of this book, please contact us at CustomerService@Harlequin.com.

Harlequin Enterprises ULC
22 Adelaide St. West, 41st Floor
Toronto, Ontario M5H 4E3, Canada
www.LoveInspired.com

Printed in U.S.A.

CONTENTS

AN AMISH MOTHER
FOR HIS TWINS

Patricia Davids

This book is dedicated to the wonderful staff of Chapman Valley Manor who have cared for my father, Clarence, during these trying times. My heart is full of gratitude. Thank you.

He healeth the broken in heart,
and bindeth up their wounds.
—*Psalm* 147:3

Chapter One

His head was ready to explode.

Nathan Weaver sat at the kitchen table in his one-room cabin with his hands pressed to his throbbing temples. He had come to Maine to live a quiet life and to forget. For six months he'd done just that. In less than a week his peace was gone. He'd never know solitude again.

Both babies were crying at the top of their lungs in their Moses baskets near his feet. His hound, Buddy, howled in accompaniment. The yellow cat, yowling to be let out, had crawled to the top of his screen door and hung splayed like a pelt on the wall. The kettle's piercing whistle was close to drowning out everything. He closed his eyes and moved his hands to cover his ears. It didn't help.

Buddy stopped howling and started barking a challenge. The abrupt change made Nathan look up. An Amish woman stood outside the screen door. For a moment his heart froze. It wasn't possible.

"Annie?" he croaked.

Was he hallucinating? It couldn't be her. Annie had died in childbirth six days ago.

The woman opened the screen door. His cat launched himself into the night, just missing her head. "Not Annie, Nathan. It's Maisie Schrock."

He blinked hard. Maisie? Annie's twin sister? She was a widow who lived in Missouri caring for their ailing father. What was she doing in Maine?

She gazed inside, an expression of shock on her face. She held a suitcase in her hand. Buddy stopped barking and went to greet her with his tail wagging. The babies continued to cry.

"Annie died." Nathan swallowed against the pain. Saying the words aloud still didn't make it feel real.

"I know. The hospital told me yesterday. I'm so sorry. My sister is with *Gott* now," Maisie said with a catch in her voice. There were tears in her eyes.

Seeing her grief propelled Nathan to his feet. He stepped to the stove and pulled the kettle off the fire. The whistling died away, but the babies kept crying.

"What are you doing here? If you've come for the funeral, it's over." Maisie lived in the tiny Amish settlement near Seymour, Missouri, where he had married her sister last fall.

"I was afraid of that. I'm sorry I wasn't here to share your burden." She focused her attention on the babies. "Boys or girls?"

"One of each."

"Are they hungry?" She crossed the room to kneel beside their Moses baskets. Gifts to Nathan from the hospital staff when they'd learned he didn't have a place for the babies to sleep. Maisie lifted a child to her shoulder and the baby quieted. Buddy, the stray hound that had shown up a few weeks after Nathan arrived in Maine, followed her with his tail wagging.

Nathan raked his hands through his hair. "I don't know what's wrong with them. I tried feeding them, but they wouldn't take much and then they started crying as soon as I put them down."

She stroked the baby's cheek and rocked her gently. "Aw, *liebling*, it's okay."

Liebling. Darling. He used to call Annie that. Before she left him with only a cryptic note a bare two months after their wedding. He still didn't understand why. He took some comfort in knowing she was trying to get back to him before she died. He would have forgiven her and taken her back, but would he have been able to trust her? Or grow to love her again?

Maisie laid her cheek against the baby's fine auburn hair. "*Ach*, you look like your mother. Your poor *mamm*. How you must miss her."

Maisie straightened and wiped her cheeks again. "I think they just want to be held."

She wrapped the blanket snugly around the baby and handed her to Nathan. He took his daughter gingerly, afraid he might somehow damage her with his big coarse hands. Maisie picked up his son, and he quieted in her arms.

Suddenly there was silence in the cabin. The pounding in Nathan's head eased. "What are you doing here?

I only wrote to you yesterday. I think it was yesterday. How did you find me?"

Maisie moved to the beat-up blue sofa he'd claimed from the side of the road where someone had dumped it. The two broken legs had been replaced with rocks. His brown-and-black hound parked himself at her feet.

"Annie sent me the money to come three weeks ago, along with your address. She said she was on her way here to make amends with you. In her letter she said she wanted her babies to grow up in an Amish family, with their father. She regretted leaving you, Nathan."

"Three weeks ago? If she knew where I was why didn't she write or call?"

While he didn't own a cell phone or have a landline in his home, like most Amish he shared a community telephone with neighbors. It was housed in a small building centrally located between the homes. The phone shack contained an answering machine, so his boss and others could leave messages.

Maisie shook her head. "I don't know why she didn't call you."

"I found out five days ago that I was a widower and the father of twins all in one breath when the bishop came with the news that Annie had died in childbirth. Eight months without a word from her. That doesn't feel like she regretted it."

"Leaving you as she did was a terrible thing. I know that, but you must find forgiveness in your heart."

"Must I? Sure, I forgive her." It was easy enough to say the words, but he didn't mean them. Not yet. Maisie knew it, too. He saw it in her expression.

Her eyes softened. "She was coming home to have your babies. She asked me to come and stay for a month or so to help her and you. Of course, I said yes. She knew twins would be lots of work."

"They are."

"But you haven't found anyone to help you."

It was a statement more than a question. He hung his head. He didn't want to depend on anyone. He'd never joined the Amish congregation in New Covenant so he didn't expect help from them. "I can raise them by myself." But could he?

"You don't have to, Nathan. I'm here now. We can get through our loss together."

His wasn't the only grief he had to consider. Maisie had lost a beloved sister. Her twin. The blow must have been devastating, but she was offering to help him, a man her sister couldn't bear to stay married to.

Did Maisie wonder what he had done to drive Annie away from her family and her faith? Did she blame him, as others had? After trying to push these questions out of his mind for months, he suddenly wanted answers.

"Did you know Annie had planned to leave me?"

Maisie glanced at the child she held. "Can we talk about this later? I'm tired and I think they need to be fed."

She looked so much like Annie. She was a painful reminder of the woman he'd loved and lost…twice. A woman who had betrayed her wedding vows and destroyed the love he'd once had for her.

When Annie left him she'd done more than break his heart. She'd taken away his dreams of a family. There was no divorce allowed in his Amish faith. He would have remained married but alone, until his death. That was why he had retreated to the wilds of Maine six months ago. He was used to being alone. He'd been alone his whole life until he'd met Annie.

Nathan belatedly recalled his duty as a host. He couldn't send Maisie away tonight. Unless her driver was waiting outside. "How did you get here?"

"I came on the bus. I was walking this way when a kindly woman stopped and offered me a ride in her car. She said she was a neighbor of yours, Lilly Arnett."

Lilly had a home about three miles down the road. She wasn't Amish but she was a good neighbor. She'd gone out of her way to bring Maisie up to his remote cabin. "Is she still outside?"

"*Nee.* She said she had to get back to do chores. Do you have bottles and formula for them?"

"The hospital sent some supplies when they dismissed the *kinder*. Formula, bottles, diapers, a couple of blankets that the nurse said she wasn't supposed to give away, but she couldn't see sending me home without a way to keep them warm."

"Clearly a woman with a good heart. I'll fix some formula if you will hold…what is his name?" She looked at him.

Nathan hadn't decided yet, for either babe. Annie should have told him what she wanted to call them. Annie should be here taking care of them. Maisie had the same flame-red hair, the same bright green eyes, and freckles across her nose. She even had the same dimples in her cheeks when she smiled. It was painful to see her and know she wasn't the woman he'd married.

He changed the subject. "Would you like some tea or hot chocolate? The water on the stove is hot. There's some bread and blueberry jam in the cupboard."

"I'll fix it. Do you want something?" She got up and settled his son in his free arm.

"Nee." He wasn't hungry.

She crossed her arms and gazed at him with her eyes full of sympathy. "When was the last time you ate?"

"I don't remember."

"Then you should at least have some toast." She went into the corner of the cabin that held a wood-burning cookstove, two cupboards, a sink and an icebox. She located the bread, then put it in the oven to toast. Next, she fixed hot cocoa for herself and opened two small bottles of premade formula the hospital had sent home with Nathan. She had a few bites of toast and a sip of the cocoa, then took the baby from Nathan and sat down to feed him.

Nathan's daughter made short work of her bottle. He glanced over to watch Maisie cooing at his son. Why couldn't it be Annie holding her own baby? Why did it have to be Maisie, who looked like Annie in every way? It was heartbreaking to see her and know she wasn't their mother.

"Don't forget to burp her," Maisie said.

He had forgotten. He took the bottle away from his daughter and shifted her gingerly to his shoulder. She burped twice and then began bobbing her head, looking for more to eat. He settled her in the crook of his arm and let her finish. When the bottle was drained, he looked at Maisie. "Should I burp her again?"

"Ja." She had his son cradled in her arms, gazing at his face, then she put him in his basket. To Nathan's amazement, the baby went straight to sleep.

Maisie turned to Nathan. "I'll put her down if she is finished."

"I think she is." He handed the babe to her and sat back, rubbing his hands on his thighs. Maisie was good with the babies. He wasn't. It was hard to imagine he was now the father of two. Nothing had prepared him for this, but he would manage. He had always managed alone.

He'd built this cabin with his own two hands. He would find a way to raise his children. Annie had at least given him back the dream of having a family. He would be grateful for that when he wasn't so exhausted.

Maisie took his daughter and laid her down. She fussed for a moment but then quieted and went to sleep.

Maisie covered a yawn. Nathan nodded toward the small loft at the far end of the cabin. "There's a bed and extra blankets up there. You're welcome to them."

Maisie scanned the rest of the one-room cabin. "Where will you sleep? I don't want to put you out of your own bed."

"I have a cot in a room down in the barn. I'll sleep there. The barn was here when I bought the place. I slept in it until the cabin was finished. It's comfortable." He didn't like being in the same room with her. She was a distressing reminder of what he'd lost.

"All right. Would you like to talk now?"

Talk about Annie and her death? He suddenly realized he wasn't ready for that. "Tomorrow."

He got up and left the cabin.

Maisie watched Nathan walk out of the house with tired, stumbling steps. She had no idea what to make of him. Like everyone in her community, she wondered what had driven Annie to leave her new husband. Why had her sister stayed away from her family and the people who loved her? From Maisie, the person who knew her best in the whole world?

The answers to those questions may have died with Annie, but Maisie wasn't ready to give up. Nathan had to have some idea of what went wrong in their marriage. Maisie needed to know the truth from him now that she couldn't learn it from Annie.

After making sure there was enough formula to see the babies through the night, she walked outside. She was tired from the long trip but too wound up to sleep. Her grief was too new and sharp.

She had boarded the bus in Springfield, Missouri, filled with joy and hope for the first time in almost a year. She was going to be reunited with her beloved sister, to meet her sister's babies and help take care of them. She was going to learn the reason why Annie had left Nathan and disappeared, something Annie said she couldn't tell Maisie over the phone but had promised to reveal when they were face-to-face again. She had no way of knowing her sister was already with God. Ten hours later, when Maisie changed buses outside of Philadelphia, she had enough time during the layover to call Annie and see if she had delivered her babies yet. Instead, a social worker at a hospital in Portland, Maine, told her that Annie was dead.

Maisie still couldn't absorb the fact that she would never see her sister again. Never hear her voice, never laugh at the same things or finish each other's sentences. It was if she had been cleaved in two and half of her was gone.

The loneliness and sorrow of those remaining horrible hours on the bus had been almost too much to bear. Only her faith and the thought of holding her sister's babies got her through the ordeal. Now she was here in Maine at last. Her life had purpose again. Nathan and the babies needed her.

The warm night air was thick with the scents of wood smoke and pine trees, and the sound of droning insects. The sky was overcast, with the drifting clouds hiding the moon and blocking out the light from the stars. When her eyes adjusted to the dark, she could just make out the outline of the barn and corral fence across the way. Two horses stood at the fence. She saw a shadow move beside them and knew Nathan hadn't gone to bed. She walked toward him, wondering what she was going to say. Buddy followed at her heels.

The awkwardness of the situation had her on edge. She wanted…no, she needed to help care for her sister's babies. They were her last and only connection to Annie. Holding Annie's child in her arms tonight had eased the hurt Maisie carried in her heart. Only, Nathan didn't want her here. How could she make him see it was best for all of them if she stayed?

He didn't seem surprised when she walked up beside him. Her head was level with his shoulder. She felt small beside him. One of the horses reached over the fence to nudge her arm. She rubbed his forehead. "Who is this?"

"Mack."

"And the other one?"

"Donald."

She chuckled. "You're joking."

"I didn't name them. That's what they were called when I bought them." His dry tone said he didn't find it funny.

"Someone had a good sense of humor," she finished lamely.

"I asked you a question earlier."

He was angry and bitter. She couldn't blame him. She had been angry at Annie, too. She still had a hard time believing her sister had done such a terrible thing. Now Annie was gone before she could explain. Maisie sighed deeply. "I didn't know my sister had plans to leave you."

"Do you know why she left?"

"I don't." It was the truth. All Maisie had was a vague suspicion—that Annie had left to be with another man. Telling Nathan would only heap more pain on a man who was already hurting, and maybe plant a seed of doubt that the children weren't his. Maisie couldn't do that to him. Like her, the children were all he had left of his love for Annie.

"How did she know to send you here?" he asked.

"She left a message with her cell-phone number on the answering machine at the phone shack of our bishop.

You had told him you were moving to New Covenant. You had given him the name of the man you planned to work for so he could contact you in case Annie came back to our community. He told me and I called her."

"What did she say? Did she explain herself? Did she know the harm she caused? I couldn't even stay in Seymour."

"She said she would explain everything when she saw me in person. I'm sorry some people in Seymour were unfair to you."

"Unfair?" The single word was almost a snarl. "They thought I killed my wife. They sent the sheriff to search my property with dogs. They didn't believe the note she left had been written by her."

Maisie flinched away from his anger. "None of the Amish community thought that, Nathan. We were all shocked to learn of her disappearance, especially me and *Daed*. It was only some of Annie's *Englisch* friends who suspected foul play." The Porters, the influential family both she and Annie had once worked for. Wealthy people who didn't understand Amish ways even though they hired them. Maisie had married and stopped working in their home, but Annie stayed another four years, until the oldest son and his children moved away after his wife's death. Then Annie abruptly married Nathan.

"The Porters were the same people who stopped buying the lumber I cut. They stopped others from buying from me or hiring me to clear land. I couldn't make a living."

"Edward Porter and his wife loved Annie like a

daughter. She was more than a nanny to their grand-children. She took care of their daughter-in-law while she was dying."

"And I loved Annie like a wife!" he shouted.

Maisie stayed silent. Finally, he drew a deep breath. "You said the hospital told you that she had passed away. How?"

"As I said, I had Annie's cell-phone number. We exchanged a few phone calls while I was preparing to travel here. She wouldn't talk about the past, only about how she hoped to make up for the pain she had caused everyone. She was excited about having twins. She wanted daughters. She said they would be as close as she and I had been." Only they hadn't been close enough.

"Did she have names picked out?" His voice broke and he bowed his head. It was too dark to see his face, but she knew he was crying.

Maisie laid a hand on his arm, fighting back her own tears. "She wanted you to name them. I know you loved her, Nathan. I know you love her children. You will give them the life she wanted for them. *Gott* will show you the way. Trust Him. Draw strength from His love."

Nathan straightened and pulled away from her hand. "*Gott* hasn't done much for me lately. Go on with your story."

There was an edge to his voice now. Was he angry with God, as well as Annie? Maisie couldn't have made it through the last two days without God's comfort and the thought of holding Annie's babies.

Nathan needed God. He would come to see that when his grief wasn't so sharp.

"I hadn't talked to my sister for over a week so I called Annie from a bus stop in Pennsylvania yesterday to let her know I was on my way. A woman who said she worked at the hospital in Portland answered the phone. She told me Annie had…died of complications following childbirth, but the babies were fine and with you. Apparently Annie was able to tell them how to contact your bishop and have him deliver a message."

Nathan sighed heavily. "She must have been the same woman who tried to give me the phone along with Annie's things when I picked up the babies. I had no use for a phone. I told her to keep it. She said she would hold on to it for a while in case anyone tried to contact Annie then she would donate it to a charity. I didn't care what she did with it."

"I'm grateful she answered even though the news she delivered was heartbreaking."

"If I'd known you were coming, I could have delayed the burial."

"I would like to visit her grave soon. To say my goodbyes."

"I'll take you tomorrow. Then I'll take you into town and get you a bus ticket home."

Startled, she shook her head. "*Nee*, I'm here to care for my sister's babies. I already love them. I did from the moment I learned they were coming."

"I can take care of them. I want you to leave."

"Nathan, be reasonable. You need help."

He faced her with his arms crossed over his chest.

The moon came out from behind the clouds, bathing his face in its cold light. "It can't be you."

"Why not?"

"Because every time I look at you… I see Annie. I don't want you here."

The bitterness in his clipped words left Maisie speechless. He walked away into the darkness.

"But they're all I have left of her," she whispered as a deep ache filled her chest. "Please don't make me leave them."

She felt Buddy lick her fingers. He whined as if he knew she had been hurt by Nathan's words. She dropped down to hold the big dog close and draw some comfort against the yawning hole of new grief she saw opening before her. How could she change Nathan's mind?

Chapter Two

The impatient whinny of a horse pulled Nathan out of a sound sleep. The call was repeated by a second horse, then a third. He opened his eyes and stared at the bare wooden timbers over his head. Why was he in the barn?

He sat up and rubbed his face. Memories of the past week came flooding back and hit him like a falling tree. Annie was dead. He had her babies to care for.

The babies! He'd left them alone! Panic pushed him to his feet. He yanked open the outside door.

The front entrance of his cabin was open across the way. He heard the voice of a woman singing a familiar Amish hymn. His racing heart slowed as disjointed images from the previous night took shape in his mind.

The babies weren't alone. Annie's sister was with them. Maisie. Annie's twin. The need to rush and check on his children ebbed away. Seeing them meant seeing Maisie. That painful moment could wait a while longer, but he couldn't put it off forever.

He should have been kinder to Maisie last night.

She'd lost her husband in a farming accident before he had married Annie. Maisie knew what it was to lose a spouse. She had moved in with her ailing father on his small farm afterward. Nathan never felt that she'd approved of her sister's choice in marrying a logger with no land or expectations. He could have built a good life in Seymour. If only Annie had stayed.

He raked his hands through his hair. His first uninterrupted night of sleep in nearly a week should have left him refreshed, but it would take more than a single night to get caught up. He yawned, closed his eyes and leaned his head against the doorjamb. He wasn't ready to face the day. Or his new responsibilities as a parent.

What he knew about being a father weighed less than a grain of wheat. It was something he and Annie should have shared together. He barely remembered his own *daed*. He'd died when Nathan was four. A logging accident, his mother had told him. He never knew exactly what happened. She was gone, too, from cancer when he was ten. Now he didn't have anyone he could turn to for guidance. He'd never been more alone.

One of his horses whinnied again. Judging by the height of the sun breaking over the wooded hills to the east, their morning grain was long overdue. He crossed the small room where he had lived last winter. It contained a narrow bed, a table, one chair and a woodburning potbellied stove. He opened the connecting door that led into his barn. Constructed of logs, the building was small but snug enough to keep his animals comfortable during Maine's long, cold winters. It needed some improvements for sure. He had planned to work on those this summer, but the arrival of the babies had put everything on hold, including his paying job.

Donald and Mack, his caramel-brown Belgians with cream-colored manes, both had their heads over the stall gates gazing in his direction with their ears forward. They knew his arrival meant their grain was imminent. Sassy, his black buggy horse, whickered softly. She was always happy to see him even if he wasn't dishing out food. He stopped to scratch her around the ears. She closed her eyes and leaned into his hand.

"Sorry I'm late again, Sass. I'll figure this out. I promise."

Figure out how to manage his small farm, his logging job and two fussy babies? Sure, he could do that. But first he had to put Maisie on a bus back to Missouri. He didn't need another distraction in his chaotic life.

He fed the horses, his milk cow and her new calf, the pigs, chickens and the ducks, then he cleaned the stalls he had neglected for the past week and gathered the eggs. When he had first arrived at this property he had dammed the small stream that cut through the corner of his pasture to form a pond, where all of the livestock could drink so he didn't have to haul water except during the worst winter months, when it was frozen over.

He had hoped to be able to harvest enough ice from it to fill his icehouse without making the four-mile trip down to the pond at the bishop's place. Instead, heavy spring rains and the runoff from a section of clear-cut forest above him had resulted in a massive amount of silt flowing in. It was little more than a big mudhole now, but his animals could still drink from the deep end. He had planned to drain it and dredge it out, but that would have to wait, along with the other improvements he had hoped to make this summer.

He washed up at the pump outside the cabin and then stared at the open front door. Maisie was still singing. Annie had had a beautiful voice. Maisie's was slightly off-key, but not unpleasant. He didn't hear either baby. The cat was sunning himself on the porch railing while Buddy sprawled across the doorway thumping his tail against the floorboards and licking his chops. The amazing aroma of fresh-baked bread and bacon drifted out and made Nathan's mouth water. His empty stomach gurgled.

There was no point in putting off this meeting any longer. He climbed to the porch and stepped over Buddy to enter the cabin. Maisie stopped singing. She gave him a tentative smile. He had to look away.

"Guder mariye," he mumbled a greeting in Pennsylvania Dutch, the language the Amish spoke among themselves.

"Goot morning to you, too. I hope you got some sleep," she said after an awkward pause.

"I did. What about you?"

Her laugh seemed forced. "I managed. They took turns fussing. As soon as I would get one quiet, the other would wake up wanting attention."

"I noticed that about them." Their baskets were propped on the couch. He stepped over to look at them. They were both asleep. The cabin had rarely been this quiet since their arrival.

Maisie walked up beside him. "Aren't they the most beautiful babies you have ever seen?"

He slanted a glance at her face. Her expression was a mixture of happiness and heart-rending sorrow as she gazed at his children. He almost laid his hand on her shoulder to comfort her but thought better of it.

"I'll get Sassy hitched to the buggy. The trip to Fort Craig takes about an hour."

"I was hoping you would reconsider, Nathan."

He hardened his heart against her pleading look. "I haven't."

She sighed and turned away from him. "Then have some breakfast before your dog snitches more of it. He's not very well trained. He took three strips of bacon off the plate on the counter before I could stop him." She scowled at Buddy, who was doing his best to look innocent.

"He's a stray. I reckon he still worries about where his next meal is coming from."

"I know the feeling," she muttered.

Nathan frowned at her. "What?"

"Nothing. Sit down. *Kaffi?*"

"Sure."

He took a seat and pulled a slice of warm bread from the plate in the center of the table. The butter melted as he spread it. Maisie filled his white mug with piping-hot coffee, then put the pot back on the stove and brought a plate of bacon and scrambled eggs to the table. She sat down across from him. He kept his eyes closed, said a silent blessing, then picked up his fork.

The eggs were perfectly done and fluffy. The bacon

was exactly the way he liked it—not too crisp. The bread was moist and delicious. He took a tentative sip from his mug. It was the best coffee he'd had in months.

He remembered the first breakfast Annie had made for him the day after their wedding. The bacon was burned, the eggs runny and the coffee weak. None of that mattered when she smiled at him. He would have happily eaten charcoal.

He grinned at the recollection. "Remember when—" He looked up and it hit him that it wasn't Annie across from him.

Maisie tipped her head to the side. "Remember what?"

"Never mind." He choked down the rest of the meal and shoved back from the table. He had to get out of the house so he could breathe. He had his hand on the doorknob when Maisie spoke.

"Nathan, wait. Please. Don't make me leave. I'm begging you. Let me care for my sister's babies. They are the only family I have left."

He stood stock-still. "Jacob is gone?"

"*Ja. Daed* passed away three months ago."

"I'm sorry. I didn't know. I liked your father."

"He liked you, too," she said softly. "I don't have family to go back to in Missouri. I had to sell the farm to pay our debts."

He couldn't let sympathy for her loss soften his resolve. He didn't want her here. "You have friends, the members of your church. They'll take care of you."

"I know, but they aren't family."

"I'm sorry. I won't change my mind." The thought of

seeing Annie every time he looked at Maisie was more than he could bear. "Be ready to leave in five minutes." He didn't look at her again. His mind was made up.

He hitched Sassy and drove his buggy to the front door. Maisie came out with the twins. He helped settle their baskets on the front seat. She went back inside and returned with her suitcase and a brown paper bag. He stowed her suitcase in the back and nodded toward the bag. "What's that?"

"Formula, diapers, burp rags, clean clothes in case they spit up. You said it was an hour trip so two hours there and back. I'm sure they'll need to be fed and changed before you get them home."

"Right."

She had brought all the things he should have thought of but hadn't. He opened the passenger-side door and helped her in. He closed the door and one of the babies started to fuss. She spoke quietly and gently rocked the basket. The baby settled.

He knew she'd never had children of her own. She and Annie had been the only *kinder* in their family. How did Maisie know so much about taking care of infants? Were women born knowing what to do?

He rubbed his palms on his pant legs. He might not know everything about caring for babies, but he would figure it out. The same way he solved every problem in his life. By trial and error. And by never making the same mistake twice.

"You will stop at the cemetery so I can say my good-bye?" she asked hesitantly.

He had forgotten her request. He glanced toward the small rise behind the house. "She's here."

Maisie's eyes filled with tears as she pressed her fingers to her lips. "Where?"

"I'll show you."

She got out. He took the baby's baskets in each hand. "This way."

He walked up the hill carrying his sleeping infants to a small clearing, where a simple white cross and a mound of dirt marked Annie's final resting place. Maisie sank to the grass beside the grave and laid her hands on the freshly turned earth. She sat in silence with her head bowed.

The morning sun beat down on Nathan's shoulders as he stood behind her. It must have been ten minutes before she sat back and folded her hands in her lap. It struck him that Maisie had always been quieter than Annie, who never could sit still. Maisie had a sereneness about her that Annie had lacked. He found it comforting.

Maisie glanced around and smiled sadly. "It's a lovely spot. It overlooks the cabin. That was a nice thought."

"I'm sorry you came all this way for nothing."

She gazed up at him. His figure against the blue sky was blurred by her unshed tears. "I wish you'd let me stay. Annie wanted me here. She knew how much work two babies could be."

"I'll manage." He avoided looking at her.

She got to her feet and dusted off her hands. "Of course you will. My *daed* used to say you were a problem solver. A man who would think on something before he acted."

He finally glanced at her. "What did your *daed* say about Annie leaving me?"

Maisie bowed her head. "He was ashamed, hurt, confused. He rarely spoke about it."

Nathan stared into the distance. "Did he think I drove her away?"

Maisie laid her hand on his sleeve. "*Nee*, he did not. Nor did I."

She hoped that Nathan believed her because she spoke the truth. Nathan had adored Annie. She knew that.

He shrugged off her hand. "How did Jacob die?"

She clenched her fingers together in her lap. "His heart gave out. I think Annie's leaving took away his will to live. If only she had written. He forgave her. I had to tell her about it when I spoke to her on the phone. I think she took comfort in knowing that." Maisie had hated breaking the news to Annie about their father's death over the phone. She hadn't shared how their father's last days had been spent calling out for Annie and begging to see her.

"Have you forgiven her?" Nathan asked.

"Of course. She was my sister. No matter how poorly she behaved, I loved her."

"We should get going."

They walked back to the buggy, where he settled her and the babies again. He got in on the driver's side and turned the horse to head down the lane. They rode in silence for the first few minutes until his rutted lane met a narrow, paved roadway. It was Maisie who spoke up first. "What is it that you do now, Nathan?"

"The same thing I have always done."

"Logging? Do you have your own business again?"

"*Nee*, I'm a feller for Arthur Davis. He runs most of the lumber camps in this area."

"What exactly is a feller?"

"I'm the man who cuts down trees with a chain saw. I've also worked as a choker, the fellow who hooks cables to the logs so they can be hauled out."

"Is it dangerous work?"

"It can be."

"It must give you peace of mind knowing that your children will be cared for by your Amish community if anything should happen to you."

"I haven't joined the church here. My job often takes me into the backcountry for weeks on end."

"That will have to change now that you have children to look after."

"I know that," he snapped. She fell silent.

Nathan's daughter began to fuss. Maisie picked the child up. She glanced at Nathan's stoic face and tried not to take his rudeness personally. He was suffering and she didn't know how to help him. She patted the baby's back. "I was wondering if you had chosen names yet. I hate to leave without knowing what to call my niece and nephew. I'll want to write to them and send cards at Christmas and such."

"I haven't thought about it."

"Your daughter looks like Annie. Maybe you could name her after her mother."

"Nee." There was no compromise in his tone.

"Well, after your mother, then. What was her name?"

"Charity." His tone softened.

"Charity. I like that. It suits her." Maisie hugged the little girl tightly. At least now she would have a name to add to her prayers.

"It's as good as any," Nathan muttered, but Maisie heard the catch in his voice.

She smiled at the baby trying to get her fist in her mouth. "Hello, Charity Weaver. I'm so very glad I got to meet you."

Nathan glanced at her. "I could call the boy Jacob, after your father, if that's okay with you?"

Maisie swallowed against the lump that formed in her throat. "I'd like that. I think Annie would have, too."

"I'd rather not talk about her."

"I know you are angry, Nathan. None of this is fair, but she was returning to you."

"Why was she coming back? Why did she leave in the first place? Why did she marry me if she didn't love me?"

"I wish I had answers for you."

"I wish you did, too."

They rode in silence until they came to the outskirts of a settlement a half hour later. Off to one side was a school where several dozen Amish children were playing at recess. Most of the children stopped what they were doing to wave. Maisie waved back. "Is this New Covenant?"

"It is."

"So this is where your children will go to school."

"I guess they will someday."

"They will be school-aged before you know it." Maisie looked back at the building as Nathan drove on down the highway. She would be able to imagine the children going up the steps on their first day of school when that day came, playing on the swings, laughing with the other children.

She brushed aside the tears that gathered in her eyes. At least she'd had the chance to hold them and love them, if only for a few hours. It was small consolation compared to the magnitude of her loss, but she was grateful, anyway.

Jacob began to fuss in his basket. Maisie laid Charity down and picked up the bag she'd brought with the formula. She opened a bottle and began to feed him. Before he was finished, Charity began crying. Maisie looked at Nathan. "Pull over, please."

"Why?"

"I can't feed two babies at once. I need you to take Jacob."

Nathan turned off the road into a driveway. A large yellow dog came loping toward them, barking excitedly. An Amish woman tending to her flower garden straightened. She walked over, pulling off her gloves as she came.

"Quiet, Sadie Sue. You'll scare the horse." The dog fell silent but stayed at the woman's heels as she approached the buggy on Maisie's side. "Can I help you?" she asked with a friendly smile.

Maisie handed Jacob to Nathan and picked up Charity. "They both decided they want to eat at the same time. I don't have enough hands."

"Twins. How *wunderbar*." The woman leaned on the door to look inside. "Boys or girls?"

Maisie glanced at Nathan, who seemed intent on ignoring the woman as he got Jacob to finish his bottle. "One of each," Maisie said.

"I'm Bethany Shetler. I don't believe we've met. You must be new to the New Covenant area."

"I'm only visiting. I'm Maisie Schrock. This is my brother-in-law, Nathan Weaver." She nodded to Nathan, who still didn't speak.

"I believe my husband, Michael, mentioned meeting Nathan not long ago. You have the place out beyond the Arnett farm, don't you?"

"I do."

"We haven't seen you at our church services yet."

"That's because I haven't attended one," Nathan said sharply.

Bethany's smile faded. "I see. You are welcome anytime. And you, Maisie, if you are still here on Sunday next."

"He's done with his bottle," Nathan said, settling the baby in his basket again. "We need to get going."

Maisie smiled at the friendly woman and waved goodbye as Nathan turned the buggy onto the highway again.

Neither of them spoke until the outskirts of Fort Craig came into view. On one side of the highway, Maisie noticed several Amish men putting together a small shed on a lot with a half dozen similar buildings.

"Is that an Amish-owned business?" she asked.

"It belongs to Bishop Schultz. He sells garden sheds and such on the side. He's a potato farmer, like most of us. He has a farm near New Covenant."

"It looks like a prosperous business." She took note of several buildings in various stages of completion. One in particular caught her attention. "Is that a little house?"

"The *Englisch* call them tiny homes. Some new fad, I reckon. The bus station is just there."

"Where?"

"In that shopping center."

Her bus driver had dropped her at the New Covenant corner yesterday, so she hadn't been to the one in Fort Craig before. There was a small sign at a convenience store with gas pumps just off the highway. Nathan pulled in and stopped. She got out with one of the babies. Nathan took the other and her suitcase. They gathered a few curious stares from the patrons in the store as they went in.

Nathan headed to a desk at the end of the room. There wasn't an attendant. A man behind the main counter looked his way. "Be with you folks in a minute."

He finished ringing up a customer and came over. "How can I help you?"

Nathan nodded toward Maisie without looking at her. "My sister-in-law needs a ticket to Seymour, Missouri."

"One way or round trip?" The man sat behind the computer and began typing.

"One way," Nathan said. "How much?"

"It'll take me a few minutes to figure the best way to get you there, ma'am."

Nathan finally looked at her. "Do you have enough money for food on the trip?"

"Ja." Annie had sent money for a round-trip fare. Maisie had spent only part of it getting to Maine.

"Goodbye, then." Nathan put her suitcase on the floor and took Charity's basket from her. He headed for the door. Maisie reached for him. She wasn't ready to say goodbye to the children yet.

"Sir, there isn't a bus going south until Friday afternoon," the ticket agent said quickly, stopping Nathan in his tracks.

"Are you sure?" Maisie asked, her hopes rising.

"Positive. There's a bus going south on Friday afternoons and Monday mornings."

Maisie grinned, almost giddy with relief. She didn't have to leave today. It was only Tuesday. She would have three days to spend with the babies. She glanced at Nathan. He was glaring at her.

Maisie didn't care. She had until Friday to prove to him how much easier his life would be with her help. She glanced at his unyielding expression again. Would that be enough time?

Chapter Three

"This was a wasted morning." Nathan tossed Maisie's suitcase into the back seat of the buggy and climbed in front beside her. She ignored his sour look. She didn't have to leave today. God was good to her.

"Next time I'll stop at the phone shack and call to make sure there is a bus before I drive for a two-hour round trip."

"It doesn't have to be wasted." She was smiling at the babies, not the least bit upset with the turn of events. She couldn't have been happier.

"What do you mean?" he snapped.

"Is there a fabric store in town?"

"Are you joking? You want to make a new dress while you're here?"

Her smile vanished as she turned in the seat to glare at him. "This may not have occurred to you, Nathan Weaver, but your children are in need of clothing."

He leaned away from the anger in her eyes.

"What are you talking about?"

"They will soon outgrow the little T-shirts that seem to be all you have for them. I will gladly spend my extra time in Maine sewing for them so they will be comfortable long into the winter months."

She took a deep breath. "I know you are not happy that I will be here until Friday. I'm thrilled that I can spend a few more days with the children, but believe me when I say I am not thrilled to spend that time watching you pout. I can't help that I look like Annie. If you think I'm going to wear a sack over my head to appease you, I won't. You will just have to bear that disappointment."

She crossed her arms tightly over her chest and turned away to stare out the side of the buggy. None of it was her fault and he was acting as if it was.

"I don't want you to wear a sack over your head," he said at last.

He waited for her to say something. She didn't.

"I'm sorry." He opened the door to get out.

"Where are you going?" she asked in a voice that trembled.

"Into the store to see if they know where the closest fabric shop is. And I don't pout."

"You had me fooled."

His eyes narrowed, but he didn't say anything. When he returned to the buggy, he got in and picked up the lines. "There's one down the street."

He drove into the parking lot in front of a shop called Sew Fine. Maisie got out without a word to him.

Inside the door, she was greeted with the smell and sight of stacks of new fabric in a rainbow of colors and prints, button displays, craft items, a bin of quilt square bundles and an elderly clerk who nodded. "Welcome. Just shout if you can't find something."

"Cotton and flannels?"

"End of aisle two, deary."

Maisie picked up a red plastic shopping basket from the stack by the cash register and headed to the back of the store. She paused to look at a solid, royal-blue polyester bolt and walked on. She wasn't shopping for herself. The bolts of flannel were jammed in together at the end of the display. Red plaid seemed to be the most popular, but she chose a few pastel colors. She carried them to the front and left them with the clerk to cut while she went in search of thread and ribbons to make the drawstring closures.

She rounded the end of the aisle and came face-to-face with her sister. Maisie stopped in shock. "Annie?"

She reached out and realized and instant later that she was seeing her own reflection in a full-length mirror on the wall beside ready-made scarves and shawls. It was heartbreaking to see her sister and realize she wasn't real. Tears gathered in Maisie's eyes. She had seldom seen herself in a large mirror. The only one at home had been a small oval one in the bathroom, where her father shaved.

She would never come face-to-face with Annie again. Maisie pressed her hand to her heart. This must be how Nathan saw her. As a painful, unreal reflection of Annie. No wonder he didn't want her to stay.

Out in the buggy, Nathan glanced at the babies and prayed they would stay asleep until Maisie returned.

His headache was back. He closed his eyes and leaned his head against the side window. Nothing was going right today. Why hadn't he thought about clothes for the children? They'd need bigger beds soon, too. They couldn't stay in the small Moses baskets the nurses at the hospital had given him. It was all so complicated. Annie should be here to take care of these things.

Twenty minutes later Maisie opened the back door and put several packages on the seat, then she got in front. She appeared subdued. He straightened and cleared his throat. "Now where?"

"A grocery store, if you don't mind. We need more formula and your cupboards are almost bare."

"I wasn't expecting to feed company." He slapped the lines against Sassy's rump to get her moving. Why did he find Maisie so irritating? Annie had never irritated him. She had been easy to get along with. If they had quarreled, he might have understood her leaving, but they never did. Not once. It made her running away that much harder to understand.

He headed Sassy out of town. He passed the local market without stopping. Let Maisie assume he didn't care what she wanted. When they passed the last of the houses along the highway, he glanced at her set face and decided it wasn't worth the energy it took to stay angry with her.

"Mr. Meriwether has a grocery in New Covenant. His prices are a little higher, but he's good to the local Amish who want to sell items at his place. I like to give him my business. In case you were wondering why I didn't turn in at the market back there."

"I was," she admitted softly.

"But you were afraid I'd snap your head off if you asked."

"Something like that." She cast a sidelong glance his way.

He allowed his sour mood to soften. She shouldn't be afraid of him. "I'll try to be less irritated during your remaining days."

A tiny smile tugged at the corner of her lips. "I shall do my best to be less annoying."

As if that was possible. He rubbed the back of his neck with one hand.

Maisie gave him a long look. "Headache?"

He nodded. "*Ja*, I get them when I'm short on sleep."

"Would you like me to drive? You can lie down on the back seat. The fabric bundles will make a decent pillow."

He glanced at her and saw concern in her eyes. For him. Guilt rushed in to push aside his aggravation. He was trying to get rid of her, and she was worried about his comfort. He shook his head. "I'll be fine, but *danki*."

"As you wish." She turned away.

When they arrived at the Meriwether Market, he pulled in and stopped. "Let me give you some money." He pulled out his wallet.

Her chin came up. "I have enough. I don't wish to be a burden."

"I will pay for what the babies and you need while you are here. Keep in mind I only have a small icebox, so don't get a lot of perishable items."

"Of course." She took his money, got out and entered the store.

Nathan massaged his neck again. His headache hadn't let up. It probably wouldn't go away until Maisie left.

Charity began to fuss. He reached over and gently rocked the basket as he had seen Maisie do. Thankfully, his daughter quieted. He wondered how long it would be before both babies slept through the night. A few weeks? Surely not more than that. He had been so overwhelmed during the first few days with them that he hadn't had time to consider what he was going to do about work.

He would need to find someone to take care of them eventually. Arthur Davis had been good about giving him time off. He had offered Nathan a month's leave, but without pay, since the other feller on the crew was experienced enough to handle the extra workload alone. Nathan hated to ask for more time, but he might have to if he couldn't find someone quickly.

He rubbed his tense neck again. Having Maisie to help would have worked, if only she wasn't the spitting image of Annie. He didn't need the added pain.

Charity squirmed in her sleep. Maisie's suggestion for his daughter's name had been a good one, though. His mother would have loved having babies to spoil. God had taken her and Annie much too soon. The Lord hadn't shown Nathan Weaver much mercy in his life.

Jacob stirred. Nathan rocked him until he settled. It wasn't so hard to care for them now that he knew what to do. Nathan sat back feeling pleased with himself. Then Charity started crying.

"I have heard that your goods are overpriced. Now I see that's true." Maisie kept a close watch on the cash register's rising total. She would show Nathan she knew how to manage money. She was a thrifty shopper.

"My prices are fair." The middle-aged man scowled at her as he rang up the container of powdered formula.

"This is at least a dollar higher than the last place I saw the same formula."

"There was a coupon for it in this week's newspaper. If you have one of those, I'll take a dollar off what you have here."

"I'm afraid I didn't see the newspaper. I'm newly arrived." She smiled at him. "Couldn't you give me the discount, anyway? The twins are going to need a lot of formula over the next few months."

He brightened at the prospect of future sales. "Twins, you say. What a blessing. All right, I will give you the discount. Keep an eye on my ads in the newspaper. You'll find some good bargains, I promise."

"*Danki*, you're very kind. The last place I lived the Amish women would travel together once a month to shop at a large discount store even though it was twenty miles away. Do the Amish women in this community do that?"

"I've not heard of it." His frown came back.

"Perhaps I'll suggest it." She cast a sidelong glance his way to gauge his reaction.

He finished scanning her items. "I'm going to deduct

five percent from the total. That's my way of welcoming you to the community."

She smiled broadly. "That's very generous of you."

And a good way to appease a troublesome customer.

"Well, folks are glad to have the Amish moving in here. My grandparents were potato farmers back in the day. They worked the land with horses the way you folks do. The old ways shouldn't disappear. Why, I can remember riding bareback on Grandpa's plow horse. His name was Dusty, which was exactly the way the seat of my pants looked when I got off of him."

Maisie grinned as she handed over her money. "Happy memories are cherished gifts from *Gott.*"

"They are indeed." He counted out her change and picked up two of the bags. "Let me help you out with these."

"Danki."

The moment they stepped out the door, Maisie heard the babies crying.

Mr. Meriwether chuckled. "It sounds as if you'll need some of that formula right quick. I'll put these sacks in the back for you." He opened the door and nodded to Nathan. "Your missus knows how to drive a good bargain. I was afraid I was going to have to pay her to take these groceries off my hands."

"I'm his sister-in-law and thank you again for the help, Mr. Meriwether."

The man left and Maisie opened the front door of the buggy. Nathan had a babe in each arm, trying to soothe them. A worried frown creased his brow. "I can't believe they are hungry already. Is something else wrong with them?"

"The long ride in the buggy may have upset them, but it's been almost three hours since we stopped to feed them. That's about normal. Let me have Charity. I'll change her and then you can feed her while I take care of Jacob. These are for you." She opened a bottle of aspirin and shook two into her hand, then laid a bottle of water on the scat.

He handed the babe to her and she dropped the pills into his free hand. He quickly tossed them in his mouth and took a swig of water. "*Danki*. How do you know they aren't sick?"

She laid the back of her hand against Charity's forehead. "She doesn't have a fever. I'm sure a dry diaper and a bottle will stop the fussing."

That turned out to be the case. Once both babies were changed and fed, Maisie held one in each arm, enjoying the time to cuddle them as Nathan drove toward home.

"How is it that you know so much about babies?" he asked.

"I worked as a nanny for an *Englisch* family." Annie had worked in the same house as a maid.

"The Porters." Nathan's tone conveyed his lingering dislike of the wealthy family that had caused him so much trouble. Edward Porter, the head of the family, had treated Nathan poorly.

"Gavin Porter, the son, had two children. His wife was sickly. I took care of her baby and two-year-old son until I left to get married."

Annie had stayed on and taken over Maisie's duties with the children. Gavin and Annie became close. Maisie had worried about her sister's attachment. She suspected Annie was in love with Gavin. Because he was a married man and Annie had already taken her baptismal vows, any romantic relationship between them was strictly forbidden. Then Maisie's husband died suddenly in an accident, leaving her with the farm to run. Between the farm work and their father's failing health, Maisie had been too busy to do or say anything about her concerns.

After Gavin's wife passed away, he moved with the children to New York. Then Annie suddenly married Nathan, a newcomer, an Amish logger she'd known only a few months. Annie's assurance that she had fallen madly in love didn't ring true to Maisie. She thought her sister was marrying Nathan help her get over Gavin. To prove she hadn't been in love with him.

"I'm surprised the Porters hired someone without experience as their nanny."

"When I was younger, I worked as a mother's helper for our neighbor after she had two of her children. She gave me a reference."

"Old man Porter took the word of an Amish *frau*? That's not like him."

"It was Gavin who hired me." Maisie had enjoyed taking care of the children. When she married, she thought she would have babes of her own, but that wasn't God's plan for her.

She gazed at the beautiful babies sleeping quietly in her arms and her heart grew warm with tenderness. It was astonishing how quickly she had grown to love them. Three days wasn't much time to prove her worth to Nathan, but the idea of leaving Annie's babies was too painful to contemplate.

She would show Nathan that she was the perfect nanny for his children. She rocked gently with the swaying of the buggy watching their changing expressions in their sleep, feeling them stretch and snuggle inside their blankets. Even when her arms grew tired, she didn't put them down. Every moment with them was precious.

"How soon will they start sleeping through the night?" Nathan asked, glancing in her direction.

"When they are five or six months old."

"That can't be right."

"I'm afraid it is."

He looked so disappointed that she felt sorry for him. She decided not to tell him about colic, teething, croup or any of the other reasons parents of new babies lost sleep. Today didn't seem to be the day to add to his worries.

When they finally arrived back at his cabin, he got out of the buggy, came around to her side and opened her door. She grimaced when she tried to move. "I'm sorry, can you take Jacob? I'm afraid my arms have fallen asleep."

"You should've put them down sooner." He leaned close to gently lift the baby from her arms.

"I didn't want to miss a minute of holding them while I'm able. They are so beautiful. Truly a gift from *Gott*."

He paused with his gaze fixed on his son's face. He stroked the baby's cheek with one finger. "They are wonderful. I wish their mother was here to see how much they've changed in just a few days' time."

"So do I, but it was *Gott*'s will." She shook her arm to clear the pins and needles, then stepped out of the buggy. Nathan took her elbow to steady her. Warmth spread from his hand up her arm. Her gaze flew to his face. A troubled expression clouded his eyes.

He stepped away abruptly. "Go inside. I'll bring the baskets."

Maisie did as he asked. She waited in the kitchen until he set the baskets on the table. She laid Charity in one and he placed Jacob in the other. Then he stood back and slipped his hands into his pockets.

"Oh, I almost forgot," Maisie said. "Here is your change." She pulled the money out of her purse.

Nathan took the bills, counted them and slipped them in his wallet. "You didn't use much. Did you spend your own money?"

"*Nee*. I was able to find some bargains. I'm careful with money." She took off her black traveling bonnet and laid it on the counter.

"Mr. Meriwether said as much. I thought it was just flattery."

Nathan went outside and returned a few minutes later with her purchases. He set them on the counter without looking at her. "I must see to Sassy. Then I have work in the barn. Don't bother fixing me anything to eat."

"You can't go hungry because I'm here. I'll fix you something now."

"I said, don't bother," he snapped and left again.

Maisie sank onto the kitchen chair. How could she prove her worth if he couldn't stay in the same room with her?

"Annie, you really hurt that man. Each time he looks at me I see the anguish in his eyes. You wanted me to be here, but you've made it impossible for me to stay."

She leaned forward to look at the sleeping babies. "I'll take good care of your *kinder* for as long as I'm able."

Maisie heard the sounds of a chain saw and an axe throughout the afternoon. Nathan didn't come in again until it was nearly dark. She'd kept a pot of stew warm on the stove for him, but the canned meat and vegetables were overdone and mushy by the time he showed up. He stopped to kiss each of the sleeping babies and then went out again. She fed the stew to Buddy.

The next morning, Nathan came in, poured himself a cup of coffee and went back out. Maisie ate some of the scrambled eggs she had made and gave the rest to Buddy and the cat. Nathan's animals would soon be fat at this rate. It wasn't long before she heard the chain saw again. Later, the banging of a hammer came from beyond the barn.

Just after noon, the sound of a vehicle coming up the lane prompted her to go to the door and look out. A brown pickup pulled into the small farmyard and stopped. She saw the words *Davis Lumber Company* on the truck door in white letters. A burly *Englisch* man in his midfifties got out. He wore faded jeans held up with suspenders, a blue plaid shirt and a brown baseball cap with the same company name stitched in white letters across the front.

He caught sight of her and pulled off his cap. "Afternoon, ma'am. I'm Arthur Davis. I'm looking for Nathan."

"I'm his sister-in-law, Maisie Schrock. I think Nathan is in the barn."

The man tipped his head slightly. "I don't recall Nathan saying he had any family."

"His wife was my sister."

"Then I'm sure sorry for your loss."

"Thank you."

"But I'm mighty glad to see he has someone to help with the babies."

"Would you like to come in for some coffee? I was just about to put on a pot."

"No thanks. I'll just go speak to Nathan." Mr. Davis started to turn away, but Nathan was already coming in their direction.

"I wasn't expecting you, Mr. Davis. What can I do for you?"

"There's been an accident at the Three Ponds camp. Ricky Burris broke his leg when a widow-maker came down on him."

"I'm sorry to hear that. Is he going to be okay?"

"The doc said he'd be off at least two months. With your situation, I was already short one feller and now I've got none. Could you see your way to come back to work starting on Monday? I know it's short notice. I wouldn't ask, but the lumber is already contracted for and I can't get behind schedule."

Nathan stared at his feet. He scuffed the toe of one boot through the gravel. "Things aren't settled here."

"I know it's bad timing on my part, and I hate to say it, but I'm gonna have to hire two new fellers to get this project in on time if you aren't willing to return to work."

Nathan looked up sharply. "Two? Are you telling me that I'm out of a job if I don't come back now?"

"The last thing I want to do is lay you off, Nathan, but I have obligations, too. I wanted to give you the opportunity to come back before I did anything. If Ricky hadn't gotten hurt I could've spared you for a few weeks, but not longer than that."

The man turned his hat around in his hands. "Look, I don't need your answer today. I'll give you some time to think it over. I'm really sorry to do this to you. You're the best feller I've had in a long time and I don't want to lose you. Think it over and let me know tomorrow. I'll stop by in the morning."

Mr. Davis settled his hat on his head, got in his truck and drove away.

Maisie wished she could do something for Nathan. He didn't need more trouble than he already had. She walked over to stand beside him. "What are you going to do?"

"There's no way I can make it through the winter with the savings I've got left after I pay the medical bills for the twins and Annie. I need my job."

"Your church will help you pay the hospital costs."

"They might if I was a member of this church. Which I'm not. I'll have to hire someone quickly to take care of the babies so I can go back to work."

He didn't even glance at her when he said it. She

couldn't believe what she was hearing. He would rather employ a stranger to look after his children than allow his wife's sister to be their nanny. The man wasn't thinking straight.

Maisie planted her hands on her hips. "Whether you like it or not, I'm staying. Those babies need me, not some stranger."

Chapter Four

"You can't stay here," Nathan snapped, wishing she would go away.

If she'd stay out of his sight instead of harping at him, he could think of what to do next. Annie had never been this exasperating. "You have a bus ticket you need to use on Friday."

Maisie stood with her hands on her hips and a stubborn look simmering in her eyes. "And you have to give your boss an answer tomorrow. Allow me to stay. What's your alternative?"

He didn't have one and he hated being backed into a corner. "Your sister was a biddable woman. I can see that you aren't."

Maisie folded her arms tightly over her chest. "We might have been twins, but we weren't the same."

Nathan didn't want to argue with her. His head was killing him. "I'm going to see Bishop Schultz. He may know of a woman who can look after the children." He was grasping at straws and he knew it. Finding someone to care for the babies full-time on such short notice was unlikely.

Maisie tossed her hands up. "Why are you so stubborn?"

"They're my children. I say who takes care of them." He started to walk away.

"You're being unreasonable."

"Enough." He raised one hand to signal the end of the conversation and kept walking.

"You're obstinate and irrational! No wonder my sister left you," she shouted.

Nathan stopped as pain seared his heart. He hung his head and gripped it with both hands. He'd gone over it a million times. There was only one explanation for Annie's actions. She left because there was something wrong with him. There was some reason she couldn't love him.

He heard Maisie running toward him. "Nathan, I'm sorry," she said in a rush.

She stopped beside him, but he couldn't look at her. He could barely breathe.

"That was cruel of me," she said softly. "You didn't deserve it."

His throat was so tight he couldn't speak.

Maisie laid a hand on his arm. "I'm sorry. Please forgive me. My temper is a fault I've tried to overcome."

He cleared the lump in his throat and found his voice. "You need to work on it harder," he croaked.

She let her breath out in a rush. "I will, I promise. I don't know why I said that. She never spoke a word against you, Nathan. Never."

He stared at the sky and blinked back tears. "I wish she had. Then maybe I'd understand. I'm just so tired and…"

"Angry. I know. I am, too, Nathan. I'm angry with *Gott* for taking her from me just when we had the chance to become close again. I'm angry with Annie for hurting you. For wounding me and our father. And for leaving her babies, though I know she couldn't help it. None of it was your fault." She tightened her grip on his arm. "Nothing gives me the right…to hurt you."

The catch in her words made him look at her. Tears streamed down her face. Her pain was as great as his own. Almost against his will, he cupped his fingers under her chin and gently wiped the dampness from one cheek with his thumb. "I reckon we're both grieving. They say healing takes time."

She nodded mutely.

Her skin was soft and warm beneath his fingers. Old longings shuddered to life in his chest. The need to hold someone and to be held. He knew the curve of this woman's jaw and the softness of her lips, but the woman whose face he caressed wasn't his wife. His feelings were for Annie, and she was gone. Maisie was only her shadow. Any warmness she stirred in him wasn't real.

More than the woman he had buried on the hill, he mourned the loss of the sweet girl he had married. The one who had left him months ago. His love for her had died a slow and painful death until there was only a hollow where his heart used to be.

How could he heal with Maisie as a constant reminder of all he had lost? It wasn't possible. He let his hand fall to his side. "I don't know where you and your sister learned to be so cruel, but I forgive you. I'll be home late. Don't wait supper."

Maisie stepped back and wiped her cheeks as much to hide the flush that heated her face as to dry her tears. Her reaction to Nathan's touch surprised and shocked her. She struggled to sound unaffected. "I'll keep something warm for you."

"Don't trouble yourself." He walked away and entered the barn.

Maisie relaxed when he was out of sight. Had he noticed the way her breath caught in her throat at the touch of his fingers? She hoped not. He had only been comforting her. It was her ragged emotions that made it seem like his touch had meant something more. She dismissed her troubled thoughts as a product of too little sleep and raw grief. To imagine there could be anything between Nathan and herself was utter foolishness. She knew better. He could barely stand the sight of her.

Now he thought she was as cruel as Annie, and she hadn't given him cause to think otherwise.

She looked up at the sky. "I'm ashamed of myself, Lord. My sorrow at Annie's death is no excuse for my words. I will do better. Give me a chance to mend my mistakes and help me bring Nathan the comfort he needs. I pray you fill my heart with kindness and hold my tongue when I would speak ill. Nathan has suffered enough because of my sister. Don't let me add to his pain. I can't change how I look, but with your guidance I can change how I act."

Walking back to the house, Maisie gave silent thanks for God's grace in allowing her to enjoy more time with the babies.

Nathan drove the buggy out of the barn and went past her. She watched him until he was out of sight. God willing, she might have even more time with them. It was wrong to hope that Nathan's mission would prove fruitless, but she couldn't help it. She didn't want to leave. The babies needed her, and Nathan needed her, too.

Inside the cabin she walked over to the sofa, where Charity and Jacob were still sleeping. Buddy was sitting alertly in front of them. He wagged his tail as Maisie sat down beside him.

"You are a *goot hund* to watch over your charges so well." His tail wagged faster. She scratched behind his long floppy ear, and he licked her hand.

"At least you are glad to have me here."

With a final pat to the dog's shoulder, she got up and began heating water on the stove to wash the glass bottles and nipples she had purchased. After that, she made up enough formula to get through the night, then put the bottles in Nathan's small icebox.

In her Amish community in Missouri they were allowed to use propane-powered appliances, so she was used to a bigger refrigerator. There wasn't any fresh milk in the icebox. She didn't know if Nathan owned a milk cow, so she had purchased canned milk that didn't need refrigeration for her cooking along with a variety of canned meats.

Did he have a garden? She had been too focused on

Annie's grave yesterday morning to notice anything else on his property. With both babies asleep, now would be a good time to explore.

She stepped outside. Buddy refused to budge from his place in front of the sofa. She closed the door and took a long look around.

Nathan's cabin was situated in a clearing surrounded by dense forest. Mostly pine trees interspersed with hardwoods. The log barn stood at the edge of a fenced-in meadow. She could see a pond at the far end with half a dozen white ducks swimming in it. Looking in the other direction, she knew what lay on the knoll above the cabin. She wasn't up to another visit there yet.

She went around to the back and was pleased to discover Nathan did have a garden, although it was somewhat overgrown. There were even a dozen young fruit trees, carefully wrapped and staked. The start of his orchard. He had accomplished a lot since leaving Missouri.

White cloth diapers flapped on a short clothesline attached to the corner of the house, but she didn't see a washer on the small back porch. Did Nathan wash his clothes by hand? The diapers were dry so she gathered them off the line.

She found his potato patch and dug enough new potatoes to make a soup later with some of the canned ham she had picked up. She spent the next twenty minutes pulling weeds and gathering what vegetables were ripe. At the far end of the garden she saw a huge blueberry bush. It had clearly been there for years. It was wild or someone had planted it long ago. The berries weren't ripe, but there would be plenty for jams and pie filling when they were.

If only she could be here to harvest them.

After checking on the babies, she went down to the barn. Curiosity made her peek into the room where Nathan had spent the last two nights. It was small but neat. His bed was made. No clothes hung from the pegs and the stove was cold.

Through the interior door, she found Mack and Donald dozing in their stalls. A brown-and-white cow occupied another stall. She had a tiny calf nursing at her side. Maisie leaned over the stall door for a closer look. "I see why Nathan doesn't have fresh milk in his icebox. He's letting your baby have it all."

The calf didn't pause in her feeding, but the cow followed Maisie's every move watchfully.

A chicken was scratching dirt in the corner of the cow's stall. Nathan had brought in eggs that morning, so he had to have several chickens. It didn't take her long to find where the others were sitting in their boxes. She left them undisturbed and returned to the house.

Inside the snug cabin, Maisie sat at the table and looked around. The furniture wasn't fancy. The table and chairs were homemade, from what looked like local wood. The one brown overstuffed chair was well-worn. The sofa was secondhand—that was easy to see—but all in all Nathan had made a good home in Maine.

Would Annie have been happy here? Maisie wasn't so sure. Hewing a living out of the wilderness would be challenging. Annie hadn't been one for hard work. She had been better at getting others to do her work for her.

It was wrong to think of her sister's faults when she'd passed so recently. Maisie wanted to remember the good times, the fun they'd had together. Those were the stories she would tell the children about their mother when they were older, even if only in the letters she wrote to them.

She took a deep breath and began to tidy up. She dusted the furniture, polished the reflective discs behind the oil lamps on the stone fireplace mantel and cleaned their sooty shades. Then she swept and washed the plank floor with a pine-scented cleaner she found under the kitchen sink.

Afterward, she fixed supper for herself, then fed and bathed the babies. She laughed at their startled expressions, and again when she was splashed by Jacob's wildly kicking legs. Once they were settled, she found a book about gardening in Maine from the stack of reading material beside Nathan's overstuffed chair. She sat in the kitchen reading by the light of a kerosene lantern and waited for Nathan to come home. She heard the horse and buggy about an hour after dark. Nathan didn't come in. Was he still upset with her? What had he learned?

She put some of the leftover soup she had kept warm on the back of the stove into a mug, fixed a ham sandwich and carried them down to the barn. Gathering her courage, she knocked on his door. When he opened it, she thrust the covered plate toward him. "It's just a bit of soup and a sandwich in case you haven't eaten."

He hesitated for so long that she thought he would

refuse, but he finally reached out and took the dish. *"Danki."*

He looked bone tired. She crossed her arms over her chest. "Do you have another headache?"

He walked over to his cot. "It's manageable. How are the babies?"

She smiled. "Manageable. Jacob loved his bath."

Nathan's eyes brightened. "Did he?"

"He kicks like a little frog."

Nathan sat on the foot of his cot. Maisie stayed in the doorway. Her smile faded. "Did the bishop know of someone you can hire?"

"He will ask around. He didn't know of anyone offhand." Nathan took a sip of soup.

"You could put an ad in the newspaper." Maisie clamped her lips shut. Why was she helping find her own replacement?

Because she wanted to help Nathan, as well as the children. She turned to leave but he spoke. "This is *goot*."

"I'm glad you like it."

"I'll come see the babies before I turn in."

She smiled softly and leaned her shoulder against the doorjamb. "Of course. You'll have to get past Buddy. He's appointed himself their guardian."

"Is that so? All he did before you came was howl when they cried."

"Perhaps he's gotten used to them. Have you decided what you're going to tell your boss?"

He took another sip of soup before answering. "I'll go back to work. I don't have much choice. It's not what

I want. I need to take care of my children. They are my responsibility. I should be the one looking after them."

"Nathan, I'm not trying to take that away from you."

He glanced at her sharply. "Aren't you?"

"I'm not. You're their father. I am only their aunt. Because I love them that doesn't diminish how much you love them." She tried to understand what was going on behind his hooded expression. "They won't love you any less because I'm here."

He stared at his sandwich without commenting.

Maisie sighed. "Come up to the house whenever you're ready." She walked back to the cabin in the darkness.

Nathan set his unfinished food aside. Was that what he was afraid of? That his son and his daughter wouldn't love him if there was someone else in their lives? Was he frightened of being abandoned again? Was he that selfish? That insecure?

How could Maisie guess what he was feeling when he didn't know it himself? Despite her temper and her stubbornness, she was a perceptive woman.

Weariness dragged at him and made him want to lie down and cover his head, but he couldn't sleep until he knew his babies were okay. He forced himself to get to his feet and walk up to the cabin.

Light spilled out the open doorway with a welcoming warmth. He stepped inside and paused. Everything was clean and brighter. The cobwebs were gone from the corners. His floor hadn't looked this good since he'd first laid it. The whole place smelled fresh.

He didn't see Maisie. The Moses baskets were on the sofa. Buddy lay sprawled across the floor in front of them. He got up when Nathan moved toward him. Nathan patted the dog's head and smiled at the sight of his children sleeping peacefully. He looked down at the dog. "They are a lot sweeter when they're quiet, aren't they?"

Nathan took one of the kitchen chairs, turned it around and placed it beside the babies. He leaned forward with his arms braced on the back of it and just watched them. Charity's eyebrows wiggled up and down as if she was trying to open her eyes. Jacob gave a small grunt and then smiled. His tiny hands grasped at the blanket. Nathan reached down and let his son wrap his small hand around his index finger. The boy's grip was amazing for his size.

He heard a sound behind him. Glancing over his shoulder, he saw Annie had come in. He realized his mistake an instant later and looked away. Maisie walked up to him. "You may hold them if you wish."

"I don't want to wake them."

"Babies need to be held."

"If you insist." It was what he needed, and somehow she knew it. Nathan reached down and scooped up his son. He settled him in the crook of his arm. The boy stretched but didn't wake.

Nathan sat in awe of the gifts he had been given. Annie had taken a lot from him, but she had given him something immeasurably precious in the end. He could feel his anger toward her shrinking. It wasn't gone, but it wasn't as painful to think about.

"I've been told that babies like the sound of familiar voices," Maisie said.

He glanced at her for the first time without resentment. "You mean just talk? What should I say?"

"You can tell him about your day or read something."

"I don't have any children's storybooks."

She sat down on the sofa beside Charity. "You don't have to read from a book. You can read from a magazine or from the Bible. Anything that sounds soothing."

"Maybe I'll just talk about my day."

He concentrated on Jacob's face. "Today wasn't the best of days. I went all the way to Fort Craig on a wild-goose chase to catch a bus that wasn't there. My boss stopped in to see me to tell me I will lose my job if I can't tear myself away from you and your sister. It was a tough decision, but I have to earn a living for you. Then I had an argument with your aunt. After that I went on another wild-goose chase to find a nanny and came back empty-handed."

He glanced at Maisie from the corner of his eye. Her eyes were downcast and her face was flushed. Embarrassment? He looked back at Jacob. "The best part of the whole day was a cup of yummy potato-and-ham soup that your aunt Maisie made for me."

He leaned down and whispered just loud enough for her to hear, "Maybe she'll leave us the recipe before she goes home if we ask nicely."

Jacob smiled in his sleep and Nathan smiled back at him.

"You left out the part where their bad-tempered auntie gave you a roaring headache," Maisie said.

Nathan realized his headache was almost gone. "I'm saving that part for tomorrow evening."

He stood up, kissed Jacob's forehead and laid him in his basket. Then he leaned down and kissed Charity's soft, plump cheek. "Sleep well, *liebling*, my little love."

He thrust his hands in his pockets as he faced Maisie. "I can take them down to my room for the night if you want some rest."

"I'm fine. We can trade off tomorrow night if you wish." The look was back in her eyes. The one that pleaded with him to change his mind and let her stay on.

He ignored it and walked to the door. He stopped and turned to her. "The place looks nice."

"Danki." She seemed surprised by his compliment.

He was a little shocked that he'd said anything, too. "Plan on staying until the bus leaves next Friday." Surely he could find someone to look after the children in a week's time.

The joy on her face took his breath away. She clasped her hands together as she smiled at him. "Bless you, Nathan."

"Don't expect to stay longer." He assumed her smile would dim, but it didn't. She nodded, but he suspected she was already thinking of ways to extend her stay.

He walked out into the night. Why had he been moved by the sight of her happiness? Because it was like seeing Annie happy again. That was all it was.

Yet something about that assumption didn't feel right.

Opening the door to his room, he stopped and looked at his narrow bed and the half-eaten supper beside it. It was quiet without the babies, but lonely. He'd lived with loneliness for months. Why should it feel different now?

He sat down and finished the cold soup, then ate his sandwich. Through the window he saw the lights in the cabin go out. Suddenly he wished he hadn't told Maisie she could stay longer. She was too unsettling to have around. The best woman for the job would be older. A grandmotherly person. Not someone with bright green eyes that silently pleaded for him to change his mind whenever he looked her way. Definitely not a woman who sensed things about him that he didn't know himself.

If the bishop didn't find someone, Nathan would use Maisie's suggestion and advertise the position in the local paper. It didn't have to be Amish women.

He realized he didn't need to wait on the bishop. He could place the ad and put up flyers in the grocery store and other local businesses. He'd do it in the morning.

Feeling better with a plan in place, he blew out the lamp and lay back in bed with his arms crossed behind his head. Maisie wasn't staying a moment longer than necessary. Not if he could help it. He wouldn't let her imploring eyes change his mind.

Chapter Five

Maisie was humming when Nathan entered the cabin early the next morning. Was she always such a cheerful soul? The smell of fresh-baked bread filled the air with an enticing aroma that made his stomach rumble. She opened his finicky stove and pulled out two beautiful golden-brown loaves. She must've been up for hours. Did the woman even need sleep?

When she turned around, he saw the answer to his question. There were dark circles under her eyes.

"Was it a rough night?" he asked.

"A little," she admitted. "They started fussing after midnight and kept it up until about an hour ago. I wonder if the different formula doesn't agree with them?"

He frowned. "How will we know?"

"They'll continue to fuss after they eat until they get used to it. If they stay fussy on it, I'll have to change back to what the hospital sent home with you. Go ahead and sit down. Your breakfast is ready. I made scrambled eggs. I hope that's okay."

"I like dippy eggs better, but that's fine." He liked to soak his bread in the runny yolks, but he wasn't going to turn down scrambled ones that he didn't have to fix himself.

He took a seat. She wrapped her apron around one of the loaves and carried it to the table. When she sliced it open, steam rose in a fragrant cloud. His mouth started watering. He loved hot, fresh bread.

Maisie pressed her hands to the small of her back and leaned backward with a grimace. Then she returned to the stove to dish up the eggs and bring over the coffee-pot. She filled his cup and then her own. Leaving it on a pot holder in the center of the table, she sat down, folded her hands and bowed her head.

He prayed silently, as he had been taught by his mother, and cleared his throat when he was finished. Maisie immediately reached for her coffee. Before she got the cup to her mouth, one of the babies began crying. "Oh, dear. That's Jacob."

He wondered how she could tell just from the sound of the child's cry. She took one sip and put her cup aside. She started to rise but Nathan forestalled her. "I'll see to him."

She shook her head. "Your breakfast will get cold."

He pushed back from the table. "I've had many a cold meal. Drink your *kaffi*. You look like you could use it."

"No flattery from you this morning."

"You should be glad I didn't say what I was thinking."

She rolled her eyes. "That I look like a worn-out hag?"

"Those are your own words."

"If I look as bad as I feel, they're accurate."

He picked up Jacob and settled him upright against his chest, then sat at the table again. Between patting the baby's back and making soothing sounds, he managed to fork eggs into his mouth with his free hand. Buddy had followed him and stood by Nathan's chair whining softly.

Jacob belched and spit up on Nathan's shoulder. He grimaced as the wet soaked through his shirt. "I reckon that was his problem."

Maisie was out of her chair and getting a kitchen towel before he could say anything else. He shifted the baby to his other shoulder while she dabbed at his shirt. He finally took the towel from her. "It's just a little sour milk. Don't fuss."

"I can take him." She held out her arms.

"He's fine where he is. Sit."

Buddy promptly sat and stopped whining. Maisie returned to her chair. Nathan glanced at his dog and then at Maisie. "That's better. Could you butter a piece of bread for me?"

"Of course." She quickly slathered a slice and handed it to him. He fed it to the dog.

"What are you doing?" she asked in astonishment.

"I'm rewarding the dog for doing as he was told even if I wasn't talking to him."

She clamped her lips together. He arched one eyebrow. "You don't approve?"

"He's your dog." She picked up her coffee cup again.

"He will never stop begging at the table if you feed him from it."

"Are you an expert on dogs as well as on babies?"

"Not at all. We never allowed our dogs in the house," she said primly.

He looked at his hound. "Did you hear that, Buddy? She might feel differently when it's thirty below outside and she's in bed with cold feet."

Her mouth dropped open, but she quickly snapped it shut. "I would rather get another quilt than allow a flea-bitten mongrel into my bed."

"Buddy doesn't have fleas, do you, boy? I put a little vinegar in his water and that takes care of them."

"Good to know." She propped her elbow on the table and settled her chin on her palm. Her eyelids began to drift lower. She jerked awake, blinked several times and then settled into the same position.

He wondered if she was going to fall asleep in her scrambled eggs. He knew how exhausting taking care of the twins could be. He had enjoyed an uninterrupted night and decided she deserved a break. He shoveled in his last forkful of eggs, washed them down with coffee and got to his feet. "I'm going to take the twins down to the barn with me this morning."

Her head popped up. "What?"

"I'm going to watch the children for a while. I suggest you use the free time to catch up on some sleep."

"I'm fine. I can look after them."

There was that pleading look again.

He hardened his heart against it. "So can I."

Rather than arguing, he simply laid Jacob on his

bed and picked up both baskets. He walked to the door. "Come on, Buddy."

The dog happily went out the door ahead of him. Nathan looked over his shoulder at Maisie. "I appreciate you making breakfast. Get some rest. You need it." He pulled the door closed and stared at it.

He shouldn't have said that, but she looked so worn out that he had taken pity on her. He didn't want to encourage her or give her false hope. He wasn't going to change his mind. Maisie was going to be on the first available bus as soon as he found a *kinder heeda*.

Maisie managed a tired smile. If he appreciated her cooking, that was a start. Maybe he was relenting.

Your words made my sleepless night worthwhile, Nathan Weaver. Danki.

She considered starting on some new clothes for the twins but realized she couldn't keep her eyes open long enough to set the stitches. She climbed the steps to the loft so she could lie down. The pillow held Nathan's scent. It was comforting and it made her feel closer to him.

She only needed to rest her eyes for a few minutes and then she would be fine.

Sometime later she heard crockery clattering in the kitchen. She sat up and looked over the low knee wall that ran the length of the open loft. Nathan was finishing the dishes. The babies were fast asleep in their beds on the sofa. Buddy sat beside Nathan at the kitchen counter, watching him hopefully. How long had she been asleep?

"What time is it?" she asked.

Nathan looked up and then quickly glanced away. "Half past noon. I'm fixing church spread. Would you like some on a slice of bread?"

He still couldn't look at her. Maisie sighed. Her resemblance to her sister was an obstacle she couldn't overcome.

"That sounds *wunderbar*." She patted her *kapp* to make sure it was on straight, then went down the steep stairs to the kitchen.

He held out a plate without looking at her. She took it and crossed to the sofa, where she sat beside Charity. The church spread, a peanut-butter-and-marshmallow cream spread, was delicious on a thick slice of her homemade bread. She licked her fingers when she was finished. Nathan stood at the sink gazing out the window while he ate. Occasionally, he broke off a piece and fed it to the dog.

"Has Mr. Davis been by?" Her voice sounded strained to her own ears.

"He stopped in."

She waited for more information, but Nathan wasn't forthcoming. "And? What did you tell him?"

He continued to stare out the window. "I told him to put me on the schedule for Monday. Now that you're up I am going into town." He turned around but only to grab some papers and his hat from the table. He stopped in the open doorway but didn't look back. "Do you need anything?"

A sack to wear over my head so that you can look at me and not see Annie.

No doubt he would be happy to bring her one. "Nothing, *danki*."

"I don't know when I'll be back. If you need anything the phone shack is about a quarter of a mile south of the end of my lane. Lilly Arnett's phone number is on the wall. She's the closest neighbor. She'll help." He went out the door without waiting for her reply.

Maisie gazed at the sleeping babies. "At least he isn't so angry today. Your *daed* won't admit it, but he can't ignore me forever."

She got up and began sorting her fabric. She had finished cutting out a pair of gowns for the babies when she heard a buggy pull up outside about an hour later. She assumed it was Nathan so she didn't go to the door. She was startled to hear women's voices outside.

She put her sewing aside as two Amish women appeared in the doorway. "Hello, sister," the older one said. "May we come in?"

Shocked to have visitors, Maisie sprang to her feet. "Of course. I'm sorry but Nathan has gone into town."

The two middle-aged women smiled brightly as they glanced about at the interior of the cabin. "What a snug little home Nathan Weaver has built," the one with wire-rimmed spectacles said. "I'm Constance Schultz. The bishop is my husband. This is my friend, Dinah Lapp. Her husband is our minister and a great help to the bishop."

"I'm pleased to meet you. I'm Maisie Schrock, Nathan's sister-in-law. His late wife was my sister, Annie."

"We heard of the tragedy only a few days ago. Accept our condolences," Dinah said. "We have come to see what we can do to help."

Maisie was moved by the sincerity and sympathy in their eyes. The Amish rallied around one another during times of trial.

"*Danki.* It's been difficult for me. Annie was my twin."

"*Gott* allowed it," Constance said softly. "We cannot understand His ways. We can only accept them."

"I know, and I pray for acceptance." She blinked back her tears. "Come and meet my nephew and niece. This is Jacob and Charity." She led the way to the sofa.

Both women bent over the baskets and cooed with delight. Constance looked at Maisie. "The little girl has such red hair. Does she have a temper to go with it?"

"Not that I have seen yet. I pray she doesn't develop one." Maisie patted her own head. "It can be a burden."

Dinah laughed. "You must meet my daughter-in-law, Gemma. She's a redhead, too."

"Would you like some *kaffi*? It won't take but a minute to put it on."

"Sounds *wunderbar,*" Dinah said.

Happy to have such pleasant company, Maisie bustled around the kitchen fixing coffee and putting slices of her fresh bread and the leftover spread Nathan had made on the table.

Constance gathered up the material Maisie had cut out and moved it to one side. "I see you're getting some sewing done."

"Nathan doesn't have any clothes for them except

what few things my sister had and what the hospital could send home with him."

"Do you have children of your own?" Dinah asked.

Maisie sat at the table while she waited for the coffee to perk. "I don't. My husband passed away some time ago. We were not blessed with children."

"That must make your sister's children especially precious to you, then," Constance said.

"It does. They are the only family I have left." Maisie felt the tears well up in her eyes.

She found herself telling the women everything about her life in Missouri, her trip to Maine, learning of her sister's death and arriving unannounced on Nathan's doorstep. She left out the part about Annie leaving Nathan. She didn't think he would want that to become common knowledge and neither did she. It didn't reflect well on Annie.

Constance leaned across the table and patted Maisie's hand. "Nathan is fortunate to have you here to care for his new babies."

"He finds my presence distressing."

"Why?" Dinah asked.

"Because Annie and I are—were—identical twins. He sees the woman he loved and lost every time he looks at me. He doesn't want me here."

"No twins are ever exactly the same," Constance said. "Surely he could tell you apart before she died."

"We didn't see much of each other before he moved here. Nathan was new to our community. He met and married my sister very quickly. I was busy taking care of my father during his illness and running our farm after my husband died. I reckon Nathan seldom saw us side by side."

"He'll soon see that you are different from your sister," Dinah said in an encouraging tone as she took another slice of bread.

Constance leaned back and folded her arms across her chest. "Is that why he asked my husband to see if anyone in the community wanted a job as a *kinder heeda*?"

"Nathan wants me to go back to Missouri."

"And what do you want to do?" Constance asked gently.

"I want to care for my sister's children. But if their father won't let me, I don't see how I can make him."

"That's true." Constance rubbed her chin. "Perhaps my husband should have a word with him."

"Nathan isn't a member of our congregation," Dinah reminded her. "Your husband's well-meaning words may not carry much weight."

"It's a family matter," Maisie said quickly. "I'd rather you left it between Nathan and myself." He wouldn't appreciate her involving the bishop. He was a man who liked to solve his own problems.

Constance nodded. "I understand. If the Lord wants you to stay in Maine, He will show you the path. Now, would you like to see what we brought?" she asked brightly.

Puzzled, Maisie rose and followed them to the door. Outside she saw their open buggy was packed with boxes, quilts and even furniture. There were two cradles and a rocking chair.

Maisie opened one of the cardboard boxes and pulled out a little sleeper. It was used but in wonderful condition. It was too big for the babies now, but in a few months it would be perfect. "This is very generous." She hugged the two women.

"If things don't work out between you and Nathan, come see me," Constance said. "There is always a place at our table for as long as you want. Now, let's get these things inside. It looks like rain."

For the first time since leaving Missouri, Maisie felt truly welcomed. She realized she wouldn't have to leave when Nathan found someone to care for the babies. With the help of friends like Constance and Dinah, she could make a life here in Maine and stay close to her sister's children.

Nathan was greeted by the sight of an unfamiliar open buggy parked in front of his cabin when he returned home. The brown-and-white pony hitched to it looked up and whinnied to Sassy. She ignored him as she headed for the barn.

Nathan unhitched the buggy and pulled off her harness before leading the mare into his corral. He rubbed her down and walked her to make sure she was cooled off before he let her drink. Giving her a final pat on her shoulder, he closed the corral gate. Sassy went to the middle of the enclosure, put her nose to the ground and turned in a tight circle before lying down and enjoying a roll in the grass.

Women's voices and laughter spilled out the door as

Nathan approached. He stopped in the doorway until one of the women noticed he was there.

"You must be Nathan Weaver." An Amish woman with wire-rimmed spectacles smiled at him from his kitchen. She was holding his naked daughter. Maisie wrapped a towel around the babe and took her in her arms.

"You've just missed bathing the babies," the second woman said as she sat holding Jacob on the sofa. There was a large pile of infant clothing and quilts beside her. "Charity spit up all over herself and her brother."

Maisie kissed Charity's cheek. "Mmm, clean babies smell so sweet."

She nodded toward the woman with glasses. "Nathan, this is Constance Schultz, the bishop's wife, and that is Dinah Lapp. Her husband is one of the ministers. Sisters, this is my brother-in-law, Nathan Weaver."

Dinah got to her feet and laid the baby in a wooden cradle Nathan had never seen before. A second one sat beside it. She turned to face him. "God's ways are beyond our comprehension, but His love and mercy will comfort you in your time of grief."

He didn't reply. There was no comfort for him, only unanswered questions.

"We were just getting ready to leave," the bishop's wife said. "I'm glad we had the opportunity to meet you. My husband is seeking someone to take care of the children for you. He hasn't found anyone yet, but he's still looking. In the meantime you are blessed to have your wife's sister caring for them. It's easy to see how much she loves them."

"I'll walk you out," Maisie said.

"I'll bring my sewing machine by this weekend," Constance said.

Maisie bit the corner of her lip. "All right, if you're sure you don't need it for a few days."

"If I do I know where it will be," Constance said with a chuckle.

Maisie handed Charity to Nathan and followed her guests out the door. He saw the women hug each other before they got in their buggy. He couldn't hear what they were saying, but Maisie nodded. She smiled and waved as the women drove away.

When she came back inside, she was still smiling.

"What were they doing here?" he asked.

"They stopped in to see how we are getting along and to bring us some things they thought we could use. They brought baby clothes and baby blankets. Even a pair of quilts for us."

She gestured toward the kitchen counter. "And they brought all that food. Freshly canned vegetables and fruit from their gardens. A ten-pound bag of flour and sugar for baking. There is even a moose-meat casserole ready to go into the oven for our supper tonight. They tell me that propane appliances are permitted in this church district, so they are able to keep meat frozen in a freezer. They also said to tell you that you are welcome to store your meat with them when you go hunting this fall."

"I didn't ask for any of this. I can provide for my family. I don't need the charity of others."

She frowned at him. "They didn't come to offer charity."

He gestured with one hand around the cabin. "Then what would you call this? Food. Clothing. Cradles for the babies and a rocking chair." He pointed to the corner by the fireplace, where he had just noticed the new piece of furniture.

Maisie folded her arms. "I call it a gesture of friendship extended to a new member of their community. Isn't that what we Amish do? We care for one another. We don't wait for someone to ask for help. We just give it. Isn't that the way you want your children to behave when they grow up? How will they learn about generosity and kindness unless they see it firsthand?"

"It's my job to teach them."

Maisie shook her head sadly. "Oh, Nathan. This is about more than your feelings of being a poor provider. We all need help sometimes. We must give it and receive it in equal measure. This is about being part of a community who live and worship together to please *Gott*. If you aren't a part of that then you aren't truly Amish and your children won't be, either."

How did Maisie find the core of his inner fears so easily? He hadn't been an adequate provider. He had failed Annie and he was failing his son and daughter.

He looked away. "What did you tell them about Annie? Will everyone know that she left me?" Shame burned like acid in the back of his throat.

"I told them that my sister was traveling to be with you when she went into labor and had to go to a hospital. She died before you or I could be with her. Nothing else needs to be said. I don't wish to besmirch my sister's reputation. She repented, and she was making amends. I'm thinking of the children and what they'll hear about her when they're growing up."

"That she took off and left me two months after our wedding with only a note that said she thought she could live Amish but she couldn't anymore?"

"They will never hear that from me. Their mother was on her way to be with their father in his new home in Maine, but *Gott* took her to heaven instead."

"You make it sound like her actions were nothing more than a trip to town. It was months of worry and wondering and never finding peace even when I prayed. Every day I waited for the mail, hoping she would send me a letter, a card, something. Do you know what that's like?"

She stepped close and laid her hand on his arm. "I do, Nathan. I prayed for the same things. I waited and bore my disappointments and cried my tears in secret, but I never hardened my heart against her. I loved her, too."

He gazed into Maisie's eyes. They sparkled with unshed tears for the grief and pain they had both endured.

Then he noticed something else about her eyes. They were green like Annie's, but Maisie had flecks of gold in hers that Annie hadn't had.

She wiped away the moisture with both hands. "I need to tell you something else, Nathan. I'm not saying this to make you angry. I'm not leaving New Covenant."

"Are we back to this again? I decide who takes care of my children."

Her face grew stoic. "That is your right," she said in a clipped tone.

"I'm not going to change my mind." He wanted to shout, but he kept his voice deliberately even.

She folded her hands demurely in front of her. "If you don't want me to be their *kinder heeda*, I must be content to be the aunt who lives down the road. I will find employment and see them as often as I can. I will bake birthday cakes and make cookies when they come to visit. I'll see them at church."

She raised her chin. "I don't care how many bus tickets you buy for me. I'm not going anywhere."

He leaned close. "We'll see about that."

Chapter Six

Maisie saw a muscle twitch in Nathan's clenched jaw. He was angry, but what could he do? She was a grown woman. He had no control over her life.

Of course, he could order her out of his house right now. She swallowed hard. He wouldn't, would he? He stared at her so long her resolve began to waver.

"You may live wherever you like," he snapped. "But it won't be here any longer than necessary."

She let out the breath she'd been holding. "I understand. If you would like your loft back I will gladly sleep in the barn."

It took a minute, but he finally shook his head. "That won't be necessary."

"*Goot*. I'll call you when supper is ready. I need to put away the things our friends have brought us."

"Your friends," he snapped, staring at his feet.

Her heart went out to him. He was so alone. There was a wall around him that he refused to let people inside. "They will be your friends, too, Nathan. Maybe not today, but when you're ready to be part of a community again."

He looked up with a perplexed expression. "How do you do that?"

She tipped her head slightly. "Do what?"

"Know what I'm feeling."

"Did you forget that I lost my husband? After John's death, making any choice was hard. I only wanted to be left alone to grieve. I avoided people. I thought I should be stronger. I didn't want others to see how broken I was. In time that passed. I found purpose in taking care of my father during his illness. I opened myself up to people again and realized that I didn't have to be strong all by myself. There were friends who wanted to help ease my way."

"I haven't made friends in this Amish community because I am ashamed of what drove me here. Being alone is nothing new for me. Annie's death didn't change that."

"Only you aren't alone anymore. You have two wonderful children who will make friends of their own someday, go to school, attend church, get into trouble, cause no end of worry for you and weave themselves into the fabric of our Amish way of life."

"I only took my baptismal vows so that I could marry your sister."

She smiled softly. "A lot of young men decide to join the faith for that reason. You need to discover what *Gott* wants from you, Nathan. He has a plan for us all if we open our hearts to it."

"You have an answer for everything."

Maisie stared at the floor. "I don't really." Then she glanced up. "Give yourself some time. It hasn't even been two weeks since you lost Annie."

His expression hardened. "You're wrong about that. I may have buried her last week, but I lost my wife months ago."

He stomped out of the cabin. Maisie watched as he picked up an axe and hiked into the woods.

She felt better that she had told him of her desire to stay in New Covenant, but their relationship hadn't improved with the telling. She grasped the ribbon of her *kapp* and wound it around her finger. There had to be a way to help him overcome the bitterness that hung like a dense fog between them. She liked Nathan in spite of his reluctance to allow her into his life. Under his gruff exterior was a good man. She was sure of it.

Perhaps what she needed to do was smother him with kindness. The trick would be keeping her temper under control in the face of his stubbornness.

Nathan swung the axe with as much force as he could muster. Wood chips flew from the pine he was cutting down. *Whack, whack, whack.*

His chain saw would have made quick work of this tree, but the rhythm of his swing and the bite of the axe soothed him. Finally, the tree came crashing down. He leaned on the axe's handle, breathing heavily. One down, three more to go.

He looked in the direction of the cabin. Maisie wasn't leaving. He would have to accept her occasional presence in his life. She had a right to see her sister's children. He couldn't deny her that. She was as alone in the world as he was. He didn't want to feel sorry for her, yet he did.

He hefted his axe and walked to the next tree he had marked. He picked the spot where he wanted it to fall and started swinging again. These trees would cure over the winter and by next summer they would be ready to be peeled and stacked. They would be used to expand his icehouse.

The tree toppled over within a few feet of where he wanted it. The satisfaction eased his foul mood. He needed a way to deal with Annie's sister just as efficiently. His current method of storming out meant he was getting more work on the farm done, but it also served to cut down the time he spent with his children. He'd be going back to work soon and that meant ten hours away from them each day. As much as he disliked being in the same room with Maisie, he would have to be in the cabin with her in order to see his babies. It didn't sit well, but he had little choice. He'd put up with Maisie's discomforting presence for the children.

Being around the woman was unsettling because she was a reminder of Annie, and because she was too perceptive, as well. When she looked at him with her green-gold eyes she saw things he wasn't ready to face.

He sighed heavily. Maisie was in his life, like it or not. Until he found a full-time nanny for the babies he was simply going to have to make the best of it.

He took down the last two trees he had marked and then headed back toward the cabin.

As soon as he came in, he noticed Maisie had cleared

out the boxes. She had everything put away except for the jars of produce that still filled the countertop. She was sitting in the rocker by the fireplace feeding one of the babies. He stepped closer to see which one it was. She held Jacob.

Charity was in the cradle beside Maisie's chair. She was squirming a little but not crying. "Has Charity had her bottle?" he asked.

"Not yet. It's warming in the sink. Jacob was the more impatient of the two. Takes after his father."

He didn't smile. "Maybe so."

"That must mean Charity will take after her mother," Maisie suggested.

That was a chilling thought. "I hope not."

He saw a flash of disapproval in Maisie's eyes, but she didn't say anything. He went to the sink and washed up. After drying his hands, he took the bottle from the pan of warm water, sprinkled some of the formula on his wrist to check the temperature, as the nurse at the hospital had taught him, and then scooped up his daughter. He offered the bottle to Charity. She latched on immediately and began to suckle.

He walked to the sofa and sat down with her. This was so much different than his first attempts to feed them. Would he and the babies have settled in comfortably without Maisie's arrival? Maybe.

No, of course they would have. He would have figured it out.

"Here." Maisie offered him a burp rag. "It will save your shirt from another milk bath."

"*Danki*, but milk might be an improvement." He picked a few wood chips from his sleeve.

"I saw the clothesline, but not a washing machine. Do you launder everything by hand?"

"The washer is in the lean-to next to the barn. I lived in the barn when I first came here. I haven't moved the machine up to the house yet."

"You don't have to do that on my account. I don't want to put you to any trouble."

It was too late for that. "It makes sense to have it here. I'll move it to the back porch tomorrow."

"I heard you chopping down trees. Are you building something new or gathering firewood?"

"Something new for next year. The trees have to dry out and cure before I can use them."

"Are you planning an addition to the cabin?"

"I'm expanding my icehouse. I'll add on to the cabin in a few years when the *kinder* are old enough to need their own room."

She glanced around. "Where would you put it?"

"Going through the wall behind the kitchen would be the easiest. That way I could add a stove to their room and use the same vent pipe."

"That's clever."

Did she really think so? "I have other ideas for the place."

"Like what?"

"I need to expand the garden and put in a root cellar."

She smiled. "That's why I couldn't find one to store those jars in. I looked everywhere."

He grimaced. "I'm not much of a cook. I usually

eat my meals at the canteen on the job site. I haven't canned any vegetables so my garden isn't big. I figure I can pay someone to preserve my produce next summer or barter fresh for canned."

"A well-stocked cellar makes keeping food on the table a lot easier." She put Jacob to her shoulder to burp him.

Nathan did the same to Charity. "At least I don't have to worry about keeping a roof over their heads. Davis pays a good wage. My potato crop will bring in extra money as long as the weather and the market cooperate. That plus my salary should see us through the winter. The hospital won't get all their money right away, but they will be paid."

Maisie swaddled Jacob and laid him in his new cradle. She gave a slight push to start it rocking and then when to the kitchen. "Are you ready to eat?"

He smiled at his little girl. "As soon as she is finished."

"I'll put it on the table. I've never had moose meat before. Have you?"

"I've had it as a summer sausage. It isn't bad."

She wrinkled her nose. "Let's hope it isn't bad in this casserole. I don't care for gamey meat."

"Annie was a picky eater, too." He assumed because Maisie was identical to Annie that she would share the same traits, but Annie never had a temper.

"I'm not as bad as my sister was but there are things I won't eat. Okra for one."

"There's none in my vegetable patch."

"I noticed when I was poking around."

He put Charity's empty bottle on the arm of the sofa and carried her to her cradle. After laying her down, he gave the cradle a gentle push. It began swinging to and fro. "Who donated the baby beds to us?"

"The bishop's brother and his wife. They have twins who are grown but not married, so no grandchildren yet to hand them on to."

"They're well-made."

"According to Constance the bishop's brother is a furniture maker. He's starting his own sawmill."

"A useful business." Nathan rubbed his short beard. "I have some hardwoods in my forest. Maybe I can sell them to him."

"You can talk to him at the service next week."

He looked at her sharply. "You assume that I'm going."

She paused in setting the table. "Of course. I'll be going. Everyone will want to meet the babies. Why would you stay home?"

"I don't want strangers staring at me and wondering what my story is."

Setting the plate down, she turned toward him. "Wouldn't the best way to avoid that be to meet the people and tell them what you want them to know? After that you'll be old news."

He hated to admit that she had a point. "We'll see."

"Goot." She smiled brightly. "When that was my *daed*'s answer, it always meant he was going to do whatever *Mamm* had asked."

"From me it means we'll see." If she was trying to

manipulate him with a pleasant smile she would find it hard going.

"As you say. I'll make sure your suit is washed and pressed just in case you decide to join us. Supper is ready."

The casserole wasn't the best he'd ever eaten but he did take a second helping. Maisie's biscuits were light and fluffy, a far cry from the bricks he knew how to make. When she brought out a plate of brownies for dessert, he happily helped himself to two.

"*Goot* supper," he said, leaning back in his chair after finishing a cup of cocoa.

"I'm happy to see you enjoying it. I was worried you'd starve rather than eat in my company."

"I worked up an appetite cutting trees this afternoon." He hesitated then said, "You remind me of things I want to forget, Maisie. I know that isn't your intent, but it can't be helped. You are so like her."

"What if Charity grows up to resemble Annie? How will you treat her? Will she be punished for her mother's sins because they look alike, too?"

"I'm not punishing you for your sister's transgressions."

"It feels like it to me."

He hadn't considered how she saw his actions. He remained silent. She cleared the table, washed the dishes and wiped down the kitchen before taking up her sewing. She sat in the rocker ignoring him. He stayed at the table, turning his cup around and around in his hands as he thought about what he should say.

"I'm sorry you feel that way, Maisie."

She plopped the little gown she was hemming onto her lap. "I'm a grown woman. I'll survive. For a child it might not be so easy."

He nodded. "Charity will look like Charity. I'll never treat her with anything but love. I promise."

"I should not have suggested otherwise." She reached over and set Charity's cradle to rocking again.

Nathan brought the wringer washing machine up to the back porch the next day and showed Maisie how to use it. It was powered with a small gasoline engine, like her lawn mower at home. It took her several tugs on the pull cord to get it started, but once it was going it was much easier than washing and rinsing diapers and bedding by hand.

The only water in the cabin was a hand pump at the kitchen sink. The two-piece bathroom used water from a roof cistern. Maisie learned the tub was an old-fashioned galvanized relic that hung on the front porch. It had to be brought in and filled by hand.

She had to heat her wash water on the stove and carry it out back to the machine. Nathan took her place caring for the babies while she caught up on his laundry, too. When she was hanging the clothes on the line she noticed several pairs of his work pants had rips in them.

After she was finished with the laundry, Nathan took off into the woods again. He seemed determined to spend as little time in her company as possible. While it was discouraging, because she couldn't bridge the gap between them, it was actually easier to work in the small cabin without his disturbing presence. She had the babies to herself and could enjoy holding and singing to them without worrying that she was upsetting him.

Later that evening Nathan was going over his farm accounts at the kitchen table while she was mending his laundry. She held up a pair of his pants. "What do you do that makes such ragged cuts in your pant legs?"

He looked at her. "I've caught them on my chain saw a few times."

Her eyebrows shot up. "While your legs were in them?"

"I've never had a serious cut."

She poked four fingers through one long slit. "The Lord has been your protector, then."

He shrugged one shoulder. "That day I did need a few stitches."

How dangerous was his job? Something Mr. Davis had said troubled her. "What is a widow-maker?"

Nathan went back to studying his account book. "Why do you ask?"

"Mr. Davis said the other feller broke his leg when a widow-maker came down. What did he mean?"

"A widow-maker is a toppled tree or big limb that is hung up or wedged against another tree. A little bit of wind can bring it down or it can stay wedged for years. You always have to be careful around them. Cutting down the tree they're leaning against can be tricky. You're never sure which way they'll fall."

"I see. Does it happen often that someone gets hurt?"

He glanced her way. "Often enough to make me a very cautious man."

She wiggled her fingers through his slit pants again. "Not cautious enough."

The idea of him being seriously hurt chilled her to the bone. She had faith in God's mercy, but she also knew how easily life could be snuffed out. One minute her husband, John, had been loading bales of hay into their loft. The next minute, he was lying on the ground with a broken neck. She shuddered at the memory.

The Lord gave, and the Lord hath taken away; blessed be the name of the Lord.

She was relieved when Jacob started fussing. She put her mending aside and picked him up. Holding him close, she rocked him until her painful memories faded. The Lord had taken her husband, her father and her sister, but he had given her two beautiful babies to love.

"Shall I fix him a bottle?" Nathan asked.

"I don't think he's hungry. I think he just wants to be held."

"You take good care of them. I'm grateful. I'll hold him so you can get on with your work."

She didn't want to give up Jacob, but she could see Nathan wanted to hold his son as much as she did, maybe more. She managed a smile. "*Danki*, that would be nice. I'll even give you the rocker."

She rose and transferred the baby into Nathan's arms. He gazed at his son so tenderly it brought a lump to her throat. She was close enough to catch his scent. Sweat, wood smoke, fresh pine sawdust, the saddle soap he had used to clean Sassy's harness that evening— a day's work all layered on top of his own unique smell.

She felt her pulse jump and beat faster as a flush crept up her neck.

She stepped back quickly. Her gaze flew to his face. Had he noticed? He was staring at her with a puzzled expression. "Are you okay?"

"I'm fine. I need to get the rest of the clothes off the line." She stumbled back another step then hurried outside. On the back porch she took a deep breath and leaned against the cabin wall until her racing heart slowed.

There was no mistaking her reaction to Nathan. As much as she wanted to deny it, she couldn't. She found him attractive, much more than she should have.

She knew what a passing fancy was. This was not something as simple as that.

How could it have happened without her knowing it? She thought back over their conversations and realized it had started the first night she arrived.

When they stood together in the darkness out by the corral—she had sensed a connection with him then. She thought it was because of their shared grief. Or rather, she wanted to believe that was the reason she felt close to him. Her mind had refused to acknowledge anything else. Until tonight.

He was her sister's husband. A man who couldn't look at her without seeing her sister's betrayal. It would be foolish of her to think he might someday care for her. He would pity her or, worse, laugh at the idea.

He had agreed she might see the children even if she couldn't be their caregiver. She didn't want to jeopardize that.

No, Nathan must never learn how she felt. Now that she recognized what was happening, she would guard her heart and not give this emotion room to grow.

She took a deep breath and went back in the house determined to act as if nothing had changed. Because it hadn't. He didn't want her here.

Keeping her wayward heart in check was harder than Maisie had imagined it would be. She tossed and turned that night long after she heard Nathan leave the cabin. It was hopeless to care so much for him. He would never return those feelings.

At least he was beginning to see her usefulness. He had thanked her for the care she gave the children. That was what she really wanted. To take care of the babies and love them as her own. If Nathan allowed that and nothing else, she would be content.

She bit her lower lip. Would she? Or was she lying to herself?

Chapter Seven

Saturday morning Maisie came down the stairs determined to ignore her irrational attraction to Nathan and concentrate on providing the best possible care to him and his children. Both infants had slept for almost five hours before getting her up to feed them. They were awake again now. Jacob was making his wants known with a loud cry. Charity was making little whimpering noises. She was more patient than her brother.

"I'm coming, Jacob. Don't holler the house down." She started into the kitchen and almost ran into Nathan coming in the back door. Her foolish heart gave a happy leap at the sight of his face. She quickly scooted around him, making sure they didn't touch.

"How are you this morning?" he asked.

"I'm fine."

"You seemed on edge last night."

It would never do for him to notice how he affected her.

"I do get cranky when I'm short of sleep." She glanced at his face. Did he believe her?

He seemed to relax. "I thought that might be the case. I will take care of the babies tonight so you can catch up on some rest."

She opened the can of concentrated formula and added the recommended amount of water from the kettle she kept warming on the back of the stove. "That is not necessary."

"I've abused your generosity. They are my son and daughter. I want to do it. If Jacob's bottle is ready, I'll feed him first since he is so loud."

"I haven't changed him yet."

"I'm not afraid of a dirty diaper or two." To prove his point he went to take care of that chore while she finished mixing the formula. She was pouring the formula into Charity's bottle when Nathan came up beside her to wash his hands at the sink. His shoulder brushed against hers. Her hand shook so badly that she splashed formula down the front of her dress.

He looked at her with a slight frown on his face. "Are you sure you're okay?"

"Don't worry. My clumsiness is not contagious," she said, sounding more annoyed than she intended.

He scowled at her. "I'm sorry I asked."

She screwed the nipple on top of the bottle. "I'm the one who is sorry. Forgive me."

He reached around her for the towel on the counter. She could smell the minty scent of his shaving cream. She closed her eyes and stopped breathing.

"There's nothing to forgive," he said as he took the bottle from her hands and went to feed his son.

Maisie turned to stare out the kitchen window. How long could she keep up the pretense that his closeness didn't affect her?

Charity began to cry in earnest. Maisie glanced over her shoulder. Nathan sat on the sofa with his boy in his arms while he rocked Charity's cradle with his foot to soothe her.

Maisie would keep her foolish heart in check for as long as the babies needed her. Because she needed them, too. She needed someone to love, and to be loved by in return. She was tired of being alone, first with her emotionally distant husband and then with her dying father, who'd constantly asked for Annie instead of the daughter who had cared for him for over a year.

Maisie straightened her shoulders and finished fixing Charity's bottle. She needed to be needed and wanted. Nathan might want her gone, but she wasn't leaving.

She lifted the baby from her cradle and settled into the rocking chair with her. Charity gazed up at her with wide baby-blue eyes.

"Guder mariye, mie lieb," Maisie whispered and kissed her forehead. "Every morning is a *goot* morning when I have you in my arms."

"They make our troubles seem insignificant, don't they?" Nathan was gazing at his son with an expression of undisguised love on his face. Maisie's heart expanded with happiness for him.

"They do," she answered. Annie had carelessly

thrown away the love of this man. Maisie had only pity for her sister. She had made poor choices.

Nathan looked up and met Maisie's eyes. Something passed between them at that moment. A shared love, not for one another, but for the children God had so graciously given into their care.

She saw his gaze slide away from her as his mouth tensed. "Annie could have been happy with me and these babies if she hadn't left. We could have had a good life in Missouri."

Maisie's heart ached for the pain he was sharing. "I think you're right. I don't believe she knew what she was giving up."

"You don't think she knew she was pregnant when she left me?"

Could her sister have been so cruel as to take away a man's children and leave him never knowing they existed? "I can't believe that she did."

"But she had to know within a month or two. Yet she didn't come back. Was there another man she wanted to be their father?"

"You are asking questions without answers, Nathan. Let it be enough that she decided to bring them to you in the end. She has gone to stand before *Gott* and answer for her life. Only He knows her heart. Only He can judge her."

Nathan drew one finger along his son's cheek. "My boy will have questions one day about why he doesn't have a mother. I don't know how I will answer him."

"You will find the words when the time comes. Until then, enjoy these amazing moments. Your children will be grown before you know it. You will never get these days back, Nathan."

"I do enjoy them." He put aside Jacob's empty bottle and raised the babe to his shoulder. He softly patted the boy's back and rested his cheek on the baby's head. Jacob drifted off to sleep, but Nathan didn't put him down. Maisie finished feeding Charity, put her back in her cradle, then slipped out of the cabin, leaving Nathan alone with his children.

She hiked to the top of the rise behind the cabin to her sister's final resting place. She sat in the soft grass beside the grave, drew her knees up to her chin and wrapped her arms around her legs. "You left so much bitterness behind, Annie, but your babies are beautiful. Charity looks like us. Happily, she has your temperament and not mine. Jacob is going to be enough to handle without adding another hothead to the mix."

Maisie plucked a few weeds that had sprouted in the freshly turned earth. "Nathan is such a good man. He's trying to be a good father. I don't understand why you left him."

She groped for answers where there weren't any. "Was it because you knew my marriage to John wasn't a happy one? Were you afraid that you and Nathan would grow apart and come to resent each other?"

Maisie thought back over the conversations she had with her sister about her unhappy marriage and wished she had kept those feelings to herself. Was that why Annie hadn't confided in her, because she wanted to spare Maisie her unhappiness?

"I never resented John. I don't believe he resented

me. We had known each other forever. Getting married seemed the thing to do. I thought our love would grow over time. I was wrong. I did care for him. I think he cared for me in his way, but he never could express that. It's a sad way to live, always wishing something would spark that love into being. Forever waiting to hear words you know will never be spoken. Children might have saved us, but I will never know, will I?"

Maisie got to her feet and brushed off her dress. "I hope you are at peace, sister. I pray you can rest easy knowing how much Nathan loves those children. Thank you for bringing them to him."

Maisie glanced around at the meadow and saw wildflowers growing near the edge of the woods. She went over and gathered an armful. Then she laid them gently on Annie's grave. "I will try to help him forgive you, for I know that's what he needs to do."

Nathan stepped outside of his room the next morning and stared at the cabin. As usual, the front door was open and he heard the sound of singing. Maisie was always humming or singing. It was the Amish off Sunday. There wouldn't be prayer services for her to attend. They were held every other week.

He glanced longingly at the forest. Only essential work was allowed on any Sunday. He might not be a member of the local church group, but he abided by the rules of his faith. His tree cutting would have to wait. He sighed heavily and started toward the house. There was a full day ahead of him that he would have to spend with Annie's sister.

He entered the cabin to see her playing with his cat. She was teasing him with a small ball of yarn. The cat would dart out from under the sofa, pounce on it and then scurry back under the furniture. Maisie would laugh and start humming as she pulled the yarn ball closer to the sofa again.

It was like hearing Annie's laugh. He shoved his hands in his pockets. "Morning."

Her smile faded. "*Guder mariye*, Nathan. Your breakfast is in the oven. I didn't know what time you would be in."

He headed for the kitchen. "When my chores are done."

She stayed silent while he ate and cleaned up quickly after he was done. She sat down with his copy of the *Martyrs Mirror* and started reading. The book contained stories of the men and women who had been martyred for their Anabaptist beliefs. They were the founders of the Amish faith.

He paced the room not knowing what to do. The babies were both quiet. He finally settled in his chair by the fireplace.

Maisie cleared her throat. "My father used to read to us on the off Sundays and in the evenings. It's a fond memory I have of him. Why don't you read to the children now?"

"Aren't they too small to care?"

"Who can say? We are born with open ears. *Gott* must want us to use them."

Nathan shrugged, got up and took his Bible down from the fireplace mantel. Maisie must have dusted it when she was cleaning because the black leather cover was shiny as new.

He carried it back to the table, moved a lamp closer and opened the cover. "What shall I read?"

"Daniel in the lions' den," she said without hesitation and picked up her yarn.

The hint wasn't subtle. "Are sure you don't mean Maisie in the lions' den?"

"Don't be silly. There is no story of Maisie in the Bible."

It had been a while since he had last opened this book. He leafed through the pages until he found the book of Daniel and began to read. When he was finished with the story, he looked over to see her smiling tenderly at Jacob. She glanced at Nathan. "His eyes are open. I think he likes the sound of your voice. Read something else."

"What would you like?"

"The Book of Job."

He turned to those chapters and started reading about Job, his suffering and his unwavering faith in God. Nathan suspected Maisie had chosen that part of the Old Testament to help him see that he was not alone in being tested. Unlike Job, Nathan's faith had wavered.

He glanced at Maisie. She had kept her faith in the face of her own painful losses. She had lost her mother when she was young, her husband when she was little more than a bride, her father and then her only sister without questioning God's plan or doubting His mercy. It was sobering to realize how strong she was. Jacob started stirring. Maisie got up to tend to him.

* * *

"Will anyone be visiting today?" Maisie asked after tucking the babies into their cradles later that day.

"I'm not expecting anyone. Why?"

She looked at him in surprise "It's the off Sunday."

"So?"

"It's a day that people normally go visit each other, families, friends. In Missouri we were always going to someone's house or expecting company on our off Sundays."

"I don't like visiting. No one comes here."

Maisie just shook her head. "I don't wonder why."

He finally looked up from the magazine he had decided to read. "What's that supposed to mean?"

"You aren't friendly with your Amish neighbors, Nathan."

"I don't have neighbors. That's why I live up here."

"Lilly Arnett is your neighbor. You said so yourself."

He turned the page of his magazine. "She isn't Amish."

"Well, who is the closest Amish family?"

"The Fishers, I reckon. They live a mile beyond Lilly's place."

"And have you been to visit them?"

"I purchased my harnesses there. Otherwise, I've never had a reason to."

"Have you been to visit the bishop and his wife? Constance is a lovely woman. I'm sure she would enjoy a visit today. I know she'd like to see the twins."

He turned another page. "It's my day of rest."

"I see. I believe I will bake a cake."

His expression brightened. "I like cake."

"I thought that might be the case." She spent the next ten minutes getting a chocolate sheet cake into the oven. Then she washed her hands and went upstairs. When she came down twenty minutes later, she had her Sunday dress on and her traveling bonnet in her hand. She checked on her cake and took it out of the oven. She began to pack some things for the babies and then moved them from their cradles into their carriers.

Nathan gave her a puzzled look. "What are you doing?"

"You may not like to go visiting, but I do. Constance Schultz was kind enough to loan me her sewing machine so I'm taking a cake to her home as a thank-you."

"I thought you were making the cake for me?"

"If there is any left, I will bring some home. Would you please hitch up the buggy?"

"It's my day of rest."

She merely arched one eyebrow and stood waiting. He threw down his magazine and got out of his chair. "If you're going to nag, I might as well get it over with. I'll enjoy my peace and quiet while you're gone."

"I'm sure you will. I'll enjoy chocolate cake and *kaffi* with my new friends."

He grumbled when he went out the door, but she couldn't hear what he was saying. She bent down to pick up the babies. "He might sound like an old bear sometimes but your *daed* is a fine fellow at heart."

She was waiting on the porch with the babies' carriers over each arm and the cake in a cardboard box by her feet when he led Sassy up to the steps. Maisie went around to the driver's side and got in without waiting for his help. She smiled at him out the open side. "Would you fetch the cake for me, Nathan? It's in that box on the porch."

He rolled his eyes but did as she asked. She put the cake on the other side of the babies. "I don't know how long I'll be."

"Be back before dark," he said sternly.

"Of course." She smiled at him and picked up the lines. "I left a piece of cake for you on the table. Sassy, walk on." The horse took off at a leisurely pace.

Nathan walked back into the cabin and stood with his hands in his pockets. The quiet emptiness was almost unnerving. Maisie was always humming softly or talking to the babies when she wasn't clattering pans or dishes in the kitchen or sweeping the floor. She was never rushed, never impatient—she simply went about her work.

She didn't jabber at him the way Annie used to in a giggling, immature way that he'd found cute, but he was always aware of Maisie. It shouldn't be that way.

He sat down in his chair and picked up his magazine but didn't open it. He stared into space and wondered if he should've gone with her. What if the babies became fussy? Would she concentrate on her driving or try to tend to them? The road out this way was narrow. It didn't get much traffic, but it only took a moment of inattention to end up in the ditch.

He looked at Buddy, who was gazing mournfully at the front door. "I'm not going to worry about them. I don't want you to worry about them, either. She's not going to give you or me a second thought. She has the babies with her, and she will be happily showing them off to everyone."

He opened his magazine and started reading until he realized it was an article he had already finished. He laid it aside and drummed his fingers on the arm of the chair.

They were his children. If anyone was going to act the happy new parent, it should be him.

He heard a sound in the kitchen and looked that way. Buddy had his front feet on the tabletop trying to reach the slice of cake in the center with one paw. His leg wasn't quite long enough. "*Shlecht hund!* Bad dog. Get down."

Nathan crossed the room and picked up the plate. "She left it for me. Not for you. Besides, I hear chocolate is bad for dogs."

He got a fork and sat down at the table to eat his treat. It was moist and delicious. He looked at the dog, who was eyeing him hopefully. "For all Maisie's faults, the woman does know how to cook."

Buddy barked twice.

"What are her faults? I'm glad you asked."

He thought for a long moment but couldn't come up with much. "She has a bit of a temper when she does get riled."

He snapped his fingers and pointed at Buddy. "She irritates me." He twitched his mouth to one side. "I don't think she does it on purpose."

Maisie didn't have many faults other than the fact

that she reminded him of Annie every time he looked at her. That wasn't something she could change.

The sooner he found a nanny for the children, the sooner he would have relief from Maisie's disturbing presence. He got up and took his hat from the peg. Maybe there was a message for him. His ad had been in the grocery store for several days. "Come on, Buddy. Let's go check the phone."

Maisie was relieved to find the bishop and his wife were at home. It turned out that she wasn't the only visitor. Michael Shetler and his wife, Bethany, were there along with Dinah Lapp and her husband, Leroy. The bishop and the men were playing horseshoes in the backyard. They left the women to provide refreshments, enjoy catching up on the current news in the community and pass the much-admired babies from arm to arm.

"I heard that Esther Fisher's sister, Julia, is planning to move here in the spring. She wants to open an Amish bakery," Bethany said. She smiled at Charity, who was yawning.

Constance frowned. "But I thought her family owned a bakery in Illinois."

"Her stepmother has convinced Esther's father to sell the business," Bethany said. "They are moving to the Amish community near Sarasota, Florida."

"Our daughter lived there for a while," Dinah said. "She claims it's a beautiful area, but I was thrilled that she decided to return home and marry Jesse." She tucked the blanket under Jacob's chin. "I couldn't bear to have my grandchildren be so far away."

"What about you, Maisie?" Constance asked. "Will you be returning to Missouri?"

"I've decided to stay in Maine."

Constance pressed a hand to her heart. "I'm so glad Nathan is letting you stay. You are the one who should be looking after his babies."

Maisie shook her head. "Nathan still wants someone else to care for the children. He wasn't happy when I told him I'm not leaving, but he has no say in the matter."

"*Goot* for you," Bethany declared.

"If you won't be staying with Nathan, where will you stay?" Dinah asked in a worried tone.

Maisie smiled with more confidence than she was feeling. "I will get a job and find a place of my own. Constance has offered to let me stay with them until I get settled. I will see the babies as often as I can. He will be gone to work in the lumber camp most days, so I don't think it will be a problem if I keep the nanny company."

Dinah took a sip of her coffee and put her cup down. "I'm sure whoever it is will be glad of an extra set of hands. I know I was when Gemma and her brother came along. Babies are wonderful but they can be exhausting."

Constance chuckled. "You are fortunate that you have twins first. That way you have no idea how much work only one baby can be."

"It's a shame Nathan has to work in the lumber camp," Maisie said softly. "I wish he could spend more time with them. They grow up so fast, and he will miss so much."

She looked up to see all the women staring at her. "What?"

"It sounds like you care for Nathan," Constance said with a strange glint in her eye.

Maisie frowned as she looked from face to face. "Of course I do. He's my brother-in-law. We may not always get along, but he's a fine man and he deserves to be at home with his children as any Amish father would hope to be. Is it wrong to wish that for him?"

"Not at all," Dinah said quickly. "You are to be commended for your concern. I mean, you say he does not want you there, so it would be understandable if you found him objectionable."

"I don't. He was married to my sister and I owe him my respect."

"That's only right. Tell me, do you think he will remarry?" Constance took a sip of her coffee.

Chapter Eight

Maisie sat stunned by the bishop's wife's question. Would Nathan remarry? She hadn't considered it. She looked away from the sharp eyes of her hostess. "It's much too soon for him to think about that."

Constance set her cup down. "Of course. I wasn't suggesting he would rush into anything, but he is going to need a wife to help raise these children. Not soon, but one day. He can't do it alone."

Maisie felt the need to defend him and looked up. "Nathan will manage on his own. He's determined to do so. And I admire him for that."

"We all do," Dinah said, giving Constance a speaking glance.

"Of course," Constance said sincerely. "A man may raise a family without a wife. I've seen it done, but I know from my years of being married that burdens which are shared are cut in half and joys that are shared are more than doubled. I would wish any parent, a man or a woman, to have a spouse to share their life with."

Maisie nodded slowly as the idea sank in. "Nathan and the children deserve to be happy."

"I understand Nathan built his own cabin," Bethany said brightly. Maisie was grateful for the change of subject.

"He did. It's quite beautiful and very functional. I know that there are improvements that could be made, but I see why log homes are so popular."

"Are they?" Constance asked with interest.

"Oh, they are. I noticed a little house on the bishop's lot where he builds sheds. Has he considered selling log homes?"

Constance became thoughtful. "Not that he has ever mentioned to me."

Maisie smiled. "It was just a thought on my part. Nathan has considerable skill as a builder, and I do wonder if it isn't going to waste simply cutting down trees for someone else."

She held her breath, wondering if she had done enough to plant the idea in the mind of the bishop's wife. If Nathan could work for the bishop, he wouldn't need to travel so far to earn a living. He could build the homes on his own property and have the bishop handle the sales.

A sly smile curved Constance's lips. "I'll tell my husband about your idea. You are looking out for Nathan's best interests, aren't you?"

"He has suffered a great deal. I fear his faith may be shaken. I know that I have depended on others when I was questioning. Knowing there are people who care about you can make all the difference during a dark time."

Bethany looked at everyone. "We have all been the recipients of loving-kindness when it mattered most."

The women nodded in agreement. Constance clasped her hands together. "I almost forgot the most important news. There is a new family coming here from upstate New York. They want to farm, and land here is cheaper than in New York, so they are bringing their entire family. They have twelve children."

Bethany laughed. "My grandfather would've been so happy with that news. He prayed that he was doing the right thing when he first came to New Covenant to start an Amish community and invited other Amish families to join him."

"Twelve children." Dinah chuckled. "They are almost single-handedly going to double our population." Everyone laughed.

Maisie stayed until early evening and then decided it was time to take the children home. Her visit had cemented her desire to remain in New Covenant. She was among friends here. They were already making her feel at home.

Only one thing troubled her about the day. She hadn't considered that Nathan might remarry until Constance asked the question. If he did, the children would become his wife's children and Maisie would have to accept that.

When she drove into the farmyard, she saw Nathan had moved one of the kitchen chairs out to the porch. He was leaning back on two legs against the cabin wall. She thought he looked relieved to see her, but she couldn't be sure. He sat in the shadows.

"I thought I said before dark?"

"It's not dark."

"Hmm. It will be before long."

She got down and lifted the babies out. "The sun won't set for another hour. We are back safe and sound. You needn't have worried."

"When you take my newborns and go wandering around the country I have a right to be concerned, don't I?"

"You are absolutely right. Does that mean you will come with me next time?"

He frowned. "We'll see."

It was a small victory. Maisie held back her grin. "Would you please put Sassy away?"

He took the horse by the bridle and glanced back. "I doubt you even brought a crumb of cake home. The piece you left me wasn't very big."

Maisie gave him her saddest look. "I didn't. Everyone took extra slices. But I did bring home half a cherry pie that Bethany made. Does that help?"

"I like apple better, but cherry pie will work."

She pressed the back of her hand to her brow and tried to sound dramatic. "I'm so glad you approve. I was terribly concerned it wouldn't do. Is food all you think about?"

His expression turned from amused to stoic. "Annie used to do that. Put her hand on her forehead and make a big drama about some little thing."

Maisie's happiness slipped away. "We used to pretend we were acting in a play when we were children."

"She was good at pretending to care. I wonder if you share her talent."

Maisie didn't know how to reply to that. "I'll get supper on."

She took the babies and hurried inside.

The following morning after breakfast Maisie was packing Nathan's lunch for the day. They hadn't spoken since the previous evening. He was sitting at the table drinking his second cup of coffee when she happened to glance over and saw he was watching her with an odd light in his eyes.

She had to know what he was thinking. "What?"

He stared down at his coffee. "Nothing. You make a good cup of *kaffi*." He took another sip.

"Danki."

"Annie's coffee was like dishwater. A little color but not much taste."

Maisie chuckled. "That's exactly what John said about my coffee when we were first married. He was the one who taught me to make it this way."

"I wish I could've met him."

Maisie looked at Nathan in surprise. "I wish you could've, too. The two of you were a lot alike."

He leaned back and hooked one arm over the top rung of his chair. "In what ways?"

"He was a thinker, a planner. He didn't like to rush into a project."

"Since you and Annie were so alike I imagine you were at his side telling him how to do it better."

She smiled and looked down. "I did, which annoyed him to no end."

"Don't I know it. I had carefully planned and built a new henhouse. I was almost done with it when Annie came out, put her hands on her hips and said, 'You have the door on the wrong side.'"

"Did you?" Maisie asked, happy to hear Nathan talking about her sister without bitterness in his voice.

"I put the door on the side closest to the barn, where their feed would be stored."

"What did she think was wrong with that?"

"It was on the side farthest away from the house. She would have to walk around to the other side to gather the eggs in the morning. We had a heated discussion about it. It was only twenty extra steps."

"That would've been an easy fix," Maisie said.

"The door was already on. I wasn't about to move it."

"Of course not."

He frowned slightly. "Annie's solution was to put a second door in the henhouse. I suppose that would be your solution, too?"

"Mine would've been much simpler. I would let you gather the eggs every morning and I wouldn't have had to walk out at all."

He chuckled. "Amazingly simple. It never occurred to me."

"What did you do?"

"I put in a second door to make her happy." His smile faded. "I guess it didn't after all."

Maisie finished packing his lunch and handed him the blue-and-white lunch pail. He took it and looked at her intently. "There was a message on the phone this morning. A woman is coming to interview for the nanny position today at noon. She's Amish. Her name is Agnes Martin."

"Oh. I see." So quickly? Maisie wasn't ready to give up caring for the twins.

"I'll leave it to you to decide if she knows enough about babies. If so, I'll talk to her myself. I think I hear Jimmy's truck coming."

She clutched her hands together to keep from reaching for him. "Be careful out there."

He crossed to the babies and kissed each of them. "Be *goot* for your aunt Maisie."

"That's the only way they know how to be." She wished he didn't have to go. Things seemed better between them this morning.

A vehicle honked outside. Nathan crossed to the door but paused before he opened it. "Make a list of things the *kinder heeda* will need to know. Feeding schedules and stuff. You don't have to take the first woman that shows up. My ad should be in today's paper. Are you going to be all right alone? I mean without me here?"

That he was concerned about her warmed her insides. "Don't worry. I know where the phone shack is. I have Sassy if I need to go somewhere. I have food, formula for the babies, water, warm clothing and Buddy to keep me company. I'll be fine. It's not like you're going to be gone a month."

He gave her a lopsided grin. "That would make you happy, wouldn't it?"

She waited until he was out the door and pressed a hand to her heart. "I'm afraid not, Nathan. I'm going to have enough trouble getting through today."

When she was sure the truck was gone, she went out and brought in the bathtub. She normally sponged off in the tiny bathroom, but if she was going to meet a potential nanny she wanted to be at her best.

Fortunately, between heating water and hauling it out when she was done with her bath, taking care of the babies, making sure the cabin was spotless and working on the storage project she was planning, she had little time to think about Nathan. When she wasn't busy, he was all she thought about. Was he being safe? Was he missing his children? Had he given her a single thought? Would he ever get past thinking that she was like her sister?

Maisie shook her head at her own foolishness. No doubt he was delighted to be back with his lumberjack companions and hadn't given her a second thought except to hope the nanny would be a good fit and Maisie would need to find a new place to live.

When Agnes Martin arrived, Maisie tried to keep an open mind. The woman was in her late fifties or early sixties. She was slender with a pinched face that seemed to be on the verge of a identifying a sour smell.

Maisie welcomed her in. "Would you like some coffee?"

Mrs. Martin untied her bonnet strings as she and Maisie sat down. "I understood that Mr. Weaver would be the one to interview me."

"I'm his sister-in-law. I've been giving Nathan a hand taking care of the babies."

"Then why does he need a nanny?"

"I'm sure Nathan can answer that question better than I can. I do know he wants someone who can take on a permanent position. I've taken the liberty of writing down some of the things you will need to know about Charity and Jacob. Their feeding schedule and such. Would you like to meet them?"

She looked around. "Isn't this a live-in position? I'd like to see my room. This cabin certainly doesn't have much to recommend it."

Maisie realized Nathan hadn't included enough information in his flyers at the grocery store. "Nathan has plans to add on to the cabin, but for now he would like you to come daily, Monday through Friday."

Agnes got to her feet. "Then I have wasted my time. I'm not driving out here to the back of beyond every day."

"I can tell Nathan that you would prefer to watch the children at your house during the day."

"I live with my daughter. I don't believe she would like two squalling infants disturbing the household."

Jacob decided at that moment to give a loud, lusty cry. Maisie hurried to pick him up and quiet him.

Agnes tied the strings of her traveling bonnet. "You should let the child cry. If you don't you are spoiling him into thinking someone will answer his every demand."

Maisie smiled as politely as she could manage. "I appreciate your advice. And I'm sorry you made the trip for nothing. I don't believe it's a position that you would enjoy."

"Tell Mr. Weaver that when he has the additional room added I will reconsider."

Maisie followed the woman to the door. "I'll be sure to pass on that message."

When the door closed behind pinch-faced Agnes, Maisie hugged to Jacob. "I think you had a narrow escape. I will be happy to tell your father we didn't suit her."

Maisie spent the remainder of the day enjoying the babies and holding them as much as she could. When they were both fast asleep, she sat down with her sewing.

At six o'clock she got up and started supper, but couldn't stop watching the clock on the mantel. It was almost seven before she heard the sound of a pickup engine. Although she wanted to rush to the door, she didn't. She took a seat on the couch with some sewing on her lap as if she wasn't on pins and needles waiting for his return.

She waited but he didn't come inside. She heard the sound of the truck leaving, but he still didn't come in. She rose and went to the door. There was no sign of him outside. What on earth was he doing? Didn't he know she had supper waiting for him? It would be his own fault if the meat loaf turned into brown brick.

She shut the door and went back to her sewing. Twice she stabbed herself with the needle because she wasn't paying attention to what she was doing. She was sucking on her smarting finger when she finally heard the door open. She turned to glare at him. "What have you been doing?"

"The chores. The horses needed to be fed. The stalls cleaned. I had to shut up the chickens and the ducks for the night. My farm chores don't vanish because I work at the lumber camp."

Maisie had seldom felt so foolish. Of course, he would do his chores before he came in for the evening. She tried to smile. "How was your day?"

He hung his hat on a wooden peg by the door. His hair was glistening wet. He'd taken the time to wash up before coming in.

"Busy. We're trying to get caught up. I spent a lot of the day repeating the story of Annie's death and my new fatherhood to different people. The *Englisch* are a curious lot. I should have called a meeting first and told everyone at the same time."

"I'm sorry if that was painful."

"After the first telling it wasn't so bad." He crossed the room to squat beside the cradles. "How were *mei kinder*?"

"*Wunderbar.* Both of them. I had them on quilts on the floor and Jacob almost turned himself over."

Nathan grinned at his boy. "Are you going to be a traveling man, then?"

"Charity is happy to lie on her back and take it all in. Nothing much upsets her. I did have to put Buddy out. He insists on licking their toes when they're on the floor."

"And what does the cat think of them?"

"He ignores them."

He stood up straight and slipped his hands in the pockets of his pants. "How did the interview with Agnes Martin go?"

"She assumed it was a live-in position. She doesn't want to drive out here on a daily basis. I told her there were plans to add on to the cabin in the future and she said to contact her then."

"I didn't plan to do that for at least another year. I didn't realize it might be a problem. Did she seem to like the babies?"

"She didn't actually ask to see them. Jacob started crying and she told me I shouldn't pick him up because it would spoil him."

Nathan frowned. "He's a newborn. Newborns cry."

"I didn't say I agreed with her. I'm merely telling you what she said."

"Then we will cross her off the list."

"You have a list? Have more people applied?"

"Not yet, but they will." Nathan settled himself in his chair and put his head back. "Something smells good."

Maisie gave a little shriek. "My meat loaf. Oh, I hope it's not burnt." She rushed to the stove, pulled the oven door open and took out the pan using the corners of her apron.

"How is it? I can eat burnt," he said.

"The edges are crisp, but it's fine." Buddy had followed her into the kitchen and sat beside her with his tail wagging and his tongue hanging out. He licked his chops hopefully. She shook her head. "There's nothing for you tonight. Go away."

She could've sworn he looked disappointed as he

padded to the door. Nathan got up to let him out. "And how was your day?" he asked, looking in her direction.

"Productive. Besides speaking with Agnes Martin, I did some housework and finished two new pants and a shirt for Jacob. They are lying on the back of the couch."

He walked over and held up the shirt. "Don't you think this is too big for him?"

"In another few months it will be too small. I wanted to give him some growing room."

"And this is for Charity?" He picked up a bonnet Maisie had trimmed with tiny pink bows.

Would he disapprove? "I know it's a little fancy, but it looks adorable on her. Do you want me to take the bows off?"

"*Nee*, I like them. She is a babe, after all, and doesn't have to dress plain."

"That's what I thought." She smiled at him. It was good to have him home. The cabin felt complete when he was in it.

He laid the bonnet back on the sofa and put his hands in his pockets. "Can we eat now? I'm starving."

"Of course. Sit down. I'll have it ready in a minute."

Maisie knew she was blushing. Nathan wasn't interested in looking at baby clothes or clean floors. He'd been working long hours at a dangerous job. The least she could do was feed him when he came home, even if it was burnt meat loaf.

Nathan finished his meal in silence. It was good to be home. He had missed his children. He had even missed Maisie a little. While it had been good to see the men he worked with again, he'd found it hard to keep his mind on his job. Even one close call with a log that slipped out of its cable wasn't enough to force him to put Maisie out of his mind. Now that she was sitting across the table from him, he tried to figure out why.

Was it because of the things she said and did that reminded him of Annie? Or was it because of the way she showered his babies with love and tried to make his sparse cabin homey? He'd noticed the clean windows and floors, and how the house always smelled like something good was cooking. It had been a long time since Nathan felt at home, even in the place he'd built with his own hands.

He went to the rocking chair and took down his Bible. He caught Maisie giving him a puzzled look.

"I enjoyed reading to them yesterday. I thought I'd read to them while you clean up."

"I think that's a wonderful idea."

When Maisie finished with the supper dishes, she sat in the rocker and began to hem a gown she had made out of a soft yellow material. He caught her yawning several times.

Before Nathan was finished reading the story of David and Goliath, Jacob began to fuss. He knew Charity wouldn't be far behind her brother in demanding her supper.

Maisie put her sewing aside and went to the icebox to get their bottles. Nathan got up and took them from her hands. "I'll do this feeding. You look tired. Why don't you turn in?"

"I can take care of them." She reached for the bottles.

He held them away from her. "I haven't seen them all day. I want to do this."

"All right. If you put it that way. I am tired. I believe I will go to bed. Don't forget to warm the milk."

"I won't. Good night, Annie." He placed the bottles in a bowl and filled it with hot water from the kettle on the stove.

He turned back to see Maisie still standing beside the icebox. "I thought you were going to bed?"

"You called me Annie."

Something in the way she said it held his attention. He had hurt her feelings. "Sorry. I wasn't thinking."

"That's all right. I know how easy it is to confuse us. I saw my reflection in a mirror at the fabric shop last week and I thought Annie was standing in front of me. It's hard to accept she's really gone. Good night, Nathan."

"Good night, Maisie."

"Thanks for feeding them."

"Sure." He watched her climb the stairs with slow, lagging steps. Was she simply tired or was something else weighing on her? It surprised him how much he wanted to know.

Would she confide in him if he asked?

Chapter Nine

Maisie felt like crying as she lay in bed listening to the sound of Nathan's voice. He talked to the babies while he fed them, telling them about his day. His voice was tender and reassuring.

He was a good father. She could imagine him teaching Jacob how to drive a buggy or handle a team. He would build the swing for Charity and push her higher when she begged him to.

She could imagine herself standing off to the side watching, not really a part of the activities. Nathan would be smiling at the children and when he caught sight of her that smile would vanish because for an instant he would see Annie standing there.

Maisie wasn't sure she could endure those mistaken looks. Nathan would glance away. He might even apologize if he knew Maisie had caught the look. In time, it might not happen as often, but Maisie knew her sister's shadow would always be between them.

A tear rolled from the corner of her eye to dampen

her pillowcase. For the first time in her life she wished she hadn't been born a twin, at least not an identical one.

Then again, she wouldn't give up any part of her childhood with her dearest friend always at her side. They seldom had to tell each other what they were thinking. Annie always seemed to know. And Maisie had read her sister just as easily. It was why Annie's disappearance had felt like such a betrayal.

Maisie should've known what her sister was thinking. She should have prevented it. Maybe then she could be watching Annie and Nathan playing with their children and standing off to the side wouldn't feel so painful.

But God allowed Annie's death. Maisie accepted that. She had come to help but she was only bringing more pain to Nathan and herself by staying. Was leaving, as he wished, the right thing to do? Maybe it was.

Eventually she fell asleep. When she opened her eyes again she saw the morning sky growing light outside her tiny bedroom window.

She sat up with a start. How could she have slept through the night without hearing the babies? She grabbed her robe and hurried down the stairs. She stopped on the next-to-last tread. Nathan was sprawled on the couch asleep. There were two empty baby bottles on the floor beside him and the cradles had been pulled up next to him.

Buddy sat up and trotted to the door. He looked back over his shoulder at her. She crossed the floor on bare feet and let the dog out as quietly as she could. When she turned around she saw Nathan was awake and watching her. She self-consciously tightened the belt of her robe. Her hair hung over her shoulder in a long braid that went past her hips. She flipped it behind her.

She stared at her toes. "You should have woke me."

"I realized you hadn't had a full night's sleep in almost a week. I know how that feels."

"I appreciate that, but you can't have gotten much rest."

He sat up and twisted his neck one way, and then the other. "This couch leaves something to be desired."

"I feel awful. I should have heard them fuss. I always do."

"I kept them close to me so I heard their first peeps. Don't worry about it. You needed a break. Now I need my *kaffi*."

She bit her lower lip. "Will you be able to work?"

"I have missed sleep in the past. It won't bother me. I've got to go do my chores." He rose and stretched out his arms.

Her breath seized and her heart started to hammer in her chest. How easy it would be to step into his embrace and have his arms enfold her.

Maisie quickly turned away and chided herself for her wayward thoughts. She had to get over this fascination with him before he noticed. "I'll go get changed."

She hurried up the stairs and pressed her hands to her flushed cheeks. There was nothing in Nathan's manner to suggest he would welcome or even understand her feelings if she made them known. How long could she keep them hidden?

The answer was simple. Forever.

Once she had her everyday work dress on, her hair up and her *kapp* pinned in place, she felt ready to face him again. She took a deep breath and went down to start breakfast. By the time he came in, she had oatmeal with brown sugar and raisins simmering on the stove, coffee ready in the pot and her emotions under control.

She sat at the table with her eyes down. If she didn't look at him it was easier to pretend nothing had changed. The oatmeal tasted like sawdust in her mouth.

"Do you need anything?" he asked. "Jimmy said he has to stop in town on his way home tonight."

She stirred a spoon of sugar into her coffee. She didn't even like it sweet. "Not that I can think of."

"You might check the machine later to see if anyone has answered my ad."

She nodded. "I will."

"Have I upset you?"

Maisie lifted her gaze to his face. "Of course not."

"Are you sure? You seem miles away."

"Too much sleep." She smiled, took a sip of her coffee and grimaced.

"Okay." He crossed to the cradles, knelt between them and laid his hands on each baby's head. "I'll miss you. May *Gott* bless and keep you both."

"Amen," Maisie said, watching his gentle goodbye.

He gazed at them and slowly shook his head. "How is it that I can love them so much already?"

The sound of a truck pulling up and honking outside brought him to his feet. "I'd better go."

"Don't forget your lunch." She got up to hand him

the small blue-and-white lunch pail. His hands brushed hers as he took it from her.

Nathan watched Maisie jerk her hand away and push it into her pocket. There was something different about her today. She seemed unhappy. Sad, even. He couldn't quite put his finger on it.

Jimmy sounded the horn again. Nathan had to leave, but he would get to the bottom of Maisie's unhappiness when he got home.

"Be safe today," she said. "I don't want to mend any more cuts in your pants."

"I'll do my best."

He went out and climbed into the front seat with his fellow logger. "Morning, Jimmy."

"Morning, Nate. How are the kids?"

Nathan grinned. "They are pretty amazing."

Jimmy turned the truck and drove down the lane. "That's what my girlfriend says, but I'm not convinced. Any success finding a gal to look after them?"

"Not yet."

"How much longer can your sister-in-law stay?"

"She says she's not going anywhere until I find someone."

"If she wants to stay, then why are you trying to hire someone else?"

"Because I don't want her staying longer than necessary."

"The two of you don't get along? I get it. I can't say I'm crazy about my girlfriend's family, either. I couldn't imagine her sister living with us if we get married. Yikes."

"*Ja*, that's the way of it." He didn't want to explain why having Annie's twin around was so painful. He was ashamed of the way his wife left him. He didn't want others to know how miserably he had failed as a husband. Thankfully, Jimmy didn't ask him anything else.

The trip up to Three Ponds logging camp was twenty miles one way. When they arrived, Nathan took off his black flat-topped hat and put on the hard hat that his boss required everyone to wear. Up here he didn't stick out as an Amish fellow. Many of the men had beards, as he did, though he didn't have a mustache. Even his suspenders weren't out of the ordinary. Many of the men wore them for comfort.

The day proved to be particularly grueling. Nathan was felling trees as fast as he safely could, trying to do the work of two men. Davis hadn't been able to take on another feller yet. Nathan would be grateful when he did.

When quitting time rolled around, he wiped the sweat from his brow and knocked the sawdust off of his shirt and pants. He saw the rip in his sleeve where he had caught it on a broken branch. He was bringing more mending home for Maisie. He knew how to use a needle and thread, but her repairs were much neater than his.

Jimmy stopped in Fort Craig and left the truck to run several errands. Nathan noticed a bookstore across the street and got out. Inside, he easily found the children's section and purchased four books. Nothing could replace reading the Bible, but it would be nice to read something the children would come to enjoy as they grew older. He hoped Maisie would approve.

He was tired enough that he fell asleep in Jimmy's vehicle on the ride home. He didn't realize he was at his front door until Jimmy shook him by the arm. He sat up to see a green car drive away from his house. He didn't recognize it. He got out with the parcel he had purchased in town.

Maisie was standing on the front porch. "Who was that?" he asked, nodding toward the car that had just driven away.

"Another applicant for your position. She wasn't suitable." Maisie turned and walked into the house.

"What makes you say that?" He followed her inside.

"Because she wasn't."

"You're gonna have to give a better reason than that." It occurred to him that she might have deliberately sent the woman away. She didn't want him to hire a nanny.

"She wasn't Amish."

He scowled. "I never said that was a requirement. Did she have experience?"

"She brought a résumé from her previous job, but I didn't care for her attitude."

"You're being deliberately vague. You could have asked her to wait another ten minutes and I could have spoken to her myself."

"It would've been a waste of your time and hers. I know the type of person who should be taking care of these babies and she wasn't it." Maisie walked to the sofa and sat down with her arms crossed tightly over her chest.

She was being deliberately infuriating. "You don't want me to hire anyone. No one will be the right kind of person in your eyes. You have taken advantage of my trust the same way your sister did."

Her eyes widened with shock. She surged to her feet. "If you feel that way you can call the woman and set up another interview. Her number is still on the answering machine. I'm going out. Make yourself something for supper. I'm tired of being your cook, bottle washer and housekeeper without getting a word of thanks. I don't know why I bother trying to please you. If those children didn't need me, I'd be gone today."

She stormed out of the house. He tossed his package on the sofa, collapsed into his chair and raked his hands through his hair. She was driving him to distraction. How much longer could he go on this way?

Fix his own supper? That wasn't a problem. He'd been cooking for himself for months. He got out of his chair and went to the kitchen to search the canned goods Maisie's friend had brought for something quick to eat. He could wash his own clothes and do his own mending, too, for that matter.

What did she mean when she said she was trying to please him? Why would she say that?

He found himself staring at an empty counter. Where had she put the jars and canned food? His storage space was limited and already full. Had she taken them out of the house to store them?

He looked around and noticed something under his open stairs. Walking over to investigate, he saw several neatly made shelves tucked underneath the stairwell.

They were lined with all the canned produce the bishop's wife and Dinah Lapp had brought over.

It was a clever idea and a good use of his limited space. He fingered the rough-cut boards. It wouldn't take much for him to sand them smooth. A coat of paint and they would be as nice as store-bought. Who knew Annie's sister was handy with a hammer and a saw? Annie hadn't been.

Maisie must've learned the skills from her husband, or perhaps her father. He glanced toward the door. Maybe he had been too hard on her. She was helping him of her own free will and at no charge. He wouldn't be able to work at all if she hadn't been here. It annoyed him that he would have to apologize. Again.

Maisie wasn't paying attention to where she was going. She found a path in the woods leading away from the house and stayed on it. She wanted to get away from Nathan's accusing stare, from his constant comparisons to her sister. She wasn't Annie, but he would never see that.

He couldn't trust her because she was like her sister. She wasn't, but he wouldn't accept it. He thought she was capable of deceiving him.

Maybe she didn't want him to hire a caregiver for the babies, but that wasn't her reason for turning away a self-absorbed *Englisch* woman who couldn't stop checking her phone for five minutes.

He would discover the same thing for himself if he interviewed Ms. Harper. Would he admit Maisie was right about her? She doubted it. He would probably hire the woman just to spite her.

She didn't take notice of where she was until there was a small bridge in front of her that arched over a brook. It was made of small logs expertly joined together. It was Nathan's work. She knew that without being told.

She walked onto the bridge and stopped in the middle. She leaned on the railing to look into the water rushing by underneath. The babbling sound began to soothe her ragged nerves. Little by little she heard the sounds of the forest around her. The birds and the insects going about their lives on a warm summer evening. It was a special place. A place for lovers to stroll along and stop to kiss where she was standing. It would be a wonderful spot to kiss someone she loved. She could almost imagine Nathan holding her close as the brook sang to them. How foolish was that thought?

"It's a pretty spot, isn't it?"

Maisie looked up to see Lilly Arnett standing on the path. "*Ja*, it is."

"Nathan built that bridge for me not long after he first arrived."

Maisie patted the solid railing. "I thought as much."

"How is he?" Lilly came onto the bridge and stood beside Maisie, looking into the water, as well.

"He's irritating, exasperating, closed-minded, stubborn and ungrateful."

Lilly threw back her head and laughed. It took Maisie a minute to see the humor in her litany of Nathan's shortcomings. She finally smiled.

Lilly leaned toward Maisie. "Enjoying your visit, are you?"

"With the babies, I am."

"Nathan doesn't get along with a lot of people. He prefers to be by himself. I understand that. I'm the same way. I wondered when I dropped you off at his place that night if he would welcome your help or send you packing."

"He drove me to the bus station the next morning," Maisie admitted with a wry smile.

"But you're still here."

"There wasn't a bus going south for three days."

Lilly chuckled. "We are remote in this part of the state. It's been longer than three days and yet here you stand."

"I'm staying. He can't make me leave." Maisie discovered a renewed sense of determination. "The babies are my sister's children. I promised to help take care of them. I didn't know that would be the last thing I said to her."

"I'm sorry for your loss. I never met her. I didn't know Nathan was married until I gave you a ride."

"They had been living apart." Maisie hoped that was enough of an explanation.

Lilly straightened. "Come down to my place. I'll fix us a cup of herbal tea and we can get better acquainted."

Maisie smiled at her. "I'd like that."

After an hour of tea, yummy butter cookies and quiet conversation, Lilly took Maisie on a tour of her extensive flower gardens, which included an abundance of wildflowers. Maisie happened to notice a glint of light through some overgrown ivy.

"What's that back there?"

Lilly looked to where she was pointing. "That used to be a caretaker's cottage when the place belonged to my grandparents. My in-laws used to stay there for the summers when my husband was alive. They are all gone now. I guess I should clean it up. It's too nice a place to let the ivy have it."

After another half hour of friendly chatter, Maisie bid her new friend goodbye and headed up the path. She had learned that Nathan had done odd jobs for Lilly in exchange for home-cooked meals when he'd first arrived. Clearing a path between the two homes had been his idea, so that Lilly didn't have to drive over to his place when she needed something. It was three miles by the winding road, but only three quarters of a mile though the woods.

Maisie stopped at the edge of the clearing when the cabin came into view. Light from the lamp over the kitchen table and from the one by the fireplace sent a warm glow spilling out the windows and the open doorway. It would be an inviting picture if she wasn't so uncertain of her welcome.

Maybe Nathan was right. It hadn't been intentional, but maybe she couldn't find someone suitable to care for the babies because she wanted so badly to care for them herself. From now on she would let him conduct the interviews and she would stay in the background.

She heard his voice before she reached the door. Pausing, she listened to him reading a story about a baby rabbit's adventures. When she stepped inside, she saw he had a babe in each arm while he balanced the book on his lap. He looked up at her.

"Don't stop," she said, coming in to sit down.

"Why don't you read? It's hard for me to turn the pages without jostling the babies."

"Okay." She took the book from him and looked at the colorful cover. "Where did you get this?"

"I stepped into the bookstore in town while Jimmy ran his errands tonight."

She sat back and began to read. "'Alejandro the cottontail spent many a wonderful hour in his rather small yard dreaming about the wonderful, spectacular thing he was destined to do one day. Of course he didn't know what that would be, but he had a spectacular imagination to match his spectacular name and he imagined all kinds of wonderful things.

"'What did a rather small rabbit imagine he could do? Well, one day he might rescue a beautiful princess and they would live in a towering castle.'"

Maisie read on through the imaginary adventures of the bunny until she came to the end of the story.

"'Late that night as Alejandro snuggled up to his mother's soft fur, she bent and kissed his forehead. Looking into her warm brown eyes, he whispered, "I love you, Mother."

"'"Oh, Alejandro," his mother sighed. "That is the most wonderful, spectacular thing I have ever heard."

"'Alejandro smiled happily as he drifted off to sleep. He had known all along that he would do something as wonderful and spectacular as his name. He just didn't know how simple it would be.'"

Maisie closed the book. "It's a very cute story."

"It's not an Amish story. But I liked the illustrations and I thought the children would, too, someday."

"I like the message, that telling someone you love them is the most wonderful, spectacular thing you can do."

"Can you take Charity?" he asked.

"Of course." Maisie laid the book aside and took the baby from his arm. He flexed his fingers and she smiled. "Pins and needles?"

"I should've put her down sooner, but I hated to disturb her. She looks so peaceful and precious when she is sleeping."

Maisie laid Charity in her cradle while he settled Jacob in the other one. Nathan stood up straight and slipped his hands in his front pockets. "I was harsh earlier. I'm sorry."

"You might have been right. Maybe I didn't like either woman because I don't want to relinquish taking care of the twins."

"I fried a can of pressed pork for supper. Would you like some?"

"I'm not hungry. I met Lilly Arnett on my walk. She fed me tea and butter cookies."

"She always has some on hand for visitors, although she claims she likes living alone. I wanted to tell you that I like your idea for extra storage under the stairs."

She glanced that way. "It's not meant to be permanent. I needed a place to store the canned goods so

I could have my kitchen counter back. I mean, your kitchen counter," she added hastily. He stood so close that she could reach out and touch him if she dared. She curled her fingers into her palms.

"You're handy with a saw and hammer. Was it your father who taught you?"

"My husband. I was curious about the things he built. He didn't mind teaching me." In his way, John had been kind to her, but not loving.

"You must've paid attention. It's sturdy." Nathan picked up the book. "I bought several like this. Would you want to see them?"

"Certainly." Maisie relaxed as he stepped away from her and picked up the books on the mantel. He handed them to her. They were all stories about baby animals with problems to solve.

Nathan's and her problems weren't solved, but at least they weren't arguing. It was a small step in the right direction.

She gave the books back to him. "You'll have to build a bookshelf for them when they are old enough to read."

He looked around the room. "Where would I put it?"

"In their bedroom, I guess, or there in the corner beside the fireplace."

"I like the idea of having it out here where I can watch them. A family should spend time together."

Maisie smiled at his enthusiasm. "I doubt that will be a problem as you only have one room in your house."

"For now, but I'll add on as they grow. I've thought about lifting the roof and adding a second story with several bedrooms."

He was looking to the future. Maisie was glad he could. He was healing. A bigger house might mean a bigger family. A wife and other children.

And no need for an aunt.

Chapter Ten

The rest of the week passed in a blur for Nathan. His workdays were long and tiring without the additional helper Davis had promised. He had breakfast with Maisie, kissed his children goodbye and didn't return home until almost dark.

Maisie took over his evening chores, feeding the animals, cleaning stalls and making sure the livestock and poultry were secured at night. She didn't ask. She just started doing it. Because of her, he had a free hour in the evenings to spend reading to the babies or simply holding them before heading to bed.

On Saturday, he worked ten hours for some much-needed overtime pay, but he told himself it was the last time. He didn't want to spend that much time away from his children again if it could be helped.

No one else responded to his ads for childcare. He had to face the fact that he still needed Maisie's help.

Sunday brought the event he dreaded most since Annie's funeral. His first prayer meeting with all the members of his new Amish community. He might have stayed home if he had been on his own, but Maisie insisted that he take her.

She was up when he entered the cabin and had breakfast waiting for him. Afterward, she gathered together the pies and cookies she had baked the night before and loaded them into a cardboard box for him to put in the buggy. There would be a meal after the three- or four-hour-long service and every family would bring something to contribute.

After loading the food, he came back in to help her with the babies.

She didn't glance his way. "Jacob is ready to go. I'm going to have to change Charity's gown. She spit up on this one."

"Are you worried about meeting more members of the community?" he asked.

"*Nee*, why should I be?"

Because I am. "No reason."

"Go on," she said. "I'll be there in a minute." She wore a white apron over a dark green dress. It was a color Annie had often worn. She once said it made her eyes look greener. He thought it was a vain reason. Was that why Maisie chose the same shade?

Why wouldn't she share her sister's vanity? They were twins.

He carried Jacob in his basket out to the buggy and settled him on the front seat. The buggy itself had been washed and swept out. Sassy had been groomed until her coat was as shiny black as a raven's wing. Her harness had been oiled and the brass fittings polished. His rig hadn't looked this good since he'd bought it. He might not be a man of means, but he wasn't ashamed of what he had.

He got in, picked up the lines and waited. He was about to call to Maisie when she came rushing out the door. "I hope I haven't made us late."

"We have plenty of time. It isn't far to the Fisher place."

"What do you know about them?" Maisie asked as she settled herself and Charity.

Nathan spoke to Sassy to get her moving. "Walk on. The father is a wheelwright. He has four sons. One of them is a harness maker. The others work with him."

"Are they married?" she asked.

He glanced her way. Was she hoping to find a husband in New Covenant? She had been a widow for more than two years. There was no reason why she couldn't remarry. "The oldest is. Gabriel, he's the harness maker. He goes by Gabe. He's married to Esther. One of the other sons is married, too, but I don't know which one."

"Have you decided on the story we should tell people about Annie's death? The truth is always best, of course. Still, I thought we should compare what we will say."

"I reckon so." She was right but he hated thinking about it. The bishop knew the whole story. Nathan had explained his situation in confidence when he asked Bishop Schultz to perform Annie's private burial service. Why did he have to say anything to the others? Why couldn't it be his business and no one else's?

Maisie folded her hands in her lap. "You and Annie were married in Seymour, Missouri, where she and I grew up. You came to Maine to start a new life. Annie was on her way to join you when she went into labor, delivered the babies and died of complications before she reached you. That is all true."

"What if someone asks why it took her so long to join me? They know I've been here for months."

"Then you will have to answer as you see fit. Not every marriage is a happy one. People know that."

"Was yours?"

Her startled gaze shot to his then she looked away. "For the most part. It's not possible to be happy all the time."

"Did you ever think about leaving him?"

"*Nee*, the idea never crossed my mind. I was married to John for better or for worse, no matter what problems we encountered."

"Why do you think Annie left me?"

Maisie's gaze returned to him. "Didn't her notes say that she had tried to live Amish, but she couldn't do it anymore?"

"That never made sense. I know she liked working for that *Englisch* family, but she never complained about giving up electricity or television or riding in fast cars after she stopped working for them. Did she ever mention that to you?"

Maisie shook her head. "I didn't see much of her after you were married. I know she missed the children that she had been taking care of. She was very close to the family."

"She didn't tell them she was leaving."

"As far as I know she didn't tell anyone. She didn't even tell me. I thought we shared everything."

She finally looked at him. "That is all in the past and can't be changed. We should leave it there."

If only that was possible. He would wonder until his dying day what had gone wrong.

The traffic was light on the highway and they saw no other buggies. There weren't any Amish families beyond his place. Sassy kept up a steady trot without urging. They arrived at the Fisher farm only thirty minutes after leaving home. They weren't the first. A dozen buggies were already parked along the lane. The horses, still wearing their harnesses, were busy munching hay, swishing their tails or dozing where they were tied to a white wooden corral fence.

The bishop's buggy was parked beside the barn, along with the gray enclosed wagon that carried the benches they would use. The backless wooden benches were transported to the family that was hosting the prayer meeting to provide enough seating.

Nathan had heard of a new Amish settlement a hundred miles south of Fort Craig that used a permanent building for their church meetings, but the New Covenant Amish still met for worship in members' homes every other Sunday, the way the Amish had done since the days of their persecution before coming to America in the 1700s.

He pulled up outside the front-yard gate. Three women came out to meet Maisie. He recognized the two women he'd met at his house. He didn't know the other woman. She was young with red hair, a babe in her arms and a toddler holding on to her skirt. Dinah Lapp introduced her as her daughter, Gemma Crump. Maisie was soon surrounded by more women and children all wanting to see the twins.

"I'll take your horse and buggy."

Nathan turned to see a boy of about fifteen at his window. The lad grinned. "I'm Harvey Gingrich. My oldest brother, Willis, is a blacksmith in New Covenant. I know who you are. What's your mare's name?"

Nathan wondered what the boy knew about him. "Sassy. I have a grain bag for her in the back. You can put it on her now. *Danki*."

Harvey moved to take Sassy by the bridle. He patted her neck. "I'll take *goot* care of her."

"*Vellkumm*, Nathan Weaver." The oldest son of the Fisher family came toward him. His eyes were full of sympathy, but he didn't mention Nathan's loss.

Nathan nodded to him. "Morning, Gabe."

"Give us a hand unloading the benches, will you?"

"Sure." Nathan would have offered without being asked, but he appreciated Gabe's attempt to include him. A man pulling a bench out turned around to greet Gabe. He was clearly Gabe's sibling.

Gabe tipped his head toward him. "My brother Seth."

"You're twins?" Nathan asked.

"Triplets, although our brother Asher doesn't look like us. He has dark hair like our little brother, Moses. We heard you have twins. Congratulations," Gabe said.

Seth grinned. "The best part of being a twin was fooling folks as to which of us was which when we were kids."

"I have a boy and a girl. I shouldn't have trouble telling them apart," Nathan said with a small grin.

Gabe chuckled and clapped Nathan on the shoulder. "Let's hope not. Grab that end of the bench and I'll get the other."

"Where are we going?" Nathan asked, as barns, sheds and outbuildings were often used for large worship gatherings.

"We're a small congregation yet, so we all fit in the house," Gabe said.

Nathan nodded and lifted out the next bench. For the next twenty minutes he met more of the men from the New Covenant Amish community. Only one, a man named Tully Lange, gripped Nathan's hand and offered his condolences. An older man with Tully touched his shoulder and shook his head. Tully seemed surprised but walked away.

The older man leaned heavily on a cane. "I'm Gideon Beachy. My son-in-law isn't familiar with all our ways. He's newly come to the Amish. I will explain to him that we seldom mention the dead once a funeral is over. To do so may be seen as questioning *Gott*'s will."

Nathan knew he was still questioning. "Tell Tully I appreciate his sympathy."

"I shall. *Vellkumm* to New Covenant. I think you'll find we are all *goot* neighbors and friends. I see the bishop and the ministers going in. Must be time for the service to start."

Nathan followed Gideon inside. The older man took a seat in one of the family's overstuffed chairs that had been set up beside a row of benches.

The seating was separated into two columns with an aisle between. Men and women sat separately. Nathan took his place among the married men sitting on the first few benches at the front, and picked up the black hymnal that had been set out for him. Behind him sat a row of beardless young unmarried men. In the last row on the men's side, the youngest boys were seated closest to the door, ready to make a quick exit when the service was over.

On the other side of the aisle were the women. He caught sight of Maisie in between two young mothers with children beside them. She seemed at ease. He didn't doubt that she had answered more questions about their situation than he had. It seemed to him that women were more curious about others than men were.

The *volsinger*, or song leader, a man near the front of the room, announced the hymn. The rustling of hymnals being opened and pages being turned filled the quiet space. When the sound faded, the man began the first hymn in a loud clear voice, and everyone joined in.

There was no musical accompaniment to an Amish prayer service. There were only voices of the faithful solemnly praising God in slow, mournful tones. The lyrics of the song were written in the hymnal Nathan held, but there were no musical notes to follow. The hymns had been handed down through countless generations, always sung from memory.

Nathan joined in the song and found a surprising peace in recalling the words he had sung since he was old enough to talk. He glanced at Maisie. She had her eyes downcast as she sang. He could just pick out her voice. Slightly off-key, but filled with enthusiasm.

How many times had he cast his eyes toward Annie during the service when he first saw her? She had been so pretty, she'd taken his breath away. If Maisie had been there he didn't remember seeing her, but she would have been sitting with the married women, like she was today.

When the last words of the song died away, the bishop and two other men entered the front of the room. They would share the preaching, taking turns throughout the next three or four hours.

Nathan glanced at Maisie again, wondering how she would fare with both babies to look after for all that time. He didn't need to worry. Less than an hour into the service another babe in the room started fussing. The young mother sent her toddler across the aisle to her father, a big burly man with black hair sitting in front of Nathan. Maisie and the other mother took their infants from the room. He heard them going upstairs.

Maisie followed Gemma to a bedroom at the end of the hall on the second story. The window was open to the morning breeze, which carried in the scent of roses. Crossing to the window, Maisie looked down and saw a trellis below heavily laden with the red, fragrant blooms. "I wondered how flowers would do this far north, but I see Mrs. Fisher has a lovely garden."

"The winters are harsh. Our summers are short, but the summer days are long this far north. That gives flowers and vegetables plenty of sunlight. It isn't a forgiving land, but it can be bountiful."

Maisie turned away from the window. "How old is your son?"

"Three months."

Maisie grinned. "He's big for his age."

"I know. He takes after his father. My daughter was premature, so I'm not used to lugging such a big fellow around. How old are the twins?"

"Two weeks." Maisie sat down on one of the twin beds in the room and lifted Jacob out of his basket, then began to change his diaper. He kicked happily.

"They grow up too fast," Gemma said with a sad smile. "It must be difficult for you. Coming so far and not finding a warm welcome from their father. Dinah told me about your situation."

"I will treasure every moment I have with them. When Nathan hires a nanny, I will look for a job of my own. I intend to stay in New Covenant. They are my sister's children, and I can't leave them. I know she wouldn't want me to."

"There is plenty of work during the potato harvest, but I'm afraid over the winter it may be harder to find a job. The area is very rural. The Amish here don't have little shops and home businesses the way they do in other communities where tourism brings in lots of people. The reason New Covenant was founded was to avoid the temptations that come with tourism and allow Amish families to tend the land the way it used to be."

"Then your husband must be a farmer."

"Jesse and I raise potatoes for our main cash crop,

but also hay and oats for our animals. For a while he worked for Bishop Schultz building garden sheds, but since we were able to acquire more land Jesse now farms full-time. It's nice to have him close by to help when I need him. Is Nathan going to stop working for Arthur Davis?"

"Not anytime soon. He has hospital bills to pay."

"I'm sure the church will help with his bills. They helped me and my husband pay for Grace's medical care."

"Nathan feels that because he isn't a member of this congregation he shouldn't ask for their assistance."

Gemma scowled at Maisie. "That's ridiculous. We help any Amish family in need. Our church has sent donations to those affected by tragedies in many states."

"Someone else will have to persuade him of that because he won't listen to me."

Gemma arched one eyebrow. "Stubborn, is he?"

Maisie smiled. "A little."

Gemma chuckled. "I'll have my husband speak to him and perhaps the bishop can. There's no shame in needing help. That goes for you, too. Taking care of little ones can be exhausting. Especially twins. Any one of us would be happy to take over and give you a few hours rest since Nathan won't be at home."

"*Danki.* I do miss my sleep."

"I know it isn't always possible, but I think it's best when a father doesn't have to leave the farm for work. Our families are second only to God in importance."

Maisie smiled at the baby she held. "I couldn't agree more."

"I hate to see you being separated from them. Are you sure Nathan won't relent and allow you to be their *kinder heeda*?"

"I'm sure he won't. Besides, it may be for the best."

Gemma's eyes narrowed. "Why would you say that?"

"It just would." Tears pricked the backs of Maisie's eyes. She quickly blinked them back. Her feelings for Nathan weren't something she could talk about. It didn't seem right to harbor such affection for her sister's husband.

"I think my boy is finished. May I feed your little girl?" Gemma asked.

Maisie managed a smile. "Please do. Her bottle is in the bag with her."

After the babies were fed, the women returned to the prayer meeting. Maisie kept her eyes down, resisting the urge to see if Nathan was looking her way. When simply talking about him made her eyes tear up she couldn't risk meeting his gaze. She didn't want him to suspect how much she had come to care for him.

When the service ended, Bishop Schultz faced everyone. "I have one announcement to make. We have a new family joining our community. Peter Yoder, his wife and their twelve children. Peter has purchased the home south of Gideon Beachy's dairy, but it isn't big enough for his family, so we are having a work frolic to build an addition onto his house this coming Saturday. Leroy Lapp has a list of needed supplies so check with him."

As everyone filed out, Maisie stayed in the house to help ready the meal along with several other women. She caught sight of Nathan waiting for her by the door.

When he started toward her, she fought down the urge to run in the opposite direction.

"Aren't you ready to go?" he asked.

"I must help serve the meal." Around her, the men were rearranging the benches and stacking them into tables where people could eat.

Nathan nodded toward the door. "Others can do that."

"I don't want people to think I am a slacker. I will do my part. We can leave once the meal is over. If you are afraid to stay longer I'm sure someone can give the children and myself a ride home later."

"I'm not afraid to stay. I just don't like standing around talking. It's pointless."

She could tell from his tone that he wasn't happy. Neither was she. He was being ridiculous, and her patience was growing thin. She wanted him to leave her alone. "Then sit in a corner and pout until I'm done."

His frown deepened, then he turned on his heel and left. She wanted to call him back and apologize but maybe it was better if they stayed at odds with each other.

So much for her plan to be kinder to him.

Bishop Schultz was coming in the door as Nathan was going out. "Nathan, I'm delighted to see you. I'm glad you could join us."

He didn't say it was about time, but Nathan heard the words the bishop left unspoken. "Maisie was keen to come." He should have let her come alone.

"My wife had only *goot* things to say about meeting her."

Nathan didn't want to talk about Maisie. The woman was exasperating. "Have you found anyone to take care of my children?"

"I confess I have not. Why don't you want your sister-in-law to stay?"

Nathan glanced over his shoulder. "We don't get along."

"I'm sorry to hear that. Division in a family is never a good thing. Most often it is the children who suffer because of it."

The bishop laid his hand on Nathan's shoulder. "I know you don't want that. Do what you can to mend your differences before it affects the children."

"I don't think we can."

Bishop Shultz bent forward to look into Nathan's eyes. "Are you sure it isn't bitterness toward your late wife that makes you say that? Her actions wounded you deeply and you will never know the reason for her choices. Forgiveness must come first, even before understanding. That is the cornerstone of our faith. You will not know peace until that happens."

"I'm afraid that's easier said than done."

"Only because you aren't yet willing to make that commitment. When you are ready, forgiveness will come easily. I must ask you one more question. It, too, may not have an easy answer."

"What?"

"Are you being fair to Maisie? Think on it. I hope to see you at the frolic."

Chapter Eleven

Nathan wanted to ignore the bishop's words, but the harder he tried to forget them, the more they stuck in his mind. Was he being fair to Maisie?

Maybe he wasn't, but he didn't want to be constantly reminded of Annie, either. He couldn't see a way to reconcile his dilemma. He couldn't escape thinking about her even when she was out of his sight.

"Nathan, have you got a minute?" Gabe asked, beckoning to him from across the driveway.

"Sure." Nathan walked toward him.

Gabe gestured toward the building that was attached to the side of the barn. "You've been in my workshop. You bought your harness from me."

"I did and I'm pleased with it."

"Glad to hear that. I've been thinking about expanding the place. I'm considering a log addition. I know you built your home from logs. I was wondering what the drawbacks would be."

Nathan pushed his relationship with Maisie to the

back of his mind. He slipped his hands into his front pockets and rocked back on his heels. "You won't find many drawbacks to log construction. Well-fitted logs provide plenty of insulation to keep it cool in the summer and warm in the winter. You can hang hooks for your merchandise anywhere on the walls. If you have your own trees, as I did, the only lumber you have to purchase is for the roof, windows and doors. In addition, a peeled and polished log interior is attractive without needing any paneling or paint. A coat of varnish will make the natural color last a long time."

At this point Gabe's dad, Zeke, had joined them. "We would need someone to point out which trees we should harvest."

"I could do that for you," Nathan said. "I'd advise against using them this season. It's best to let them dry out over the winter. Are you in a hurry to expand?"

Zeke chuckled. "My sons are always in a hurry. Why don't you take a look around our forest and see if we have trees that are worth harvesting before we take the idea any further."

"I've started back to work for Arthur Davis so it will have to be next weekend before I can get out here."

Zeke looked at Gabe and then nodded. "That's agreeable."

"If you have the right kind of timber, will you cut it yourself or will you need a logger?" Nathan asked, hoping for a little extra income.

Gabe lifted his hat and combed back his blond hair with his fingers. He settled his hat on again and looked at Nathan. "We can't conduct business on Sunday. We'll discuss that when you come to look over our trees. How about a game of horseshoes? Cowboy can join us. He loves the game."

Nathan cocked his head to the side. "Cowboy?"

"That's what we call Tully. He was an Oklahoma cowboy before he found us. Ask him to show you some of his rope tricks."

"Is he any good?" Nathan asked.

Gabe laughed. "He was an *Englischer* who roped himself an Amish wife. That takes real skill."

"If he has joined our faith, I'd say it was the wife who possessed considerable talent in bringing him around."

"Nee." Zeke shook his head. "Tully says *Gott* used Becca to give his life purpose. The Lord makes use of us all in ways we may never know."

Maisie came out of the house and walked toward Nathan. He focused on the ground. She stopped a few feet away. "I'm ready to go if you are."

He cleared his throat. "Spend some time with your new friends. I can wait."

"Are you sure?" she asked hopefully.

"Ja. We will go when everyone is done eating."

"Danki. I'm sorry about earlier."

"Forget it."

She gave him a tight smile before she turned and walked back to the house.

Nathan looked up to find Gabe staring at him. His father was heading toward the barn. Gabe arched one eyebrow. "Trouble between you and Maisie?"

"What makes you think that?"

Gabe shrugged. "My wife, Esther, is deaf, and she's

very good at reading body language. I've picked up a thing or two from her."

Nathan sighed. "Maisie is my wife's identical twin."

"So?" Gabe asked.

Nathan wanted someone to understand what he was going through. Gabe was a twin. Perhaps he could see Nathan's point. "It's like looking at the woman I lost every time I see her."

"I take it you didn't know Maisie well before this?"

"I saw her briefly at the wedding and a few times at different gatherings." He'd only had eyes for Annie back then.

"As a triplet I can say my brothers and I are confused by people who don't know us well. We may look alike at first glance, but we're totally different people. Your grief is new, Nathan. It colors your thinking. That's only natural. As you get to know Maisie better you'll see that she isn't so much like her sister. Come on." Gabe tipped his head toward the barn. "The horseshoe pit is this way."

Nathan thoroughly enjoyed himself for the next hour as he and Gabe played against Zeke and Tully. He didn't have their skill level. He hadn't played in a while, but everyone looked like amateurs when the bishop played against the big black-haired fellow Nathan learned was Jesse Crump. Both men were highly skilled, but the bishop inched out a win at the end of three games. The older men congratulated the bishop while Gabe, Nathan, Tully and the other Fisher brothers commiserated with Jesse.

"Admit it," Moses said. "You let him win."

A wry grin appeared on Jesse's face. "You will never hear those words from my lips. It's my opinion that the Lord is on the bishop's side." He slapped Nathan on the back. "I hear you're a lumberjack. Kind of small for that line of work, aren't you?"

Nathan stood several inches taller than the Fisher brothers, but he didn't come close to Jesse's height. "With a sharp chain saw in hand the tree doesn't care how big the man is. It falls just the same."

Gabe laughed. "Jesse doesn't use a chain saw. He just bites the trees off and uses the splinters for toothpicks."

Jesse took the teasing good-naturedly. "Sometimes it takes two bites. Walnut is a lot harder than pine."

Nathan realized he had missed the camaraderie of other Amish men since leaving Missouri. He had friends among his *Englisch* coworkers in the lumber company, but there was something special about the dry wit of Amish men that another Amish fellow could appreciate.

"I had best round up my family and head for home," Tully said. "The cows haven't learned how to milk themselves." He walked over and spoke to his father-in-law and then to Harvey. The boy nodded and jogged toward the horses. He untied one and led it to one of the parked buggies.

Nathan looked toward the house. Maisie was probably becoming impatient. He walked into the kitchen and heard voices coming from the living room. He looked in and saw her sitting cross-legged on the floor. She was holding Charity against her shoulder while Jacob lay snuggled in the nest of her lap. Two young girls, who looked to be eight or nine, were lying on the floor with their chins propped on their hands beside Maisie, admiring Jacob. Maisie was chuckling at the antics of the toddler playing peekaboo with a teenage girl in the center of the room.

Maisie looked up and caught sight of him. Her bright smile vanished. Because of him. He suddenly wished he knew how to restore it. What did the others think of their relationship?

"I'm ready if you are," he said, avoiding her eyes.

"I am. Annabeth and Maddie, would you fetch the baskets for the babies?"

The girls beside her popped to their feet and raced up the stairs. Maisie held Charity out for Nathan to take, then transferred Jacob to her arms and rose.

The two girls came downstairs and set the baskets at Maisie's feet. She settled Jacob in one then held out her arms for Charity. Nathan handed over his daughter. Maisie swaddled her and tucked her in. "There we go, *liebling.* Snug as a bug," she said softly.

Maisie was so at ease handling them. She seemed at home with the other women in the room, too. He felt oddly out of place and wondered if they had been talking about him.

He picked up Jacob's basket. "We'll be in the buggy."

"I won't be a moment. Goodbye, everyone."

"Don't forget to let us know if you need anything," Gemma said. "We'll be out to check on you soon."

Nathan paused in the doorway when he heard that. Check on her? Why?

Maisie nodded. "I appreciate that. I'll see you then."

"Bethany will bring some of her cinnamon biscuits because I love them," Gemma said.

"You should learn to make them yourself," another woman said. Nathan recognized her as Bethany Shetler. They'd met on the day he was taking Maisie to the bus station.

Gemma sighed heavily. "I've tried. Yours are better."

"I'll fix cinnamon coffee to go with them," Maisie said.

"*Ach*, that sounds *goot*. How is it made?" the bishop's wife asked.

Maisie glanced at Nathan and then back to the women. "I'll show you when you come. Goodbye."

Outside, he found Harvey had brought Sassy and his buggy to the front door. Nathan helped Maisie in and then handed her Jacob. He went around to the driver's side and got in. "Why are they coming out to check on you?"

"Because that's what they do for new mothers. I know I'm not the children's mother but taking care of them and the house can be exhausting. The women will clean and bring ready-made meals so I don't have to cook as much." She settled Jacob's basket next to Charity on the seat so that both babies were between them.

"That's *goot*. I won't be so concerned about you while I'm at work."

Her gaze snapped to his. "You don't need to worry. I'll take every care with them."

"Oh, I know that." In fact, he was sure of it. He picked up the lines and clicked his tongue to get Sassy moving.

* * *

Maisie watched the slowly changing countryside as Sassy trotted toward Nathan's home. Fields of potato plants were sandwiched between areas of dense forest, giving the land a patchwork appearance in varying shades of green. There were a few wheat fields and cornfields, too, but for the most part the farmable land grew potatoes. It was the staple crop for the area.

She looked at the babies, who were both sleeping peacefully, and smiled. The worship service and the companionship of new friends had succeeded in lifting her spirits. She glanced at Nathan, determined to keep things casual between them. "I thought all three of the preachers did a *goot* job, didn't you?"

"*Ja.*"

He didn't elaborate. "Did I miss anything important while I was upstairs with the *kinder*?"

"*Nee.*"

"Was meeting people as hard as you feared?"

"It wasn't."

Two words that time. He was getting quite talkative. "No one asked about my sister. I think Constance and Dinah must have shared what I told them with everyone. Did anyone ask you about Annie?"

"I spoke to the bishop. He knows the whole story. Only Tully Lange offered his condolences and asked about her. His father-in-law was quick to explain that Tully was newly come to our faith and didn't know it was improper to speak of the dead."

"His wife Becca told me Tully was *Englisch*. I've never known one of them to join our faith, have you?"

"I have not."

Maisie stared at her folded hands. "I guess I shouldn't mention Annie anymore. *Gott* allowed her death. I accept that, but I'm not ready to let her go. We were so close once."

"If you need to talk about her I will understand," he said, surprising Maisie.

"Danki."

Not knowing what else to say, she went back to watching the landscape. In the distance, she saw a black shape loping up the side of a hill.

She sat up straight. "Is that a bear?"

Nathan looked her way. "Where?"

"Near the top of that rise?" She pointed to where she was looking.

"I see it. That's a black bear, all right."

Nathan's home was less than a mile away. "Are they dangerous?"

"They avoid people so make noise if you are walking in the woods."

"What do you mean make noise? What kind of noise?"

"Talking, singing. Anything to let the animal know where you are."

"I'll remember that. I should climb a tree if I see one, right?" She shivered at the idea. What if she was out with the children?

"They are excellent climbers so that won't deter them."

Walking in the woods was definitely out of the question now. "Have you seen them near your home?"

"Occasionally. Buddy will warn them away if they come around."

"He's not a very big dog."

"His bark is loud enough. I reckon mine has been, too. For that I'm sorry."

Was he apologizing for the times he had snapped at her? "At least you don't bite."

"I'll do better in the future."

"As will I."

A smile pulled up one corner of his mouth. "Haven't we had this conversation already?"

"You less irritated and me less annoying? I believe we have."

"Perhaps we'll get it right if we keep trying."

"I'll be less irritated from now on. You can be less annoying."

"It's a deal."

Jacob began crying. Maisie tried to soothe him but he wasn't having it. She hadn't packed more formula because she thought Nathan would have returned home by now. Nathan turned into his lane and Sassy picked up the pace. He stopped her in front of the cabin.

Maisie picked up Jacob and his head bobbed angrily against her shoulder as he tried to find something to suck on. His grasping hand found the ribbon on her *kapp* and he pulled it toward his mouth.

Maisie winced and tipped her head. "Ow! Stop, honey, that's pinned to my hair." She tried to open his fist, but he hung on tight, pulled harder and yelled at the top of his lungs.

"Let me help." Nathan opened her door and leaned

in. He took hold of the baby's hand. His own fingers brushed against Maisie's neck. "Let go, *sohn*," he coaxed.

Maisie felt the heat rush to her face at Nathan's nearness. "It's fine. I can manage."

"I've got it." He gave a tug that pulled her *kapp* crookedly over her eye, but the babe let loose.

Nathan tried to smooth her head covering back in place. Suddenly he paused with one hand still touching her face. Maisie looked into his eyes and saw confusion. Her heart began to beat faster. What did he see? What was he thinking? Was he remembering the times he had touched Annie's face with tenderness? She looked away, but the feelings she held in her heart didn't subside. If anything, they grew stronger. She didn't want to be the cause of his pain or a reminder of sweet things that passed between a husband and wife.

She wanted Nathan to see *her*. She could tell he didn't.

A knot formed in Nathan's chest. Maisie's hair was thick and soft. The sun-dried smell of her linen *kapp* mixed with the scents of lavender and clean babies. He realized he was looming over her when she pulled away. He slowly withdrew his hand and took a step back. "He's got a good grip for such a small fellow. He'll be able to hold an axe, for sure."

She cradled the crying boy in her arms and slipped out of the buggy without speaking. Her shoulder brushed against Nathan's chest, causing the knot in him to tighten. He took another step back and watched her rush into the house. Once she was out of sight, he was able to take a breath.

His reaction to Maisie's nearness amazed him. It should have been because she resembled his wife, but he hadn't been thinking about Annie in that moment.

He couldn't be attracted to Maisie. The idea was ridiculous. Besides being his sister-in-law, she didn't even like him.

He shook his head to clear it. His reaction had to be because she looked like Annie. The affection he'd had for his wife had withered during the months following her vanishing act, but he had loved her once. The moment with Maisie must have sparked the memory of those tender feelings. He would have to take care that it didn't happen again.

Charity began to squirm in her carrier. Nathan realized he'd forgotten about her. He lifted her out of the basket and cuddled her against his chest. "Sorry, *liebling*. Your *daed* isn't thinking straight today."

She curled into a ball against him. So tiny and precious. His heart expanded with love for her. "May *Gott* grant me the strength to protect you always."

Would her life be difficult without a mother? Nathan could supply many of her needs, but what about the things a little girl learned at her mother's knee? How to cook and sew and make a home, even how to care for younger brothers and sisters. All these things, and so many others, he wouldn't be able to teach her. Perhaps her nanny, when he hired one, would show her all those things.

He glanced toward the house. Maisie could teach

her what she needed to know and would love her, too. Every child needed to be loved.

The bishop's words came back to him again. He was being unfair to Maisie, but was he being unfair to his children, too? Didn't they deserve to be loved by her?

He shook his head and kissed the top of his daughter's bonnet. "Your *kinder heeda* will love you and your brother. How could she not?"

He walked into the house determined to avoid a repeat of his closeness with Maisie. Dredging up old memories of Annie was exactly why he didn't want Maisie around.

The afternoon passed pleasantly enough. He thought Maisie took pains to stay out of his way. She cooked a light supper of boiled beef and cabbage from his garden. He liked the way she seasoned it. He couldn't recall Annie ever making the dish.

After supper, he got down the Bible and sat in the rocking chair between the babies to read to them. Maisie sat at the kitchen table mending his socks. He didn't have a pair without at least one hole in them. He was grateful she had noticed.

After half an hour, he closed the book. Maisie looked up from her mending. "Shall I fix you a lunch for tomorrow?"

"I can eat at the canteen on site. You don't need to go to any trouble."

"Is the food *goot*?"

"It's food."

"I see. So, *ja*, I will fix you a lunch." Her tone said

the subject was closed. She put her mending aside. "I believe I will turn in now."

"I think I'll stay up a while. I like to watch them sleep. You don't have to stay up with me," he added quickly.

She smiled softly. "Remain as long as you like."

"*Danki*, Maisie. For all you have done for my babies," he said, wanting her to know he meant it.

She smiled at him. "It's what Annie would have wanted me to do." She crossed the room and climbed the stairs to the loft.

The bishop's question came back to Nathan. *Are you being fair to Maisie?*

He wasn't. He wasn't being fair to his children, either.

He should let Maisie be their nanny, but how was he going to make that work?

Chapter Twelve

Maisie was relieved when the weekend was over and Nathan started back to work again. It meant she only had to see him for brief times during the day. She fixed his breakfast and his lunch with a cheerful smile on her face. It wasn't until he went out the door that she fell to pieces. She tried to put him out of her mind, but it was like making the sun go down in the east. Impossible.

When she was with him, she noticed everything about him, from the way he smiled at his babies to the way he didn't smile at her. It was hopeless. He was growing dearer to her every single day.

The evenings were the worst, when he read to the babies or worked on some project at the kitchen table. Sometimes she caught him watching her and her heart would begin to race, but he always looked away. He never said that he cared for her, too. She took to going up to bed early just so she wouldn't have to face him and hide her feelings.

She longed for and yet dreaded the coming weekend, when he would be home for two whole days.

Friday evening she sat in the rocker after supper and picked up Charity. The babe wasn't hungry so Maisie just rocked her and hummed a children's song she had learned when she was in school.

"I remember that one," Nathan said. He was sitting in his chair with an open book in his lap.

"I think all schoolchildren must learn it." She traced Charity's dainty eyebrow with the tip of her finger.

"Davis finally hired another feller. The man is every bit as good as Ricky was."

"I'm glad to hear that."

He cleared his throat nervously. "I've been reconsidering your situation here."

She stopped rocking. "What does that mean?"

"It means I've decided that you should be their *kinder heeda*. I'm not going to look for anyone else."

She could barely believe her ears. "Do you mean it?"

"I have to think about what's best for them. It's clear you love them. You're a sensible woman. I think you're the best person for the job."

Tears sprang to Maisie's eyes. "Oh, Nathan, how can I thank you?"

"You've been caring for them and doing it well in spite of my objections. You might as well be paid for the position."

Her heart was so full of joy that she didn't know what to say. She bent and kissed Charity on the cheek. "Do you hear that? I'm going to take care of you for as long as you and your brother need me."

"We should discuss living arrangements." Nathan rubbed his hand nervously on the arm of his chair.

"Okay."

"You can't continue staying here. It was understandable when you first arrived, but now you will need your own place."

He didn't want her here. He had made that abundantly clear from the start. It shouldn't hurt to hear him say it again, but it did. "How will you manage to take care of them through the night and still work if I'm not here?"

"I've been thinking about that. If you agree, the babies can spend the nights with you through the week and then with me over the weekend. Say Friday, Saturday and Sunday nights."

"That sounds reasonable. I'll have to start looking for a place to rent. Nathan, I can't tell you how happy this makes me."

"Then all we have to do is agree on your salary."

"I can't take money for watching my niece and nephew."

"You can't live on air. I don't know how you are set financially, but I suspect you aren't wealthy."

That made her laugh. "Hardly."

"Then you must treat this as a paying position. Will you be going to the frolic tomorrow?"

"Of course. And you?"

"It's time I started helping my fellow man again. I've been holed up for long enough."

"I'm glad to hear you say that." It was what she

wanted for him. For him to move forward with his life and leave the bitterness and unhappiness behind.

"I reckon I'll see you early in the morning, then." He rose and left the cabin, taking Buddy with him.

Maisie got to her feet and twirled around once, still holding Charity in her arms. "Do you hear that? I'm going to be taking care of you forever. Or until you start school, whichever comes first. You know what this means? It means your father is accepting me as part of his family." It wasn't what her heart desired, but it was close enough.

Nathan nailed another sheet of siding in place on the new addition for Peter Yoder's home. All around him, men were working in concert to complete the project by the end of the day. Gabe came down from his place on the roof. "We're almost done."

"It was a good day's work," Nathan said. He paused to look for Maisie and saw she was sitting in the shade with a group of women. Peter Yoder's oldest daughter, a girl of eighteen, had both his babies in her arms.

"My wife tells me you have decided to let Maisie look after your children. What brought about your change of heart? The last time we spoke you said the two of you didn't get along. What's changed?"

Nathan wasn't surprised the news had gotten around so fast. He gave Gabe a wry smile. "I guess I have changed. You were right. The more I'm around Maisie, the more I can see that she is different from her sister."

"Things are better between the two of you, then?"

"We've found some common ground."

"Aha." Gabe grinned.

Nathan glanced at him. "What's that supposed to mean?"

"Nothing. It's just that I've noticed the way you look at her. And the way she looks at you."

"It's nothing like that. We both want the best for the babies. That's all."

"That's understandable. One more row of shingles and we're done. I'd better get a move on."

Nathan looked toward Maisie and met her gaze across the lawn. He raised his hand in a brief wave. She smiled softly and nodded to him, then looked away. There was nothing unusual in the exchange. What was Gabe seeing that Nathan didn't see?

"He's a handsome fella," Kathrine Yoder said with a giggle in her voice.

Maisie glanced at the cheerful teen. "Who is?"

"Nathan Weaver."

Maisie hoped she wasn't blushing. "He's well enough, I reckon."

"And hardworking, too. *Mamm* says that's the first thing a girl should look for in a man."

"Your mother is a wise woman. He's a little old for you, isn't he?" Maisie suggested.

"Oh, *ja*, but not for you."

"Me?" Maisie's voice squeaked in surprise.

"You can't stop looking at him except when he's looking this way," Bethany said.

Maisie looked around at the faces of the women she was sitting with. Bethany, Gemma, Dinah and Constance were all grinning at her. She was shocked. "*Nee*, you are mistaken. He's my brother-in-law."

"Was your brother-in-law," Constance said.

"There's nothing between us. I take care of his children. That's all there is."

"If you say so." Kathrine giggled again.

"I do," Maisie insisted. "I'm looking for my own place. Does anyone know of a small house or apartment that I can rent for a reasonable price?"

They all shook their heads, but then Bethany snapped her fingers. "I do. Your neighbor, Lilly Arnett, came in to have a clock fixed. She told Michael she had been thinking about taking in a renter at her place. She has an empty caretaker cottage or something. Do you know her?"

"I do. I'll talk to her. *Danki*."

"Its *goot* you are leaving Nathan's cabin," Constance said.

Maisie sobered. "I hope there hasn't been any gossip about us."

"Nothing like that," Constance assured her. She looked toward Nathan. "I was just thinking that absence makes the heart grow fonder."

Maisie didn't laugh as the other women did. Her absence from Nathan's house was the only hope she had to mend her heart, because being with him every day was breaking it in two.

Something was different about Maisie this morning. Nathan couldn't put his finger on it, but something wasn't right.

She made a breakfast of dippy eggs, toast and oatmeal for him without comment. She fed the babies and dressed them in the new gowns she had sewn for them, while he ate instead of joining him. Not once did she meet his eyes.

As she was cleaning up, it struck him what was different. She wasn't humming or singing the way she normally did in the mornings.

"Are you feeling ill?" he asked.

"I'm fine." She kept her back to him as she worked at the sink.

He wanted to understand what was wrong. "Did the babies have a fussy night?"

"No more than usual. Are you going to be in here for a while?"

He had already finished his chores before breakfast and had even turned the cow and her new calf out into the pasture for the first time. "I reckon I can be."

"*Goot.* I'm going to go visit Lilly." She dried her hands, lifted her shawl off the peg near the door, flung it over her shoulders and went out.

"Beware of—" The door closed behind her before he could finish his warning. There had been occasional bear sightings in the area. He got up from the table. The dog was asleep under it. He nudged the hound with his toe. "Buddy, go outside with Annie."

Nathan winced and curled his fingers into fists. How long before Annie's name didn't roll off his lips? Not until her constant reminder lived somewhere else.

Buddy sat up. Nathan walked to the door and opened it. "Go keep an eye on Maisie."

The dog trotted out. The hound would alert her to any bear or moose in the area. Nathan closed the screen door behind the dog, leaving the wooden door open so he could enjoy the morning breeze. The air was distinctively cool. Summer was on the wane. Another month and he would be harvesting his potato crop. He wondered if Maisie would help or if he would need to hire someone. One of the Fisher brothers perhaps.

Gabe had it wrong about Nathan and Maisie. He wasn't interested in her romantically. When they weren't squabbling, she was fun to have around. She took wonderful care of the babies. He liked her cooking, but that wasn't the same as liking the woman.

Outside he heard Maisie shout followed by Buddy barking. He should see what was going on. Or maybe not. She had obviously wanted to get away from him. He cast a glance at the sleeping babies. Now was as good a time as any to get ready to go back to work on Monday. His chain saw needed sharpening. It was essential work. He headed to the barn to fetch it knowing the task was simply his excuse to check on Maisie.

He heard the cow bellowing loudly. Buddy's barking rose in volume. Nathan looked across the pasture. The cow was pacing frantically back and forth by the pond. He didn't see her calf. When she stepped far enough to one side, he saw Maisie up to her waist in the water with her arms around the calf's neck in the shallow end of the pond.

He vaulted the fence and hurried toward her. The cow decided he was an unwelcome intruder and tried to knock him aside. Buddy rushed in to nip her nose and distract her. "What are you doing?" he yelled at Maisie.

"There was a bear by the fence. I chased it off, but the calf became so frightened she ran into the pond. Now she is stuck in the mud."

Of course, Maisie would chase off a bear without calling for his help. His blood ran cold at the thought of how badly that could have ended. "I see she is stuck. Why are you in there?"

"She can't get out. I tried to free her, but it's no use. I'm afraid if I let go of her head she'll drown."

He started to wade toward Maisie, but quickly became mired in the mud himself. He stretched out his arm as far as he could. "Grab my hand."

She reached for him but her wet, muddy fingers slipped out of his grasp. The movement made her sink even farther. She shook her head. "Get back before you get stuck, too. We need a rope or a long branch."

"Hang on. I'll get something. Try not to struggle."

"That's what I keep telling this baby, but she won't listen." The calf continued thrashing her head back and forth, bawling pitifully for her mother. Her struggles were sending Maisie deeper into the mud.

Buddy was still doing his best to keep the cow away. Nathan looked at Maisie. "If you can't save the calf, save yourself."

Maisie turned her face away from the splashing water the calf's movements sent flying. "Get a rope and save us both."

Nathan bolted for the barn. He grabbed a coil of rope from the tack room, opened the door to Donald's stall and led the big horse out into the pasture at a trot. At the edge of the pond, he quickly tied one end of the rope to Donald's halter and then waded toward Maisie. If he got stuck, the big horse could easily pull him free. The struggling calf had pushed her farther out. He paused with a coil in his hand. "Can you grab the rope if I throw it to you?"

"I'll try." She was up to her chest in the muddy water. He had no idea how deep the mud was where she was standing. If her legs were stuck, she wouldn't be able to swim.

He carefully tossed the rope toward her. She made a grab, but it floated beyond her reach. He quickly pulled it in and tried again. This time it landed across her arm. "I've got it," she shouted.

"Hold on and I'll pull you out." He started drawing the rope toward him.

"Let me get it around the calf first." The ensuing struggle had her up to her chin in the water. "Pull now," she said.

"Back, Donald. Back, back."

The big horse began walking backward until the rope was taut. Nathan kept pulling, too. The calf came slowly toward him and then popped up like a cork. He hauled it to shore as quickly as he could. Once the baby's legs touched dry ground, it collapsed in exhaustion. Nathan picked it up and carried it away from the shore so the heifer's mother could reach her. He hurried back to the water.

Maisie's pale face was barely above the surface. She held up one hand. "Hurry, Nathan."

He waded out until he was as close as he could get. It took him two tosses to get the rope near her hand. He started breathing again when she got hold of it. "Wrap it around your chest if you can, Annie."

She pulled the rope underwater. A few seconds later she gave a tiny nod. "Pull."

"Donald, back, back!"

The rope went tight, and her head went underwater. Nathan hauled on the rope, stepping even farther out and sinking above his knees in the muck. Suddenly she came up and slammed into his chest. He hung on to her as his horse dragged them both out of the water.

"Whoa, Donald. Whoa, boy," Nathan shouted from his back on the grass. The rope went slack. Donald walked up to sniff at Nathan. He reached up to rub the horse's nose. "*Goot* boy. Very *goot* boy."

He lay still for a few moments, relishing the weight of the woman in his arms. He could feel her rapid breathing. Her head was pressed against his chest. She must be able to hear the pounding of his heart. He looked down at her mud-covered face. "Are you hurt?"

"Nee." She rolled to the side, sat up and began struggling to get the wet rope untied. He got to his feet. Suddenly he was furious with her for putting herself in such danger. "Annie Jean, that's the most foolish stunt you have ever pulled," he shouted, then realized his mistake.

Maisie surged to her feet, shimmied the rope to her ankles and kicked it aside as she glared at him. "I don't know how you could possibly know that, Nathan whatever-your-middle-name-is, since I am not *Annie*!"

She stormed past him, leaving a trail of dripping mud and water in her wake.

No, she was definitely not Annie.

"You're welcome," he shouted.

She stopped for a moment but then kept walking. He coiled up his rope, untied it from Donald's halter and led him to the barn. Nathan gave the horse an extra ration of oats and then followed Maisie to the house. The memory of the feel of her in his arms wouldn't fade.

He tried the door, but it was locked. He knocked. "Maisie, let me in. I'm sorry. It was the heat of the moment and her name just slipped out."

"Go away. I'm taking a bath."

He glanced along the porch and saw the galvanized tub still hanging on the wall. He unhooked it and knocked again.

"What?"

"Would you like to use the tub?" he asked, trying not to laugh. He was dripping wet and cold but he didn't care.

The door flew open. She had her *kapp* off. Her auburn hair hung down in long wet strands over her muddy dress and her eyes danced with green fire. *"Danki."* She pulled the tub from his hand and shut the door.

She opened it a second later. "And thanks for saving me and the calf." She closed the door before he could reply.

He looked down at his sopping clothes and knocked one more time. The door opened. A shirt followed by a pair of pants, a towel and a bar of soap came flying out. "Now go away," she shouted and slammed the door in his face.

Buddy came trotting up and scratched to be let in. Nathan looked at the dog. "I don't reckon she wants you right now. Might be for the best. She's touchy today."

Buddy scratched again. The door opened a crack. He wiggled inside before it shut.

Nathan picked up his dry clothes, the towel and the soap and headed to the pump to wash up in the cold water. No, she was definitely not Annie.

He had been angry because Maisie put herself in danger, but he realized how angry he still was with Annie. That feeling kept him from accepting Maisie as a person in her own right. Maybe it was time to let go of his bitterness.

After washing up and putting on dry clothes, Nathan walked up the rise to Annie's grave and squatted on his heels beside it. He saw the fresh flowers that had wilted and knew Maisie had put them there.

"I see your sister tends the dead as well as the living. Maisie is a born caretaker, but I reckon you knew that."

It felt odd but right to put his feelings into words.

"I'm at a loss, Annie. I'm angry. I'm sad. I'm bitter, but none of that affects you, does it? Only the living suffer. I've made Maisie's life miserable because she reminds me of you in so many ways, but I'm starting to see she isn't much like you at all. She's taking *goot* care of the babies. She has been showing me how to love them. How to give them more than food and shelter. If they learn to be caring people it will be because she has shown them how it's done. You were right to ask her to come."

He picked up a handful of dirt and let it trickle through his fingers. "You hurt me, Annie. You broke my heart, made me doubt myself. You caused me to shut myself away from my faith and those who would help me. I'm never going to know why, am I?"

He rose to his feet and slipped his hands in his pockets. "The bishop here said forgiveness must come first, even before understanding. That's a hard thing to wrap my brain around. I wanted answers before I forgave you, but I'll never have them. I can't live my life with this weight on my soul. Those around me deserve better."

He wiped at the wetness on his cheeks. "So I forgive you, *liebling*. Rest in peace."

He turned away and walked down the hill with a lightness in his heart that he hadn't known for nearly a year. At last, he was free.

Maisie washed the muck and pond smell from her long hair at the kitchen sink with cold water while she waited for her bath water to heat up. She had every pot full of water and the stove on high.

She shouldn't be this upset. Nathan hadn't meant to call her by Annie's name, but it hurt, anyway. Closing her eyes, she faced her sad desire. She wanted to be back in Nathan's arms just for a moment. Even if they were both exhausted and soaking wet in smelly pond water. She chased the image from her mind. Had he been holding her? Or had he been holding Annie?

She wanted his concern to be for her, but she would

never be sure if he was thinking about her or if he was thinking about her sister.

She wasn't going to ask him. She wasn't going to beg for his attention the way she had begged for John's in a hopeless effort to make her marriage into something it hadn't been.

What she needed was to get away. Not from the babies, but from Nathan. She needed her own place, where she didn't have to hide her feelings. She could pretend for the few minutes that they would meet each day that she was fine.

She took a quick bath in lukewarm water because she was too impatient to wait for the water to get hot. She would go see Lilly today. She prayed her friend hadn't already rented the little ivy-covered cottage. It would be perfect for her and the babies and close enough to the cabin to make it easy for her to share their care with Nathan.

She dried off, emptied out the tub and took her clothing out to the washing machine. She saw Nathan's clothes piled on a chair beside the washer. She tossed everything in together and went back to clean up her mess in the kitchen. She had no choice but to wear her hair down. It wouldn't dry if she put it up or braided it. She used a kerchief to cover her head and tied it at the nape of her neck. Then she went to the front door, took a deep breath and stepped out. Nathan was waiting on the steps.

His uncertain smile made her traitorous heart turn over in her chest. Why was she falling in love with a man who couldn't care for her because of how she looked? She put her shoulders back, determined to go through with her plan. "Would you bring the buggy around, please? I'm taking the babies to visit Lilly. She hasn't seen them yet."

"Are you okay?"

"Of course I am. Why wouldn't I be?"

She was embarrassed to have him see her hair hanging down her back. A woman's hair was her crowning glory, to be viewed only by God and her husband.

"I was afraid the rope might have hurt your skin."

"I'll have a bruise or two, but otherwise I'm fine. The buggy, please?" She turned on her heel and went back inside before he could ask her anything else. She put the babies in their carriers and waited outside until Nathan brought Sassy and the buggy around. She got in and picked up the lines. "I'm not sure when I'll be back."

She put Sassy into a quick trot. The sooner she was away from Nathan, the sooner she could gather her scattered wits and decide what to do next.

Chapter Thirteen

Nathan heard a horse and buggy a short time later and wondered if Maisie was returning already. He put down the harness he was cleaning and opened his door. He was surprised to see the bishop step out of the buggy.

Nathan pulled his door shut and started walking toward him. "Good day, Bishop Schultz. What can I do for you?"

The bishop turned around and smiled. "I came to see how you are getting along, brother."

"Well enough." Nathan nodded toward the barn. "I have coffee down in my room if you'd like some."

The bishop looked puzzled. "In your room?"

"I sleep down there. That gives Maisie and the babies more room in the cabin."

The bishop's eyes widened. "Of course."

Nathan suddenly felt self-conscious about the arrangement. "Come in. Maisie and the children have gone to visit Lilly Arnett." Nathan walked ahead of Bishop Schultz and opened the cabin door.

The bishop stopped on the porch to look the building over. "I understand you built this place yourself."

"With my team and an occasional hand from the men I work with at the lumber camp."

"It looks solid."

"The first winter will be the real test. Nothing like a wind-driven snow to find the cracks and poor joints." Nathan walked inside, hung his hat on a peg and indicated his chair. "Have a seat."

The bishop hung up his own hat. "Show me around first. I see you have a loft. How wide is this place?"

"Twenty feet."

He walked to the center of the room and turned around. "And how long?"

"Thirty-five feet."

"And could you make it smaller?"

"Smaller is easier than making it bigger. Why?"

"The *Englisch* are looking for smaller homes now. They call them tiny houses. I have built a few and they have sold well. I think there is a certain appeal to a log home, especially here in Maine. How long would it take you to construct one that was twelve feet wide and, say, twenty feet long with a loft like this one?"

"It would depend on the weather and if the materials were readily available. In the right conditions, I think eight weeks for the shell."

"It's an interesting thought." He turned to Nathan. "But not why I am here today."

Nathan sat on the sofa and waited until the bishop took a seat. "Why have you come?"

"I haven't found anyone to work for you, I'm sorry to say. I heard that your last candidate wasn't suitable."

"Maisie did not think so, but I took your advice and asked her to care for the babies as their *kinder heeda*."

"She has invested her heart in her sister's children, hasn't she?"

Nathan leaned back. "That she has."

"And how are the two of you getting along?"

"Fine. She takes good care of my home. She's a fine cook. She keeps an eye on my livestock, too." Nathan grinned at the memory of Maisie up to her neck in muddy water.

The bishop was watching him intently. "So you get on well?"

"I would say so. I try not to be irritated and she tries not to be aggravating for the most part."

"Worthy goals. And you find her trustworthy?"

"I would not leave my children in her care if I didn't."

"Is she a devout woman of faith? Will she instill a love of *Gott* in the children?"

"Absolutely. Her faith is rock-solid." And stronger than Nathan's, but he knew his faith could grow and flourish now.

"That's reassuring to hear from someone who knows her best. We didn't have a chance to talk much at your wife's funeral. I could see that you weren't ready. You did say that she had left you and you didn't know where she was until I brought you the news of her death."

Nathan leaned forward and clasped his hands together, propping his elbows on his knees. "That's right.

She left me with only a note. I didn't know I had children until you came that day."

"When was the last time you saw Annie?"

"Last December. Two months after our wedding."

"You grieved the loss of her then, didn't you?"

"I guess I did. Except I held on to a small measure of hope that she would return."

"That's understandable. It's what any man would want. I ask because what I'm about to suggest may seem unusual. Especially to those who don't know your story."

Nathan didn't understand. "Unusual how?"

"Your children are going to need more than a nanny. They're going to need a mother. Have you considered remarrying?"

Nathan held up one hand in surprise. "*Nee*, I'm not ready to look for a wife."

Would he ever be ready to trust his heart to another woman? It was hard to imagine.

"A broken heart is sometimes slow to heal," the bishop said. "But not every marriage is based on romantic love. A marriage can be successful if it is based on love of *Gott*, mutual respect and shared goals. Love between two people can grow out of friendship over time. There are several young women in our community who would make wonderful mothers for your children, but I think you already know the best candidate."

Nathan shook his head. "I don't know who you're talking about."

The bishop arched an eyebrow. "I think you do. Maisie."

Nathan was thunderstruck. "Maisie? You think I should marry Maisie?"

"I am not in the habit of playing matchmaker. That is something my wife enjoys. It was her suggestion that I speak to you on the subject."

This was unbelievable. Nathan got to his feet, walked to the door and opened it. "Please, tell your wife I appreciate her concern, but I have no intention of taking a wife. Especially not Maisie."

The bishop rose, walked over to get his hat and stopped beside Nathan. "I will tell her what you said, but she's going to ask me why 'especially' not Maisie?"

"She's too much like Annie."

"Your own words belie that. You said she keeps a fine home, loves the babies, she's a devout member of our faith, she's even a good cook. Which of those qualities are too much like those of the wife who broke her vows and abandoned you?"

Nathan clenched his jaw so hard his teeth ached. The man didn't understand. "Good day, Bishop. It was kind of you to call," he said when he had his temper under control.

The bishop tried to hold back a smile. "I found it very enlightening myself." He nodded to Nathan and went to his buggy.

Nathan shut the door and leaned against it with both hands. "Of all the ridiculous, unbelievable, preposterous ideas. Me? Marry Maisie?" What was the man thinking? Of course, she was like her sister. They're twins.

He remembered Maisie's furious face when she'd shouted, "I am not Annie."

His anger faded. She wasn't Annie. Annie hadn't had a temper. Annie never sang in the mornings. She never suggested that he read from the Bible in the evenings or enjoyed visiting with friends. She told Nathan that he was enough for her, but she had broken the vows she made before God and their community.

He forgave Annie, but that didn't mean he could forget what she had done or want to replace her. The children had Maisie and they had him when he could be with them. That would be enough.

Besides, Maisie would laugh at the suggestion of marrying him.

Wouldn't she?

It didn't matter. He wasn't about to ask her.

Grabbing his hat, he went out and headed down the lane. He had told the Fisher men that he'd be out to look at their trees to see if they had enough harvestable wood to build an addition on Gabe's shop. Now was as good a time as any and he could use the long walk.

Lilly came out to greet Maisie as soon as she stopped Sassy outside the front gate. "Maisie, how wonderful to see you again. Do come in. I just took some banana bread out of the oven."

Seeing the welcome in Lilly's eyes made Maisie feel better. "I'm glad you're home. I have brought some visitors with me."

Lilly's expression brightened even more. "The babies? Oh, how wonderful. Bring them inside. Will your horse be okay out here by herself?"

"She'll be fine. Give me a hand with these chubby

children. I can't believe how much weight they have put on since I first arrived. These little baskets won't hold them much longer."

She handed Charity to Lilly and got out with Jacob. Lilly was smiling tenderly at the little girl. "She certainly looks like you."

"She looks like her mother."

Lilly immediately appeared contrite. "I'm sorry. That was thoughtless of me."

"It's okay. If she looks like her mother she has to look like me, too."

"My gracious, woman, look at all your hair."

Maisie blushed. "I hope you don't mind my wearing it down. I washed it and I'm waiting for it to dry."

"I don't mind at all. It's a beautiful auburn color. I shouldn't say that, should I? The Amish don't want to be called handsome or beautiful. They want to be plain."

"Because it isn't our outward looks that please God."

"That is so true. Well, come in. I want to hold that little boy, too."

Maisie followed her into the kitchen, which had bold yellow stripes on the walls, white cupboards with yellow daisy-shaped pulls and numerous paintings and sketches of different flowers on the walls. "Your kitchen is colorful."

"I know it must seem gaudy to you, but I like it." She placed Charity's basket on one of the white wooden chairs.

"Did you do the paintings?" Maisie asked, impressed with the quality of them.

"Most of them I purchased from local artists. Several

of them I got from Esther Fisher. Gabe's wife. She and I share a love of wildflowers. I like to grow them. She likes to sketch and paint them. How is Nathan?" Lilly asked, suddenly serious.

"As well as can be expected." Maisie concentrated on lifting Jacob out of his basket. She handed him to Lilly, who took him tenderly. Talking about Nathan was the last thing she wanted to do.

Lilly smiled at the babe in her arms. "It's been ages since I've held a newborn. You forget how tiny they are. What a perfectly wonderful way God chose to start a person."

"They certainly have their own personalities already. The reason I came today was because I heard you are renting out your cottage. I'm looking for a place and it would be close to Nathan's."

Lilly's face fell. "Oh, no. I wish I had known."

"You've already rented it to someone else?" Maisie struggled to hide her disappointment.

"I'm afraid so. Mr. Meriwether knows a gentleman from Philadelphia who is looking for a weekend getaway home. He's going to take it. I'm so sorry."

It had been too good to be true. Maisie managed to smile. "All things are as God wills. I'll keep looking. If you hear of anything, please let me know."

"I will. Now can I interest you in a slice of banana bread and some milk?"

Maisie nodded. "That sounds wonderful."

"Let's have it out on the patio so the sun can dry your hair."

Maisie enjoyed Lilly's treat and her company for another hour while Lilly admired the babies, but Maisie knew she was simply putting off her return to Nathan's cabin. What could she say to explain her outburst over something as simple as being called the wrong name? She couldn't tell him the truth. That she was falling in love with him and she wanted him to care for her, not her sister.

Nathan wasn't home when Maisie returned. She was glad of the reprieve but knew it was only that. She stabled Sassy and took the babies inside. They weren't ready for their feedings, so she settled them in their cradles and fixed a roast with new potatoes and carrots from the garden and put it in the oven. She had time to make a salad of fresh greens to go with the roast before Jacob began fussing.

She fixed his bottle and settled in the rocker with him. "I'm beginning to think Agnes Martin was right about us. You demand attention and I jump to take care of you. I think I'm spoiling you." She bent to kiss his forehead. When she looked up, Nathan was watching her from the doorway.

Nathan stared at Maisie as if seeing her for the first time. It wasn't her resemblance to Annie that caught and held his attention. It was a look of love in her eyes when she gazed at his son. He didn't know it at the time, but this was why he had built this cabin. To someday see a gentle, sweet woman rocking his baby by his hearth.

A sense of wonder filled him. This is what he wanted, what he had always wanted—a family of his own.

How could he have been so blind as to see only Annie

when he looked at Maisie? Their similarities were minor things. It was Maisie's inner beauty that filled his heart with happiness. This felt like coming home.

He was afraid if he spoke that feeling would vanish, but he couldn't stand in the door all night. "Did Lilly enjoy meeting our *kinder*?"

"She did. I had a hard time prying them out of her arms. Nathan, about before—"

"Forget it. I have."

"I was very rude to you and I'm sorry."

"Nothing to be sorry for." He picked up Charity and sat in his chair. "Aggravating and irritated, I reckon we'll do that to each other now and again. It doesn't matter as long as we share this quiet joy together."

She smiled softly. "They are a blessing, to be sure. Where were you this evening, if you don't mind my asking?"

"I walked over to the Fisher place to look through their forests and see if they have enough usable timber to build a log addition on Gabe's shop."

"Do they?"

"They do, but some of it is going to be hard to reach with heavy equipment, which I'm guessing is why the bigger trees haven't been cut already."

"What about using horses?"

"It is certainly possible. It would take a little longer but the impact on the land would be a lot less. In fact, they offered me the job."

Her bright smile did funny things to his stomach. "Are you going to take it? What about the lumber camp?"

He studied Charity's face as he stroked her cheek. She turned her mouth toward his finger and opened her lips. "I would still need to work for Davis. This would be a side job. I think this little girl is ready to eat."

"Her bottle is warming on the stove."

He got up to get it.

"I went to see Lilly because I heard she had a place to rent," Maisie said.

He froze. They had talked about her getting her own place, but he didn't think it would be so soon. "It would be close."

"Someone else had rented it before I got there."

His relief was startling. She wasn't leaving him yet. "I hope you know there's no rush. I'm perfectly comfortable where I am."

"I appreciate you saying that, but I do feel odd sleeping in your bed while you sleep in the barn."

He returned to his chair with the warm bottle of milk, picked up his daughter and began to feed her. "In that case, we can trade beds. You can have the cot up there and I'll haul the big bed down to my room."

Maisie laughed. "There isn't enough space in there. You would have to walk sideways to get to the stove."

"That's true. I guess you're stuck with the better bed."

"You could move Mack to your room and put the bed in his stall. There'd be plenty of room then."

He laughed. "No way. Donald snores. I'm not sleeping next to him."

She grinned. "I guess it would make the cow and her calf jealous if Mack had a stove and they didn't."

He tried to sound serious. "We could have a barnyard revolt on our hands before we know it."

"The roosters might start crowing at midnight in protest."

He smacked his hand on the arm of his chair. "That settles it. Mack is staying in his old stall no matter how upset he gets."

She giggled and he loved the sound. It was good to see her being carefree, even for a little while.

"Both babies are awake and not crying. You should read to them," she said.

"Why don't you sing instead? There is a lullaby my *mamm* used to sing to me. *'Schloof, Bobbeli, Schloof'*—do you know it?"

"'Sleep, Baby, Sleep.' Of course I know it. I've sung it many times." She put her head back in the chair and began to sing softly. He joined in and their voices blended in a pleasant harmony. By the time the song ended, both babies were sleeping. She put Jacob to bed and then took Charity from Nathan's arms and tucked her in.

He leaned back in his chair and glanced toward the kitchen. "Something sure smells *goot*. What's for supper?"

"Is food all you think about?" she asked, still smiling.

"I reckon," he replied, but it wasn't true.

He was thinking about the reason for the bishop's visit. Marriage. Maybe it wasn't such a far-fetched idea after all. There would be advantages to a more permanent relationship.

But could he get Maisie to see them?

Their relationship had been rocky at best. Only when they were with the children did they seem of one accord. He couldn't do much to improve the situation unless he was home.

He got out of his chair. "I'm going down to the phone. I should leave a message saying the nanny position has been filled in case anyone calls about it."

"Okay, I'll wait supper on you."

"Danki."

He got his hat and went out. When he reached the phone booth, he recorded a new message and then dialed the number for his boss.

Maisie followed the smell of frying bacon down to the kitchen early the next morning. Nathan stood in front of the stove with a large blue apron over his clothing.

"What are you doing?" she asked.

He turned to her with a breathtaking smile. "I thought I would make breakfast for a change. I hope you like hearty eggs."

This was different. "And what are hearty eggs?"

"Eggs with diced onions, grated cheese, grated potatoes, crumbled bacon and hot sauce to top it off. One of the guys at the lumber camp showed me how to make them."

"That all sounds fine except for the hot sauce. Is it optional?" she asked hopefully.

"Of course, but you'll never know if you like something new unless you try it."

She was almost convinced but thought better of it. "I'll have mine less hearty than yours."

"Don't tell me you're a fraidy-cat." He shook his head and make a tsking sound. He brought the plate to the table and sat down.

After saying grace, she cautiously tried a spoonful and found it was quite good. He pushed the hot sauce toward her.

She sprinkled a few drops on her next spoonful and regretted it as soon as it touched her tongue. With her mouth open, she tried to fan the heat away. "Water," she croaked.

He put a glass of milk in front of her. "This is better."

She didn't care what it was as long as it was liquid. After several moments, the heat died away. She frowned at him. "Why would anyone want to eat something painful?"

"It wasn't that bad. Admit it."

"I admit nothing. I believe I'll have some toast."

He pushed the plate where she could reach it. "The Fishers are hosting a frolic on Thursday to build a greenhouse. I thought you might want to go."

"I'll see. It depends on the babies and if I feel up to it. It's a pity you can't go. I know you've become friends with Gabe."

"Who says I'm not going?"

She frowned. "What about your work?"

"I told you Davis hired another feller. I called him last night and asked to use the rest of the time off he'd promised me when I told him about Annie and the babies. He agreed."

"But what about your pay?"

"I'm not getting paid time off, but I can cut and haul the timber for Zeke Fisher and make up the difference. I want some time with you and the babies before you get your own place. Last night was nice, wasn't it?"

Smiling at the memory, she nodded. "It was a pleasant evening." Following a stressful day.

"*Goot*. We should have more like that one." He winked at her. Actually winked. "Without the squabbling first, *ja*?"

Chapter Fourteen

Maisie poured coffee refills into the cups for her guests. "Have either of you heard about a place for rent nearby?" Bethany and Gemma had surprised her with a visit on Thursday morning.

Both women shook their heads. "How are you and Nathan getting along?" Bethany asked.

Maisie grinned. "The change has been like night and day. I don't know what happened. Well, maybe I do. I gave him a frightful scolding last Sunday. Nathan has been so nice to me these past few days that I'm tempted to scold him once a week."

"That's what I do to Jesse," Gemma said, hiding a smile with her cup. Since Jesse towered over little Gemma, the thought of her shaking her finger at her mountain of a husband made both Bethany and Maisie chuckle.

Gemma leaned forward. "Did Agnes Martin really apply for the babysitting job?"

Maisie nodded. "I'm sure she's a nice woman but she didn't seem a good fit for the twins."

"You made a wise choice," Gemma said, sharing a speaking glance with Bethany.

"Agnes wanted Gemma to be shunned when she first returned to us," Bethany said. "After the bishop had granted her forgiveness."

"I was pregnant but not yet married," Gemma explained shyly.

"Agnes isn't the kindest soul," Bethany said. "I don't think she would have been right for the job."

Maisie shook her head. "You should have met the *Englisch* woman who came with her résumé. She couldn't stop checking her phone the entire time I was talking to her. I was shocked. Who would hire someone like that to watch their children?"

"Nathan chose the right woman when he chose you," Bethany said. "We can all see how much you love those babies. They will never know another mother except you."

"Unless Nathan remarries," Maisie said quietly. Neither of her friends said anything.

Maisie pasted a smile on her face. "Are you going to the frolic at the Fishers' today?"

"I wouldn't miss it." Bethany set her cup in the saucer. "I made a cherry pie for dessert. What about you, Maisie, what are you bringing?"

"Nathan said he likes apple. I think I'll make two of those. One for the frolic and one to leave here."

Bethany rolled her eyes. "I hope he knows how fortunate he is to get a *kinder heeda* who cooks and cleans, too."

"We should get going," Gemma said. "Jesse loves watching the children for me but for some reason the house is always a mess when I get back. We'll see you this afternoon."

As much as she enjoyed their company, Maisie was glad to see them on their way. She had pies to make because she knew Nathan would enjoy them. He loved the smell of something good cooking in the kitchen and she liked doing it. It was a small thing, but it made her happy to make him happy.

Until she found a place of her own, she reminded herself. And then he would be cooking for himself again unless she took pity on him and cooked something while he was at work. It was getting harder to contemplate making that break from him. His recent kindness had her puzzled, but perhaps he realized how unfair he'd been to her in those first few weeks.

She wanted to think they could come out of this as friends.

Nathan paced in his small room as he tried to decide what to say to Maisie. He was going to propose today. Things had been good between them since Sunday. He was afraid if he waited any longer something would happen to derail his plans.

Her friends had left nearly ten minutes ago. If he waited much longer his courage was going to fail him.

He left the barn and walked up to the house. Outside the door, he stopped to take several deep breaths.

This was a good idea. He'd thought it through carefully so why was his stomach churning?

It was the logical thing to do. Maisie would understand and appreciate the advantages when he pointed them out. She wasn't the most logical of women—he'd seen that—but she had a good head on her shoulders when she wasn't angry. He was sure that she had gotten past being upset with him.

Nathan rubbed his suddenly sweaty palms on the sides of his pants. This was as good a time as any. He opened the door and stepped in the house.

She was in the kitchen slicing apples into a clear bowl with cinnamon and sugar. Two pie pans with unbaked crusts were sitting on the table. He walked up beside her and leaned against the counter. He crossed his arms because he didn't know what to do with his hands.

He cleared his throat. "Making apple pies?"

A smile twitched the corners of her lips. "What gave me away?"

"Yeah. It's pretty obvious." For some reason the collar of his shirt suddenly seemed too tight. He gave a small tug on it.

"Did you want something?" she asked, reaching for another apple in the bowl beside her. She deftly peeled it and started slicing until only the core was left. She tossed it in the garbage can beside her.

"There's something I'd like to talk to you about. I think you'll see that it's also an obvious solution." Did he tell her it was the bishop's suggestion? He decided not to mention that.

"So talk." She reached for another apple.

His hand shot out to cover hers. "Could you stop doing that for a minute?" Her hand was so small and soft compared to his. A tingle skittered up his arm, centered in his chest and made his breath catch in his throat. He jerked his hand away.

A tiny frown creased her brow as she looked at him. "I have to get these in the oven if they are going to be done in time for the frolic."

"This won't take long."

She laid the knife on the counter and dried her hands on her apron. "You have my attention. What is it?"

"I've been thinking about our situation." He swallowed hard. Was it hot in here? From the stove. Of course.

"And?"

"I have a solution. Please hear me out."

She crossed her arms. Her eyes narrowed slightly. He could still see the gold flecks in her green irises. He hadn't noticed before what thick eyelashes she had and how they framed her eyes so beautifully.

"Do I have something on my face?" She rubbed her cheek.

"Nee." Should he tell her that she had beautiful eyes? Maybe not. It had nothing to do with their situation. He needed to ease into this conversation, point out the advantages for her.

She tapped one foot. "I'm waiting."

"You have pretty eyes."

A blush crept up her cheeks. "That's kind of you to say. Is there anything else?"

"I think we should get married."

Her eyes widened with shock. "What?"

"There are so many advantages," he said quickly. "You won't have to look for a place to live. You can live here. We can live here. You won't just be a nanny to the children—you'll be their mother. I know you would like that. You would never have to be parted from them. I know you already feel in your heart that they are yours."

She half turned away from him and braced her hands on the counter. "I do love them. What about us?"

"Us?"

"*Ja*, us. As in you and me. Together."

Why was she making this so hard? A simple *yes* was enough.

All the things he wanted to say ran through his mind. *Marry me so I can take you in my arms and kiss you. Let me hold you close and tell you my hopes and my dreams and hear you whisper that you understand. That you care for me.*

He would say those things in time, but he wasn't sure she was ready to hear them. "We get along pretty well now. You have a bit of a temper, but you also have a generous heart. I don't see a reason it won't work." He stared at his toes. "I wouldn't make any demands on you," he said softly.

She was silent for several long, uneasy moments. He saw her fingers splayed on the counter curl into her palms and then slowly open again. She drew a deep breath. "Getting my own place is a better idea."

He jerked upright. "But I thought you liked it here. You have ideas for how to make the cabin a better home. You are going to expand the garden."

She picked up her knife again. "I have to finish these. We don't want to be late."

"You don't want to marry me?"

"Nee."

Why did that one word hurt so much? He had trouble drawing his next breath. What else could he have said? What could he offer her? Maybe he was rushing her. "If you want to think it over, I don't have to have an answer right now."

She whirled to face him. "I'm not a replacement for my sister. I'm a person with my own thoughts and my own feelings. Did you really expect me to jump into your arms and be thrilled at the idea of stepping into my dead sister's shoes?"

"That wasn't what I was thinking. Look, I have rushed you. I'm sorry. Take some time and think it over. I believe you'll see it's best for both of us and the babies."

"You have my answer. Now please get out of the kitchen and let me finish these pies." Her voice broke and she threw the apple core into the trash hard enough to make it bounce out and land at his feet.

Nathan let his hands drop to his sides. She didn't want him. Just like her sister hadn't wanted him. A sick feeling seeped through his body. What was wrong with him? Why wouldn't she give him a chance to make it work between them?

It didn't matter. He could see her mind was made up. "Fine. Call me when you're ready to leave. I'll be in the barn."

He stormed out of the kitchen and slammed the door,

wishing he could somehow leave the pain behind, too, but it stayed like a ball of broken glass in the center of his chest.

Maisie covered her face with her hands as her sobs broke free. She sank to the floor in a heap of misery as hot tears flowed down her cheeks. He had ruined everything. She couldn't pretend that he was starting to like her. He had only been nice because he thought that would persuade her to accept his proposal.

He could bring himself to marry her, but he didn't love her. He couldn't say the words she needed to hear. She was a solution to his problem. Not someone he loved. She cried until there were no tears left and then she hauled herself to her feet and washed her face at the sink.

God forgive her, she had almost said yes. She loved him. He had offered her everything she wanted except the one thing she could never have. His heart. Annie had ruined him more completely than she could have known.

As much as Maisie had grown to love Nathan, she knew she couldn't fix him. Couldn't change him. She had tried with John and only earned more heartache.

She was greedy. She wanted more. She wanted to be loved because she was Maisie. Nathan would never see her as anything but a pale imitation of Annie.

The magnitude of Maisie's grief hollowed out a place where her heart should have been. She wouldn't be able to stay here. Constance had offered to let her live with them. That's what she would do. Nathan was going to be off work for several weeks. The babies would be fine with him, though the thought of leaving them was unbearable. She needed time to decide what to do next.

She wouldn't be able to look at Nathan every day and know she could have been his wife if she had been willing to accept his proposal.

It wasn't fair. She had already endured one loveless marriage. She would not subject herself to that humiliation again.

Nathan hit the nail with as much force as he could muster. The head of his hammer slipped off and the nail bent. It was too far in to be pulled out so he hit it over and over until he smashed the bent part into the wood.

"What did that poor nail ever do to you?" Gabe asked from his position a few rafters over.

"It's not the nail," Nathan grumbled.

"Oh, it's the woman." Gabe chuckled.

"What are you laughing at?"

"I've been where you are and I'm happy to say I got through it."

"I asked Maisie to marry me."

"Did you? That's a surprise. What did she say? I ask, although I think I already know the answer."

"I don't understand the woman. I offered her everything that I have. Everything she wants and she still said no."

"That was going to be my guess. Maybe she is in love with someone else," Gabe suggested.

Nathan scoffed at the idea. "If I thought that I wouldn't have asked her to marry me."

Gabe drove in his nail then slipped his hammer into the loop on his tool belt. "I don't know what to say. When a man tells a woman that he loves her, he expects her to feel the same and sometimes it doesn't happen that way."

"I didn't say that."

"You didn't what?"

"I didn't tell her that I love her."

"Okay. That might have been your first mistake." Gabe scratched the side of his head. "You asked a woman you're not in love with to marry you?"

"I didn't know I was in love with her. I thought I admired her. I respected her. I thought she'd make the perfect mother. It didn't hit me just how much I needed her until she said no."

"You didn't know you were in love with her then, but you do now?"

"Of course, I'm in love with Maisie. She's everything I need. She's as wonderful and spectacular as her name."

"So why can't you tell her that?"

Nathan drove in the next nail, then he looked at his friend. "Because she won't believe me. She thinks I'm still in love with her sister. She thinks I see her as a substitute for the wife I lost."

"And why would she think that?"

Nathan hung his head. "Because that was what I saw when she first arrived. I couldn't bear to look at Maisie because I saw Annie."

"Let me guess. You may have mentioned that to her at some point."

"So now you see why I can't just tell her that my feelings have changed and that I love her for who she is and not because she looks like my dead wife."

"You have a problem, Nathan."

"Tell me something I don't know." He hammered in another nail.

"Well, you're a fool for one thing."

Nathan shot him a sour look. "That didn't help."

"If she thinks you only see Annie when you look at her then you have to convince her otherwise."

"It's too late for that. She is willing to take care of the babies while I'm at work but otherwise we won't see each other."

"Ours is a small community. You will have to see each other at church services and gatherings."

"I know, I know. I'll see her every day when she comes to stay with the children. I don't know how I'm going to endure that. I don't want to take them away from her. She loves them as much as I do."

"Then perhaps you should let her raise the children."

Nathan jerked upright. "I'm not going to give away my flesh and blood. I want my family with me. I'm not going to abandon them."

"Then you'll have to convince Maisie that you see her and not her sister."

"Any suggestions on how I do that?"

"Pray about it. God is all-knowing. He has the answers if you're willing to listen."

Gabe got down, leaving Nathan to wonder if God would listen to a man who had turned his back on Him and was only now stumbling back into his faith.

* * *

Maisie brought out a plate of fried chicken and set it on the table already overloaded with food. Constance came out and rang the dinner bell. Maisie shaded her eyes with her hand and looked toward the building site. All the men wore the same clothing—the same dark blue pants with suspenders and light blue shirts—but she didn't have any trouble picking out Nathan. Her heart foolishly ached at the sight of him. He was on the rafters. He left off working along with the others as they all made their way toward the food.

Would she ever be able to look at him without wanting to be in his arms?

She moved her plate of chicken over and pulled a bowl of baked beans next to it. A second later, she moved them back. Then she stood staring at them.

"What's the matter with you?" Gemma asked, setting a bowl of coleslaw beside the baked beans.

"Nothing. Why do you ask?"

"Because you've been staring at your plate of chicken for a long time. Is there something wrong with it?"

"Everything is wrong with it." Tears sprang to Maisie's eyes. She covered her face with her hands and started crying.

She felt Gemma take her arm. "I don't think this is a conversation your chicken should overhear. Come with me."

Maisie allowed Gemma to lead her around to the other side of the house and into the garden. Gemma sat down on a wooden bench and pulled Maisie down beside her. "Okay, I know it wasn't about the food. What's really bothering you?"

Maisie looked into Gemma's sympathetic eyes and blurted out the truth. "Nathan has asked me to marry him."

"That's wonderful news."

Maisie shook her head. "No, it isn't."

Gemma became instantly sympathetic. "Oh. You don't love him. How awkward for you."

"I love him. I love him with all my heart."

Gemma took Maisie's hand and patted it. "I'm missing something. You love Nathan and he has asked you to marry him, but that isn't good news?"

"Don't you see?"

"Not right this minute. Perhaps you could explain."

Maisie shook her head. "Nathan said he could give me a home. I could help him raise the children. I'd never have to be parted from them."

"It sounds wonderful. What did he miss?"

"The one thing he can't give me. Love. He didn't say that he loved me. Nathan is still in love with Annie. He sees me as a replacement for her. Not an original but almost as good. Sometimes he even calls me by her name." She jumped to her feet and began to pace among the flowers.

Gemma followed Maisie and put an arm around her shoulders. "Now I understand. So you turned him down, didn't you?"

"Of course I did. I deserve to be loved because I am who *Gott* made me. I'm not an Annie replacement."

"What will you do now?"

"Stay with Constance and the bishop, I guess, but I don't want to leave my babies." Her voice broke. "I love them more than my own life. They are part of my heart and soul. I don't know what to do."

"Our Lord will find a way through this for you. You must have faith. In the meantime you can stay with Jesse and me."

"*Danki*, but I need to be with the children. Can someone take us home?"

"Certainly. Jesse will take you."

"If anyone is going to take my family home it will be me," Nathan said. He was standing at the side of the house with his hands clenched into fists.

How much had he heard? Maisie turned away.

"I'm going to go help serve the food," Gemma said brightly.

"Don't go," Maisie begged, reaching for her friend.

"You don't need me, and Nathan would rather I left, wouldn't you?"

"Jesse married a smart woman."

"I tell him that all the time." Gemma gave Nathan's arm a squeeze and walked around him.

"You and I need to have another conversation," Nathan said. "Do you want to do it here or shall we go home, where we won't be interrupted?"

"I don't know what else there is to say."

"A lot, actually. Things I should have said before. Things I didn't know I needed to say."

She didn't want to rehash her heartache, but she saw the determination in his face and nodded. It was better to be humiliated in private. "I'll get the babies."

Chapter Fifteen

The silence in the buggy during the ride back to the cabin was stifling. Even the babies seemed to pick up on the tension. They whimpered and squirmed in their baskets. Maisie kept rocking them, trying to reassure them, but it didn't help. She dreaded what she knew was to come but she was thankful when he turned into his lane. It was better to get it over with sooner rather than later.

When they drove into the yard, she saw there was a dark gray car sitting beside the house. Maisie didn't see anyone around. She looked at Nathan. "Do you recognize the car? Is it one of your logging friends?"

"It looks too high-dollar for the lumberjacks I know." He got out and came around to open Maisie's door.

She handed out the twins in their baskets and noticed movement up on the rise near Annie's grave. A man was kneeling by the marker. It was Gavin Porter.

"It's someone Annie and I used to know. I'll go talk to him," she said.

"You and I need to talk."

"We will." She clasped her hands together tightly as she stared up the hill.

"Do you want me to come with you?" Nathan asked softly.

If what she suspected was true, Nathan deserved to hear it firsthand. She nodded. "I think you should."

Maisie walked slowly up the rise and stopped a few feet away from the kneeling figure. "Hello, Gavin. I'm sorry we weren't here to greet you."

He stared at the small white cross bearing Annie's name. "I'm sorry for a lot of things."

He got to his feet and faced them. "Hello, Maisie, and you must be Nathan."

"I am." Nathan eyed him suspiciously.

"And these are Annie's babies?" Gavin smiled at the carriers. "May I see them?"

Nathan laid the baskets in the grass and opened them wide enough for him to peer in.

"Charity and Jacob," Maisie said. "I wrote to your parents to let them know about Annie's passing, but I didn't know how to contact you."

"They called me. I wish things had turned out differently." He glanced back at the grave. "She was the light of my life."

"She was with you, then?" Maisie folded her arms and looked down. "I wondered as much, but when your parents didn't know where she was I thought I must be mistaken."

Nathan scowled. "Annie left me to be with you?"

"We fell in love when she worked for my family,

but I was married to a dying woman. After my wife passed away, I didn't think I had the right to ask Annie to choose between me and her faith. So I moved to New York with the kids. I thought I could start a new life, but all I could think about was how much I missed her. I wrote to her and asked her to come be with me and the children. I didn't know she had gotten married or I never would have asked. When she told me, I was shocked, but I didn't want to lose her again." His expression was so earnest that Maisie believed him.

She took hold of Nathan's arm. This had to be so painful for him. "Why the secrecy, Gavin?" she asked. "Why not let your parents or me know that she was with you?"

"Because she was ashamed. She made me promise to wait and not tell anyone until after her divorce became final and we were married."

"Divorce?" Maisie was shocked. "Our faith does not allow divorce, Gavin. Annie might have remarried but Nathan never would have been able to. She knew that."

"She never filed for her divorce," Gavin said.

"Why not?" Nathan's words were as brittle as glass.

"She learned she was pregnant. She couldn't come to terms with having left you and taken your child away, too. If we had married the child would have been legally mine, and before you ask, yes, they are yours, Nathan, and not just because you were still her legal husband when they were born."

Nathan looked at Maisie and gave her a half smile. "It would make no difference. They are part of my heart and soul now."

Gavin shoved his hands in his pockets. "I tried to make her happy, tried to find a way to keep her with me, but I could feel her slipping away. I know she loved me and my children, but her guilt eventually drove a wedge between us. Finally, she told me she was going back to you. I didn't want to lose her, but I wanted her to find peace, so I let her go. I should have been with her."

"I'm sorry for your loss," Nathan said, surprising Maisie.

A tear slipped down Gavin's cheek as he looked at Nathan. "Thank you. I came here to say goodbye to her, but also to ask for your forgiveness. We wronged you and I am so, so sorry."

Nathan held out his hand. "You have my forgiveness and so does she. There is no need to ask for it."

Gavin took Nathan's hand and nodded but didn't speak. Then he walked away.

Maisie picked up one basket and Nathan picked up the other. Together they walked down the hill as Gavin got in his car and drove away.

"At least we have some answers," she said as she paused at the door of the cabin. What was Nathan thinking? She was ashamed of her sister's actions, but love made people do foolish things.

"I'm glad to finally understand what made Annie leave me, but it doesn't change what I have to say to you." He gazed at her intently. "I'll put away the mare and then we'll talk."

She flushed and hurried inside. Once the babies were in their cradles, they relaxed and went to sleep. Buddy curled up in his usual place between them.

Maisie was anything but relaxed. She went into the kitchen and saw her apple pie sitting on the counter. Tears pricked the backs of her eyes, but she refused to let them fall. She was done crying over Nathan Weaver. She had her own life to live.

She crossed her arms and leaned against the counter, waiting for him to come in. It wasn't long before he walked through the door and hung up his hat.

"How much of my conversation with Gemma did you overhear?" she asked before he could say anything.

He walked slowly into the kitchen and leaned back on the counter beside her. "Enough, I think. I heard you tell Gemma that you loved me. Did you mean it?"

She tried to brazen it out. "What does it matter?"

"It matters more than you know. I never expected to hear you say those words."

"I never expected to feel that emotion. I tried not to."

"Why?"

She bit down on her lower lip until it stopped quivering. "Do you really have to ask?"

"If I'm going to get this right, I need an answer. We already know how badly I messed up when I tried this on my own."

"If you're going to make me say it, I didn't want to love you because I knew you would never feel the same toward me."

He ran a hand through his hair. "Yesterday I would've said that you were right."

"So there. It's out in the open. I don't want your pity."

"Of all the emotions running through my head right now I can promise you pity is not one of them," he said.

"Are we done? Because I'd like to go lie down for a little bit. I have a headache."

"And your headache's name is Nathan."

"Those are your words." She started to walk past him, but he took her arm. "Maisie, look at me."

She couldn't. She was afraid he would see how close she was to breaking down.

"Maisie, I want to marry you," he said softly.

She cringed inside. He had no idea how much he was hurting her. She longed to say yes but she knew it would only bring her heartache. "We've been over this."

"We have had this conversation but that was before."

"Before Gavin came?"

"Before you opened my eyes. I heard what you were afraid of when you were talking to Gemma. But you haven't heard what I'm afraid of."

She looked at him then. His face was grim. "I have been afraid since I was young that no one really wanted me. My father died when I was four. My mother died when I was ten. I went from home to home, never really being a part of the family. For one reason or another none of them could keep me. I thought it was my fault. I thought I was different. I believed it was better to be alone. Then I met Annie."

"I know you loved my sister."

"I surely did. Then just when I thought God had led me to the place where I finally belonged, she left. It did more than break my heart. It shattered my faith in God. Watching you care for the babies and for me over these last days gave me a glimmer of hope. My faith started mending. Maisie, I don't want to marry you for the sake of the babies or because it's the sensible thing to do. I want to marry you for my own sake. Because I love you and I don't want to live without you at my side."

Maisie could feel her resolve weakening but she couldn't let go of her doubts. He didn't mean it. He couldn't. "You love Annie. Every time you look at me, you see her. That's who you are in love with."

"I thought so, too, but I was so wrong. You once told me that you and Annie were twins but you weren't the same." He cupped her chin and lifted her face. "I see you, Maisie."

"You see her shadow."

"I don't. Maisie has flecks of gold in her green eyes." He leaned forward and kissed her eyelid. "Maisie has a freckle right here that Annie never had. Maisie has amazing faith. She has a wonderful and spectacular heart. The likes of which I have been searching for my whole life."

Maisie was afraid to believe what she was hearing. She couldn't speak for fear she would say something that would drive him away and she didn't want him to go.

"I haven't convinced you?" There was a smile in his voice.

"You haven't."

"Maisie has a temper."

"I'm working on overcoming that."

"Don't work too hard at it. I find I admire a woman who can give me a piece of her mind and argue with me and still make me want to kiss her."

Maisie pressed her lips tightly together. She wanted

to be kissed but not because she looked like the woman he loved.

"Oh, Maisie, what can I say that will make you hear me and not your doubts? You see into my heart. You know what I'm feeling the way Annie never did. I see a hundred ways in which you are different from your sister and I love every one of them."

"You said you loved my sister, too. How can I be sure this love is for me and not something left from loving her?"

"I did fall in love with your sister. I will never tell you differently. As I have gotten to know you, I have grown to love you. I didn't *fall* in love with you. My love grew so slowly I didn't know it was happening. Then it was there, like a sunflower forever turning its face to the sun. You are the woman who loves my children as much as I do. A woman who has a strong and endur- ing faith in God. I love you, Maisie. Not because you look like Annie or because you cook for me and keep my house, but in spite of all that. More than anything, I trust you will always love me and never leave me."

"How can you be so sure?"

"Because I have seen what kind of woman you are. I see your love for me in the way your eyes light up when I walk into the room. I feel it when your hand touches mine. I hear it in your voice even when you're scolding me. It took me a while to figure it out, but I'm sure now. I love you, Maisie whatever-your-middle-name-is. I'm going to kiss you. Speak up if you have any objections."

It was all happening so fast. "I'm sure something will occur to me."

He smiled. "Until it does." He pulled her close and pressed his lips to hers.

Every doubt and worry she had fell away as her heart soared with happiness. She slipped her arms around his neck and returned his kiss with all the joy in her soul. She loved him and he loved her. She would never doubt it again. When he drew away, she reluctantly let him go.

He sighed and tucked her head beneath his chin. "Have I convinced you?"

"Not totally."

He chuckled. "I should've known. What will it take?"

"If you would hold me like this forever and never let me go I might be convinced."

"Oh, if only I could but the *kinder* will want to be fed soon. Will you marry me, Maisie?"

"I think I will have to." She leaned back to look up at him. "How else can I show you how much I love you?"

"You could start with another kiss?"

She cupped his face with her hands. "Far be it from me to argue about such an important issue."

He gave her a quick peck on the lips. "Is this how I win one of our squabbles?"

She pressed a finger to his lips. "*Nee*, but I suspect we will have fewer in the future."

He laughed and hugged her tightly. "I'm not so sure about that, my love."

"We should notify the bishop of our decision soon. He'll be surprised."

"Don't be too sure. It was his idea."

She pushed back to look at him. "What was?"

"He suggested to me, because his wife suggested to

him, that I should marry you and give the children a mother instead of a nanny."

"Did he really?"

"I thought it was a preposterous idea."

"Oh, you did? Was that why you proposed?"

"Something tells me I'm slipping onto thin ice again. What's for supper?"

Maisie burst out laughing, as he hoped she would. He wasn't the least bit interested in eating. He wanted to kiss her again. Nothing she baked could come close to the sweet taste of her lips. He laid his forehead against hers. "*Gott* took us on a roundabout path to each other, didn't he?"

She reached up to brush a lock of his hair off his face. "Perhaps that was so we will never take each other for granted."

He captured her hand and kissed her palm. "How soon can we marry? I don't want to wait another day to call you my own."

"Since we have both been married before we won't need a big ceremony. Two weeks after he reads the banns I'm guessing. We can join the church here at the same time."

"Do you want a big wedding?" He would give her whatever her heart desired.

"I had that. I don't need it again. Just a few of our new friends and neighbors will be fine."

"Then let's go see the bishop in the morning." He wanted to go now, but he knew she wouldn't want to wake the babies and take them out again.

A knock at the door made her move away from him. "Whoever it is, they have terrible timing," he muttered as he crossed the room and opened the door.

Lilly Arnett stood on the porch. "Is Maisie here?"

He stepped aside. "She is. Come in."

Lilly was grinning from ear to ear as she made a beeline into the kitchen. "I have the best news. The man who was going to rent my property has changed his mind. It's yours if you want it, Maisie."

His love laid one finger alongside her lips. "Did you hear that, Nathan? I can have a place of my own. What a tough decision."

He frowned. She was teasing him, wasn't she? He caught the twinkle in her eyes and crossed to her side. "Shall I help you pack?"

She laughed. "*Danki*, Lilly, but I won't be needing a place."

Lilly's face fell. "Oh. I'm sorry to hear that."

"I'm going to marry a lumberjack with a nice cabin that needs only a few minor improvements."

Lilly grinned. "The cabin or the lumberjack?"

Nathan chuckled as he draped his arm over Maisie's shoulders. "She'll improve both."

"Congratulations," Lilly said, taking Maisie's hand. "The two of you deserve every happiness."

"Can you do us a favor?" Maisie asked suddenly. "Could you stay with the babies for a little bit?"

"Oh, I'd love to."

"*Danki*, we won't be long." Maisie took his hand and pulled him toward the door.

He followed her outside, curious as to where she

wanted to go. There was a full moon rising in the east, giving enough light to see by. She chose the path that led to Lilly's house. Where was she going?

When they reached the bridge, she stopped. The moon shone down, making the rippling brook sparkle with reflected light. The sound of the stream rushing over the rocks drowned out everything but the beating of his heart as she gazed at him in the moonlight.

She cupped his face with her hands. "The first time I saw this bridge I knew you had built it."

"How?"

"I just did. I thought then it would be a wonderful place to kiss the man I love."

He drew her close. "Shall we see if it is?"

She smiled and wrapped her arms around his neck. "I thought you would never ask."

"What did I do to deserve you?"

She rose on tiptoe and whispered in his ear, "Only *Gott* knows that. I'm just following the path he set my feet upon." Then she kissed him, and he knew his heart was truly home.

* * * * *

THEIR SURPRISE
AMISH MARRIAGE

Jocelyn McClay

Always, I thank God for this opportunity.

Kevin, there could never be a more amazing
service-oriented hero. I'm glad you're mine.

Thanks to Dad, I was raised around cattle,
although they were beef, not dairy.

Thanks to two dairy-farming uncles
who let me trail after them at milking time.

Brother-in-law Craig,
thanks for sharing your experience with broken ribs.

Audra, I watched you handle a twin pregnancy
with much mental, if not physical, grace.
I watch you display the same grace as you parent
my grandchildren, twins Eli and Amelia
and older brother Judah, who bring me much joy.

As far as the east is from the west,
so far hath he removed our transgressions from us.
—*Psalm* 103:12

Chapter One

She had to tell him. Stealing a glance at the dark-haired man across the grove, Rachel Mast rested her hand against her stomach. She didn't know if this bout of nausea was exacerbated by the thought of telling Benjamin, or just another round in the seemingly endless succession she'd had lately. In this case, it was most likely just the thought of talking to Ben. They hadn't exchanged a word with each other since the day Aaron left. Since the day they'd… Swallowing against the prickling sensation at the back of her throat, Rachel pressed her hand more tightly against her stomach. She had to tell him.

Mired in thought, she flinched when words were spoken just off her shoulder.

"I'm so glad Ben came today. His appearances at these events have been about as rare as yours." Rebecca's comments told Rachel her younger sister's attention was also on the man chatting with a young Amish woman while he tapped a spile into a maple several trees away.

Turning her back on the couple, Rachel took the clean pail from Rebecca to hang its handle on the hook tacked via a spile to their tree. "We were both baptized into the church this fall. Maybe we've felt ending our *rumspringa* meant no longer attending the *youngie* gatherings." Or maybe Ben felt the same guilt and shame she did. In the past six weeks, it'd been a race to see who'd depart a room the fastest when the other one appeared.

"But neither of you are married."

Rachel felt the blood drain from her face. Rebecca's mittened hand flew to her mouth. "I mean... I know you thought you'd be married to Aaron by now. I'm... I'm sorry I mentioned..." Reaching out, she touched Rachel's shoulder before turning to hurry back to the sled, parked in the middle of the grove behind two winter-coated Belgian horses. Rachel knew Rebecca's haste was more an embarrassed escape rather than a need to gather additional pails for the clusters of young people tapping the nearby maple trees for syrup.

Upon reaching the sled, Rebecca anxiously glanced in her direction. Rachel sighed. She couldn't blame her sister. Rachel had been counting down the days until her and Aaron's wedding announcement could be made. All plans were in place for a customary late fall wedding. Until Aaron had been kicked by a horse on baptism Sunday, spending the morning at the hospital getting a complicated fracture set instead of becoming a member of the church along with Rachel.

Although sorely disappointed, Rachel hadn't despaired. Aaron would surely be baptized sometime after the Christmas season so they could be married. No one, least of all her, expected him to disappear into the *Englisch* world in January, a few days prior to doing so. And she couldn't follow him—even if she knew where he went—as having been baptized, she'd be shunned if she left.

Inconsolable, Ben—also stunned by his brother's departure—had given her a ride home so they could commiserate in private. Rachel flushed as she recalled the shock and grief that had extended to comfort being sought. And offered. Which had led to…

Sagging against the tree, Rachel warmed chilled hands on her now-heated cheeks as she watched the clear liquid spilling down the spile into the bucket, an indication the maple sap was indeed running. She wished everything were just as clear to her. How naive she'd been, when her life had seemed so simple a few months ago. *Oh, Aaron, why did you leave? When are you coming back? Are you coming back?*

If Ben had heard from Aaron, surely he'd have told someone who would've mentioned it to her?

Rachel pressed her fingers against her throbbing temples. Even though the late February afternoon was just above freezing, she began to perspire. "Be sure your sin will find you out." *Ach,* the Old Testament verse was certainly true in this case. Rachel swallowed against another bout of nausea. Being sick in the snow would only raise questions she couldn't answer. And she had enough of those herself. What would Ben say?

Would he believe her? Would he ask her to marry him? What if he didn't? What if she wed Ben and Aaron came back? Marriage was for life. Her nose prickled with the threat of tears. There seemed no good options.

What if she waited, and didn't marry, leaving her to face even more shame? And Aaron never returned? Pressing her cheek against the rough bark of the maple tree, Rachel panted shallowly, the crisp winter air a contrast to the bile at the back of her throat.

She was running out of time. She had to tell Benjamin.

Benjamin Raber gently tapped the spile into the maple tree, listening—without hearing—to the constant chatter from the woman at his elbow. He was glad Lydia Troyer had clung to him like a cocklebur to a horse's mane upon his arrival at the *youngies* outing. It kept him from talking with others. It helped keep his eyes from straying, like they did now to the tall brunette woman across the way, currently resting her head with its neatly pinned *kapp* against a tree.

Frowning, Ben stilled his hands as his eyes narrowed. Was Rachel all right? He shifted his weight in her direction before, tightening his lips, Ben continued with his task. Rachel didn't need his help. Not that she'd tell him either way. She was like a startled deer whenever she came in sight of him now, the way she'd jump and dash off. Besides, he wouldn't know what to say to her anyway. Lead congregated in his stomach. Or what he'd say to his brother if he ever saw him again.

"Are you all right?"

He blinked at Lydia's question, having momentarily forgotten she was there.

"*Ja.*" Ben redirected his hammer, glad he'd been tapping gently instead of swinging away when he hit his hand. Of course, a whack to the head might be just what he needed. Firming his jaw, he took the bucket from Lydia and set it on the hook. A whack to the head was surely what he'd needed weeks ago when a teary-eyed Rachel had curled against his chest and whispered, *I'm so glad you're here with me. Could you just hold me?* Ben stared unseeing at the silver lid as he fastened it to the top of the spile. Of course he had. He'd dreamed of holding Rachel for years. When she'd looked up at him, it'd seemed the most natural thing in the world to kiss her. And when she'd kissed him back...

"Wait up!" He could hear Lydia crunching through the snow behind him as he stalked to the next tree. "I thought you said that tree was big enough to support another tap and bucket."

Ben grunted. "Sometimes just because something is possible, it doesn't mean you should do it. It leads to... trouble." Plucking the drill from where he hooked it on his belt, Ben placed it against the bark, angled up so when the sap flowed, it would drip down to the bucket.

Lydia placed her mittened hand over Ben's bare fingers. Furrowing his brow, he looked up to see her simpering smile at a very, very close distance.

"I hope you don't really feel that way. Because I'm hoping it's possible you give me a ride home today."

Ben's fingers flexed and the sound of the power drill cut into the crisp afternoon. Lydia jerked her hand and herself back. Thankful to have borrowed the drill from the furniture shop where he worked, Ben shifted his attention back to the tool in his hand. He sighed as he continued his task. He wished he had the glib tongue of his friend and former coworker, Samuel Schrock. Samuel would know how to flirt back. Or did before he was married. Ben's brother, Aaron, also would've known how to respond. Only too well. Ben's hands tightened. He winced when the drill bit cut farther into the maple than he'd intended. Carefully withdrawing it, he patted the tree, silently apologizing.

Clearing wood shavings from the edge of the newly drilled hole, he gave Lydia what he hoped passed as a smile. "I need to get back home. Got to help with chores tonight."

He didn't have to; it was the quickest excuse he could think of. But, having said it, it's what he would do. That was the way Ben worked. His folks would surely be surprised to see him home early today, as he was only here this afternoon because his mother had basically kicked him out of the house. *Things need to go back to some semblance of normal around here. We don't know why Aaron left, when or even if he's coming back.* She'd pinned Benjamin with a look. *I'm tired of you pacing around the house like a lonely goat when you're not at work. Aaron is gone. That doesn't change our lives. We have to go on.*

Ben's younger siblings were attending the event, an activity planned when the late February weather finally warmed up enough during the day to prompt the sap to run. Ben had wanted to come, while simultaneously wanting to avoid it. The reason for his conflict was leaning against a tree several yards distant.

Except that she wasn't. Not anymore. A stolen glance revealed Rachel had straightened and was staring in his direction. Ben fumbled the spile and hook he was pulling from his pocket, almost dropping them into the snow. This was the first time she'd looked at him in weeks. Surprisingly, she held his gaze. He felt as frozen as the snowman some of the younger attendants had rolled up in the small clearing.

Was she as embarrassed and ashamed as he was? Was she all right? Her face was almost as white as the snow layered on the branch of the tree above her head.

"Are you ready for this yet?"

Reluctantly, Ben turned to see Lydia holding up the bucket she carried. His gaze dropped to the recently bored hole. The one that held no hook or spile. The one obviously not ready for a pail. The only thing obviously ready was this woman for his attention. Lifting his eyes again to Lydia, he saw her gaze shift from his face to somewhere over his shoulder. In the direction where Rachel stood.

"I wonder what Rachel is going to do now that Aaron left. I mean, everyone knew they were going to get married. The Masts' garden was full of celery this summer, planning for a wedding. I heard she even had her blue dress made. If I were her, I'd feel rejected. No wonder she was crying her eyes out that day."

Ben carefully set the spile, with the hook behind it, at the edge of the new hole, his teeth gritted. Rigidly controlling his actions, he gently tapped it in. The one he wanted to reject was Lydia. But it wasn't her fault. She'd just stated the obvious. He knew the pain Rachel had felt. Was surely still feeling. Pain he wanted to take away. His stomach soured at the knowledge that he'd made it worse by his actions in trying to do so.

"Ready for the pail."

After Lydia hooked the bucket under the spile, Ben attached the lid that would keep precipitation or other debris out of the pail. A quick glance over his shoulder showed Rachel was still looking in his direction. Inhaling deeply, Benjamin warmed up his smile and turned to try it on Lydia.

He injected fabricated enthusiasm into his voice. "Looks like we'll need some more buckets. And I could certainly use a cup of the hot chocolate if they still have it."

The red-haired young woman's immediate return smile dipped to a frown when she saw the congregation surrounding the sled and the thermoses brought along for the outing. "Be right back."

"Take your time," Ben called as she tromped through the snow to join the growing line. After another considering look at Rachel, he started walking through the trees, away from the crowd, and at an angle that would converge with her. Should she decide to take a stroll. A sideways glance revealed she had. Ben's heart rate accelerated. It was a struggle to prevent his pace from doing so, as well.

Their paths intersected about thirty yards deeper into the trees. Here, oaks interspersed with the maples, creating a denser wood, and therefore a less attractive destination to any potential tappers. The snow was shallower. Ten pristine feet of it separated him from Rachel when they both slowed to a stop.

It was the closest he'd been to her in almost two months. This girl, who unknowingly had been his secret childhood longing until she became his brother's girlfriend. Their relationship, although stilted, had remained cordial. It'd had to. She was going to be his sister-in-law. Even though it tormented Ben to see her with his brother. And now they were…awkward. Uncomfortable. Embarrassed. *Ach*, had they sabotaged their friendship beyond any salvaging?

Frowning, Ben silently regarded Rachel. Framed by her pale face, her brown eyes, normally so lively, seemed bigger and darker above hollow-appearing cheeks. Her arms were crossed over her torso. If she hugged herself any tighter, she'd turn inside out.

"Are you cold?" Ben crossed his own arms to keep from reaching out to comfort her. If she were looking for something like that, she wouldn't have stopped ten feet away. Not that he would offer it again. Succumbing to the urge to give comfort had gotten them to this unhappy place.

Rachel slid her arms down to her sides. "*Nee*."

They stared at each other across the snow for a few more moments.

Ach, it'd been quite a long wait for those few important words. Ben grimaced and shifted his weight. There was so much he wanted to say to her. But where to start? Perhaps with the obvious, but not the one particular obvious he wanted to ask—are you all right after what we did? Perhaps he could leave it at *are you all right?* But even that currently sounded too personal.

He settled for something that was surely on both their minds, "Have you heard from—" stopping when he heard her ask the same question.

Her *nee* was a softer echo of her previous one. He shook his head at her hopeful gaze.

Refolding her arms across her chest, Rachel looked down to where she was making semicircles with one foot in the snow in front of her. "Benjamin…"

Ben crept a few steps closer in order to hear, her voice had dropped so low.

"About that day…"

He flushed with embarrassment. What about that day? Could they get past their shame and bear to be in the same room with each other once more? Had she decided she never wanted to see him again? That seemed more consistent with her actions the past several weeks. Ben braced himself for her next words. Whatever they might be, he would abide by them out of respect for her. He could see from Rachel's expression that the unspoken words were difficult to share.

Previously perspiring, now a chill prompted him to flip up the collar of his coat. Still, Rachel's words were nothing like he'd expected.

"I'm going to have a *boppeli*."

Chapter Two

The blood drained from Ben's face at a pace likely exceeding all the sap running from the recently tapped maples. Stumbling to a nearby oak, he braced an arm against the furrowed bark of its trunk. Of all the things he'd thought of that night, and he'd thought a lot, he hadn't considered this. But he should have. He lived on a farm where managing livestock supported their livelihood.

Lifting his head, he stared at Rachel, whose white face was surely a reflection of his. "You're sure?"

Avoiding his gaze, she bobbed her head once. "*Ja.*" The whisper drifted to him across the feet separating them.

Inhaling sharply, Ben straightened from the tree. He stepped toward Rachel, only to halt abruptly at a call from behind him.

"There you are! Here's your hot chocolate. Although hot probably won't describe it any longer."

Ben pivoted to see Lydia descending upon them, a

smile on her lips while her hooded eyes shifted rapidly between him and Rachel. The hand he'd been extending toward Rachel reluctantly moved to accept the unwanted cup of chocolate. Not knowing what else to do, Ben concentrated on keeping his tremors under control so the dark brown contents didn't splatter over the snow as he carefully brought the cup to his lips and took a sip.

"*Denki*," he choked out as some of the lukewarm liquid went down the wrong tube in his tight throat. Thanks was not what he wanted to tell Lydia. Ben's gaze swept over the woman he longed to talk with— *needed* to talk with—then returned to the one he needed to sidetrack from her. Stepping between the two females, he reluctantly gave his physical attention to the one, while his awareness and emotions were fixed on the other.

The sound of Rachel's deep sigh reverberated through him. It was followed a moment later by the crunch of the snow as she walked away. It took all his willpower not to look in her direction as he headed back toward the gathering by the sled, Lydia walking close enough beside him for her arm to brush his elbow. Her dangling hand bumped against his own. Shifting the cup to that hand, Ben lifted it out of range.

"Thanks again for the chocolate. It's just what I needed before the drive home."

"Are you sure you don't want company?"

Ach, he surely did. Just not hers. "I'm *gut*. Got a few more things to take care of this evening than I expected." Like dealing with the concept of becoming a father. Ben stumbled at the realization, the hot chocolate arcing out in front of them to drop like a dark rain onto the snow.

To his chagrin, Lydia used the excuse to latch on to his arm. "Are you all right?"

Nee. He was far from all right. He'd betrayed his brother. He'd put himself and a friend he'd always cared for—*even loved?*—in a precarious situation. Ben's feet continued to move of their own accord while the arm Lydia hung from was as stiff as the oak tree he'd recently leaned against.

Rachel was going to have a baby. Ben's heart began to race. *They needed to get married.* His heart rate picked up even faster. Marrying Rachel had been his dream for years. The breathless smile that lifted the corners of his mouth froze. *But what about when Aaron comes back?* Ben had reluctantly watched the relationship between his brother and the girl he loved develop from the time she'd started her *rumspringa* at sixteen. Aaron Raber and Rachel Mast. Amish courtships were usually kept secret but the knowledge of those two together was so ingrained in their Plain community in the past four years, it was like saying salt and pepper.

What if Rachel wouldn't marry him? What if Aaron came back to wed Rachel and he had to watch his brother raise his child? Ben's steps slowed. The plastic cup crumpled in his suddenly tightened fist, the remainder of the cold chocolate dribbled from his hand. At his shoulder, Lydia glanced at him with a furrowed brow.

Ben shook his head, warding off her questions. "*Ach,* just a lot of things to do tonight. Much more than I expected," he murmured. Much, much more.

Lydia nodded, patting his coat-covered arm with one of her hands that encircled it. "I suppose Aaron's departure has prompted some changes."

Ben's breath whistled out through clenched teeth.

He couldn't agree more.

Even though the temperature had dropped with the setting sun, firmly lodging itself below freezing, Ben's gloveless hands were sweating. He wiped them down the sides of his pants as he walked up the sidewalk to the Masts' front porch.

He'd known Susannah Mast for years. He'd always respected Rachel's *mamm*. She'd witnessed and laughingly forgiven him for many youthful transgressions when he'd played as a youngster in a group with her daughters. Ben's ears burned. She wouldn't be laughing about this one. Swallowing hard, he mounted the stairs and crossed the porch. He took another deep breath before he could rap his knuckles on the door.

The dim glow of an interior lamp shone through a window, advising folks were home. Still, Ben flinched, conscious of the last words they'd spoken, when the door opened to reveal Rachel. The solemn expression on her lovely face told Ben he'd been expected. But was his presence welcomed? He'd soon find out.

Thoughts of how to handle the unsettling situation had overwhelmed Ben as he helped his father—who was surprised with his unexpected appearance—with chores. As he'd flung bales of hay to the cattle, Ben had practiced proposing to them. None had accepted. He was afraid he'd get the same response from Rachel.

But he had to try. Marrying her had been his dream. But not like this. Not in a situation that was surely a nightmare to her.

Rachel stepped back, opening the door farther to allow him entrance. Ben swept off his knitted winter cap, wondering if he should've worn his black felt hat for the occasion. What was the proper protocol for proposing to his brother's girlfriend? Ben stifled a snort. There surely wasn't anything related to the topic in the district's *Ordnung.* He bit the inside of his cheek at the thought of the community's set of rules they'd obviously disobeyed. A confession—perhaps, even probably a public one—was required of both of them. Ben's stomach churned at the thought.

Susannah looked up from where she stood at the sink washing milking gear and smiled. Along with keeping bees, the Masts milked some goats that Susannah and her family used to make soaps and other items to sell.

"Ben, how nice to see you. Do you think we'll have a good year of sugaring? I asked Rachel, but she hasn't said much about the day."

"*Ja.* Sap seems to be running pretty *gut.*"

Susannah shook water from her hands and reached for a dish towel. "What brings you over this evening?"

Ben wadded the knit cap in his fist. "I… I was wondering if Rachel would like to go for a drive."

Raising an eyebrow, Susannah looked from him to her silent daughter and back again.

"I'll grab a blanket and my cloak."

Ben's tense shoulders dipped in relief at Rachel's words. He couldn't tear his eyes from her as she hastened to collect the items from the room. She was with child. Did she look different? His gaze lingered on her face. There was no evidence of the animation that normally lit her eyes. Her eyes looked tired. She looked tired.

He was aware that under her furrowed brow, Susannah's thoughtful gaze followed them out the door.

"Does she know?" Ben's voice was quiet as he trailed Rachel down the porch steps.

"*Nee.*" Her words and a waft of condensation drifted over her shoulder. "No one knows but you."

Ben sighed as he watched her black-cloaked figure precede him through the yard's gate. Folks might not know now, but with Rachel's slender form, it wouldn't be long before they would. He stopped to free his mare, Sojourner, from the hitching post. Ben's tongue felt as tied as the knot he fumbled with. He wasn't good with words. Would he find enough appropriate ones to convince Rachel to marry him?

The prospect wasn't looking good when he climbed into the buggy to see Rachel sitting so far on the opposite side she was in danger of falling off the seat. The blanket she'd brought was piled between them like an instant mountain. Backing his horse away from the post, Ben studied his passenger's profile. He didn't speak until they pulled out of the lane and onto the country road. His pounding heart greatly exceeded the steady clip-clop of Sojy's slow jog.

"*Denki* for coming out. And for…telling me."

Her soft sigh carried to him on the quiet night. "I had to. Much better sooner than later."

"No word from…?"

Rachel shook her head before her chin dipped to rest against her chest.

Ben's fingers flexed on the leather reins. "I know I'm not the one you wanted, but, since you're having a *boppeli*… I'll marry you." He cringed as he heard the words fall out of his mouth. He'd done better proposing to the cattle. Another deep sigh from Rachel. Ben counted sixty-seven beats of Sojourner's hooves before she spoke.

"I'd like to make our confession to John Stoltzfus."

At least it wasn't an outright *no* to his question. It was a better outcome than he might have hoped, given the way he'd bungled it.

"Sounds *gut*. When?"

"If it's all right with you, I'd like to get it over with."

Ben nodded. When they reached the intersection, he turned the mare in the direction of the Stoltzfus dairy farm. "How are you feeling?"

Rachel turned to him with a weak half smile. "I've been better."

What did that mean? Had she been sick? Years ago, Ben might have coaxed her to expand upon her short answer. But that was before she and Aaron became a couple. When their relationship became apparent while other Amish courtships were usually kept under wraps, Ben's comments when he was with them had dwindled. The pair seemed to have so much to say to each other that, when they were all together, his contributions to the conversation weren't needed. Even the evening after Aaron's disappearance, he hadn't said much. He'd just wanted to be there to offer Rachel support. But while he may not have said much, he'd unfortunately done plenty. Ben's head sunk lower as he hunched his shoulders. Apparently, the less he said and did the better.

Twenty minutes later, and with fewer words than that spoken between them, he turned Sojourner into the Stoltzfuses' lane. Upon drawing to a stop, Ben descended and hurried around the buggy to assist Rachel down. How much help did a woman six weeks with child require anyway? He didn't recall any of the times his *mamm* had been with child. He had younger siblings, but he'd been pretty young as well when they were born. If the Amish kept courtships under wraps, they definitely didn't speak of pregnancies. Ben flushed at his ignorance. Things would seem normal, then there'd be some excitement and female company, and the next day there'd be a *boppeli*. He didn't know anything about being a husband to a woman with child. That knowledge, or lack of, had him breaking a sweat.

By the time he reached Rachel's side of the buggy, she was on the ground, twisting her hands together. "Do you think they'll put us under the *Bann*?"

"I don't know. In past situations, if they have, it hasn't been for long. We might be out for a Sunday or two."

At Rachel's anxious expression, Ben hastened to assure her, "I think you made a wise suggestion in choosing to confess to John Stoltzfus. I'd rather face him than Bishop Weaver or another minister."

"He was a friend of my *daed*'s. I thought he might

be more…sympathetic." She grimaced. "But he might be more disappointed, as well."

Ben winced. The minister would be one of many in the community. "Well, we're here now."

Glancing about the surrounding farmyard in the early dusk of the February day, Ben's attention sharpened on the dim glow visible through the windows of the large barn. With his help, their farm's chores had been early, but the Rabers didn't have as many cows as the Stoltzfuses did. "Looks like he might be in the barn. I don't know what time he normally milks. Shall we go see?"

When he returned his gaze to Rachel, Ben bit his lip at the forlorn figure she made. Knowing how he felt, and that she felt the same or worse, he strove to provide whatever support he could, extending a hand toward her. Glancing at it, Rachel frowned before looking toward the barn and crossing her arms. With a deep sigh, Ben let his hand drop.

Rachel longed to take Ben's hand. But not if it would lead her into the barn. On top of being anxious and physically miserable, she felt so stupid. What kind of Amish girl was afraid of cows?

Ach, this one was. When she was a little girl, she'd been so excited to see a newborn calf she'd rushed into the pen and gotten too close to the new mama and her baby. The protective cow had knocked Rachel down, stepping on her several times in the process. Rachel had been terrified of cattle ever since, particularly Holsteins, one of the larger of the dairy breeds. Fortunately for her, unrelated to her harrowing adventure, her folks had traded out the cow for some goats shortly afterward. She hadn't been around cattle since, which was more than fine with her.

"Hello?" The call came from the house, where Mrs. Stoltzfus had stepped onto the porch to investigate the new arrival.

Returning her wave, Ben quietly asked, "Do you want to wait in the house?"

Rachel gave him a heartfelt smile. "*Ja. Denki.*" The weight of his gaze followed her as she made her way across the ruts of the yard, where slush was refreezing after the warmth of the day. Mary Stoltzfus ushered her inside. The minister's wife obviously had other folks drop in to see her husband and thankfully didn't ask any questions. She and Rachel chatted about community events until the door opened and the men stepped inside. Although Ben met her gaze with an encouraging smile, any ease Rachel had developed with Mary's comfortable conversation evaporated at their arrival.

After getting her husband a cup of tea, Mrs. Stoltzfus made herself scarce. Rachel tipped up one side of her mouth at the unmistakable scent of cows wafting from the older dairyman. The odor didn't bother her at all. It was just the animal itself that scared her witless.

Settling into his chair, John Stoltzfus wore a smile on the weathered face above his graying beard. "Benjamin said you wanted to speak with me?"

Rachel had always liked her *daed*'s friend. The two had been ministers together in the district, up until Vernon Mast passed away. From John Stoltzfus's curious expression, he wasn't sure why they were there, but looked hopeful that it was for some positive occasion.

Unfortunately, that wasn't the case, although she supposed weddings in the Amish community were always considered a positive event. But was she going to marry Ben? Rachel hugged her arms to her chest. She hadn't answered him, and in his Ben-like manner, he hadn't pushed her. This wasn't his fault. She'd felt jilted, abandoned, deserted when his brother had left. Aaron had become so much of her identity. What was she without him? The night he'd left, she'd reached out for comfort, some type of affirmation, and Ben had provided it. He was a *gut* man and didn't deserve this situation.

Still, she didn't know how to answer her *daed*'s old friend. Clearing her throat, Rachel sent a beseeching glance to where Ben sat motionless in a nearby rocker. She saw his hands tightened on the ends of the chair's wooden armrests before he shifted and straightened in the seat.

"Um...*ja*. We need to make a...confession."

"A confession?" Mr. Stoltzfus frowned. Brow furrowed, he considered them both, his gaze darted back and forth between her and Ben before his face drooped into sorrowful lines. "*Ach*. I'm sorry to hear of the need. Best tell me though."

Haltingly, she and Ben separately confessed to their sins, Rachel reddening as much during Ben's confession as she had during her own. To her surprise, Ben was adamant that he was the instigator of the regretful situation. She slid a glance at him from below lowered eyelids, knowing it wasn't true. Still, she appreciated his actions. That was Ben, always stepping up to take care of things.

"And do you repent? Are you sorry for your sins and seek forgiveness?"

"Most assuredly." Their fervent responses were in unison.

"That's *gut*. And now, are you getting married?" The minister pinned Ben with a gaze as pointed as the tines of a pitchfork.

"I…uh…" Rachel saw Ben's throat bob as he swallowed. "I've asked. That will be Rachel's decision."

"And are you getting married?" Now John Stoltzfus's intent yet sympathetic eyes focused on Rachel. It was the sympathy from her *daed*'s friend that did her in. That and the hopeful look on Ben's face before he quickly controlled his expression. He was the father of the child she carried. She should be married to the child's father. And she knew Ben. He would make a good *daed* and husband. But could she make a *gut* wife for him? When she'd always love another man? A man who was his own brother?

Rachel flinched when the clock struck the hour, the sound overly loud in the silent room. Time was something she didn't have. She longed to wait on the decision, as marriage was for life. What if Aaron came back? But would he even marry her, knowing she carried his brother's child? The threat of nausea had her throat bobbing in a hard swallow. Flicking a piece of lint off her skirt, she shifted her hand subtly to rest against her stomach. She glanced across the room to the baby's father. Ben met and held her gaze. Again, so like him. Ben Raber would always be steady and true. Rachel drew in a deep breath, knowing whatever she might feel she needed to be fair to the two lives now connected to hers.

"*Ja,*" she exhaled. "*Ja.* We're getting married."

Both the men in the room sighed, as well. Ben's was accompanied by eyes that drifted closed.

John Stoltzfus thoughtfully rubbed his hands together. "A sin confessed is a sin forgiven. As you've freely confessed and asked forgiveness of your sins, I don't see a need for this to go any further. The situation will obviously—" he grunted uncomfortably "—impact your wedding plans."

Rachel knew what he meant. They'd be punished, not directly, but subtly, through diminished celebrations. She also knew the minister's leniency had a great deal to do with the friendship he'd had with her *daed*. Still, she was so relieved not to be placed under the *Bann* she almost slumped in her chair. Her lips twisted. Of course, her desire to collapse could be due to the perpetual tiredness that shadowed her lately. Only sheer will kept her on her feet some days.

As for the wedding, it wouldn't be the one she'd dreamed of anyway. Neither would the marriage. Nor the groom.

A glance at Ben revealed his dark head was bowed. Surely he was as relieved as she not to be placed under the *Bann*? Or had his sigh been more one of discouragement that he was now unexpectedly saddled with a wife?

Rachel bowed her head as well to hide the tears congregating behind her eyes. This couldn't be the marriage he'd hoped for either. How could they possibly make it work?

Chapter Three

"Why do you keep watching the door? Everyone's here who can be here because of..." Rebecca flushed, "Well, you know."

Rachel grimaced as she sat with her sister, Ben and a few other *newehockers* at the *eck* table in the corner of her family's home. She certainly couldn't tell her sister she'd been watching the door in hopes Aaron would come through. Although now it wouldn't make any difference. It was too late. She'd said her vows to Benjamin this morning and she would never break them.

And yes, Rachel did know. Although they hadn't had to make a public confession in the few weeks since their visit to the minister, the smaller assembly was the district's way of punishing her and Ben for breaking the rules of the *Ordnung*. That, along with diminished festivities, fewer attendants and more limited decorations than she'd anticipated for her...other wedding.

All changes seemed insignificant to the fact that a different groom sat on her right at the corner table set up for the bridal party. She was Rachel Raber as she'd dreamed of for years, but she was married to a different Mr. Raber.

The reduced activities were intended as a disgrace for their sin, but Rachel didn't think she could be more shamed than when she'd had to face her *mamm* about the situation. Ben had offered to come in with her when they'd returned from seeing John Stoltzfus. Rachel had declined. It was time she left her youthful illusions behind and shouldered the responsibilities going forward. Besides—a flush rose in her cheeks—it would've made her more embarrassed to have him there.

Susannah Mast hadn't said anything. She'd looked up with a questioning smile when Rachel came through the door. As Rachel haltingly and tearfully explained where they'd gone and why, her *mamm* had slowly stood, her expression subsiding into a sympathetic frown. And then she'd opened her arms. Shaking with sobs, Rachel had walked into them.

There might be fewer sidesitters that joined her at the *eck* table than she'd planned to invite, but Susannah Mast had worked to ensure her oldest daughter had a memorable event. The farmhouse almost gleamed from intensive cleaning. Their corner table was laden with roast chicken, mashed potatoes and gravy, creamed celery, coleslaw, applesauce and fruit salad, with various desserts to be picked up from a side table later.

Rachel eyed the banquet before her ruefully. With fatigue and nausea continuing to plague her, she had little appetite for any of it.

Ben glanced over to give her a shy but supportive

smile. His blue eyes were concerned when his gaze lingered on her barely touched plate.

He scowled. "Was it the mousetrap we found in the salad?"

Rachel's lips twitched at the common Amish wedding prank. "*Nee*. Actually, I was expecting something like that. Our friends have been known to pull a trick or two at these events."

"At least, as it's winter, hopefully they won't put the bed in the middle of the field." His eyes met hers. Rachel watched a flush that surely matched her own color his cheeks.

Ben suddenly found something of interest on his empty plate. "Well, I hope they won't."

Rachel cleared her throat, wanting to recall the brief moment of comradery. "I seem to remember being at weddings where you were an integral party to that activity."

With a rekindled twinkle in his eye, Ben returned his regard to her. "Probably more than my share. It seems to have gotten out that, as a furniture-maker, I'm pretty quick about disassembling and reassembling pieces wherever they might be needed."

Rachel was grateful for the shared smile. It was something she desperately needed today when she felt as if she were holding herself together with the straight pins that secured her wedding dress. When Ben's eyes softened, she found herself leaning imperceptibly closer.

"I meant to tell you that you look very…nice."

Rachel's eyes widened at his unexpected compliment. "I… *Denki*."

Plain people didn't believe in using words like *pretty* or *beautiful* in regard to one another. To do so might make the recipient proud, or *hochmut*. Rachel soaked up Ben's words like a shriveled plant in a hot August. Affirmation, another thing she desperately needed today. It was something she'd really loved about Aaron. He'd showered her with positive comments all the time. But this was the first time she'd heard one from Ben. Warmth spread through her, permeating the edges of her tension and fatigue.

Reaching over, she touched his hand where it rested between them on the table. He inhaled deeply. Slipping his thumb away from his fingers, Ben shifted it to capture the tips of hers. The flare of warmth expanded. This was the first time they'd even held hands, if that's what they were doing. Rachel's heartbeat accelerated. He was her husband now. Her breath caught on the thought. *Her husband.* These past few weeks, she'd thought about getting married to Ben, not about being married to him. What would happen to their relationship after this afternoon?

The sound of a crash jerked her attention to the center of the room. A young man and woman stood glaring at each other, the dark liquid from a broken cup of coffee splattered over the linoleum at their feet, along with the fragments of white china. It was obvious the pair didn't get along. Which was regrettable, as they were husband and wife. It was common knowledge their relationship was as splintered as the porcelain scattered across the floor.

The warmth seeping into Rachel dissipated, replaced by a chill. The couple now the center of the room's attention started out the same way, for the same reason, as she and her new husband. She glanced at Ben's somber profile, his attention also fixed on the red-faced and thinned-lipped couple. Would the same happen to them?

"I hear they won't even be living together pretty soon," he murmured.

Rachel tugged on her hand. Ben's thumb tightened against the ends of her fingers for an instant before it fell away. Returning her hand to her lap, Rachel clenched it there in the folds of her blue wedding dress. A dress made when she was dreaming of a happy married life with another man. For the Amish, marriage was for life. If the relationship didn't work out, there was no way out unless one became a widow or widower. Please, please don't let them end up like the couple now assisting her *mamm* and other women in cleaning up the floor. Ben's hand remained on the table, tightened into a white-knuckled fist. How would she and Ben clean up the mess they'd made of their relationship?

Picking up her fork, Rachel prepared to take a bite of potatoes, just for something to do in the awkward situation. "I don't know if I ever thanked you for the china. It's a lovely set."

In lieu of an engagement ring like the *Englisch* did, an Amish man generally gave his intended something practical, like a clock or china. Along with the dishes,

Ben had also presented her with a table and set of chairs he'd made.

"Hopefully that wasn't one of the pieces."

"*Nee*," she hastened to assure him. "My *mamm* had been collecting this china from resale shops this past year in anticipation…" Rachel's words dried up. The dishes had been collected in anticipation of her wedding to his brother. She closed her eyes in frustration. Almost every topic led to a pitfall today.

Ben smiled wryly. "Your *mamm* was always wise that way."

Rachel strove to veer the conversation in another direction. "Well, she'll have them ready to share at a future barn-raising or community frolic."

Ben couldn't sit anymore. "I'm going to see if there's any coffee left. Can I get you something while I'm up?" Scooting his chair back, he shot to his feet. His mind had been constantly churning the past few weeks with regard to their future. The mention of a barn-raising reminded him of his next primary concern after the wedding. He had to find them a place to live.

New Amish couples typically spent the first several months at the bride's parents home while they established more permanent living arrangements. He and Rachel hadn't talked about theirs. Ben snorted as, wearing the expected smile for those he passed, he crossed the room to where the coffee urn was located. The two of them barely talked about anything.

Given the stiffness of their current relationship, Ben wondered how they'd survive one night, much less many months, living under someone else's roof without their stilted marriage becoming a community discussion. Not that Susannah would talk, but the Amish grapevine was such that the footfalls of someone limping across the floor on one side of the district echoed in conversations on the other side within a few hours, prompting folks to either whittle that person a cane or talk about how clumsy he was.

Ben didn't have the money to buy a place right now. He hadn't expected to be married this soon. He'd figured that, after watching Aaron wed the woman he wanted, it would be a while before he could even imagine settling on someone to marry. But *Gott* had another design. Looking across the room, Ben's heart ached at the sight of his bride. He was thrilled to adjust his plans to *Gott*'s, but it would take time. Maybe a second job? He'd ask around, but still, it would be months at best before he could afford a place, even if one was available. And they'd need one with enough room for the *boppeli*... Ben's eyes widened at the reminder.

"I sure didn't see this coming. As soon as the one was out of sight, she latched on to the other. I don't think even ticks jump to another body that fast." The sharp female voice siphoned through the clatter of dishware and background hum of conversation in the room.

"Then you obviously weren't paying attention. Ben was making calf eyes at Rachel even before I was married."

Swiveling, Ben saw two women on the other side of the big coffee urn, their backs to him. He could tell from the color of their *kapps* that one was married while the other wasn't. A moment later, Lydia Troyer's profile was visible as she frowned toward the *eck*.

Ben pressed his lips together. He was surprised any single man, in or out of the district, had missed her attention. If there were a prize for flirting, she was the perennial winner, including, to his chagrin, him the day of the sugaring, when he'd welcomed her distracting company at first.

Lydia's sister had been more subdued in her flirtations, but apparently not subdued enough. She was the female member of the couple who'd broken the coffee cup. Ben's ears burned as he reminded himself that, like the story in the *Biewel*, he certainly couldn't cast the first stone.

What pained him more than the parallel of how the couple's marriage began was the current status of it and the corresponding fear he and Rachel would end up the same way. Ben's arm jerked, sloshing coffee over the edge of his cup. He'd seen how her gaze had constantly flicked toward the door during the marriage service this morning, obviously hoping his brother would show. He'd been watching for the same person as well, with the opposite desire. Switching the cup to his other hand, Ben snagged a napkin and dried the coffee from his fingers. They were married. He vowed to do whatever was necessary to make the relationship work.

Dropping the napkin in a nearby receptacle, he raised his voice so the pair on the other side of the table could hear him. "*Denki* for coming. I appreciate the…respect you're showing by celebrating with us on this special day." He propped a smile onto his lips, but he couldn't make it reach his eyes.

Whirling to face him, Lydia flushed until her cheeks were as red as her hair. "*J-ja, denki* for having us," she muttered, looking everywhere but at Ben. "*Ach,* looks like they're clearing this seating to get ready for the next. I should go…and see if I'm needed for help." Ducking away, Lydia headed for the kitchen. Ben watched to make sure the young woman didn't go near Rachel. With an embarrassed, conciliatory smile, Lydia's sister left, as well. Ben knew Lydia was a gossip, but she probably wasn't saying much more than a few others were about his unexpected wedding. His troubled gaze followed the two women into the kitchen before it shifted, equally concerned, to where Rachel sat at the corner table.

He almost jumped at the hand that settled onto his shoulder. Turning, he looked into the steady regard of his employer, Malachi Schrock. "You're a good man, Benjamin Raber. Nothing is going to change that. And if your bride doesn't know it now, she'll soon figure it out."

Ben tried not to be embarrassed that the man, who he greatly respected, had witnessed the previous exchange and apparently interpreted some of Ben's unease.

Reaching up, Ben patted the hand still resting on his shoulder. "*Denki.* Those words are the best gift I could have gotten today."

"Don't judge your situation by others. She's not Rachel and the husband isn't you." Malachi's fingers tightened reassuringly on Ben's shoulders before he dropped his hand. "And I've never known anyone to work harder than you to make things right."

Ben wished he had the confidence in himself that his employer had. Still, the words encouraged him as he made his way back to his bride.

Hours later, Ben stared at the wooden door to Rachel's bedroom. Should he knock? After today, as per Amish custom to live in the bride's parents' home, it was his bedroom too. Rubbing a hand over the back of his neck, he swallowed. It was a custom about to be broken.

He eyed the door's handle like it was a wasp nest he needed to stick his hand into. "We've already tossed some of the more essential ones aside." His mouth hooked in a rueful smile. It wasn't as if theirs was a normal marriage. If they were to make it one, it might be best to do so without an audience.

Ach, well, he'd solved the situation. Hopefully his... wife agreed.

His wife.

He tried the word on again, speaking it softly. His wife, Rachel Mast, now Raber. Ben's hands flexed as he acknowledged the realization of a dream. Now that was definitely something his wife wouldn't agree on. Which was why he would never tell her. Far better to be silent and appear a fool to her than to speak and remove all doubt. His mouth snapped shut at the sound of footsteps from inside the room. Nothing like having his wife open the door to find him talking to himself like he was *narrish*. Although it was crazy to have loved his *bruder*'s girlfriend. Even crazier to have married her.

Firming his shoulders, Ben rapped his knuckles on the wooden panel. The footsteps stopped, then...nothing. He held his breath in the ensuing silence. Was she going to leave him outside the door, feeling like more of a fool than he already did?

"*Ja?*"

Exhaling at the quiet word, Ben twisted the doorknob. He took one step inside and stopped short. If he'd felt breathless on the other side of the door, he now felt like the time he and his three brothers had climbed upon one of his *daed*'s Percherons. When they'd all fallen off, Ben had landed at the bottom, with his brothers piling on top of him. He'd had no air. He had none now either. He'd never seen anything as beautiful as Rachel, with her dark hair streaming down over the shoulders and the back of her white nightgown. His jaw dropped. Along with his breath, gone were any intelligent words he'd planned to say. He hastily stepped back into the hallway.

He remained rooted there until a soft, "Come in," drifted through the open doorway. When he warily stepped through, Rachel, pale of face, stood by the window. Her hair was pulled behind her and under the quilt that was now wrapped about her shoulders. She offered Ben a quavering smile.

"I..." He pointed awkwardly toward the hallway. "They told me to come up. For the night." He swallowed. "Which I did." His toes curled inside his shoes, newly purchased for the occasion. He probably couldn't sound more *dumpkoff* if he tried.

Shaking his head, Ben's lips twitched into a self-depreciating grin. "Obviously, becoming a husband hasn't made me any wiser. Except," his smile evaporated as his gaze flicked around the room, "that I don't think it's a *gut* idea for us to be here together while we're still…" he twisted his hand back and forth, searching for a word "…uncomfortable with each other." The look of surprise and relief that swept across Rachel's face was unflatteringly obvious. If he'd felt the same way, it would've been comical. Instead it was more evidence of the missing foundation necessary to build their relationship.

"So. After it gets quiet downstairs, I'll go out to the barn and spend the night."

Rachel's eyes rounded. "You can't do that. You'll get caught."

"I'll be careful, but it's only for tonight. After we help clean up from the wedding tomorrow, I'll start work on moving us into our new place."

"New place?" Rachel frowned, her brows lowered in confusion.

Ben hoped she wasn't too disappointed not to be traveling around the community over the next few weeks, calling on friends and collecting wedding gifts. She'd seemed strained enough just with today's events. Given the situation, he'd assumed she might want to avoid the other activity for now. It'd be difficult to hide that they weren't sharing a room if they stayed with everyone they visited, as was customary.

He couldn't sneak out to all the barns in the community. She was right—it'd only be a matter of time before he was caught.

Which was why Ben was so excited about his news. He struggled to contain the enthusiasm in his voice. "*Ja.* I was just talking with Isaiah Zook. He recently bought an *Englisch* farm. It'll be a few years before any of his daughters are old enough to marry, so the house will be available for a while. He's moved his dairy steers and some of his Holstein bulls over from his own place, as he'll be expanding his cow operation there."

Ben had always enjoyed working with cattle. He couldn't believe their *gut* fortune. "In exchange for lower rent, we'll just need to do a few chores around the place. Isn't that *wunderbar?*" An economic place to live in private where he and Rachel could establish a stronger foundation for their marriage. It was more than he could've hoped for.

Sagging, Rachel braced a hand against the windowsill. Her face paled further until she was as white as the *kapp* sitting on the dresser beside her. Ben tightened his grip on the door handle to steady himself in the deluge of disappointment. Obviously, his wife thought living alone with her new husband was anything but *wunderbar.*

Backing out of the room, Ben pulled the door shut behind him as he stared blindly down the narrow hallway.

Chapter Four

Rachel cleared the breakfast dishes from the table as Ben finished the last of his coffee. They'd developed a routine of sorts over the last four weeks. She'd come out from her bedroom to start breakfast while Ben came out of his to head for the cattle chores. By the time he returned to the house, she'd have breakfast on the table. They'd eat a quiet meal together before he'd leave for work. In the evening, they'd do it in reverse. He'd come home, do chores and come in for a quiet meal before they'd head for their separate bedrooms.

Running water into the sink, Rachel snorted. Good thing the rental house had more than one bedroom, or maybe that'd been the plan. Ben had moved in the day after the wedding, with the excuse of needing to start taking care of the livestock. When he'd shown her the house, his jaw tight while he avoided her gaze, Ben had murmured that as things currently stood, he figured she could take the master bedroom and he'd use the one across the hall. Just until they got settled.

Whatever settled was. Apparently, they weren't there yet. Rachel felt a mixture of relief and…concern at the current situation. Surely this wasn't normal for married couples. It wasn't living in separate houses, but still… She certainly hadn't mentioned the discussion again, and neither had Benjamin.

Another thing he hadn't commented on was her tendency to break into tears at the drop of a hat. It frustrated Rachel, as she wasn't normally a weepy person, but for some reason, she couldn't keep the waterworks at bay. Whenever she started to cry, Ben's blue eyes would go solemn as he found her some type of tissue. But he never said a word. In fact, Ben hadn't commented on a lot of things, except to talk about the dreadful cattle and to tell her about his work at Schrock Brothers' Furniture when she asked.

Still, she found an odd sort of comfort having breakfast together before he'd harness Sojourner and head for town. It wasn't the marriage she'd dreamed of but, Rachel had to admit, it was better than she'd expected. It was tolerable. More, she had to admit, because of Ben's efforts than hers.

"What are your plans for the day?"

Rachel heard the scrape of his chair and the rattle of dishes behind her as Ben collected them to bring to the counter. He was always doing that. Taking care of little things she knew she should be doing. Rachel bit her lip, wondering if it was because he didn't think she was capable of keeping up with the housework by herself.

She squirted soap into the water. "I thought I'd be overly optimistic and plant some of the garden."

Ben's mouth curved in a small smile as he set his plate and cup on the counter. She'd told him of her delight in gardening and the canning associated with it later in the summer. Although he'd raised his eyebrows at the abundance of seeds she'd purchased, he'd borrowed a team and, with their landlord's permission, tilled up a large area on the place for her. "As long as you don't mind the risk of replanting if we get another frost."

"I'll take my chances." Anything to keep busy and not be constantly reminded of the large black-and-white cattle constantly milling about on the other side of the white rail fence beyond the driveway. And speaking of fences… "Why did you put up a fence in the garden?"

"*Ach.*" To her surprise, his cheeks reddened. "I thought if you'd plant your cucumbers beneath it, the vines would grow up the woven wire. That way," Ben dropped a quick glance at her expanding waistline before rubbing the back of his neck, "you wouldn't have to bend over later this summer when it's…harder to."

It would make it a lot easier for her. Rachel blinked in surprise at his thoughtfulness. She wasn't used to that. While Aaron had showered her with sweet words, he'd rarely done something thoughtful like that for her. And Rachel hadn't expected it. Her *daed* had never done things like that for her *mamm*.

"*Denki.*" She gave him a soft smile.

When she reached for his dishes, a flurry of activity outside the window caught her attention. A few of the cattle were wrestling with each other. Their roughhousing was standard activity. What wasn't normal was when the biggest one—a huge mostly black beast Ben had pointed out as the Zooks' prized young bull—used his broad head to butt a smaller steer in the pen. The steer was knocked onto its back into the wooden feed bunks that lined the fence. Rachel watched open-mouthed as four black-and-white feet flailed in the air.

"What is it?" Ben looked out to the window to see what had drawn her attention. "Oh, no!" He bolted for the door. Rachel followed in his wake to the front step and watched, wadding her apron in her wringing hands, as he sprinted toward the pen. Cattle scattered from along the fence as Ben vaulted over it, although a few, including the big black bull, didn't go far.

The bawl of the distressed steer cut through the chilly spring morning as Ben dashed to where it struggled in the wooden bunk. If he didn't get the animal off its back in time, the heavy weight of the steer's stomach would suffocate it. He couldn't abide the thought of losing an animal of his own. He definitely didn't want to lose someone else's livestock when he was responsible for it. Reaching the bunk, he tried to help the young Holstein get repositioned, taking a few kicks to the shoulder in their combined frantic efforts. It was no good.

Stepping back an instant to reassess, Ben's alarm increased as he heard the steer's breathing begin to strain. His eyes darted along the worn wood of the bunk. He had to break it to get the steer out. Now! Grabbing the top board with both hands, he jerked on it with all his strength.

"Rachel! Bring me the small chainsaw from the shed!" Splinters cut into Ben's fingers as he wrenched at the board. Although it moved a fraction of an inch, the nails groaning in their holes, he couldn't tug it farther. The steer emitted another pitiful bawl, weaker this time. Its white-circled eyes were bulging in its head.

"Rachel!" Ben spared a brief glance up to see, despite his urgent calls, his wife hadn't moved from the stoop. She wasn't going to help him. He didn't have time to race to the shed himself. The animal would be dead before he could get back. Frantically looking about for some type of tool, Ben spied the sledgehammer he'd recently used to pound in the steel posts for Rachel's garden. He'd set it down by the fence last night, intending to put it away when he finished chores, forgetting about it on his way to the house. Now the omission was his only chance to save the steer.

Dashing down the fence to where the hammer was propped against a post, Ben scrambled up the railings to lean over the fence top and grab its handle. With his adrenaline, the heavy head arced over the fence at his tug to bump, at the end of its swing, against the hip of an animal that'd come up to investigate the activity. Ben recognized Billy, the big young bull, as he raced back along the fence to the bunk where the steer struggled feebly.

Great, I let one animal die and injure Isaiah's prize bull. He'll probably kick me off the place. Positioning himself where his efforts wouldn't hit the trapped animal, Ben pounded away at the bunk's outer boards. To his great relief, after a few hard swings, the top boards moaned in protest before breaking away from the end of the bunk. Dropping the sledgehammer, Ben pushed them out the rest of the way. He jumped back into the bunk between the fence and the steer, who was laboring to breathe. Finding purchase, Ben groaned mightily as he wedged the animal out of the bunk. With the boards now gone, the animal tipped over the edge to drop the short distance into the churned mud of the pen, landing with its feet underneath it.

Ben sagged against the fence, gasping in unison with the now freed steer. His legs were rubber. Sliding his back down the fence, he sat in what remained of the bunk as he anxiously watched the steer. When, after a tense few moments, the steer slowly lurched to his feet and ambled away, Ben closed his eyes in relief. When he opened them, Billy was watching him from ten yards away.

Figuring him as the culprit who created the situation, Ben admonished the young bull. "Don't do that anymore. He's no threat to you." Easing himself out of the bunk, Ben began to collect the pieces of the broken lumber while keeping an eye on the animal. Turning a back on a bull, particularly a dairy one, could get you killed. Any species of breeding male on a farm was always a danger, but bulls, with their size and unpredictability, were particularly dangerous. Dairy breeds, due to the way they were raised around people, were worse than beef bulls, because at maturity, they could perceive humans as their subordinate rivals.

Keeping a watchful eye on Billy, Ben ensured he'd accounted for all the nails that could've come loose with the boards. He didn't want one going up a hoof and injuring one of the cattle. With a last look at the young bull, he climbed over the fence. He needed to remind Rachel to keep well clear of Billy and the two other young bulls in the pen.

Glancing toward the house, he saw she'd gone back inside. Ben frowned as he carried the sledgehammer to the shed. He'd clearly requested Rachel's help. Hadn't she heard him? Was he expecting too much from her in her condition?

Or did her actions show she wanted him to fail? Did she want them to have to leave the farm and return to her mother's home? Was that what all the tears were about?

Or were they because he wasn't his brother?

With compressed lips, Ben headed to the barn to harness Sojourner. He was late for work. He may not be the one she wanted, but he was supporting her. At least that was something he could do right.

"Rachel." Ben spoke quietly from where he sat at the table following a quiet meal that evening, another in a string of quiet meals between the two of them over the weeks they'd been married. But this one had an added level of stiffness that made even *please pass the salt* an uncomfortable statement. What had they done to each other? Could they ever recover the easy comradery they'd had when they were young, or at least the somewhat amicable relationship they'd had when she was his brother's girlfriend?

At the sound of her name, Rachel's shoulders

hunched where she stood with her back to him at the sink. Sighing, Ben steepled his fingers, tapping the tips of them against his mouth. He'd thought about this all day. This being their awkward relationship. Although he'd always dreamed of more, he'd thought they could at least work together enough in their marriage to make a reasonably comfortable life. Had he just been seeing what he wanted to see? Or did she actually want him to fail so she could justifiably think he was, and always would be, second best?

Closing his eyes, he took a deep breath. *Please let me say the right thing this time.* Opening his eyes, he studied her rigid back. "I'm sorry if I expected too much of you this morning when I asked for your help with the cattle."

Bowing her head, Rachel curled her fingers over the edge of the sink. "It wasn't that." The words, spoken to the window, were barely audible from where he sat.

"What was it then?" Sliding back his chair, Ben stood, bracing his palms on the table as he prepared to hear her lament that Aaron would never have let something like that happen, that everything would be better if only he'd been the one to leave instead of his brother.

Turning toward him, Rachel knuckled away a tear. "I just feel so foolish being an Amish farm girl who's afraid of cows."

"What?" Ben's weight sank onto his hands as he blinked in surprise.

Rachel sniffed. "When I was a little girl, I ran up too close to a cow and her newborn calf. The cow charged me. I've been petrified of them ever since."

What she confessed was so different from what he'd been expecting. Ben hissed out a shaky breath in relief.

"See? Even you think it's silly." Her lower lip quivered.

"*Nee.* Not at all." He straightened from where he'd slumped at the table. "I'm just so glad you told me what was bothering you. I can understand why you didn't want to come closer this morning." Circling the table, Ben approached where Rachel stood at the sink. Although he wanted to put an arm around her and draw her close, he settled for carefully cupping his hands about her tightly knotted ones.

"It probably would've helped to know this before I moved you onto a place where you have to face them every day." He tipped his head toward the window that looked out on the pen full of cattle. "I'm sorry. Is that why you're always crying? Because of the cattle? Is there some way I can help you work through your fear? Or..." he caught his breath "...do you want to move?"

"Oh, *nee,* we don't need to move." Rachel quickly shook her head, but the beginnings of a smile touched her face. "And," her cheeks pinkened, "I think the crying has something to do with the *boppeli.*" She wrinkled her nose. "But, regarding the fear, I... I don't think I'm ready to confront it yet. I still feel a bit foolish about it."

Ben's heart rate sputtered when she twisted her hands to entwine them with his. "You shouldn't. We all have fears. Sometimes we know the reasons for them, sometimes we don't. Everyone is afraid of something. Even me."

Rachel rolled her eyes. "I can't believe that. You? The local hero? Who jumped into a frozen pond to rescue an *Englisch* boy who fell through the ice?"

Ben's lips twitched into a half grin. He'd forgotten about that day when he and Gideon Schrock had come upon the alarming situation. Thank *Gott* Gabe Bartel of the local EMS service had gotten there in time to resuscitate the boy after he and Gideon pulled him out. "I didn't have enough time to think of being afraid then."

He was delighted when Rachel's dark brown eyes teasingly narrowed under her delicate brows. "When you have time to think, what are *you* afraid of?" she challenged.

His smile evaporated. "Depends on the hour," he joked.

Ben's hands involuntarily tightened on hers before he gently disentangled them and took a step back. His greatest fear was never far from his mind.

I'm afraid you'll never love me like you love my brother.

Chapter Five

"Have you seen her? It's growing more obvious by the day why someone had to marry Rachel so hastily."

Rachel paused beside the endcap displaying various boxes of crackers in the Bent 'N Dent store. Normally, she wouldn't have hesitated to move past other shoppers in the next aisle who were deep in discussion, usually with a reciprocating smile and nod, but in this conversation, her name was mentioned. And the conversation wasn't complimentary.

Things had been comfortable between Ben and her in the five weeks since the incident with the steer. While it was far from what she'd dreamed of, she could live with comfortable. Theirs may differ from a normal marriage, but she'd almost forgotten how it'd initially gotten started in the day-to-day work of keeping up a household, particularly during gardening season.

With that and dealing with her body acting in new and odd ways, she hadn't thought much about the community at large, other than to see folks at church. And be seen.

Rachel cast a self-conscious glance downward. Where she'd always been slender as a reed, now it was apparent she...wasn't. While the Amish seldom spoke of a pregnancy, it didn't mean all were ignorant when confronted with an obvious one. Rachel hadn't considered what some in the community might think of her unexpected relationship turn. Her hands tightened on the handle of her basket as she blinked back tears. How did the old saying go? Eavesdroppers never hear any good of themselves?

Taking a step back, she was tempted to retreat to the far end of the aisle and slip past hopefully unseen. But then the speaker mentioned Ben's name. Rachel bit the inside of her cheek as she brushed a hand over the roundness under her apron. The community, or the few in it that liked to gossip, could say what they wanted about her, but she didn't want them saying anything about Ben. Whatever she'd expected when their marriage started, he'd been nothing but kind and supportive thus far. Indignation flared in her that he'd be maligned when he had ten, no, twenty times the character of the speaker. Sucking in a deep breath, she straightened her shoulders and stepped around the corner.

Already knowing whom she'd be facing as she'd recognized the voice, Rachel was prepared to meet Lydia Troyer with a bland smile. The smile wavered a bit when she saw the speaker's audience. She'd grown up with the young woman and thought of her as a friend.

When the girl flushed redder than the coffee can behind her and murmured, "Sorry," before quickly excusing herself to hurry down the aisle, Rachel was reminded she'd only heard one person speaking. She'd been trapped a time or two in an unwanted conversation before. Now knowing how it felt to be the object of the discussion, she vowed to speak up and never be party to that kind of situation again.

Lydia flushed as well, but not as deeply. Rachel knew the young woman's embarrassment was due more to being caught gossiping than the gossiping itself. Still not accustomed to the roller coaster of her hormones, Rachel was grateful her tears had evaporated under a flash of heat directed toward the red-haired busybody who was discussing her private life.

"Please do go on, Lydia. I'm very curious as to what comes next."

Lydia's eyes widened in surprise at the unexpected comment from her supposed victim. Rachel's polite smile solidified. She knew she wasn't going to be able to prevent the girl from gossiping, but at least Lydia would know she wasn't going to be cowed by it.

Uncharitably, Rachel noted the red-haired woman's attractiveness greatly diminished when her mouth sagged like a carp instead of sporting her counterfeit simper. Of course, she wouldn't waste that on Rachel, who wasn't her preferred audience. Lydia snapped her mouth into a thin line as her eyes narrowed.

Rachel felt a moment of unease as her anger ebbed and threatened to take her courage with it. *Please don't fail me now*. Lydia's eyes darted to Rachel's midsection. Rachel braced herself.

"You didn't waste any time. Was that the way you tempted Ben to marry you?" Her expression slid into a sneer.

It was too close to the truth. Rachel's ears burned that someone else might overhear their conversation. She'd never been close to Lydia, although it hadn't been intentional. They'd interacted with other female friends while in school until eighth grade. Once out and into their *rumspringa*, Rachel had immediately coupled up with Aaron, while Lydia had flirted with anyone and everyone available in broadfall trousers. Rachel had noticed Lydia casting a few frowning glances in her direction at Sunday night singings and other functions, but she'd never thought the other woman actively didn't like her. Until now.

She dipped her chin to hide its trembling. "Whatever we've done, we've made our confessions. As to why, you'll have to ask Ben."

"One Raber *bruder* wasn't enough?" Lydia looked her up and down as if she didn't see anything special.

Shifting her feet, Rachel fought the urge to cross her arms over her middle. She didn't know why Aaron originally turned his attention to the shy, awkward girl she was when she entered her *rumspringa*. She'd just been dazzled that he had.

"If you and Aaron were such a pair, why didn't you go with him?"

Rachel furrowed her brows. "I couldn't. I'd been baptized. If I'd left, I'd have been shunned." Besides,

Aaron hadn't asked. He hadn't even told her he was going to leave.

The other woman looked like she wouldn't mind shunning, if the recipient was Rachel. "There're few enough eligible men in the area. You didn't have to go rushing after Ben as a consolation prize, stealing him from other women. Maybe he had someone else in mind to walk out with before you flaunted yourself at him." Lydia's lips twisted. "But you didn't care."

But she hadn't gone rushing after Ben. She had just… Rachel caught her breath, recalling that awful day. She had sought Ben out. When he'd seen her, he hastened to determine the reason for her distress. He'd received permission to leave work due to his *bruder*'s unexpected departure. And her distraught self. Was sobbing in someone's arms about his missing *bruder* who happened to be her beau flaunting?

Ben had always been a friend, until he was relegated more to Aaron's *bruder* while she and Aaron were dating. She hadn't paid much attention to what Ben was doing at singings and such. She'd been totally absorbed with Aaron. Had Ben been courting someone? Had he been secretly walking out with another girl in the district? Rachel hissed in a breath. With Lydia? Surely not? But he'd been with her that day in the woods while sugaring. The day she'd finally advised him of her situation. With a troubled frown, she regarded the pinch-faced woman before her.

Nausea, different from the normal kind frequently troubling her lately, uncoiled in her stomach. Had she unintentionally stolen Ben's future happiness with his chosen one because hers had been yanked from her? He'd never said a word.

But he wouldn't.

Rachel swallowed against the bile threatening the back of her throat. Whatever Ben and her situation was, it was now permanent. They were married. Even if Lydia had been walking out with Ben before, the relationship couldn't be changed. But it could be one without joy. Particularly, if Ben had been interested in someone else. As much as the thought troubled her, and even as she knew she should forgive and forget, Rachel couldn't give Lydia the satisfaction of feeling she'd been successful in bullying her prey.

Though she was tempted, Rachel ensured her smile wasn't a gloating one as she lifted her head. "I care for Ben. No matter how we came together, we're now married. And nothing is going to change that." Glancing down into Lydia's nearly empty basket, she continued, "I hope you find what you're looking for."

With a slight nod, she turned and walked down the length of the aisle and over to the checkout counter. Whatever else she'd come into the store for was forgotten as her mind roiled with the realization she'd gone into this relationship thinking only of what she'd lost. She hadn't given any consideration to what her new husband might've given up.

Tossing her single bag into the buggy, she grimly climbed in behind it. She'd been proud of herself for thinking of the great job she'd been doing to tolerate the unfortunate situation she and Ben found themselves in. What if she wasn't the only one just trying to tolerate it?

* * *

Susannah Mast looked over from the goat pen as Rachel turned her horse into the lane. Rachel's shoulders slumped in relief at finding her at home. For some reason, the sight of her *mamm* brought her to tears. Snorting as she knuckled one away from her cheek, Rachel acknowledged almost anything could bring her to tears lately. So it wasn't surprising a little self-realization and guilt that she wasn't the only one in her marriage whose dreams had dissolved could turn on the waterworks. As had the guilt that, if disappointed, Ben had been doing a better job of making the best of it. Or at least appearing to do so.

Sniffing back the remaining tears, she drew the horse to a stop and set the brake as Susannah secured the pen's gate behind her.

"This is an unexpected pleasure," Susannah called in greeting, a smile on her already sun-darkened face. Climbing down from the buggy, Rachel fought the urge to rush into her *mamm*'s arms. Instead, she strolled to the pen's fence to rest her elbows on the top rail.

"I was at the Bent 'N Dent and thought I'd stop by on the way home."

Having mirrored her actions, with her elbows resting on the fence beside her, Susannah raised her eyebrows. Rachel could understand. Her old home was far from a direct route between the store to where she now lived. With her husband. Who might be just tolerating their relationship. Her chin quivered. Stilling it with a frown, she focused on the multicolored goats in front of her.

"Kids all arrived for the year?"

She felt her *mamm*'s quiet regard before the older woman turned her attention to the pen. "Have a few stragglers. They should be coming soon." Susannah put a hand on Rachel's elbow. "You aren't here to talk about the goats. So what *are* you here to talk about?"

Turning to face the sympathetic brown eyes that matched her own, this time Rachel couldn't prevent her chin from quaking. "How did you guess?"

"I know my *dochder*. Do you want to stay out here with the goats, or would you like a glass of tea?"

"Tea would be nice." Rachel felt heat bloom up her neck. She cleared her throat as she tried not to touch her midsection. She knew her *mamm* knew, but so soon after the confrontation with Lydia, it was still embarrassing. Pivoting, she followed her *mamm* across the yard and into the kitchen. Here, amongst the familiar surroundings, tension immediately began to seep away. With shaky knees, she sank onto a worn kitchen chair.

Susannah retrieved a pitcher from the refrigerator and poured two glasses of tea. Setting one in front of Rachel, she pulled out a chair on the table's opposite side and sat down. After taking a sip of tea, she set down her glass, rested her hands on the table and gave Rachel an understanding smile. "It's a lot to adjust to in a relatively short period of time."

Rachel shook her head against the tears that again welled in her eyes. Lifting her apron, she dabbed at them, laughing without humor as she repeated, "How did you guess?"

"I was a new bride once. And an impending mother."

Her lips twisted wryly. "And one quick upon the other, but not quite as quick as you."

Sniffing, Rachel put the apron to use again. "I don't feel quick at anything anymore." She gestured to her stomach. "Definitely not quick on my feet. Not quick keeping up with the garden and housework." Face contorting, she hitched in a breath. "And not quick to have anything more than an awkward companionship with my husband." Embarrassed at her outburst, she mopped up tears until the apron felt damp in her clenched hands.

There was an audible sigh from across the table. "You have to work at your marriage. You're two different people who suddenly formed a union, but you're two different people who now need to work together to make a single unit."

Rachel dropped the apron to meet her *mamm*'s compassionate gaze.

"You've driven draft teams before. Surely you've noticed the teams that pull together evenly get work done more efficiently and seem happier doing it. I know he isn't the one you thought you'd be in harness with. But that doesn't matter, you're a team now and there's no changing that. No matter what you feel for him, he is your husband, whether you care for him or not."

"I know that. And I do care for him."

"I'm glad to hear it, for he's a very *gut* man."

"It's just that…" Rachel didn't continue. She wasn't sure how to express her feelings.

"It's just that what?"

She should've known her mother would be persistent. "Well." She furrowed her brows. "With Aaron,

I knew how he felt. And how he made me feel. He was always saying nice things to me. I liked that. Ben doesn't say much, and definitely doesn't use the sweet words that make me feel he cares for me, although he's always doing things for me."

"Saying nice things doesn't get the work done."

Rachel frowned. "*Daed* would always say nice things to you."

"*Ach*." Her *mamm* shook her head. "As I said, saying nice things doesn't get the work done."

Rachel knew she must've looked as stricken as she felt, as Susannah hastened to continue. "Your *daed* and I loved each other. Have no doubt about that. But people show love in different ways. People look for love in different ways. Your *daed* was *gut* about telling me how the sunlight gleamed in my hair and how he appreciated all the work I did around the place." Susannah smiled ruefully. "But there were times that instead of hearing about my hair, I'd rather he'd have done more doing and less appreciating."

Rachel thought back on what she knew of her parents' marriage. There'd never been harsh words. But now she thought about it, when he'd been alive, her *daed* had been fishing many a morning when her *mamm* had been working with the bees or the goats. As Rachel knew the farm had come from her *mamm*'s father, she'd assumed that played a part in the work quotient. Now she wondered. She loved her *daed*, but his heart had seemed more in the ministry he'd later been selected for and less in the farming. Until now, she'd never heard her *mamm* say a negative word about him.

"I always liked it when *Daed* would mention how well I'd done at school. Or tell me how *gut* the meal was that I'd fixed while you were outside working." Rachel's confession was hesitant. "Or how *gut* a job I was doing taking care of Rebecca while you were with the *boppeli*." Her voice faded away on the last word.

Her expression falling into sorrowful lines, Susannah reached across the table to grab Rachel's hand. "I'm so sorry. I didn't think about what a burden it might've been for you when all my attention that wasn't on the farm while they were ill went to them."

Rachel returned the comforting squeeze. "I feel guilty remembering how his words made me feel appreciated when—" She stopped short at the stark look on her *mamm*'s face.

"When I didn't have time to even acknowledge your presence, other than to give you instructions for the day. You were young to be burdened so. I shouldn't have done that. We should've kept a hired girl longer. And I should've been the one to say *gut* words to you."

"It's all right, *Mamm*. I understood. I knew they needed you."

Susannah's eyes closed. She pressed her lips in a line that was as firm as it was fragile. When she spoke, her words were barely audible across the table. Rachel felt more than heard them. "We lost them anyway."

Rachel had been very young, but she still remembered the babies. First a little *bruder*, then about a year later, a little *schweschder*. So excited at first for a new *boppeli*, it hadn't taken long to see something was wrong. Even as newborns, when they'd open their tiny unfocused eyes, the backgrounds would be yellow, not white. Their skin was an unnatural golden. They both died very young.

It was only after they were gone that Rachel had heard the words *genetic disease* mentioned in hushed tones between her parents. Nothing more was said about the *boppeli*. The Amish way was not to grieve overmuch when someone dies, as to do so would be questioning *Gott*'s will. But for a long while, her *mamm* hadn't returned to the no-nonsense cheerfulness that usually personified her. The winter Rachel turned ten, she'd noticed Susannah had grown especially quiet. Rachel smiled, realizing now her *mamm* had been expecting her little *bruder*. Only after Amos had arrived, with enormous blue eyes in a perfectly white background, had Susannah brightened.

Rachel's breathing slowed. She hadn't thought of her lost siblings for years. Or the hereditary disease concerns the Amish were prone to, beginning as they had with a handful of families and usually marrying within their group, therefore limiting the gene pool. Pulling her hand free from her *mamm*'s loose grasp, she wrapped her arm protectively around the bump under her apron. "What if—" She cast a wide-eyed gaze across the table.

Pushing back her chair, Susannah circled the table to put her arm around Rachel's hunched shoulders. "*Ja*. There is a chance. But whatever happens will be *Gott*'s will. I've learned fretting about it doesn't help you or the *boppeli*. Has Ben spoken of any issues in his family?"

"*Nee.*" Neither had Aaron. But they'd never talked about it. She and Aaron had talked of frivolous things about marriage, not thinking about *boppeli* at the time. And she hadn't mentioned her deceased siblings. To either of them. As they'd all been young at the time, they might not remember them.

"Well." Removing her arm, Susannah gave Rachel's shoulder a last pat and returned to her seat. "Whether the *boppeli* is affected is entirely up to *Gott.* The success of your marriage, on the other hand, is something you have an impact on. So what really brought you here today?"

Her *mamm*, as usual, was right. Their discussion about the *boppeli* had reduced to insignificance Rachel's distress over the confrontation with Lydia. "I just realized that Ben might not have wanted this marriage any more than I did at the time."

"And what brought that on?"

Rachel shrugged sheepishly. After their previous topic, it seemed so trivial. "I overheard Lydia Troyer talking about me in the Bent 'N Dent. About how I went so fast from one Raber *bruder* to another. About how someone had to marry me. Quickly." The words still stung.

Susannah huffed. "If my horse ran as fast as that girl's mouth, I'd get to town in half the time. The *Biewel* has something to say about gossipers. Why do you let her bother you?"

Rachel bowed her head. "Is it gossip if it's true?" She swallowed. "I did go very quickly from Aaron to Ben. And he did have to."

For a moment, the only sound in the kitchen was the ticking of a wall clock. "Has Ben given you any reason to think he didn't want this marriage?"

Rachel thought back over Ben's actions from the time she told him about the *boppeli*. She shook her head. "*Nee.*"

"Benjamin Raber strikes me as one who knows his mind. You're married to a fine man. One who's no longer available to other single girls in the community. No wonder Lydia is upset. She's been dangling after anyone in suspenders since she got out of braids. She's seen girls younger than her make *gut* matches while with her; the available men shop but don't buy. She'll find something else to talk about before long. Besides, those who listen to such drivel don't matter and those who matter don't listen."

When Rachel raised her head, it was to meet Susannah's narrowed eyes. "You mentioned *at the time*. Not that you have a choice, but do I understand you want this marriage now?"

"*As* you'd pointed out, he is my husband." Rachel hunched a shoulder. "But, *ja*, I want it to be more than…more than what we have right now." Poking a finger in the condensation gathering at the base of her glass, she drew a short line on the table. "He doesn't say the words I liked to hear like Aaron did. But he does things in his own way that are…special." Twisting her lips, she continued, "And as for work you mentioned earlier, it seems we're both working all the time. I don't see how we could be working any more."

"You're working. But are you working on your relationship? From the way your feelings are beginning to change, it sounds like Ben is. Are you?"

Rachel pulled another line of moisture from the ring at the base of the glass. She thought back over the past few months. Was she? She was tolerating the cattle. She didn't say anything more about them, but then neither had Ben since she'd told him of her fear. She thought of the work he'd done for her in the garden, and many other thoughtful things she'd never commented on. And she'd done...? Other than keep up with the housework and ensure there were meals on the table, had she reciprocated in simple thoughtful gestures? Or just absorbed his like a dried-up sponge?

Sighing, she leaned back from the table. She'd been selfish. Drumming her fingers on her stomach, Rachel reasoned she had the excuse she'd had many new things going on in her life. But so had Ben. But he'd been finding ways to put in extra, unselfish effort. It was time she did too.

She raised a wry glance to Susannah. "*Mamm*, how come every time I'm around you, you put me to work in some fashion?"

"Habit, I guess. Makes me wonder why you come around."

"Habit, I guess. And one I hope to never break. But now," Rachel pushed up from the table, "I need to go home and," she wrinkled her nose, "work."

Rachel was surprised at the moisture that seemed to glimmer in her *mamm*'s eyes as she also stood. "I'm sure you'll do as well there as you always did here. And I'll be just as proud."

Minutes later, after a final wave, Rachel gathered up her bay's reins and directed him down the lane. Encouraging words from her *mamm* might've been rare while growing up. But, Rachel smiled broadly as her heart swelled, she couldn't imagine they would've felt any better than those few words did right now.

Now to go home and apply her *mamm*'s advice. And wonder if Ben would notice her efforts.

Chapter Six

Who knew that concentrated effort on her marriage would begin with a trip to the feed store the next day? When Ben tentatively asked as she was cleaning up the breakfast dishes if she'd like to ride along, Rachel figured it was the closest she could get to doing something with him regarding the wretched cattle while staying far away from the beasts. Regardless of her motivation, they'd barely turned out of the lane when the beauty of the late spring day called to her, making her glad she'd come. That and the shy smiles her husband kept sending in her direction. Although their conversation centered on the clear, sunny sky after the previous week's rain and the blooming vegetation along the side of the road, it was as pleasant as the lovely weather.

They ran into Gideon Schrock, Ben's coworker at Schrock Brothers' Furniture and good friend, coming out of the feed store as they went in. He stayed around to help load the bags of soybean meal pellets Ben was picking up on Isaiah Zook's account into the flat back of the open buggy Plain folks in the area used in warmer weather.

When the men had stacked the last of the bags, Gideon leaned on the top one as he considered them. "You two have lunch plans? If not, would you like to join me at The Dew Drop?"

Ben, after a glance at Rachel, declined his friend's invitation to join him at the town's main restaurant with a regretful shake of his head. "*Ach*, as I did chores first this morning, we're not that long up from the breakfast table. Also, as this belongs to Isaiah, I want to get it safely put up in the barn before there's any chance the weather changes. Besides," he secured the short board across the end of the wagon, "fine as the cooking is at The Dew Drop, Rachel's is better."

Gideon turned to her with a smile. "High praise indeed. I hope you have a touch for frying mushrooms. They're one of Ben's favorite foods. I'm surprised he didn't give a test on fixing them before you two were married."

Rachel flushed. There hadn't been a discussion on cooking skills, much less anything else besides the forthcoming *boppeli* when she and Ben had determined to marry. She smiled tepidly in response to Gideon's teasing. Not fond of mushrooms to begin with, as touchy as her stomach still was months into her condition, the memory of the edible fungi's heavy smell while cooking made her ill. The thought of frying morel mushrooms several times during their current growing season made her want to run behind the store and retch.

She swallowed against the growing nausea. Her

mamm had advised she needed to work on her marriage in order to make it succeed. Right now, success would be getting her and Ben back to a comfortable friendship. If that meant holding her breath and ignoring her rebellious stomach while she cooked what was her husband's favorite food, it was a start. At least walking in the spring-growth woods together would be pleasant. And frying up his favorite food—Rachel tipped her face away and managed to control her grimace at the thought of the smell—could definitely be considered work on her part.

When she turned back, she found her husband watching her. "Would you like to go mushroom hunting? I know a good spot to find them." He glanced at Gideon. "A location I'll never divulge."

Sighing inwardly, Rachel propped up the corners of her lips into a smile. "*Ja.* Sounds *gut.* Do I have to keep it a secret too?"

Gideon nodded. "First rule of a good marriage is to not reveal the location of secret morel patches."

Given the situation of their marriage, the absurdity of the requirement made Rachel's lips twitch for real. Rules of a good marriage? How about not to expect a *boppeli* with your intended brother-in-law before getting married? She wasn't sure, but probably sleeping in the same bedroom once wedded might be a candidate for the list. Maybe talking with your spouse more than *please pass the salt* or a stilted *how was your day?* might be included. In all likelihood, it wasn't a rule, but not being terrified of something your husband enjoyed would be helpful.

Even though she'd prefer to have the whole church district and some of the *Englisch* neighbors as well tramp through the secret mushroom-hunting ground so there would be none to find, take home to prepare and—she shuddered—eat, if it would help in laying the foundation of a good marriage with Ben, she'd go find, cook and try to eat a mushroom.

"My lips are sealed." Reaching up, Rachel tapped her mouth. A glimpse at Ben revealed his attention was lingering on her lips where her fingers rested. The look in his blue eyes made her grateful there was a spring breeze that stirred against her heated cheeks. He looked away when she lowered her hand.

On the way home, Ben gave her an out. Keeping his eyes directed on his horse Sojourner, he murmured, "We don't have to go if you don't want to. I've got work I can do around home."

Although instantly tempted, Rachel responded. "*Nee*. Sounds like fun. It looks like a lovely day to walk in the woods." *You'd be proud of me, Mamm.*

Ben looked more excited than she'd seen him in some time. "Sounds *gut* then. If you want to grab some baskets and knives, we'll go as soon as I unload the feed."

An hour after reaching home, Ben was filling her in on mushrooms as they approached his clandestine hunting grounds. "When the daytime highs are in the sixties and the lows stay above forty degrees, the morels start coming out." They pulled off the county blacktop onto a short well-shaded lane. Fifty yards farther, Ben drew the bay mare to a halt in a small clearing.

Scanning the area for some place to secure Sojourner, he continued talking. Rachel suspected he knew she didn't have that much interest in the topic, but she appreciated his enthusiasm and efforts at conversation, preferring it over their continued silences.

"They like well-drained sandy soils. And areas around oaks, ash and elm trees. A lot of times, they grow around dead or dying trees. I look extra close if I see an area where the bark is slipping off the trunk." He guided Sojourner to a small bush among the trees that ringed the clearing. Snagging the lead rope, he climbed down to secure the mare to one of its branches.

Grabbing the two baskets they'd brought along for the mushrooms Rachel hoped would stay empty during their exploration, she joined him. Sojourner was already nibbling on the bush when Ben relieved Rachel of one of the baskets. "Just keep your eyes on the ground. Once you find one, slow down and search the area carefully. There're probably more."

That's what she was afraid of. Rachel didn't mind the hunting of mushrooms. It was the thought of soaking whatever they found in water for a couple of hours to clean them and wash out any bugs living inside the hollow mushrooms that made her shudder. That and the reaction of her currently delicate stomach to the strong smell as they were sautéed or cooked however Ben might prefer.

But I'm trying, Mamm. She had to admit, it was less awkward between them as they were actually doing something instead of avoiding eye contact across the table. Besides, it was a pretty spring morning to walk in the woods.

Last fall's leaves rustled as Ben shuffled through them a short distance beyond her. Rachel kept her attention on the ground, more so to not trip over a branch than to find a mushroom. She wasn't looking hard for morels and didn't expect to find any.

But there, between her right foot and the deteriorating wood of a fallen log, she instantly recognized the tall honeycombed cap and stem. A closer scrutiny of the surrounding area yielded several more. Tightening her grip on her small basket, she stole a glance at Ben. With the downed log between them, he couldn't see the small but bountiful patch. Rachel gnawed on her lip. With the toe of her shoe, she nudged some surrounding leaves and bits of bark around the area until even the tips of the mushrooms were barely visible.

She jumped when Ben called from where he was searching roughly fifteen yards away. "Finding anything?"

"*N-nee.*" Rachel inched away from the now-concealed mushrooms.

"That's funny. This is usually a pretty good spot for hunting."

"Maybe it's still a little early for them?" she offered halfheartedly as she angled away from the fallen log.

"Maybe. Might have to come up with something else for supper."

"I'm sure we'll think of something." The words couldn't tumble out of Rachel's mouth fast enough.

* * *

Ben rubbed a hand over his mouth and chin to hide his smile. It still startled him to find the beginnings of a beard, identifying him as a married man, every time he touched his face. A furtive glance in Rachel's direction ensured she was facing away. With his booted foot, he carefully shifted leaves over the prolific gathering of morels before him. He didn't think Rachel would search this way, but just in case, he camouflaged the earth's bounty.

He'd seen her kick leaves over the patch she'd found. His grin widened. He'd been wrong in his expectations for their outing. He'd figured Rachel wouldn't try too hard. She was trying hard all right, trying hard not to find any. Well, two could play at that game.

Her face had turned a bit green at the mention of frying mushrooms. The past few months, he'd watched her blanch at the smell of certain foods before hurrying to the bathroom. Causing her distress was the last thing he wanted. But she'd agreed to come. Ben had been surprised and encouraged. *Ach*, more than encouraged, he was thrilled.

And she seemed to be enjoying herself. Ben nudged some leaves over another trio of morels. So was he. Immensely enjoying not finding mushrooms with his wife.

Compared to what it could be, while not good, things had been all right between them these last few months. When he didn't see Rachel in profile, he'd even forget the original reason they married. Although she'd often try to hide them, he'd noticed a decrease in the frequency of her tears.

Even if they didn't share a bedroom, at least they were still living in the same house, unlike the couple from the wedding. Word was Lydia's sister and her children were in their farmhouse, while her husband had moved into the *daadi* house on the place, usually reserved for the older generation once the grandparents are ready to move out of the main house.

Ben didn't like gossip. He figured one shouldn't talk about someone what you wouldn't say to them. But when he'd heard the couple's woes mentioned, he'd pricked up his ears, as the fear of a similar fate in his marriage was a frequent companion.

So he was satisfied their relationship could be defined as all right. To intentionally try to change that brought risk. Risk he wasn't prepared to take. He glanced over to where Rachel was shuffling along through last autumn's fallen leaves, now with a stout walking stick in her hand. His lips twitched at the possibility she was using the stick to press mushrooms back under the leaves. Although he winced at the loss of a tasty mushroom, he was charmed she'd think of that. Charmed that she cared enough to come today. Charmed enough to express his feelings to her?

The prospect made his heart pound. Taking a couple deep breaths, he reminded himself he was fortunate for what he did have. They were married. It was more than he'd ever imagined. *Don't risk it.*

Ben grimaced. Because he'd saved the boy in the pond, folks thought he was brave. Those things were easy. He had no fear of risking his life or limb. But his blood ran cold at the thought of risking his heart. Of expressing feelings that could be ridiculed or not reciprocated.

So he couldn't say things. He wouldn't say things. But he couldn't help but show his feelings. Hopefully Rachel wouldn't notice. She never said anything about the things he did for her. Maybe she didn't care. He could live with that. He didn't want to think about not living with her. Or living with her pity if she didn't feel the same way.

"I thought you were supposed to be such a *wunderbar* mushroom hunter." Rachel made an exaggerated swing of her basket to display its emptiness.

"Must be the company." Ben grimaced comically as he turned his own basket upside down.

"Well, I guess I'll have to provide then. I think I'll be able to at least find some eggs when we get home so we won't starve. Would you like them fried, boiled or scrambled for supper?"

As they approached the clearing where they'd left the buggy, Ben figured his grin couldn't stretch any wider. Instead of enduring Rachel's teasing, he was relishing it. This was the Rachel he'd grown up with. The one he'd fallen in love with. Not the quiet, subdued Rachel he'd lived with the past several weeks, although he'd admired and respected that woman. And, he sighed with satisfaction, this was the way she'd acted around his brother, whom she'd loved. Was it possible she was growing to care for him?

"We'll have to see how many eggs you actually find. You might walk by a dozen right under your feet." As had been the case with the morels. His secret spot had been so prolific with them, the challenge had been guiding her away from the patches without either of them admitting they saw the iconic mushrooms.

He blinked against the sunlight as they left the shade of the budding trees.

Rachel stopped and glanced around the empty clearing. "Speaking of finding, are you sure we found our way back?"

"*Ja,*" Ben said as he surveyed the area, as well. He was certain of it. But a horse and buggy were pretty difficult to miss. Where had Sojourner gone? Walking the perimeter of the empty clearing, he found proof of where the rig had been parked. Fingering the now stripped bush, Ben discovered the method of her escape. He wiggled what was left of the branch of the bush he'd tied the mare to.

"*Ach.* Looks like she chewed herself free. I should've secured her better." He'd never made a mistake like that before. But his mind at the time had been on the encouraging smiles of his wife and the hopes those smiles had wrought.

He ran an assessing eye over Rachel as he considered the situation. While she'd seemed fine for their tromp through the woods, he didn't know how long they might now be on foot. He didn't want to tire her out. Rachel was tall, but even so, there was extensive rounding under her apron. Ben squinted at the sight, trying to recall how many months with child she would be. Three? *Nee.* It would be slightly more than four now.

His eyes narrowed further. Ruth Schrock, his boss's wife, had delivered a baby girl early this year. Although no one spoke of the pregnancy, Ben remembered when she'd come in to visit the business where she'd previously worked. Ruth was a much shorter woman than Rachel. Still, there'd not been a suspicion she was with child until much closer to when the baby had been born.

By his calculations, Rachel's child would arrive in the fall. And a profile of his wife already indicated there was no question about her condition. Why would she be so advanced? Frowning, he mentally counted the months again. He froze as Rachel's words that day when they were tapping the maple trees came back to him. She'd said she was having a *boppeli*.

She didn't say she was having his *boppeli*.

Was it possible…

"How far do you think she went?"

He flinched at Rachel's question. She was frowning now, as well. Ben shook off his troubling thoughts. Right now, the priority was to find their transportation. And equally important to him, regain Rachel's smiles.

He propped up the corners of his mouth. "*Ach,* fortunately for us, she should be easier to see than the morels were. But I don't know how long she's been gone or how fast she was going. Do you want to stay here in the shade and wait for me to come back with her? Hard telling how far she went."

Rachel dipped her chin shyly. "I'd rather go with you."

Ben smiled at the admission, but he hesitantly nodded toward her middle. "Are you sure you feel up to walking some more?"

"*Ja.* I'm *gut.*"

"Well, at least in this, you don't have to even think about bending over. Although perhaps we'll find more mushrooms on the road than we did in the woods."

Bumping his basket with hers, Rachel smiled at his teasing. "I'll let you get them then."

They turned in accord toward the lane on the far side of the clearing. Ben shifted his basket to his outside hand and let the other one dangle between them. "Think she went all the way home?"

Rachel's eyes widened, probably thinking as he was of the several miles distance. "I hope not." She bit her lip. "Is she an ambitious type?"

Ben thought of his mare. "Not generally. She has a nose for good grass though. I'd even have called her a picky eater." He grinned again. "Until she ate the scrub bush."

To his delight, his wife grinned back at him. "Maybe it was an intentional escape." To his further delight, she shifted her basket to her outside hand. Her now free one brushed against his as they started under the tree canopy of large oaks that draped over the lane.

"Hmm. I don't know. Hopefully it doesn't become the fugitives of the farmyard. What next? The cows?"

Rachel giggled at his bad joke. Their hands brushed. And lingered together. Ben hooked his little finger around hers. His heart beat accelerated when she didn't resist. Or let go. "Of course, that might not be something you get too upset about."

"Now, I disagree on that."

Ben's grin faded at her serious tone.

"I'd be highly upset if they came into my garden instead of heading down to the road," she continued.

"Can't have them walking through the zucchini. I'll check the gates. And if Sojy's become an escape artist, maybe I better check the hitches around the community. She might choose to use one of the wooden posts for a toothpick."

Rachel giggled again. When they'd walked out of the woods to find an empty clearing, she'd held her breath. She was prepared for what Aaron's response might have been confronting the situation. It likely wouldn't have been Ben's comic banter and the two of them giggling together like children on an outing. What normally would've been undesirable circumstances was actually fun, because of the man beside her. Granted, her feet hurt and she was tired. But what had started out as something of a chore had turned into a joy. Rachel slanted a glance at her husband, her lips lifted at his engaging profile. Of their own seeming volition, the rest of her fingers eased into his until their clasped hands swung easily between them.

Maybe when you worked at marriage, it didn't seem like so much work after all.

Fortunately, they hadn't gone much more than half a mile when they saw Sojourner in the distance, halfway up an *Englisch* farmer's lane, her head down as she grazed on the lush green lawn that lined it.

"We've found the fugitive."

"Is her choice of farm going to give us any problem?" Rachel was apprehensive. Some *Englischers* weren't fond of having Amish neighbors.

"*Nee*. It's *gut*. I know this farmer. He won't have a problem. If he's home, he'll just probably tease me about our predicament."

"You don't think she's considering leaving the Plain life for the *Englisch* one, do you?" Rachel looked up at Ben, expecting him to joke back. She watched the amiable expression fade from his face at the same time he loosened his hand from hers to flex his fingers and let it swing at his side.

"*Nee*. She's got a good life with the Amish. Besides, her Pennsylvania Dutch is much better than her English." He paused, before adding in a quiet murmur. "And she'd let me know if she had plans to leave."

Rachel's brow furrowed at his abrupt change. Until she remembered who'd left for the *Englisch* life without telling anyone. Aaron. She stumbled, bumping into Ben before she recovered her balance. How could she have forgotten? His departure was what'd prompted the basis of her life now. She loved the man. Something she'd totally forgotten while basking in an unexpectedly delightful afternoon with her husband. But why was she feeling guilty? Shouldn't she be forgetting Aaron? He couldn't be a part of her future. But he'd been so much a part of her past. Years of it. And she'd forgotten because of the man beside her.

She was trembling when she felt Ben's strong grasp under her elbow. "Are you all right?"

"*Ja*. Just…tired." When Ben swung her up into his

arms, she gasped. "You shouldn't! I'm too heavy," she protested.

"I should've thought of this before." Ben adjusted his grip to hand her his basket before shifting his arm back under her knees. "And you're no heavier than some bales of hay I've thrown."

Rachel had to admit, it was a relief to be off her feet. "I feel like I'm shaped like one. I'm huge." Her face was close to his shoulder. From his shirt, a whiff of the soap she used for laundry, warmed by the man wearing it, drifted to her. Blushing, she retained a grip on the basket handles in one hand, resting them over her rounded stomach as she looped her other arm around the back of his neck for support.

The muscles of Ben's neck stretched under her hand as he looked down. Rachel glanced up with a tremulous smile, expecting to share it with Ben. His pensive expression as he considered her midsection sent a chill through her. When his blue eyes met hers, they were troubled. He abruptly looked away. Startled by his reaction, Rachel remained quiet as they closed the distance to the lane.

Fortunately, Sojourner didn't wander farther as they approached. Ben situated Rachel in the buggy and they drove up to the house. The *Englisch* farmer wasn't home. Rachel wished he had been. At least then it might have prompted a conversation during the quiet ride home when her husband's eyes repeatedly flicked to her stomach.

Chapter Seven

A boppeli. Not *his boppeli.*

Rachel's words when she'd first told him of her condition that day in the maple grove were all Ben had been able to think about for the past week.

He'd never thought about them before, realizing after what they'd done, the situation was possible. At her concern regarding her size last week when he'd picked her up, and after furtive glances since then at her profile, he did now. Was her pregnancy further along than he thought?

If that was the case, it couldn't be his child.

It was Aaron's.

His wife was going to have his brother's baby.

Ben shifted his position so he could look over Gideon Schrock's shoulder to watch Rachel, several yards away, as she, along with other women of the district, began removing the side dishes from the table after the picnic's stragglers had gone through for their second or possibly third helping. His lips felt bloodless, compressed as they were in a line firm enough to build a barn upon.

It wasn't the surprise that hollowed him to the core. It was…disappointment? But what had he expected? He'd stolen his brother's girl. Now he'd stolen his brother's life. And whatever happened, that couldn't change. Marriage was for life. Aaron, wherever he was, might be a father someday, but not to this one, his oldest child.

Shifting his eyes toward Gideon, Ben noted that although his friend nodded in response to whatever the two men standing with them were saying, he was frowning in Ben's direction. Lifting a hand to his mouth to cover it and rub his tight jaw, Ben nodded distractedly, as well.

It was Aaron who should be experiencing the wonders of seeing his wife grow with their child. Who should be experiencing the joys and fears that come with pending fatherhood.

But Ben would raise this child the best he could, no matter who the father was. Because he loved his brother. And loved the child's mother.

Ben couldn't blame Rachel for what she'd done. With his brother gone, she'd been in a terrible situation. Even if she hadn't told him, he'd have asked her to marry him as soon as he'd realized the circumstance. And she hadn't lied to him. He'd been the one to jump to conclusions. After that initial shocking announcement, they really hadn't talked much about the baby. There'd been so many other things to do.

"Everything all right?"

Ben blinked when Gideon placed a hand on his

shoulder. Glancing about sheepishly, he realized the other two men who'd been with them had drifted away. He flushed under Gideon's raised eyebrow regard.

"It's okay. We just figured you were a man with a pretty bride and a...pending life change."

"You could say that," Ben murmured rueful agreement.

Gideon's eyes narrowed as he considered his friend. "You're not happy?"

Ben made sure he was smiling when he met his friend's concerned gaze. "*Ja.* Just a lot to think about."

Gideon dropped his hand. "*Ach.* You have cause. Lot of changes within a few months. It even surprised me when you two married. You'd never mentioned Rachel once between the time Aaron left and the wedding was announced in church. Believe me, I would've remembered, because you never talked about any girl."

Ben's smile was getting harder to keep in place. "Sometimes things just take us all by surprise." He debated sharing his concerns with Gideon, a coworker who'd become a *gut* friend. This recent discovery was feeling like a heavy burden to bear. He needed to discuss it with someone. Whereas before—with everything except the topic of Rachel—on the rare occasions he felt moved to speak of what was bothering him, he'd talk with Aaron. It hadn't been an option, for various reasons, on this topic.

A quick glance around confirmed no one was within listening distance. Inhaling deeply, he opened his mouth to divulge his apprehensions, only to close it again as he watched his younger *schweschder* hurrying toward them with a disturbed look on her face.

Gideon turned when Sarah joined them. She glanced briefly at the blond man before giving Ben a look that indicated she needed to speak with him. Alone. As it was out of character for the young woman, Ben furrowed his brow in her direction but didn't hesitate.

"Gideon, be glad you don't have *schweschder* here to nag you. I'm sure it's some task she wants me to do. I don't know why my younger *brieder* can't address whatever needs to be done, but as she's come to me, I'll assume it's because I'm the one who'll have to take care of it."

"That's all right. Actually, I wouldn't mind having my *schweschder* move up from Ohio. They haven't said anything, but I'm beginning to feel like a third wheel with Samuel and Gail, when they're more interested in a two-seater cart. With a place for Lily, of course. And I'm thinking, if they're wanting an extra mouth to feed soon, it's not me they have in mind. If Miriam came, maybe we could find a place together."

Sarah rolled her eyes at his friend's words. "You just want her to take care of the house and cook for you."

Gideon grinned. "Well, that did come to mind first."

Sarah turned her back on him to look meaningfully again at Ben. He'd been glad of their banter. It'd helped him relax. But he took her hint. "Seems this is a private discussion. I'll catch up with you later."

Gideon tipped his head in farewell. Ben watched him saunter off to join another group of men before turning his attention to his sister. "What's so important it couldn't wait nor have an audience?"

"I assumed you'd want to know that Lydia is telling all who will listen, and loud enough that those of us who don't want to will hear it anyway, that Rachel—" Sarah paused. Her eyes dropped as color rose in her cheeks.

Tension seeped into Ben. He straightened from his previously casual stance. "That Rachel?" he prompted.

"That Rachel..." She faltered again, her head still bowed. Drawing her shoulders back with a deep breath, she lifted her head. Her blue eyes were fierce when she met Ben's troubled gaze. "That it's Aaron's."

Ben felt like when he'd accidentally bumped up against an *Englisch* neighbor's electric fence. He blew out a steadying breath. It was one thing for him to speculate, to know, about his and his wife's situation. To even think about sharing it privately with a close friend. It was quite another for someone, whose business it wasn't, to be sharing it about the community.

"Did Rachel hear?"

Sarah shook her head. "I don't think so. She wasn't in the area, at least not when I was around."

Ben discovered his fists were clenched. He carefully extended his tightly curled fingers. "Where is Lydia?"

Sarah's worried glance moved from his face to his hands.

"It'll be fine. Where is she?"

"Before I left to find you, I heard her say something about taking dishes to her buggy."

He nodded. "*Denki* for telling me. You did the right

thing," he reassured her. Knowing she was troubled about the situation, Ben reached over and awkwardly patted her shoulder. Sarah was the next oldest behind him and Aaron. The three of them had once been close. Maybe instead of talking with Gideon, he should be talking with her. But, his mouth settled into a grim line, right now, he needed to be talking with someone else.

With one last pat on Sarah's shoulder, he pivoted and strode toward the field where the buggies were parked.

He caught up with Lydia between the rows of black buggies as she was heading back toward the picnic area. To his relief, she was alone. Although, with as much as she'd apparently been talking, what he was going to discuss with her wouldn't be news to anyone. Still, he'd rather have his say in private.

The look on Lydia's face when she saw him revealed the red-haired woman had no idea what was on his mind. Ben didn't understand. Had she no shame, greeting him with an eager smile when she'd just been gossiping about his wife and *bruder*? Didn't she know he would take care of his family? With a few quick glances, she apparently noted their solitude and her smile shifted, giving Ben a look that implied she wanted him to forget the vows he'd made before *Gott* to his wife.

Ben was left a little breathless with shock. He'd never betray Rachel that way. He knew Lydia was a flirt. There'd been ample evidence over the years of her *rumspringa*. But he'd never thought she would extend her activities to that level. He stopped behind one of the buggies in the long rows that stretched across the field. The triangular orange and red sign hanging on the buggy's back reminded him to go slow, be cautious, as he watched the young woman sashay closer.

If she was willing to tempt him, a married man, did that indicate she might have no qualms as a married woman forsaking her own vows? Lowering his brow, Ben frowned. He'd never taken Lydia's attentions seriously, as he'd always had his eye on Rachel. But some of the other targets of her flirtations were his friends. Although his own marriage was far from ideal, he didn't want to think of his friends being trapped in a relationship like one with Lydia might be.

"Ben, what a pleasure to see you," she cooed, stopping a few feet away.

"You might not think so after our discussion."

"Oh, I doubt that." Stepping closer, she placed a hand on his shirt.

Ben jolted in surprise. He knew, unless someone else was out in the field, the buggies blocked anyone seeing them from the picnic area. But still, he was dismayed by her boldness. Encircling her wrist with careful fingers, he pulled it from his chest. "Stop gossiping about my wife."

Lydia batted her eyelashes and dropped her jaw in attempted innocence. "Has she been complaining? If folks are discussing her…hasty romances, it has nothing to do with me."

Releasing her wrist, Ben wiped his hand on his sleeve like he'd touched something unpleasant in the barnyard. "You're right. It has nothing to do with you.

So that's enough. And if anything more is said, I'll know where it came from."

To his relief, she dropped the guile. "Why are you defending her? From the looks of it, it's not even your own *boppeli*." Her lips twisted into a sarcastic smile. "I forgot. Just like always, Ben comes along to fix what his older *bruder* left undone. Don't you ever get tired of it?"

A fireball of suppressed emotions erupted within Ben. Guilt, shame, fear, protection—he felt the sting of them all. Knowing she'd notice and gloat if he showed any reaction, he kept his expression neutral and hands loose. Catching his tongue between his teeth, he inhaled and released a quiet breath. "I get tired of worrying that my friends or younger *brieder* would be fool enough to walk out with you. Makes me think I'll have a little discussion with them. Remind them that just because the fish are practically leaping out of the pond to bite, it doesn't mean anything you snag is worth keeping."

The smile faded from her face.

It was an improvement, but not enough. "Almost wish I were still going to Sunday night singings, just to see everyone be too wise to give you a ride home at the end of the evening."

Her eyes narrowed. "I'll tell my *bruder*."

Ben worked with Jacob Troyer at Schrock Brothers Furniture. Although not close friends, he respected the man. "Go ahead. I'll tell him what you've been saying about my family." Ben was slightly embarrassed about the sharkish smile that lifted his lips. "And what some of my friends have been saying about how eager you are for the rides home."

Along with being surprised that she still could, he felt a little bad when her face flushed. The comment had been a reach—his friends weren't ones to kiss and tell—but either Lydia didn't know that, or had done more than he knew with them, and others. He figured the latter. "No more talk about my wife. Or my *bruder*."

At her stiff nod, he pivoted and headed with relief toward the gathering. Ben made the walk back at a slower pace than when he'd come out. He was grateful it was a bit of a distance, as he had much to think about. He still didn't know what he was going to do about his marriage. Or the rumors he believed had truth to them. But at least now, they'd hopefully just be his and Rachel's business to deal with, and no one else's.

The rest of the afternoon, until he noticed subtle signs that Rachel was getting tired and needed to get off her feet, he kept a wary eye on where Lydia was and what she was doing. The redheaded woman kept her mouth mainly closed. Her gaze slanted to him a few times, more in the manner she was aware he was watching than that she was saying something she shouldn't.

When Rachel idly asked where he'd gone during their ride home, Ben just shook his head. "Had some… bad apples that needed addressing."

The ribbons of Rachel's *kapp* danced about her chin as she cocked her head to consider him. "At the picnic? That's odd. But always good to sort them out as soon as possible, I guess. They can spoil quite a few surrounding ones if you wait too long."

"That's what I figured." Their marriage had enough internal challenges without outside rumors and opinions weighing on it.

He could see Rachel's profile from the corner of his eye. Was she ever planning to tell him? Ben noticed his knee bouncing as his foot kept tapping on the floor of the buggy. To still the restless movement, he crossed the other foot over his ankle. Did it matter whether she told him or not? It might take a while to sort out his feelings, but the knowledge wouldn't have changed his actions.

What would Aaron think if he came back and found his brother raising his child? His fingers tightened on the reins, causing Sojourner to toss her head and jangle the bridle. Relaxing his hands, Ben reminded himself it didn't matter who'd fathered the babe.

Still, he wanted to know.

Chapter Eight

"I'm nervous." Rachel's apron was wadded in her hands.

"I suppose that's normal." Ben rubbed his own sweaty palms together as, looking out the window, he watched the Mennonite midwife who served the district drive her car up the lane.

"I'm glad you suggested it was time to contact Mrs. Edigers. I didn't know how long I should wait before we did. Some women wait longer when they are with child." Dropping the apron, Rachel rested a hand on her stomach. "But maybe not with their first?"

She was chattering. Rachel never chattered. Was she worried about what the midwife's visit might reveal? She was also looking at him like she thought he had answers. He certainly didn't. But he wanted to. It wouldn't change the way he felt about Rachel. Or the coming baby. But he wanted to know. Was this baby coming much sooner than they'd thought? Correction, than he thought? He glanced at Rachel's anxious yet excited face as she watched the Mennonite woman and Hannah Bartel, an Amish woman now apprenticing with her, get out of the car. Would Rachel do that to him, knowing he would raise the child as his own, regardless of whether he was the father, or…the uncle?

Ach, hopefully they would soon know. Forcing down a swallow, he strode to the door to open it to the two women and their armloads of equipment.

Over the next fifteen minutes, Ben slowly paced the house as Mrs. Edigers asked Rachel questions regarding family history, her own health history, what she'd been eating and how she'd been feeling amongst other things while Hannah took his wife's pulse and blood pressure. He turned his back but remained hovering at the door when Rachel lay down on the bed.

"Now what does that do?" he heard her ask.

"We're listening for the baby's heartbeat," was the midwife's calm answer.

Ben straightened from where he'd been leaning against the doorframe. A heartbeat? The thought of a separate heartbeat made the child so much more real. He twisted so he could see the trio at the bed. Mrs. Edigers had the device on Rachel's stomach, her eyes narrowed as she listened intently. When he saw the midwife's eyes widen, he turned fully, stiffening as he watched her shift the device to different areas of Rachel's exposed stomach. Was everything all right? He fisted his hands. *A boppeli* or *your boppeli* didn't matter at all as long as Rachel and the babe were all right. Please, *Gott*, let them be all right.

Ben released the breath he hadn't been aware he

was holding in a loud exhale when the older woman's face softened into a smile. Glancing in his direction, she winked. Ben jerked his head back. What did that mean? Had she sensed his concern and was advising him everything was okay?

The Mennonite woman straightened. Handing the device to Hannah, she nodded toward where she'd been listening. With a perplexed expression, Hannah bent over Rachel's midsection. After a few moments, her eyes widened, as well. Ben was two steps farther into the room before he realized he was moving.

Mrs. Edigers helped shift his wife so she rested with her back against the headboard. "Rachel, good thing you're sitting down. Maybe you want to as well, Ben. I have some big news for you." The older woman chuckled as she patted Rachel's shoulder. "I heard not one heartbeat, but two. You're having twins."

Rachel gasped as her round-eyed gaze swiveled to Ben. "Twins? Two *boppeli*?"

Ben dazedly figured her dropped jaw and stunned expression mirrored his. "Are you joking?"

Mrs. Edigers's smile expanded. "Yes, two babies. No, no joke. I imagine you've been quite tired. That would also explain why you're a bit bigger than you might have expected. From your measurements and what you've indicated, they should arrive sometime early October, as multiple babies usually come a few weeks earlier than a single pregnancy."

Everything else the midwife was saying was lost in the buzzing in Ben's ears. Two babies? They were going to have two babies? His heart was racing. He staggered out of the room to sink into his cushioned chair. Arriving in early October? That meant… Ben's ears reddened. Twins in October meant he should never have doubted his wife. His fingers curled over the smooth oak arms of his chair. It didn't matter. It wouldn't have mattered. He would be husband to Rachel and father to the child regardless. But now, he'd be father to two. And they were his. Not his brother's. Ben slumped with simple joy and relief at the thought. Two babies at once? His head flopped back on the chair. He didn't know how to be a father to one.

Hopefully *Gott* knew what He was doing, as Ben certainly didn't.

"How are you doing, new *daed*?" Still dazed ten minutes later, he hadn't heard Hannah Bartel enter the room.

Blinking to clear his vision and rein in his galloping thoughts, Ben saw her smiling down at him. "I don't know yet. It will take a while to sink in. I was still getting used to one *boppeli*. And now to have two?" He'd seen multiplies before with sheep and cattle. He'd remembered in the last few moments there were other twins in the district, but he'd never thought he'd belong in that group. His bemused grin ebbed and his brow lowered as he tried to recall any issues those with twins had experienced. Sometimes twin calves didn't thrive. He sat up abruptly. "What does carrying two *boppeli* do to the mother? Will two *boppeli* be all right?"

"I don't know enough at this time to give you advice on either of those questions. This is my first set of twins. But I'll learn and I'll let you know. I'm sure the *boppeli* will be smaller than a single birth. As for how it affects the mother?" Hannah shook her head. "I just don't know yet."

Pushing to his feet, Ben nodded vaguely. Surely Mrs. Edigers had some answers, but, whereas he'd grown up with Hannah and might discuss the topic with her, he didn't know the midwife well enough to feel comfortable yet asking these questions. Peeking through the door to his wife's bedroom, he saw her cradle her rounded belly in wonder. The ends of Ben's lips tipped up at the sight. He would find out the information though. He'd do whatever was needed to take care of his family. It's what he did.

"Maybe you should sit down. Can I get you anything?"

Rachel, standing at the sink, looked over to where Ben came in the door from doing the evening cattle chores. This was the first he'd had a chance to speak to her after their big—he raised his eyebrows at the understatement—news. He'd waved from the barn when Mrs. Edigers and Hannah left. The livestock had needed tending and he'd had too much nervous energy with the afternoon's shocking revelation to stay put in the house.

Her smile still held more than a hint of wonder. "Physically, I feel no different than when I woke up this morning. But mentally?" Rachel shook her head. "I can't wrap my mind around it." She accepted Ben's hand as he led her to sit in a chair by the table.

"Well, that explains why you are…" With his hands, Ben vaguely shaped around his stomach.

"As big as some of the milk cows on Zook's farm?" Rachel offered helpfully.

Ben grinned as he sat across from her, "*Nee*. But maybe bigger than other women with child are at this stage." Rachel eyed him quizzically. His smile drooping, Ben rubbed the back of his neck. "Not that I go around looking at women who might be…" Squirming, he brought his hand around to rub over his mouth and looked down, finishing in a mutter, "But you seemed bigger. And I thought…"

When he raised his head, Rachel regarded him with a frown. "You thought…" Then her eyes widened. "You thought it was Aaron's baby," she whispered.

Ben simply nodded. He wished to look anywhere except at her, but he knew it would be cowardly so he kept his gaze on her stark expression.

"I would never do that to you." Her eyes were dark with hurt.

Ben wanted to reach for her. Instead, inhaling raggedly, he clasped his hands together and hid them under the table. "I… It wouldn't have made any difference. I still would've married you. Regardless. I would have loved the child as my own. No difference."

"I never… He and I never…"

Ben's gut clenched at the tears welling in her brown depths, making her beautiful eyes glisten.

"I can't believe you thought that of me." Rachel's voice trembled as much as her lower lip.

He couldn't stand it. Ben reached out a hand toward

her, for what purpose, he didn't know. It didn't matter anyway. Ignoring it and him, Rachel pushed to her feet and returned to the sink.

"Supper will be on the table in a few minutes if you want to take the time to wash up." She didn't turn. Her posture was as stiff as her voice.

With a slumped head, Ben rose from his chair and trudged to the bathroom. What he wanted to wash was his mouth out with soap. Why hadn't he just stayed quiet about his concerns? Either way, they wouldn't have made any difference. Was it because he was just so elated to have that concern lifted? To know he really hadn't been used, just because he was available and had a habit of cleaning up after his brother? It wouldn't have mattered. His actions would've been the same. Still, as he'd reminded himself earlier, it was better to be silent and appear a fool than to speak and remove all doubt. Look where this acknowledgement had gotten him.

Now his wife was distressed. Ben turned on the water at the sink, washed his hands and splashed water on the back of his neck. Glancing in the small mirror above the sink that he used when shaving, Ben fingered the beard that marked him as a married man as he frowned at his reflection. He knew Rachel's character from way back. Deceit wasn't in her nature. He should've trusted *Gott* and trusted his wife. Shaking his head at his reflection, he thought back over the afternoon.

Twins! He hadn't fully grasped the concept of one *boppeli* yet.

A gasp and crash from the kitchen had him bouncing off the doorjamb as he dashed from the bathroom. Hurrying across the room, he took in the plate on the floor and the sight of his wife, one hand braced on the counter and the other touching her rounded apron.

Avoiding the broken plate, Ben skidded to a halt before her. "Are you all right!"

She turned toward him with a dazed expression. "I think so."

"What happened?" Ben bent to pick up the pieces of the broken plate and carry them to the trash.

"I think I felt…" Rachel's cheeks and the shell of her ears, exposed by her *kapp*, were a charming pink. "I think I felt the *boppeli* move."

Taking a step back, Ben braced his hip on the table. He needed the support of four legs as his two were unsteady. "Are you sure?"

"I'm not too sure of anything right now, but I've never felt anything like it before. According to Mrs. Edigers, I should be able to feel them soon." She gave a breathless giggle. "I guess this is soon."

Ben sagged more heavily against the table, gazing in amazement at his wife's midsection. First a heartbeat, and now movement. The vague concept that'd prompted their marriage was becoming real at the speed of stampeding cattle. Lifting a hand toward her, he instantly jerked it back. Crossing his arms, he tucked his palms into his armpits to keep from touching her.

Rachel didn't seem to notice. "I don't feel it on the outside. Only on the—" if possible, her cheeks turned even more crimson "—inside. It's a sort of fluttering. Like a butterfly." She shook her head. "Two. Oh, my…"

Astonishment faded to be replaced by the dawning of concern. "The midwife said they'd be smaller than a single baby. I hope they're all right."

"I know. But whatever happens is *Gott*'s will." Even as he said the words, Ben couldn't help hoping it be *Gott*'s will that the two, becoming more real and so precious to him, would be safe and healthy, even if he didn't know what to do with them once they arrived. But one thing he knew he should and could do, was make it right with their mother.

"I'm sorry, Rachel. I should never have thought…" Ben's shoulders lifted in a guilty sigh "…what I did. I should've known you'd never do something like that. I'm sorry I ever doubted you."

With a glance at a few plate chips remaining on the linoleum floor, she carefully stepped around him to get the broom and dustpan from the closet. Dropping his arms and straightening from the table, Ben took the dustpan from her to squat down and place it next to the plate pieces on the floor. When the broom didn't move, he looked up to see a rueful twist on Rachel's lips.

"Was it because of the rumors?"

He couldn't prevent a wince. "You heard about those?"

The broom went into brisk motion. "I think that was the intention."

After the last whisks into the dustpan, he rose and dumped the contents in the trash. He met Rachel at the closet door. Reaching out, she grabbed the edge of the dustpan and held it between them until she had his full attention.

"*Denki*. And you're forgiven." She put the tool away and shut the closet door. "I know Plain people don't generally speak about a woman with child. That doesn't mean some aren't thinking and watching. And given my size, you probably aren't the only one to think what you did."

Still whirling with relief at her first words, Ben almost didn't hear her last ones. When he didn't speak, Rachel grimaced. "I'm sorry on that, as it affects you, as well."

He shook his head. "I can handle myself." Recalling his conversation with Lydia, a slow smile slid over his face. "And I don't think that person will be saying anything more." As for him, he wouldn't doubt his wife again. "What do you want to do now? Let this news trickle into community knowledge? Or let them continue to wonder?"

Rachel grinned impishly. "I'm tempted to let them continue to wonder." Her expression faded a bit as she continued, "But if they've heard the rumors, I don't want to do that to my family or yours. Besides," her bright smile returned, "I can't wait to let my *mamm* know she'll be a *grossmammi* to two."

"I wouldn't mind telling my folks the news, as well. We'll let things go from there as they will then." Although he longed to do more, Ben limited himself to taking one of her delicate, deceptively strong hands in his. "And Rachel, one, two or ten *boppeli*, I know you'll make a *wunderbar* mother."

She blushed, her hand momentarily tightening on

his. "*Gut* thing I helped care for my younger *schweschder* and little *bruder* when I was growing up."

"You have the advantage over me. I have far more younger siblings than you, but I have to admit, when they squalled or smelled, I'd race out of the house to the barn, leaving Sarah to help *Mamm* while I shadowed *Daed* and—" Ben caught himself before he said Aaron's name. His gut clenched as he cleared his throat. "And learned what to do in the barn and fields." He forced a grin. "If there's anything with the *boppeli* that requires a pitchfork or feed bucket, make sure you let me know."

"I think with two, you'll be called upon to learn a few new things."

"With two," Ben echoed, shaking his head. His smile became natural. "Oh, help."

Rachel nodded understandingly at the common Amish phrase. "Oh, help indeed."

Sharing a warm gaze that jolted Ben almost as much as news of the twins, they slowly released their clasped hands. Rachel turned to the cupboard to get a plate to replace the broken one. Ben sat in his chair and eyed the contents on the table. The potatoes were no longer steaming. The gravy looked a bit congealed. The dressing had slid off the cucumbers. But to Ben, it seemed like the best meal he'd had in a long, long time. It was the first one where it finally seemed there was just him and Rachel in the marriage, without his brother's shadow hanging over them.

Chapter Nine

Rachel glanced out the kitchen window at the clatter of hooves coming up the lane. She smiled when she recognized her sister Rebecca's rig. Rinsing the quart jar she'd just washed, she set it upside down on the rack to dry and shook the water off her hands. Grabbing a dish towel, she finished wiping them as she walked to the door. Rachel's smile dimmed at the expression on her sister's face as Rebecca hurried up the steps.

"Is everything all right? Is *Mamm* okay? And Amos?"

"*Ja, ja.* I'm sorry, I didn't mean to make you worry." Rebecca gave her a quick hug as she came through the door. When Rachel closed it behind her and followed her into the kitchen, Rebecca withdrew an envelope from the waistband of her apron.

"This came for you at home. I wasn't sure what you wanted to do with it. Or whom you might want to see it. So I brought it right over."

Brows furrowed, Rachel took the long white envelope from her sister's outstretched hand. She stiffened as her fingers pinched the slender missive. Although there was no return address, Rachel recognized the handwriting that scrawled her maiden name and previous address across the front of the envelope. He'd written her before a few times while they'd been walking out. Why would Aaron send her a letter now, after all this time?

She looked up to find Rebecca watching her expectantly. With a tight smile, Rachel shook her head. "I'll read it later." She tucked it into the waistband of her own apron. Her sister's expression briefly revealed her disappointment but she nodded understandably.

"*Denki* for bringing it over. I have no idea what it might say, but you're right. Until I do, it's probably best that no one knows he sent it."

Intentionally changing the subject, she walked with Rebecca out into the garden and picked a few summer squash to send home. Although she greatly enjoyed her sister's visits, today the minutes weighed as heavy as the letter tucked into her waistband until the younger woman indicated it was time for her to go. Upon waving goodbye as Rebecca drove down the lane, Rachel returned to the house. With damp palms, she retrieved the envelope and stared at it.

Why now? She'd almost forgotten him. Her life was so full with just learning about the two babies a week ago and... Ben. A twinge of guilt flickered over her face. She could barely remember what Aaron looked like and she'd intended to marry the man for years. He was dark-haired and blue-eyed like his brother, but whenever she tried to visualize his face, instead of a square jaw, she saw a cheek that dimpled with a rare shy smile. Rachel tapped the letter against her palm. What could it possibly say?

There was one way to find out.

With a sharp inhale, she slid a finger into the edge and tore the flap open, the crackle of the ripping envelope causing a small shudder to run up her spine. Pulling out the single sheet of paper, Rachel unfolded it and quickly scanned the contents.

Dear Rachel, I've been thinking of you. I didn't intend to hurt you. I do care for you. Aaron.

She stared at the simple pen strokes, the words becoming blurry as the backs of her eyes prickled with tears. That was it? And after all this time, what did it mean? One tear dripped, dampening the paper as memories of the relationship that'd meant everything to her during her *rumspringa* flooded through her. Memories of the man whose sweet words had made her feel special. Whom she'd thought was *Gott*'s chosen one for her. Why did Aaron have to send this now, when things had been going well between her and Ben? With one last look at the brief words, she refolded the letter and slid it back into the envelope.

Any way she could think of it, this would not help her relationship with her husband. There was no news about his brother she could pass on to Ben. It didn't say where Aaron was, why he left, or when or even if he was coming back. Only that he was thinking of and cared for her. The envelope crinkled as her hand tightened around it. Her. Who was now his brother's wife. Did Aaron know that? Opening her hand, she ran her thumb over the address. Obviously not, as he'd addressed it to her maiden name.

Smoothing out the wrinkles she'd created, Rachel gazed at the wastepaper basket. If there'd been something in it to share with Ben, she would have. As it was, there was no reason to keep the missive. Still—she pressed the letter to her chest—she couldn't let it go. When she'd moved out of her old home, she'd thrown all mementos of her relationship with Aaron in a tearful purging. This was the only thing from him she had now. Although troubling, it brought back memories, good ones, of a carefree girl romanced by a charming fellow. Instead of being a new wife in a tenuous marriage, heavy with child and the responsibilities of running a household. Could she ever totally let go of that carefree girl?

Rachel tapped the envelope against her side a moment before she crossed to her bedroom and opened the drawer of the nightstand next to her bed. Dropping the envelope in, she shut the drawer again with a rueful sigh. *Oh, Aaron. You did hurt me. Everything has changed because you left. And can't return to what it was. If you return to confront the repercussions of your abrupt departure, there'll be more of us hurt. Maybe it's best if you stay away.* Her heart clenched at the thought. She reached for the drawer again, only to curl her fingers into a fist before opening it. With a resolve to dispose of the letter at some point—just not yet—Rachel returned to the kitchen to continue preparations for the day's canning.

When Ben asked that evening about her day, she told him about the canning and her sister's visit, and nothing else.

Waving a casual farewell to coworkers still harnessing their horses after work, Ben guided Sojy down Main Street, his thoughts already turning toward Rachel. He snorted with self-derision. He was always thinking of Rachel. But now, amongst the silent longing and muted joy was a tinge of worry. She'd been quiet the past few days. Rachel wasn't a loquacious woman anyway, and he knew she was often tired when he got into the house after work and chores at the end of the day, but the past couple days since she'd mentioned Rebecca had visited, his wife had been exceptionally subdued.

Had Rebecca brought bad news? Ben sighed, sick at heart that he and his wife still didn't have the relationship where they could talk easily together. Surely she would've told him if something was wrong at her *mamm*'s farm? Had Rachel and her *schweschder* argued? Ben didn't want to get into the middle of two sisters bickering, but, his lips flattened grimly as he passed The Dew Drop restaurant where Rebecca worked, he'd do whatever was necessary to protect his wife. Whether or not she was growing more burdened by day with carrying his two children.

Maybe that was the reason. Maybe she was even more fatigued, as there were two *boppeli* instead of one. Rachel never complained, but he'd detected winces and grimaces crossing her face when she didn't think he was watching. Was she worried now that they knew there were two? Did she know something about multiples that he didn't? Pregnancy and childbirth were very normal in the Amish community, as they welcomed and rejoiced in large families. That didn't mean there weren't occasional problems. In fact, their neighbor Jethro Weaver had lost his wife and unborn child last fall due to a pregnancy-related issue.

After they'd been advised of the twins, Ben had noted all the twins existing around the district. Although somewhat rare, there were a few. Did carrying twins bring increased risks for the mother? His stomach began to churn at the thought of losing his wife and children like Jethro had. Was there something Rachel wasn't telling him that had her silent with worry?

He was approaching the cheerfully colored awning of the quilt shop where Hannah Bartel, the apprentice to the midwife, still occasionally worked. Slowing his horse, Ben peered into the windows of The Stitch. To his relief, he saw Hannah inside. Before he could talk himself out of it, he guided a surprised Sojourner to the curb. Hopping out, Ben secured the mare and headed for the shop door, his step slowing when he noted other shoppers were inside.

Pausing outside the door, he debated his hasty decision. He knew all the women visible in the shop, but still, he didn't want them to hear his questions for Hannah. Drumming his fingers on his thigh, he weighed his and Rachel's privacy against settling his concerns regarding her and the *boppeli*. He glanced at the shop hours stenciled on the door's window before narrowing his eyes at the clock visible inside on an interior wall. A few moments until closing time. Hopefully the women would soon finish their business and leave. Ben shifted his feet when he saw that he'd drawn their curious attention. Heaving a sigh, he pushed open the door and stepped inside.

The three women at the counter smiled as he stepped inside. His boss's wife, Ruth Schrock, called out the first greeting.

"*Guder Nummidaag*, Ben." Although her expression remained bland, he recognized the impishness in her eyes. "When did you start quilting?" Having grown up with Ruth and worked with her at Fisher Furniture when her *daed* owned the shop before Malachi bought it, Ben wasn't surprised at her teasing.

"Good afternoon to you, as well. And this is nothing new—you always have me in stitches." The trio of women giggled at his response. He strolled toward them through the rows of fabric. Might as well brazen it out now. "She's grown." He nodded to Deborah, the baby girl, dressed just like her *mamm,* who peered curiously at him from the safety of Ruth's arms. He swallowed hard at the thought, the hope, that one like her would be nestled in Rachel's arms sometime in the future.

"She certainly has. It's a race between Deborah and Rascal as to who can scurry over the floor faster now."

Ben nodded to Ruth's companion, another woman he'd grown up with. He'd been glad when Hannah's *schweschder*, Gail Lapp, now Gail Schrock as she'd married Malachi's *bruder* Samuel, had returned to the community with her young daughter. "And how are you, Lily?" He nodded toward the little blond girl currently petting Socks, Hannah's Border collie and frequent companion.

Eyeing him warily, the girl gave the dog a few more strokes before solemnly stating, "*Ich bin gut.*" She glanced up at her *mamm.* "I said that right, didn't I?"

Rubbing a hand over his mouth, Ben hid a smile. Whereas most Amish children spoke the Pennsylvania Dutch dialect at home and didn't learn English until they attended school, Lily had it backward, having lived in the *Englisch* world for the first few years of her life and only returning with Gail to Miller's Creek last summer. Lily tugged on her *mamm*'s apron. "Can we go home? I want to watch *Daed* work with the filly."

Ben's grin behind his hand grew larger. Samuel Schrock, also a previous coworker before he'd become the horse trader for the community, was going to have his hands full with this *maedel.* Ben couldn't wish it on a better man. And nothing would be said, but as was evident by Gail's profile when her apron had been tugged, Samuel was also going to be a *daed* again at some point. Ben was thrilled for his friend.

But now he wanted to ask the midwife apprentice about his own wife's condition. Hannah met his eyes and smiled in understanding. She turned her attention to the little girl. "I think you're going to have a lovely new dress with that material, Lily. Will you be wearing it next church Sunday?"

Gail Schrock picked up a bag from the counter. "I don't know if it'll be done by then, because I'll have to get someone to stand still long enough to take measurements before I can make it. Come on, Lily, let's go see how the filly's training is coming." With a wave of fare-well, she followed her skipping daughter to the door.

When the little girl departed, Socks trotted to the dog bed in the corner and settled on it. Ben watched as she stretched out her black-and-white legs and rested her head upon them.

"Where's Nip and Tuck?" Hannah and her husband, Gabe, had rescued the two Border collie pups during one of Gabe's EMS calls this past winter.

Hannah shook her head with a smile. "They're out at my folks' farm until we can get a bigger place. The apartment upstairs was getting a little too small for all of us."

Ruth snagged a small bag from the counter. "We need to be heading out as well as we're riding home with Malachi. We're supposed to meet him at the shop after work. As you're here, he may be ready to go, as well." She squinted at Ben. "Although I'm still trying to figure out why you are here."

"You keep thinking on that. It should entertain you for a while."

She flashed him a smile, but after studying his face for a moment, Ruth's expression grew more serious. "It's *gut* to see you joking again, Ben. We've been wor-ried about you."

"*Ach*," Ben ducked his head as his cheeks reddened. "I'm fine. I'll always be fine."

"*Gut* to know." Ruth reached out to briefly touch his arm before she shifted the girl in her arms, bid him and Hannah farewell and left the shop.

"I'm guessing you're here because you're worried

about someone else. I'm also guessing from what she said, you haven't shared the news about the twins."

"Only to our parents, because of the..." he scowled "...rumors. Everyone else will just have to find out when they arrive."

Hannah frowned, as well. "When they come early, as multiplies frequently do, some might not know that. They'll count the months and still wonder."

"Those that want to will do that. I can't change what they think. They're not my business. Rachel is. What have you learned?" He prompted the apprentice midwife.

He wasn't encouraged when, frowning further, she sighed. "Well, there are greater risks for complication with twins. Although that doesn't mean they'll happen," she hastened to assure him.

"Like what?"

"*With* the *boppeli* in all likelihood arriving early, it means they'll have low birth weights." She met his somber gaze. "Along with corresponding issues."

Ben grew up with livestock. He knew about runts and their struggle to thrive. He pivoted to stare blindly at the far wall, the bright-colored quilts that adorned it counter to his bleak thoughts. Amish districts differed. Some tended to reject extraordinary measures to save a life, since such measures may attempt to interfere with *Gott*'s will. As Amish carried no health insurance, relying on the church and community to cover member's incurred bills, expenses born by his family would affect the whole district. What were they to do if the babes were born too small to survive? Would *Gott* punish him through his children for his sin of being in love with his brother's intended? For stealing her for himself? Ben's head lowered as his eyes closed. With hands pressed to his chest, he emptied his mind and opened his heart. *Gott, please forgive me. It is my sin, and my sin alone. I am in awe that You've brought Rachel and these children into my life. Please forgive me of this sin against my brother.*

With a shuddering sigh, Ben opened his eyes and lifted his head. A good part of the *boppeli* staying healthy depended on the health of his wife.

"What about for Rachel?" He directed the question over his shoulder.

Hannah hesitated before continuing softly. "Some frequent issues of women carrying twins are higher risk for gestational diabetes, anemia and preeclampsia."

Ben hissed in his breath. Eclampsia had been determined as the cause of death for Jethro's wife and child.

"More morning sickness."

"*Ach*, she's certainly had that." He turned to face Hannah.

"I'd always heard so, but having now seen her numerous times in action, I can vouch for the fact that Mrs. Edigers is very *gut* at what she does. She'll take *gut* care of them."

"As I'm sure that you'll be as talented as well, by the time you finish your apprenticeship." He smiled ruefully.

"I hope so. I'll certainly strive to be."

"Well, I should be going. I have chores and Rachel will be expecting me. *Denki* for the information, Hannah. I can't say it's comforting to know, but I'd rather know than be ignorant. Tell Gabe hello for me." He turned and began weaving his way back through the brightly colored rows.

"Will do and we'll keep a close eye on any issues with Rachel and the *boppeli*. It might be difficult convincing her, but as she gets closer to their arrival, it would help her to get off her feet. *Sehn dich scheeder*, Ben."

"*Ja*. See you later," he echoed, the bell above the door jangling as he exited.

Ben's brow remained furrowed as the familiar countryside breezed by during the drive home. He had to take care of his wife. Always his intention, the need pulsed through him with this new information. How to do so? If he didn't know she'd already have supper on the table, he would've returned to The Dew Drop to take something home for them. He blinked and shifted on the seat. Why hadn't he thought of that before? He'd tell Rachel he'd pick something up for them tomorrow so she wouldn't have to cook.

How else could he care for her? There were a few hours of daylight after supper. He could go to the garden instead of reading the paper and do the hoeing so Rachel didn't have to.

Ben's customary glance toward the kitchen window as he drove up the lane turned worried when Rachel didn't appear there to wave. With a frown, he scanned the garden. She wasn't there either. Directing Sojy to the barn, he left her in front of its big door as he hurried toward the house.

It was quiet when he entered. "Rachel?" he called softly. The kitchen was empty, albeit the table was set for two. A garden salad sat on the counter. A steaming casserole was visible in the oven, although the appliance was off, its door open a crack.

He found her in her rocking chair. Ben's air was stranded in his throat, until he saw the steady rise and fall of her breathing. She'd fallen asleep. She'd spared a moment during the day to sit down and had fallen asleep. Her hands rested across her midsection. Her head was tipped to one side against the back of the rocker. A few strands of dark hair had fallen from under her still neatly pinned *kapp* to drape across her cheek. Her eyelashes fanned over the dark circles under her eyes.

For a moment, Ben just watched her sleep. For years, he'd never been able to look his fill at Rachel. First, it would've drawn teasing from his fellow schoolmates if they'd caught him watching one of the girls. Then, when she was Aaron's, it hadn't seemed right. After he and Rachel were married, the way their relationship had begun, and stood, he knew it would make her uncomfortable to gaze at her as he wanted to.

When she didn't stir, he gingerly unpinned her *kapp* and took it with him into her bedroom. Setting it on the nightstand by the bed, he turned down the handmade quilt and cotton sheet. Returning to the rocker, Ben gazed down at her again with a soft smile on his face. Rachel hadn't been sleeping well. He could hear her moving around when he wasn't sleeping. He longed to guard her rest, because when the babes came, from what he'd heard, neither of them would get much sleep at first. She was always working. Even though she was tired, she never complained.

Bending down, Ben gently curled his arms about her and lifted her from the chair. Her head lolled against his neck. Ducking his chin, Ben tenderly kissed her forehead. Resting his head against hers, his eyes drifted closed as longing to be able to do that freely rippled through him. With a regretful sigh, he carried Rachel into her bedroom and carefully laid her down on the bed. Conscious of the day's warmth, he pulled the sheet only over her, tucking it at her shoulders.

"I know I'm not the one you want to hear it from. I shouldn't say it. But I can't hold the words back. You're beautiful. I don't understand why *Gott* saw fit to make you mine. But I'm so thankful He did. And I'll do everything in my power that someday, hopefully, you'll be thankful, as well."

He froze as she murmured something and shifted to her side. When she resettled, he placed one last kiss on the coiled length of her hair and quietly left the room.

Chapter Ten

Ben leaned the bag of feed against the wall, grabbed the tab at the top and jerked it open with a resulting *brr* sound as the heavy thread ripped loose from the reinforced paper. As he poured the brown pellets into two pails, his thoughts were far away from his task.

His earliest memories regarding chores on the farm had been of tailing after his older *bruder*. Aaron had been the one to show him how to carefully maneuver about in the corn bin. He'd been the one to show him how to harness their pony. Aaron had taught him how to tie his first boots when it'd gotten too cold in the fall to go barefoot. How to put a worm on a hook, how to take a fish off and how to get one on in between. Ben had been two steps behind the older *bruder* he'd adored all the time when they were young. Their folks had even commented on it, joking, Gut *thing we named them with the first letters of A and B, as Benjamin's always following Aaron.*

Unhooking the barn door, Ben slipped through

carrying the first two pails of corn he'd filled earlier. "Hey, back off," he admonished the numerous black-and-white heads crowding around him. "You'll all be fed soon if you're just a little patient. Just let me get through." Bumping the buckets against some noses that got a little too close, he made his way through the restless steers to the feed bunks. Ben grimaced as he noted the end bunk he'd destroyed weeks earlier to save the steer. *I need to get that fixed. Always something to do, particularly with livestock.* Pouring the two buckets in a long line down one of the other two bunks, he hurried back to the barn for two more pails of corn. The cattle, except for a few, were jostling for position at the first bunk, freeing his path to the second.

He glanced over to where Rachel was working in the garden. Although breakfast had been more leisurely this morning as he didn't have to go to town for work, they still hadn't talked much. She'd been charmingly disconcerted and apologetic about falling asleep before supper last night. And about finding the kitchen cleaned up when she'd awakened this morning.

Enjoying her rosy cheeks, he'd assured her it was fine. And it had been. More than fine. He'd treasure those quiet moments for some time, never knowing when he'd have a chance to store up more.

Emptying the buckets, Ben returned to the barn, his gaze still on Rachel in the garden. The first time he'd wondered about gardening was when his *grossmammi* had called him and Aaron two peas in a pod. That's the way they'd remained growing up. At home, at church, at school, where Ben had expressed little interest because he was shy and much more intrigued with any other aspects of life. But anything Aaron could do—except for schoolwork—Ben strove to emulate his hero older brother.

For sure and certain, they'd been competitive. They'd played baseball on opposite teams, raced horses, competed eating the most pancakes and throwing hay bales the farthest. But he and Aaron had been best friends, even though his older *bruder* seemed to always have been a little better, a little faster, a little smarter.

Until Aaron entered his *rumspringa*.

Then everything changed. Ben was left behind as Aaron's close friends became the ones he met at the parties he was either attending or continuously talking about. With those, and other *Englisch* pursuits as his main interests, he was frequently distracted from his work on the farm. Then it was Ben that came along, finishing up tasks or correcting errors so Aaron didn't get into trouble when he'd head out early to meet up with guys driving cars to parties. A cell phone and charger were tucked into the dresser the two shared, along with magazines on mechanics and *Englisch* blue jeans. Aaron no longer sported a bowl cut, his hair was now trimmed shorter under a ball cap instead of a straw or felt hat.

The only Amish thing Aaron seemed to enjoy was courting Rachel. When Ben finally entered his *rumspringa,* his *bruder* had already paired off with the girl he'd always admired. Although he was glad to spend time with his Amish friends, the only reason Ben had gone to singings and *youngie* parties was to see Rachel. And torture himself that she was now with Aaron.

Nudging the barn door open with his shoulder, Ben carried out the two pails of pellets. He'd been shocked Aaron had left Rachel. But even though they'd taken baptism classes together, although he'd been disappointed and heartsick at Aaron's disappearance, Ben wasn't really that surprised his *bruder* had left for the *Englisch* life he'd seemed so fascinated with. As Ben climbed into the first bunk to walk between the cattle's broad heads and sprinkle the pellets on top of the rapidly disappearing corn, he wondered what Aaron would've come up with to delay baptism into the church if he hadn't been kicked by the horse and broken his arm that Sunday morning. Aaron had left without being baptized. He could therefore return to the community without severe consequences. Had that been his plan all along? If he'd left after having been baptized, he'd have been shunned if he came back. The fact that he hadn't been baptized left the door open for a return. The now empty pails banging against his legs, Ben glanced again at his wife's profile as he climbed down from the bunk.

Ach, maybe Aaron's consequences of departure, if he planned to return, had been rather severe after all.

Rachel straightened and arched her back before resting a hand on the underside of her burgeoning middle. As this was mid-July and the midwife had mentioned early October, she couldn't imagine how she'd be able to work closer to when the *boppeli* would arrive. While she was still wrapping her mind around the thought of two, her body well knew the burden she carried.

Heaving a sigh, she considered the wall of vines climbing up the woven wire ahead. She appreciated Ben's idea of the fence for the cucumbers more than he'd know. Gathering her apron into a basket, she dropped the summer squash into it and trudged toward the end of the garden, curling her bare toes into the sun-warmed tilled earth. Rachel relished in the sensation, but when she recognized the beginning of a waddle in her gait, she winced.

Her face warmed as she recalled that she'd slept while Ben had taken care of her and the supper chores. Although she appreciated his constant solicitousness, it always seemed directed toward her as a woman with child. *Ach*, Rachel sighed, it would be hard to see a woman who walked like a duck as anything but that at the moment.

She wanted to be seen as a woman who was attractive to her husband. But it understandably would be hard for him to see her that way when the whole of their marriage, she'd been a swirling mess of emotions and physical changes. Surely a man didn't find his wife attractive when she was red-eyed with weeping, or wearing a deathly pallor as she raced for the bathroom. Or looking like she'd swallowed a watermelon whole instead of tending to its vines.

At least with Aaron, she'd known where she stood. Like her *daed*, he'd praised her in one way or another. As the oldest of a growing family who strove to do everything right to gain her busy parents' attention, she'd craved affirmation. Although not proud of the need, Rachel recognized that praise had made her feel less invisible.

She blinked in the morning sun. Was that what prompted her to fall for Aaron? Certainly, he was very handsome, but really, when she thought about it, no more so than Benjamin. Had she been enamored by the way he automatically filled her subconscious need for validation with his flowery compliments?

Rachel considered the wall of green interspersed with pale yellow blossoms in front of her. She wished she knew where she stood with Ben. Besides just as a responsibility. She wished she knew if her husband found her attractive. Because she did find him attractive. Rachel blushed at the acknowledgment. She might want words, but Ben's continual practice of doing things for her was starting to grow on her. Maybe her *mamm* was right. Words were sweet, but they didn't get things done. There were definitely many things that needed doing around a farmstead. To her surprise, she'd found doing those things brought a feeling of partnership to a couple. One more deeply rooted than one based on flowery words?

She certainly didn't feel invisible with Ben. She felt…cosseted. Was that because of responsibility to the mother of his children? Or because he cared for her as herself?

Rachel plucked a robust green cucumber at waist-height from a vine. Maybe she should tell Ben how much she appreciated his thoughtfulness. Things had been better between them lately. Weeks ago, he'd apologized about not trusting her. She'd understood. Given the situation, she'd have wondered the same thing.

She sighed. The rare kind word from Ben meant so much to her. Even though he never said anything, it probably worked in reverse. Her lips twitched. Was this part of the *work* in marriage her mother had referred to?

Adding the cucumber to her apron, she glanced over to where Ben was feeding the cattle. Rachel had to admit, he was certainly putting in the effort. He was always doing thoughtful things for her. If they were sitting at the table and she'd forgotten to put the butter on, before she could shift in her chair, he was up like a jack-in-the-box and rushing to the cupboard. When he was home, she couldn't climb into the buggy without his steadying hand under her arm, whether she needed it or not. When he wasn't home, and he found out she'd gone out, harnessing her horse by herself, he'd narrow his eyes in dismay. The next time she went to the barn, the harness was hung with lower pegs on the wall, making it easier to reach. He'd even mentioned getting a pony and cart for her to get around, reasoning that the babies would need one at some point anyway.

Snorting, Rachel worked her way down the fence to where she spied another cucumber hiding amongst the green leaves. How did he expect her to get around when he wasn't here if she didn't harness the horse and hook up the buggy? The babies hadn't affected her arms and legs. Although—she shifted at a twinge in her hips— they definitely were affecting other things. Still, it was sweet of him to be so attentive.

She should tell him. He wouldn't say anything, but

his blue eyes might soften and his lips might lift in that endearing half smile she was beginning to watch for. A smile on her own lips, Rachel glanced again toward the cattle pen, where she could see Ben from the hip up as he walked along inside in the bunks, pouring something from the buckets he carried.

The cattle were jostling each other to get close to the feed. Her eyes narrowed as she noticed they were steering clear of the big bull, Billy. Through the rails of the fence, she could see slices of his large black profile. The bull's massive head was lowered. One cloven hoof was digging into the dirt, throwing clods of it over his shoulder.

Rachel's breath caught in her throat as she turned to fully face the pen. A *rrumph, rrumph* bellow rumbled to her through the quiet summer morning. Openmouthed, Rachel's horrified gaze swiveled to where Ben had just climbed down from the last bunk and turned toward the barn, the empty pails swinging from his hands.

Frozen, Rachel watched the bull sprint across the pen. She willed herself to shout a warning, but no sound escaped her throat.

But something had alerted Ben. Turning at the last moment, he threw the pails toward the charging bull, giving him a second to try to dodge from its path. With a toss of Billy's colossal head, the pails went flying over his broad back. He struck Ben a second later.

Ben's hat sailed in one direction while he went flying in another. When he disappeared from her view, Rachel found her voice. She screamed so harshly, her throat was instantly raw. Rooted there in the garden, she kept screaming. Numb fingers dropped her apron. Vegetables scattered around her as she raised her hands to cup her face and scream, her horrified gaze locked on the pen. Through the space between the two lower boards of the fence, she saw a glimpse of Ben. He was belly-crawling toward the bunks along the side of the pen. Black-and-white legs milled around him as the steers tried to scatter from the wheeling bull.

Rachel's heartbeat pounded in her ears when she caught a flash of Ben's blue pants as he struggled to roll under the bunks amidst the churning feet. She shrieked anew when the bull slammed into the bunk. Unfazed, the huge Holstein rammed it again with his head. The sharp crack of splintering wood cut through the air.

A black blur flew into her peripheral vision. Gasping through her burning throat at the fear it might be one of the other bulls, Rachel swiveled in its direction. Gravel flew as their neighbor's rig raced up the lane. Jethro Weaver launched himself from the buggy while it was still rolling. Yelling at the top of his lungs, he sprinted toward the fence. Whipping off his flat-brimmed hat, he threw it at Billy. With an ominous bellow, the animal turned in his direction. Jethro scrambled up the fence, continuing to yell at the big Holstein. Snagging a heavy stick leaning against a post, Jethro waved it at the bull. Shaking his massive head, Billy snorted. A few tense moments later, he lunged toward the shouting man. Keeping up his verbal onslaught, Jethro held his ground. With a final bawl, the bull veered off and trotted hostilely to the center of the pen.

Keeping his eye on the agitated animal, Jethro called over his shoulder. "Rachel! Rachel, can you hear m-me?"

"*Ja.*" Rachel's mouth formed the word but she was voiceless. She'd screamed herself to hoarseness. Struggling to find enough saliva to swallow, she tried again, wincing at the pain in her throat as she got sound out. "*Ja.*"

"Can you get in m-my rig? You need to ride d-down t-to the phone shack and call 911." Attention still on the pen in front of him, Jethro was slowly moving his way down the fence toward the bunks.

Only knowing the need for urgency kept Rachel from collapsing into the tilled earth of the garden. Bracing an arm under her stomach, she ran for the untethered buggy. The horse, in its confusion, had headed for the barn. Flinching at the rough gravel under her bare feet, Rachel raced across the driveway toward it. She barely had breath for words as she clambered up the buggy steps. "Is he…?"

"Hurry, Rachel!"

Jethro's tone didn't invite further questions. Seizing the dangling reins, Rachel wheeled the buggy. She gasped as, from her perch, she spied Ben's motionless figure sprawled under a bunk. With a slap of the reins, the horse lurched down the lane. Careening onto the road, they raced the mile to the nearest phone shack.

Tumbling out of the buggy, Rachel barely caught herself when her feet hit the ground. She hadn't allowed herself to think during the frantic drive, just kept urging Jethro's Standardbred faster. She didn't stop to tie him. The horse's head was lowered as he panted for air, his bay coat flecked with lather.

Throwing open the shack's door with a bang, she stumbled inside. Her fingers trembled as she punched the emergency number. With an equally shaky voice, she relayed what she knew of the situation to the calm dispatcher.

Following the call, it took Rachel two attempts to get the handset back into its cradle. Once it rattled into place, she sagged against the bare wood wall of the shack. She'd told them what she knew, but what she didn't know was the status of her husband. Or if she still had one. They might rush out to find it was too late. She might be too late. *Oh, Ben, please let me have a chance to tell you how* wunderbar *a husband you've been, and what a* wunderbar *father I know you'll be.* Cradling her rounded belly, Rachel slid the rest of the way to the linoleum-covered floor.

Was he still alive? Please, please, *Gott*, let it be so. Tears flowed down her cheeks to drip onto her collarless dress. Her eyes squeezed tight at the memory of the shock, followed by wonder and joy in his face when he'd heard they were going to be parents of twins. Wonder and joy she'd shared. Quiet, endless support she'd known he'd give. Please, *Gott*...

The steady *clip-clop* of hooves gained in volume as someone passed by on the road. Sniffing, Rachel wiped her face on the sleeve of her dress and pushed to her feet. She wasn't doing any good here. Jethro might need her help. Ben—if he was alive—would need her. On shaky legs, she exited the phone shack. Jethro's horse, head up but still blowing slightly, eyed her warily.

"It's okay," she murmured, patting his sweaty side as she hurried past to the buggy. Please, *Gott*, let it be okay. Climbing onto the seat, she swung back onto the road. At a slightly less frantic speed, she drove back toward the farm.

The wail of a siren came up behind her. Rachel closed her eyes with a sigh of relief. Guiding the horse to the edge of the road, she pressed her lips together to keep from crying anew as a truck with a blue light flashing on its dash raced by. Recognizing Gabe Bartel's vehicle, she urged the horse to a faster speed. Turning into the lane, she slumped on the seat at the sight of Billy grazing placidly in the pasture with the steers. Somehow, Jethro had gotten him out of the pen. At least now they could safely reach Benjamin. But what would they find when they did?

Even burdened with the bags he carried, Gabe was scurrying up the rails of the fence when she drew the horse to a stop. Jethro waved him to where he stood by the bunk. Setting the buggy's brake, Rachel dropped the reins and scrambled down from the seat. Pressing a palm to the hitch in her side, she hurried over to where the bunks lined the fence. Kneeling, she peered between the first and second rails to see underneath the weatherworn wood of the feed bunks.

Ben lay motionless. His head was turned away from her.

"Is he…" She drew in a ragged breath, unable to finish.

At her voice, Ben groaned and slowly swiveled his face toward her. Rachel's heart ached as he obviously tried to give her a smile, any hint of dimple hidden in the smeared dirt on his cheek. She burst into tears at seeing him alive.

"Like… I…told…you…" There was no air behind his wheezing voice. He grimaced before continuing. "Don't…ever turn…your back…on a bull."

"That's good advice. Advice you should've taken." Gabe was working from Ben's other side. "Now for my advice. Let's not move until we have a better idea of what we're dealing with here." He ducked his head below the bunk to glance at Rachel. "The ambulance is on its way. Ben the bullfighter here needs some X-rays so we can determine the extent of internal injuries."

Rachel's eyes widened. Sniffing back her tears, she rubbed her wrist under her nose.

Watching her face through pain-hazed eyes, Ben flinched as he inhaled. "I don't…think…"

"Yeah, you're not thinking if you don't let us take you in. You need to be up and around to help her with those babies in a few months. For all I know, you hit your head. You're not in the best position to decide. So we'll consult the next of kin." Gabe glanced up from the gauge he was monitoring to meet Rachel's eyes. "Rachel?"

Her gaze traveled over Ben's white face and down the dirt-smeared shirt and pants of his sprawled and motionless body. One suspender strap dangled over his shoulder, its clasp broken. Swallowing, Rachel nodded. "I'll go down to the end of the lane and wave them in."

Shifting from her knees to rock back on her feet, she used the rails of the fence to leverage up to a standing position.

She paused at the sound of Ben's feeble voice. "Don't…hurt… Billy. Bloodlines…too *gut*." Glancing over the bunk, she saw Jethro's lips thin as he shook his head.

Keeping a hand on the top rail, Rachel walked several yards down the fence until she felt steady enough to leave its support and cross to the driveway. Her eyes were focused on the sleek mostly black monster unconcernedly grazing in the pasture. For a moment, he became blurry as her face contorted and her eyes filled with tears. At the faint whine of a siren, she turned her head toward the road and hurried down to the end of the lane.

Chapter Eleven

Rachel rose from her chair when she saw the white lab-coated woman come through the gray swinging doors. Ben's *daed* leaped up, as well. Although they stayed seated, her *mamm* and Ben's dropped their knitting into their laps. Other members of the community who'd been trickling into the designated waiting room over the last hour halted their quiet conversations as they all turned toward the doors.

The gray-haired woman smiled at them. "You're here for Mr. Raber?" After their varying nods, she made eye contact with Rachel and motioned her closer. "Rachel Raber?" When Rachel hastened forward, the doctor continued in a lower voice, "Your husband is a very fortunate man. He has some broken ribs and a number of cracked ones. Although slightly bruised, his organs appear all right. Luckily, although there're some jagged edges, none of the fractures punctured a lung. He also has a badly sprained ankle, but considering he was outweighed more than ten to one, it could've been so much worse. Just to be on the safe side, we're going to keep him overnight to monitor his organs and lungs. He'll be restricted in some movements for several days, and will be limited to lifting only a few pounds for several weeks, but should make a full recovery."

Clasping her hand to her mouth, Rachel closed her eyes and sagged against the wall. *Denki, Gott! Denki* that it was His will that Ben would live. Whether because of the coming *boppeli* or something else, she cared deeply for Ben. Was it love? It didn't matter. What mattered was that she now had a chance to find out.

She hadn't seen Ben since she'd watched with quaking limbs as the ambulance team braced his neck and carefully loaded him on a backboard for the trip to Portage. Gabe Bartel had given her a lift to her *mamm*'s house and had then taken them both to the hospital. When they'd arrived, Ben was nowhere to be found. Gabe, familiar with the facility and personnel, discovered Ben was being x-rayed. Rachel and Susannah had sat down to wait, joined shortly by Ben's parents, Elmer and Mary Raber.

"May I see him?"

"Absolutely," the older woman assured her, "he's been asking for you."

Rachel followed the doctor down the hall, her shoes squeaking on the shiny tile floor. When the doctor smiled and pushed open a wide door, pointing a thumb in its direction before heading on down the hall, Rachel peeked into the room. Her gaze immediately locked with Ben's. When he saw her, he shifted upright in the inclined hospital bed. He abruptly froze, his face going as white as the pillow supporting his dark-haired head. Rachel winced in sympathy before cautiously stepping into the room.

"Are you all right?" Focused on the unnatural beeps and hisses of the medical equipment, Rachel almost jumped at his quiet question.

She stopped along the raised silver rail that extended the length of the bed. "Am *I* all right? You're the one who was tossed like a doll by a bull."

He grimaced, then his face went slack as if he were concentrating before a dimple came into play along with a half smile. "Surely I looked more manly than that."

The tanned V of his neck, now displayed by the loose neck of his hospital gown, was in sharp contrast to the pale skin surrounding it. One of his always-capable arms was connected by tubes to a tall silver pole, a clear bag half-full of liquid suspended from its top. Another device was on a nearby pole, revealing lines and numbers in green. Without his always-present work shirt and suspenders, she barely recognized her husband.

"Well, your hat went one way and you went the other. Then I couldn't see you…" Rachel compressed her lips as her chin started to quiver. She squeezed her eyes tight against the prickling that threatened the backs of them. She didn't want to be a blubbery mess in front of him.

She opened her eyes at an abbreviated sigh from the direction of the bed. "I was afraid of that. That hat was just getting to be a perfect fit. I suppose there's no salvaging it?"

Sniffing, Rachel shook her head.

"Come here." Ben started to raise his arm before instantly stopping with an inhaled hiss. Rachel reached a hand through the rail of the bed and clasped his fingers where they'd returned to rest on the beige blanket. Rotating his wrist to grasp her hand more fully, Ben returned the pressure. "I don't suppose this helps the way you feel about cattle."

Rachel snorted through her tears. "*Nee*. It doesn't help at all."

"Understandable." His lips twisted. "I suppose that means you won't be doing the cattle chores while I'm laid up for a few days?"

Tears were forgotten as her jaw dropped open. When she tried to jerk her hand back, he gently tightened his grip, keeping her fingers trapped.

"How could you think—" She paused at the sight of his smile.

"Stopped you from crying."

She sniffed again. "It isn't funny."

"I know." Releasing her fingers to carefully touch his side, he closed his eyes and sighed. "*Gut* thing, as I'm thinking it'll be a bit before I find the courage to try laughing."

Ben cautiously shifted his position on the bed. Rachel watched his face as flickers of reaction swept over it. He settled into place with a frown and lowered brow. He must be in terrible pain to reveal anything at all. Again, she sent up a silent prayer of thanks to *Gott* that, according to the doctor, Ben would make a full recovery. That time currently seemed far into the future.

"Your *daed* and *mamm* are here, along with several others. Your *daed* has already spoken with the bishop. He said not to worry about the bills. The church will figure out some way to pay for it."

Ben's frown deepened.

Rachel tried not to take pleasure in her next words. "And it'll probably be more than a few days before you're taking care of the cattle. The doctor said you'll be restricted for several days and won't be able to lift anything more than a few pounds for several weeks."

His eyes still closed, Ben grimaced more at this news than the physical pain when he'd moved abruptly. "She say when I'd be able to come home?"

"*Nee*. Not exactly. Only that they were keeping you overnight for observation."

Ben's eyes finally opened. "I doubt I'll be doing anything interesting enough that they'll find it worthwhile observing."

Rachel smiled at his feeble joke as he'd intended. "Do you want me to stay?"

After a quick glance around the sterile hospital room with its one stiff-looking chair, Ben frowned as he looked back at her. "*Nee*, I'd feel better if you went home. It'll be a more comfortable night for you there."

Focusing on keeping the hurt from her face, Rachel nodded slowly. He didn't want her there. He figured he'd be better without her. And why not, they didn't share a room at home. Their relationship was such that the overnight proximity would be both mentally and physically awkward. Dry-mouthed at the rejection, she forced a swallow. "I'll see you tomorrow morning then?"

"*Ja*. Hopefully with the doctor's permission to bring me home soon after. Will you be all right by yourself at the farm?"

"Of course." She shrugged half-heartedly. "I grew up on a farm. There were surely a few times I wouldn't have minded having the place to myself in order to have some peace and quiet. Besides, it's like a night off, as I don't have to fix you supper." Her joke must've been more feeble than his, as there was no ensuing lift of his lips.

"*Gut*. Hopefully you can get some rest. I'll see you tomorrow." There was a thread of gentleness in Ben's solemn voice as he held her gaze. Still, Rachel couldn't help but feel dismissed. With a jerky nod, she hurried out of the room. Entering the sterile corridor, her steps slowed when she saw the gathering of Amish community members in the waiting room. She hadn't asked Ben if he wanted more company. But she wasn't going back in there now. Resolutely, she headed for the expectant group. If he didn't want them, he'd have to turn them away himself. Just as he had her.

Ben's gaze was fastened on Rachel's straight back and the dangling ribbons of her *kapp* as they disappeared around the closing door. Shutting his eyes, he dropped his head back against the pillow. His face twisted in pain. Not the physical pain that stabbed through his body at any unwary move. That could be abated by the painkillers he suspected were dripping through tubes into his system. This ache was excruciating and would be harder to diminish. The hurt he'd seen in her face. The tears she'd shed. He'd caused them. Regardless if they were for him, or because of him, the fact he'd brought her distress pained him.

He shook his head against the pillow, about the only thing he could move right now without being jolted with breath-stealing reminders of why he was there. Despite his intent, he'd taken his wife's greatest fear and exacerbated it. Would she even want to stay on the farm? With his growing family, could he afford the higher rent if they had to move somewhere else or he no longer did chores for Isaiah?

Even if he could leave the hospital tomorrow—his aching chest clenched at the thought they wouldn't let him go—given the tightness of the skin he felt around his ankle and the twang of pain generating there whenever the sheets bumped his foot, he wouldn't be on his feet for a few more days.

The door swung inward. Opening his eyes, Ben eagerly lifted his head. Was Rachel returning? Had she determined to stay with him? At the sight of the white lab coat, he dropped his head back against the pillow.

The doctor quickly scanned the room. Her eyebrows rose. "Has your wife gone already? I thought she'd stay longer, as frantic as you were to see her."

Ben didn't have a reply.

"Well, can I trust you to follow instructions, or do we need her back here to ensure that you do?"

It depended what the instructions were. Ben forced a weak smile. "We're good."

The physician eyed him dubiously, gauging his sincerity before she began. "We don't wrap ribs anymore. We found it counterproductive. Although it might be uncomfortable, it's important to take occasional deep breaths and cough once in a while to prevent pneumonia. You'll have some whoppers of bruises. Most help we can offer on that is some pain medication and to recommend icing the area for a while." She frowned. "Do you have access to ice?" At his token nod, she continued, "You'll need to take it easy for several weeks. Be cautious on how much you lift in that time. Nothing very heavy."

"I don't want pain medication."

"I appreciate your concern, but we need to manage your pain enough that you can take deep breaths and cough occasionally. Not fully inflating your lungs is detrimental to their far ends. The blow you took probably bruised your lungs, which puts you at even higher risk of developing pneumonia, as the lung itself is injured. It might be painful at first, but I recommend you walk around the house several times a day if you can."

The information hit Ben harder than the bull had. "Around the house? I have work to do outside."

The doctor shook her head. "I wouldn't suggest it for the next four weeks at least. It usually will take six to eight weeks for a bone to heal."

"I can't." Ben shook his head at the absurd possibility.

"You can, unless you want worse problems." The

physician pinned him with a pointed gaze over her glasses.

Ben closed his eyes as frustration swamped him. He'd always been the one who took care of things. Now he'd be a burden instead. How was he supposed to do cattle chores twice daily, along with anything else the animals might need? How was he supposed to do his work at Schrock Brothers' Furniture? How was he supposed to assist his wife and the ever-increasing burden she carried? Unthinking, he shifted in bed, hissing in a breath as he stiffened in shock at the pain that shot through him. His fingers curled around the smooth cool rails of the bed. Just the thought of trying to roll over made him sweat.

He opened his eyes to the doctor's sympathetic gaze. "We want to get you whole and back in business as soon as possible too, but you need to follow instructions to make it happen. I'll check back with you tomorrow morning and we can hopefully let you go then. Do you have any questions?"

Ben shook his head wearily. None the doctor could answer.

With a commiserating nod, the woman exited. Beads of perspiration dotted Ben's forehead in the air-conditioned room. Not only might he not be able to take care of his own financial responsibilities, the hospital stay made him a financial burden for others. The Amish didn't carry health insurance. The community had always taken care of its members when they were in need, somehow raising funds to cover costs. They'd only just recently paid off hospital bills from the bishop's heart attack episode earlier in the year. Ben had always been on the giving end. He didn't know if he could handle being on the receiving one.

How could his wife care for him if he failed in every way of taking care of her?

With a scowl, Ben pushed against the cane to lever out of his chair. He felt like a *grossdaddi*. Worse than one. Because if he was old enough to be *en alder*, he probably wouldn't be watching fretfully as his very expectant wife went out to hoe the garden, or wince when she bent over to pick the green beans, or hold his breath as she harnessed the horse. He should be doing work for her, not causing her extra work. Shuffling to the window, he looked out to where Jethro was feeding the cattle. And that was another thing. Jethro had enough to do at his own place. Having folks do things for him when he should be doing them in reverse pained Ben more than his sore ribs. He should be paying Jethro the discount he was receiving for rent for the work he'd been doing these past few days since the incident.

Hands braced on the edge of the sink, Ben wedged himself higher so he could see over the rise of the hill in the pasture. There, grazing contentedly, was Billy. Even though the bull had hurt him, Ben was glad Isaiah Zook had been convinced not to sell the animal. Ben didn't want anyone else to be hurt, but he'd have felt worse if his carelessness in turning his back on the animal would've deprived Isaiah of good bloodlines to improve his dairy herd. But he understood Isaiah's dilemma. People had been killed before by rogue dairy bulls. It was frequently a one-and-done offense. The bull would be sold as he might be likely to do it again.

It was decided that Billy, until he was needed to sire cows, would be a fixture in the pasture and not in the pen with humans and the more docile steers. The two younger, smaller bulls kept him company.

Before climbing into his rig to drive down the lane, Jethro waved a farewell to Rachel, who stood leaning against her hoe in the garden. Ben turned from the window in frustration. His elbow banged against the plastic pail on the counter, shifting the five-gallon bucket closer to the edge. Jerking up a hand to catch it, Ben hissed in response to the pain that flared in his chest at the action, his fingers curling over the rim of the bucket.

When the pain ebbed, Ben stared at the bucket's contents. Extending one of the fingers curled over the pail's rim, he flicked the end of one of the green beans Rachel had picked earlier in the day that filled the bucket. His gaze shifted down the counter to the collection of clear quart jars, waiting to be sanitized and filled tomorrow when Rachel put up the beans.

Beans that weren't yet snapped.

Ben's eyes narrowed as he regarded the full bucket of green beans. His chest and foot might be bunged up, but his fingers still worked. Eyeing the pail, he gauged its weight. Too heavy for him to move. He snorted with disgust at his limitation in doing something he wouldn't have thought a moment about before. And the way his ankle was already starting to ache, he wouldn't even be able to stand up for long.

Glancing about the kitchen and living area for inspiration, his gaze landed on a tall stool. One that, to his apprehension, Rachel climbed to reach infrequently used items in the upper cupboards. If he could nudge it along the counter closer to the pail without twinging his ribs, it was tall enough that he could sit on it. It wasn't much, but at least snapping beans, he'd be of some use to someone.

Shuffling down the counter, Ben leaned to grab the stool's seat and immediately froze in place as his torso complained. Loudly. Resting his hands on the counter, he panted as he hooked a leg of the stool with the foot that had the bum ankle and tried to tug it toward him. He was glad Rachel wasn't in the house to hear the squeak he emitted at the flash of white-hot pain. Grimacing, he reevaluated the situation.

Working his way back down the counter, he snagged a large bowl from the dish drainer, along with a smaller one. Setting them on the counter in front of the stool, Ben limped back to the pail. Elbows protectively tight against his chest, teeth gritted in preparation of rogue pain spikes, he used both hands to carefully tip the bucket so green beans spilled over the counter toward the bowls. As he returned to the stool, Ben swiped more beans in that direction. With a sigh, he eased himself onto the stool and went to work, the *snap, snap, snap* of fresh green beans echoed about the otherwise empty kitchen while he watched his expectant wife work in the garden.

* * *

That was where Rachel found him when, hot, sweaty and with her back and hips aching more than she wanted to admit, she entered the kitchen. Her gaze shifted in amazement from the bowls and bowls of evenly snapped beans to the empty bucket sitting on the floor next to the door.

She slumped a hip against the doorjamb. "How?"

Ben rubbed his fingers together. "Billy didn't get ahold of these." He pointed farther down the countertop. "I saw you heading this way. There's a glass of lemonade for you by the refrigerator." Eyes on her face, he frowned. "You're flushed. You need to sit down."

Rachel nodded toward the sink, where the lunch dishes were now stacked haphazardly in the drainer. "What about you?"

"I've been sitting. And sitting. And sitting." Quickly masking a grimace, Ben levered off the chair. "So why don't you sit for a minute with your drink. I don't promise that it'll be much more than just edible, but I'll find us something to eat for supper." He grinned, his dimples making a brief appearance. "It just won't be green beans. I'm tired of looking at them."

Rachel picked up the glass before gratefully sinking into the chair at the table. Taking a deep drink of lemonade, she raised her eyebrows at the tartness of it—Ben had a heavy hand with the powdered mix—but the taste was perfect for how hot and tired she was. Sighing in contentment, she scanned the cluttered countertop. It looked like he'd used every bowl in the kitchen to contain the snapped beans. Rachel didn't care. She'd been dreading spending the evening snapping beans. A task that needed to be done, but not one she cared for. She'd much rather pod peas. Actually tonight, she'd much rather sit and do nothing. Or just hand sew the little outfits she'd been making for the babies. And now she could.

Taking another sip, she studied Ben's back, broad between the bands of his suspenders and his lean, corded forearms, the dark tan of them sharply contrasting with the rolled up sleeves of his white shirt as he pulled a carton of eggs from the refrigerator. His brother, Aaron, might have frequently filled her ears and soul with sweet words, but right now, Rachel couldn't think of anything sweeter or more satisfying for her body and soul than what her husband had just done for her.

Chapter Twelve

"It pains me to watch you walk across the room, so I can't imagine how you're feeling." Ben's eyes were worried when Rachel glanced over at his comment.

She shifted her unconscious grimace into a weak smile. "Well," she pressed one hand against what seemed the constant ache in her back and hips and the other under her greatly rounded midsection, "I must admit, it pains me too."

"Why don't you sit down?" Ben patted the chair he was passing. "How long before…they arrive?"

"They'll come when they're ready. But the midwife says that twins usually arrive three weeks or so before single babies. It's September so maybe in another few weeks?" Her tentative glance met his.

Ben's eyes widened. He looked down at her stomach, then back to meet her gaze. Rachel knew what he was thinking. She was thinking the same thing. How much bigger would she get before the babies came? How much bigger *could* she?

"Do you—" he swallowed "—do you regret not doing the pictures and procedures like the *Englisch* people do?"

Stifling a groan as she shifted position, Rachel twisted her hands together. "It's not our way. I don't care whether they're boys or girls, but—" she started to inhale deeply, flinching when she was reminded it wasn't possible to do so anymore. "I'd like to know how they're doing. To know they're…all right." Her voice ended as breathless as she felt.

"I know. But whatever happens, it's *Gott*'s will." Ben quietly echoed her thoughts.

Rachel steered her mind away from what wasn't hers to control. "And I can't sit. There's too much to do."

"I can help."

"*Nee*. When? You returned to work weeks ago, probably sooner than you should've. Now that the doctor reluctantly cleared you to feed the cattle after six weeks, with that and all the other livestock chores you persuaded Jethro to leave for you." She shook her head. "You won't have time for much more."

"You need some help. We'll need to hire a helper after the babies are born anyway. How about hiring one now?"

Rachel blinked at the possibility. Employing a hired girl after a baby's arrival was common practice in the Amish community. Rachel didn't know about having one come before the child was born, but the way her hips and back constantly bothered her and the sleep she wasn't getting at night was beginning to wear on her. She shuffled over to the chair Ben had indicated earlier and sank down into it.

"Who would you suggest?"

Ben sat down in his chair as he pondered the question. "Your *schweschder*?"

Rachel shook her head. "Rebecca likes her job at the restaurant. She's worked there for years. I couldn't ask her to quit to help me for a short time and risk not getting her job back."

"*Ach*, the same with mine. With two of us in the family recently gone—" Rachel shared his wince at the words, knowing he was referring to Aaron "—they're needed at home, at least until winter."

They sat in silence. Rachel figured Ben, like her, was trying to think of available young women in the community.

Ben straightened in his chair. "Jacob mentioned at work that his sister was looking for a job. Perhaps…"

"I don't think so."

Ben grinned at her quick denial and flat tone. "No?" Rachel could see his dimples flash. She raised her eyebrows at him so he knew she didn't appreciate his teasing.

"No," she reiterated empathically.

"Why ever not, I wonder." Folding his hands together, Ben thoughtfully considered the ceiling.

Rachel snorted. "I'd rather do everything myself before and after the *boppeli* are born than have Lydia Troyer in my house." Just the thought made her want to shudder. "Besides, do you want everyone in the district to know what goes on in our house?"

Ben was still smiling when he glanced back at her. "I'm sure someone will come to mind before we have to resort to certain considerations. But as far as gossip, it's not like we're really that interesting…" His voice trailed off as his gaze touched on their separate bedroom doors. "I suppose not."

Rachel's attention rested on the wooden doors as well. What would happen after the *boppeli* were born? Would she and Ben continue to stay in separate rooms? Shifting in her seat, she carefully avoided looking at him as she felt her cheeks warm. Now, the way she constantly twisted and turned in a futile attempt to find a comfortable position for the night, she'd keep anyone else in the room awake, as well. But after the *boppeli* arrived… Rachel flushed further as she realized she wouldn't mind sharing a bedroom with her husband. The two rooms, an embarrassing and adamant necessity when they'd moved in immediately after their awkward wedding, now didn't seem quite as necessary. Needing to do something with her hands, Rachel picked up the dark blue cloth on the petite table next to her chair and searched it until she located her sewing needle.

"Probably a *gut* thing about Lydia."

Frowning at the mention of the woman's name and the memories it stirred, Rachel looked over in question at Ben's overly casual remark.

"As Jacob said the job she's looking for is in Pennsylvania."

Rachel sat forward abruptly, or tried to with the burden of her stomach. "What?"

"Going there to live with a cousin. Seems she thinks the opportunities might be more plentiful there."

Rachel's lips twisted, although they were on their way to a smile. "The opportunities to chase men, you mean."

"Think I ought to warn them?" Ben picked up the paper from the small table beside his chair. "I could run an advertisement in *The Budget*. Sort of like a public service announcement."

Her chuckle expanded to a laugh, followed by a groan when she couldn't find enough air to support her giggles. "*Nee*. She might be just what someone is looking for."

"That's a frightening thought. Even to inflict on Pennsylvanians."

Rachel giggled some more, her hands bouncing on her rounded belly. When she regained composure, she mused, "I hope for even Lydia to find her chosen one. She wants a husband very much."

Ben met her smiling gaze. "Well, we don't always get what we want." If the room weren't so quiet, she wouldn't have heard his following words as he lifted the paper and turned his attention to it. "Although sometimes it's possible."

Rachel continued to study him, her smile softening. Although she certainly hadn't thought it at the time, she was realizing more and more that Ben was surely *Gott*'s chosen one for her. She was sure she'd been in love with Aaron. But Ben just grew on you over time. Her hands on her stomach shifted to identify a knee here, an elbow over there. Kind of like her little passengers. Who would soon be arriving.

Refocusing on potential hired girls, Rachel considered the young women in the community. But any that came to mind either had jobs, were needed at home or were perhaps too young. Which was quite young indeed, as many Amish girls in large families were already well accustomed to taking care of younger siblings and household chores at an early age.

Ben's sigh drifted to her as she picked up her sewing. He was apparently running into the same roadblock. With his work-roughened hand, he began stroking his short beard. Rachel hid a smile at the sight. After all these months, he still didn't seem used to its presence. But, seeing his eyes narrow as he stared at the wall, perhaps the action was thought-provoking.

"Gideon Schrock mentioned wanting to get one of his sisters up to Wisconsin. He's been living at the farm with Samuel and Gail since they were married, but Gideon figures when they start growing their family, they'll want the place to themselves. He's not opposed to moving out, but not if he has to fix his own meals and take care of housework." Ben grinned. "Apparently, he and Samuel weren't too successful at that before. But if a sister moved up, they could share a place."

Rachel paused in the middle of a stitch. She liked the Schrock brothers, who'd moved into the area a few years back when Malachi Schrock had purchased the furniture business where Ben worked. If the sister was anything like her brothers, Rachel figured they could deal pretty well together.

"Weren't they from Ohio? Do you think she'd move that far from home to come up here?"

"I don't know. I'll ask Gideon or Malachi. From what he said, I know Gideon would be all for it. Do you think she'll be able to care for two *boppeli*?"

Wrinkling her nose, Rachel resumed her sewing. "I don't know how well I'll be able to care for two *boppeli* and I'm going to be their *mamm*."

"I think you'll be a *wunderbar mamm* to them."

Rachel flushed under his warm regard. Her husband may not say sweet words to her very frequently, but when he did, she knew they were heartfelt and all the more precious. Her gaze darted about the picked-up living area, cleaning that she hadn't done. Another thing he just quietly did for her. Ben's kind words might be the frosting on the cake of all she was discovering he did for her. And, to Rachel's surprise, she was discovering, between the two, she'd rather have the cake.

Rachel's heavy sigh echoed across the quiet room. Ben looked up from reviewing local livestock sales listed in The *Budget*. Someday, when they had their own place, he'd liked to get a few cattle. If his wife could tolerate them. "What's wrong?"

"I left my scissors in the bedroom." Shifting awkwardly, she placed her hands on the edge of the chair to lever herself up.

Ben was relieved the twinge that stung his chest when he bounded out of his seat was minimal. "You stay put. I'll get it."

"*Denki,*" she murmured gratefully as she sank back into her chair with a soft smile.

"Where am I looking?" Ben called over his shoulder as he headed for her bedroom.

"I was working the other night when I couldn't sleep. Should be somewhere on the stand by the bed? Maybe in the drawer?"

When he lit the lamp on the nightstand, the only other items on the otherwise neat surface were a spool of thread and a half-finished outfit, similar to the one she was currently working on in the other room. Ben smiled. Rachel had started two, reasoning that, with twins, many outfits would need to be completed. Having projects in both rooms saved walking back and forth if she happened to carefully settle where one wasn't within reach. Lifting the dark blue fabric to confirm the scissors weren't hidden underneath, Ben marveled at its miniature size, at the wonder that it could soon hold his son or daughter. He was flooded with emotions he wasn't yet ready to share with his wife. Tempted, as things had been so *gut* between them lately, but not yet ready.

Closing his eyes, he brought the tiny garment to his chest and pressed it against his heart. *Gott, denki for this dream I never figured could be realized. The chance to love this woman. To raise a family with her. Although I feared at first, I believe that we can make it. That in time our marriage can thrive and not just exist.* His fingers tightened around the garment. *That these will be the first of many children. Help me to be the husband and* daed *I need to be.*

Raising the fabric to his face, he pressed his lips to it before carefully setting it down. Not finding the scissors on top of the nightstand, he tugged on the nob of the simple single drawer below. It slid out easily, revealing the scissors and a few spools of thread. Relieved at the discovery, Ben picked them up and started to slide the drawer shut. He froze when he saw what lay beneath the scissors.

Inside the drawer, its few contents neat like the surface of the stand, was an envelope. Instantly recognizing the handwriting that scrawled Rachel Mast across the front of it, Ben's breath had locked in his throat. As brothers sharing a desk at school, they used to tease each other. Aaron had liked to write as much as Ben hadn't. Sometimes he would write Ben's homework for him in exchange for Ben doing chores. Until the teacher noted Aaron's handwriting, as Ben did now.

After a moment, his eyes shifted to the empty white corner. No return address.

His *bruder* had written his wife. And she hadn't said anything about it.

Unconsciously straightening, Ben put a few more inches between him and the drawer, his eyes still fixed on its contents. When had the letter been sent? The postmark was smudged. Had she brought it over when they'd moved? It was addressed to her family's farm. It could be an old communication. Aaron was good about that. Writing letters. Saying sweet things. They'd had a long romance. Aaron could've sent several letters and she'd only kept this one. That was history.

But still, she'd kept this one.

His heart rate accelerated as his stomach twisted. Things seemed to have been going so well between them lately.

He shouldn't look at it.

But it could be recent. It could reveal where his *bruder* was. What he was doing. Ben reached toward it, his hand pausing an inch away. If it was recent, it could be something he didn't want to see. What could be good about his wife communicating with the man she'd thought she'd marry? What could be good about her keeping secrets from her husband?

Ben jerked his hand back. He swallowed before snorting softly. He'd been less cautious when he'd once encountered a rare Massasauga rattlesnake while clearing brush.

"Did you find it?" He flinched as Rachel's voice floated in from the other room.

"*Ja.*" He responded hoarsely. He'd found it, all right.

He'd rather deal with the snake. Tentatively, as if it was the poisonous reptile, he lifted the envelope and turned it over. It was open. Whatever was in it, Rachel had read it. She knew what it said. His breathing shallow, Ben opened the flap and pulled out the single sheet of paper. Flicking it open, one ear tuned to the door in case Rachel decided to see what was keeping him, he scanned the words. His *bruder* had written so little. Said so much. Folding the paper with a slow exhale, Ben returned it to the envelope.

No word of where his brother was. Only that he was thinking about Ben's wife and regretted hurting her. No word of whether he was coming back. It'd been sent to Rachel's home address. Did he know she was married? Did Aaron know Ben had taken his wife? His life?

Speaking of secrets, didn't Ben have his own? His hand clenched, reminding him of the forgotten scissors when the edges of the blade cut into his palm. Slowly, carefully, he pushed the drawer shut. Rachel was to have been Aaron's wife. Her children should've been Aaron's. He'd stolen his brother's life.

Gott's opinion on coveting was well-known. Ben swallowed as he backed away from the stand. His silent prayer now was quite different. May *Gott* forgive him for what he'd done. Hopefully sooner than he could forgive his wife and himself. As for his brother? If he returned, Ben didn't figure Aaron would ever forgive him.

"*Denki.* You're a tremendous help to me. I'm fortunate to have you." Rachel's words drifted over her shoulder as she worked at the sink.

Ben paused in the action of clearing the supper table to absorb her words. They warmed him like a glowing stove in January, particularly after finding the letter two weeks ago. His lips twisted. When had he become so maudlin? You'd think he was now the one with child, he was so out of balance with emotions.

He watched Rachel shift her position a few times before she plucked another tomato from the sink. Remembering Hannah's words that it would help his pregnant wife to be off her feet, he frowned as he crossed to the counter.

"Are you doing too much so late in your condition?"

He nodded toward the collection of already full jars farther down the counter and the sink full of tomatoes.

Rachel's expression was bland. But Ben knew she'd become quite adept at masking her discomfort over the past several weeks. "It's not work when you like doing it."

"You like doing this?" His tone revealed his surprise.

"Oh, *ja*. It gives me great pleasure to see the shelves filling up with food for the winter. In fact, if Isaiah doesn't mind, I'd like to expand the garden next year."

Ben grunted as he retrieved another paring knife from the drawer and joined her at the sink. She shifted to make room. He reached in the water for a tomato and began to peel. "We might have to buy our own draft horses if I expand it much more."

Rachel grinned. "If we expand, I can add some different vegetables and herbs or plant more of what I did this year so I'd have enough to sell." She looked up at him with such enthusiasm in her face that Ben would've put the horse collar on his own shoulders and tugged the plow across the ground himself just to keep her expression in place.

"Then I can help earn some money. Maybe to get a place of our own sooner?"

"You just want a place where you can put in an even bigger garden. Sounds like it needs at least forty acres of cleared flat ground just for your vegetables. I guess I need to make that a four-horse team and get a cultivator as well as disk and plow."

She giggled.

He shared her smile as he dropped the peeled tomato

into the bowl with the others. It warmed him to be talking about the future with her. Talking and smiling about plans she had. Plans that included him. Reaching into the sink for another tomato, Ben froze when his hand connected with Rachel's grabbing the same bobbing target. She went still, as well. Striving to control his suddenly elevated breathing, he carefully loosened his fingers to seek out another objective. Plucking one, he shook the water from it and began to peel. Plans that included him only because his brother was no longer in the picture.

Ben's hand tightened on the tomato as he recalled the letter. With a squirt of juice, it slipped from his fingers and fell back into the water with a plop. "Sorry," he muttered. Fishing it out again, he scrapped the knife across its surface, peeling off the skin that'd been loosened by the blanching. Who knew when that letter had been sent? Although he'd always been aware of their actions while they were courting, he hadn't been involved in her and Aaron's relationship. They could've had a falling out before and the letter had been sent when Aaron was still living at home.

Since he'd found the letter, he'd given Rachel ample opportunity to mention it. All without mentioning Aaron. He'd dropped associated topics. Discussed letters that'd come in the mail. She'd never said a word. It only made him worry more. Ben thought about his last interaction with Lydia. He would never break his vows. But if Aaron ever came back, would Rachel? Would she meet secretly and intimately with his *bruder*? Would she betray him that way? Would Aaron? Grimly, Ben remembered that he, not Aaron, was the cowbird that came in to steal the nest Rachel had been planning to build with a husband.

But Rachel was now smiling while talking about future plans with him. Surely that meant something?

He slid a sideways glance at her. Tendrils of her hair, damp from the steamy heat of canning, curled about her flushed face. One clung to her cheek. Her hands busy, Ben watched as she tried to blow it free with a puff from pursed lips. Lips he wanted to kiss. But the situation never seemed right and, his stomach churned as the letter and what it might mean had taken root in his mind, she might not want his affection. Ben didn't know what made him feel worse, that she would avoid any overtures he might make, or that she would accept them unwillingly. Either way, he would keep his hands and lips to himself, if not his heart. It was too late for that.

Searching for distraction from his dismal thoughts, he glanced out the window. In the pasture, Billy was wrestling with one of the smaller bulls. Head to head, the big bull easily pushed the lighter one back. With a final lunge, he knocked the other to its knees. Ben stiffened, watching carefully as the smaller bull scrambled to its feet and scampered safely away from the big animal.

Rachel glanced out the window in the direction of his gaze. Ben heard her disturbed sigh when she noticed the bull.

"I wished you hadn't started doing chores again."

"The doctor said my ribs were healed enough to

handle lifting the weight of the pails. Besides, I didn't want to put Jethro out any more than I had already."

Any sign of smiles was gone. Her lips were tight as she dropped her tomato into the bowl and jerked another one from the water. "I liked it better when Isaiah took Billy to his place for a while. I was sorry to see him come back."

Putting his tomato in the bowl, Ben picked up another. "The cows needed him. I'm glad Isaiah didn't sell him. I made a mistake. Billy made a mistake. We're even. I'd feel bad if I'd deprived Isaiah of good genetics when I'm supposed to be the one taking care of the animals."

"The cows might need him, but I need to see him as hamburger. He could've killed you."

Ben's lips twitched, secretly delighted with her concern. "He'd be a lot of hamburger. Almost enough to go with all your canned tomatoes."

To his regret, she didn't smile at his joke. "Speaking of which, I'll need more jars from the basement. I'll go get them if you want to finish these up?"

Putting his finished tomato in the bowl, Ben set down his knife and rinsed his hands by swishing them through the water. "I'll get them. I don't want to think about you going down those steep stairs any more than you have to. Or coming back up with a boxful of jars. Quarts or pints?"

"Quarts. We're a growing family." This time a smile accompanied her words.

He raised his eyebrows. "Not growing that fast. I

hope these keep a few years. I'm thinking the *boppeli* won't be eating tomatoes for a while."

"Okay," she relented. "A mixture of quarts and pints."

He dried his hands on a nearby dish towel. "Why didn't you plan a canning frolic here with some of your friends? I know you've been to a few this summer."

She wrinkled her nose. "Maybe next year. This year, I just wanted to settle into my own kitchen. I know some folks have bigger dreams, but mine was always just to have my own home, sharing it with children and—" She halted abruptly as she stared down at the tomato in her hand. "And taking care of it and them," she finished awkwardly.

Ben strode to the basement door and jerked it open. "I'll get the jars," he tossed over his shoulder. He descended the stairs to the concrete-floored basement, his heart as heavy as his tread, his mind echoing with the word she didn't say. That she was going to say. *My own home, sharing it with children and... Aaron.*

Rachel watched as Ben disappeared through the door to the basement. She'd been so glad she'd caught herself in time. Before she finished with, *and the man I love.* Because she was beginning to think she loved Ben. But she wasn't ready to share that, as he hadn't given any indication he felt the same way.

He'd been quiet lately. Ben was generally quiet, but he'd seemed particularly withdrawn lately. Was he worried about being a *daed*? Dropping the last tomato into the heaping bowl, she bent and leaned an elbow on the edge of the sink. Now that he wasn't watching, she reached to press a hand against the small of her back, which had been aching for some time. Along with her hips, but that was nothing new. They'd been aching for the past month, particularly the past two weeks.

Not only Ben, but the *boppeli* were quieter, as well. What was it with her family recently? They'd been as active lately as Standardbreds coming down the home stretch, but today, their movements were more subdued. Rachel smiled faintly. She could tell them apart. She didn't know who they were yet, or, she grimaced ruefully, what they would be called—another thing she and Ben hadn't talked about—but she could tell who was where. Not only had they not talked of names, but Ben had never felt them move. Other than that first time just after they'd learned there were two when he'd seemed intrigued, he hadn't indicated an interest. Sure, she'd catch his gaze on her in the evenings when she'd exclaim after one of the *boppelis'* particularly rambunctious bouts, but he'd never said a word and, although she'd wanted to share their movements, she was afraid to ask if he was interested. In case he wasn't. In case, although he seemed to be tolerating their marriage, he wasn't really excited about the reason it had come about. At least, not like Rachel was. She couldn't wait to see their little faces. To hold them in her arms. To assure herself they weren't affected by what had taken her two siblings. As another spasm surged across her back, she pressed her hand more forcefully against her spine and bit her lip.

Hearing Ben's step ascending the stairs, Rachel

straightened from her slouch against the sink and smoothed her features. Pulling the sink's plug, she drained the initially cool water where the tomatoes had been transferred after their hot water blanching.

"Find some?" Efficiently cleaning out the sink, she prepared to wash the new jars.

Jars rattled in the cardboard box as Ben carried them over. "You and your *mamm* must've hit every auction this spring and summer to collect so many of these. Did you outbid everyone in the district?"

Glancing over as he set the box down on the counter, Rachel assessed whether he was truly upset. Seeing a welcomed hint of his dimple, she began putting the jars in the rising soapy water. "Only the ones that weren't quick enough. I hope you don't mind. I told *Mamm* I'd share some of the canning so she wouldn't have to put up as much. I used to do it at home as she was busy with the goats and bees. She has a new hired hand now." Rachel frowned as she washed and rinsed a jar and set it upside down in the drainer to dry. "But I don't know that he's working out that well."

She raised her eyebrows when Ben picked up a dish towel and began to dry the jar. "Well, I hope Miriam Schrock works out for us. Gideon said the other day that he was picking her up from the bus station tonight." Setting the dried jar on the table, Ben reached for another one from the drainer. "I think, or at least hope that she was a good choice as a hired girl. If she's anything like Malachi, Samuel and Gideon, I'm sure she'll work out fine. Still, I look forward to getting to know her a bit before the *boppeli* arrive and she moves in."

Under the concealing suds, Rachel clenched her hand around a pint jar as another spasm seared her back. She panted quietly through pursed lips. She was afraid they might not have a chance to even meet Miriam before the *boppeli* arrived.

Chapter Thirteen

"Ben..."

Instantly awake, Ben sat up at the sound of Rachel's voice outside his bedroom door.

"Coming," he called as he swung his feet to the floor. Flicking on the flashlight on his nightstand, he pointed it at the small clock there. It wasn't so much the time that concerned him—shortly after midnight—it was the tone of her voice. The tight, anxious tone. Hastily he donned his clothes and was swinging open the door a moment later.

Her tone—and her face. Rachel's face, its paleness emphasized by the fall of her dark hair that framed it, was tight with pain in the glow of the lamp she held. Garbed in the loose gown above her bare feet, she bit her lip as her wide eyes met Ben's.

When she grasped his hands, he was surprised at the crushing pressure of her fingers. "The midwife?"

She nodded.

Lifting their clasped hands to his lips, Ben kissed

the slender back of his wife's. "I'll be back from the phone booth as fast as I can."

When he would've let go, Rachel clung to his hand. "I want my *mamm*."

Ben hissed in a thoughtful breath. While it was only a mile down to the local phone shack, it was several more miles to Susannah Mast's farm. He didn't want to leave Rachel alone long enough to travel there and back. Opening his mouth to say so, he slowly closed it again at the pleading evident in her dark eyes.

"*Ach*, I already owe Jethro more than I could ever pay. I might as well add this to the list. I'll see if he'll go to your farm and bring your *mamm* here to you. Is that agreeable?"

Grimacing, she hunched over in mid-nod. Wincing himself, Ben helped her back into her bedroom and assisted her onto the bed. "I shouldn't be gone too long. Do you need anything before I go?"

"Just Mrs. Edigers and my *mamm*." As he loosened his arms from about her, Rachel reached up to palm his cheek. "And you."

He was momentarily stunned at the words and the touch of her hand. Once she removed it, Ben nodded so hard he was afraid his head would snap off his neck. Leaving her on the bed, he rushed to the door, only to stop and turn when he reached it. "I'll be right back."

Dashing out the front door, he was halfway down the sidewalk before he quickly retreated to put on his shoes. A short minute later, he was bridling Sojourner before launching himself on the back of the startled mare. At his urging, the confused horse broke into a gallop as soon as they cleared the barn.

"I'll probably never get you back to just trotting with the buggy," Ben muttered into the mane flying into his face as he leaned over her neck. "I can live with that, if you get us there and back double quick tonight." After the breathless moonlight run, he vaulted from Sojourner's back as she slid to a stop in front of the phone shack.

Flinging the shack's door open, he was dialing the phone a second later. Mrs. Edigers's number was taped inside the phone shack, useless in the current darkness of the booth. Fortunately, Ben had the digits memorized from the first time they'd met with the woman. The midwife answered on the second ring.

"The *boppeli* are coming!" Ben didn't identify himself, but either Mrs. Edigers recognized his voice or she'd noted the plural.

"I'll grab some things and contact Hannah."

Ben recalled how restless Rachel had been when he'd come home from work yesterday. Several times over the evening before they'd gone to their separate bedrooms, he caught her absently rubbing her back. He'd seen her struggle through various discomforts in the past months. Her face tonight told him she'd been in pain for quite a while. "I think she's been… I think this has been going on a while."

"Hmm. All right, we'll be there shortly."

At her calm, steady voice, Ben took his first normal breaths since hearing Rachel's tense summons at his bedroom door. Hanging up the phone, he stepped out of the booth. Fortunately, Sojy hadn't wandered off following her wild ride when he'd dropped the reins. Patting her neck, he gathered up the leads and swung onto her back. He turned her in the direction of Jethro Weaver's small farm, another mile farther up the road.

Although it took a moment for his neighbor to come to the door, Jethro immediately swung it wide upon seeing Ben. He began putting on his shoes as Ben explained why he'd burst in on him in the middle of the night. Without further question, Jethro headed to the barn. Mission accomplished, Ben leaped back onto Sojy and sped home.

Trusting the mare wouldn't go any farther than the barn if she wandered, Ben left her at the yard gate and raced into the house. Panting, more from suppressed tension than expended energy, he halted at her partially closed door.

"Rachel?" His intended whisper came out much harsher than intended in his concern.

"Come in." He swung the door open to see her neatly stacking the nightstand with towels, sheets and other paraphernalia. His eyes widened to discover she'd changed into the white birthing gown she'd shyly made in the last few weeks. Her hair was now neatly pinned under a *kapp*.

"Are you all right?"

"*Ja*. Just glad you're back. Is my *mamm* coming?"

"Jethro's on his way there now. The midwife's on her way too." He scrutinized her from the doorway. Although flushed and sweaty with slight anxiety in her eyes, she otherwise appeared calm. "If you'll be okay for the moment, I need to take care of Sojy." At her nod, he turned from the door, only to spin back around at the breathless sound of his name.

"Ben, we're finally going to meet them. I can't believe we'll be parents soon."

Sharing her bemused smile before he ducked out of the doorway, Ben found himself nodding giddily as well as he crossed to the door.

Although he'd only been back in the house a few minutes after tending to the mare, it seemed like forever before Ben heard a car in the drive, alerting him that help had arrived.

He met them at the door. Mrs. Edigers and Hannah Bartel gave him encouraging smiles as they hurried past, laden with equipment. When they disappeared through Rachel's door, he paced the living room, listening for the clatter of hooves on the driveway that would hopefully mean Jethro had been successful in delivering Rachel's mother.

When they arrived thirty minutes later, Ben was out in the yard in time to help Susannah down from the buggy. Her searching look at Ben was seemingly satisfied with his ragged nod. The sight of the midwife's car made her more so.

"Don't go too far," she instructed him as she crossed the porch. "You'll be needed as a catcher. Even more important when there are two."

Both men's gazes followed her into the house. At the click of the door behind her, Ben turned to Jethro. "*Denki*. I can't thank you enough for bringing her."

"Glad t-to help."

"Seems I can't thank you enough, period, Jethro. I don't know what I'd do without you lately."

"It's what neighbors are for." The man brushed off the gratitude. "You'd d-do the same for m-me."

"Whenever I have the chance. Do you want to come in?"

Glancing at the door, Jethro shook his head like inside the house was the last place he wanted to be. "*Nee.* I need t-to get home."

Although he wanted to be with Rachel whenever she might need him, Ben understood the sentiment. "Can I get you anything before you go?"

"*Nee.* I'm *gut.*" Before turning his horse down the lane, Jethro cast another look at the house.

Ben furrowed his brow at the obvious longing in the man's gaze, until he remembered Jethro had lost a wife and unborn child. The realization was a blow to his midsection. Pivoting from the rig already clattering away, he hurried into the house and quietly crossed to Rachel's bedroom door to peek inside.

There was an intense purposefulness in the room. To his relief, the three women appeared calm and confident in their actions. A glance at Rachel's contorted red face however, escalated his concern.

Seeing him hover in the doorway, Mrs. Edigers motioned Ben inside. "Go wash up well with plenty of soap." She swept a gaze over his attire, which Ben knew was soiled from his quick journey and care of Sojourner. "And put on a clean shirt."

Ben hastened to do as instructed, his heart beating so rapidly his fingers fumbling over the fastenings in the transition. Up to this point, the *boppeli* seemed real in an abstract manner as they'd prepared. Rachel had sewn blankets and several sets of clothes for them. He'd made two cradles, mainly while he was laid up from doing other things. Although he'd seen his wife touch her middle with an expression of wonder on her face when she'd felt them move, he hadn't had the courage to ask to feel them himself, and she hadn't offered. The babies' existence had just primarily been the unlikely reason he and Rachel had married.

Now with their imminent arrival, the realization there'd soon be two little ones in the house, depending on him, shook him to the core.

Failing twice to get the clean shirt fastened, Ben held his hands before him, dismayed at their trembling. He, who was steady and sure with detail work in furniture making, in fact was steady and sure in most aspects of his life except being a husband, couldn't fasten a shirt. Whereas Rachel had grown up caring for little ones, how could he handle being a *daed* to not just one but two? Drawing in a shaky breath when he heard Mrs. Edigers call his name, he tackled the task a third time. He was about to find out, whether he was ready or not.

A short time later, Ben held his tiny son. Although he squirmed, the little one didn't make a sound. Mrs. Edigers quickly took the baby from Ben's dazed hands. The midwife's back was turned to Ben when he heard what sounded like the bleat of a baby goat. He looked over Mrs. Edigers's shoulder to see her and Hannah vigorously rubbing the baby with a towel. Ben's heart clinched as he caught the look the midwife shared with

Hannah as they bent over the little one, attending to its immediate needs.

There was trouble. He was too small. They didn't think his son was going to make it.

"I want to see my *boppeli*." Rachel struggled to sit up.

Wrapping the baby in a clean blanket, Mrs. Edigers carried him to the head of the bed. "For a brief moment. We aren't done yet. You've got some more work to do."

If he hadn't loved her already, Ben would've fallen hard as he watched Rachel take their child into her arms and look down at his tiny face with a sense of wonder. Ben dodged the others until he was beside her at the head of the bed. Determining the bustling women in the room were busy with other tasks, Ben leaned down and gently kissed Rachel's hair, visible before the edge of her *kapp*.

He had to tell her. "I love you" he mouthed, knowing he was safe, that Rachel wouldn't see his words as she was focused on their tiny son in her arms.

She looked up, almost catching him. "Do you want to hold him?"

Ben's heart thundered in his chest. After confirming the midwife's approval, he nodded. He couldn't even speak to the affirmative. Silently, Rachel handed their son to him. He felt like reverse gravity, the miniature bundle was so light. It seemed impossible that a son, *his* son, who would someday stand shoulder to shoulder with him, was wrapped up inside.

If *Gott* willed it.

He forced himself not to tighten his arms in protection around his precious bundle, afraid he might accidentally crush his oldest child. This tiny person, who surely weighed no more than the dandelion fluff that blew through the pasture. *Please don't blow through my life that fast. I know whatever happens is* Gott*'s will, but I hope His will is that you grow strong and tall to work beside me.* The *boppeli*'s hands were tucked under his chin, just visible at the top of the blanket. In awe, Ben brushed the newborn skin with the tip of his finger. Tiny fingers with delicate fingernails moved to curl partway around his calloused thumb.

Mrs. Edigers paused beside him to scrutinize his son. The *boppeli* blinked owlishly. "We're getting ready for baby B. Are you going to be okay with him?"

"*Ja*," Ben breathed. "Is it all right if I step outside?"

The midwife nodded. "That's fine." Before she returned her attention to Rachel, she held Ben's gaze in a meaningful exchange. "Call me if you need anything."

Ben tried to nod, but couldn't. With his son in his arms, he stepped out of the bedroom, leaving the door ajar behind him. He was wandering about the living area, introducing his son to everything he could think of, when minutes later, there was no question that the sound now coming from the bedroom was a *boppeli* crying. He turned to see Susannah at the bedroom door.

"You have a *dochder*, as well," she informed him, a gentle smile on her face. "She's *gut*. Healthy. Already loud, as you can hear. And no apparent jaundice on either." The last was said with a heartfelt murmur.

Ben blinked rapidly against the unexpected tears

that filled his eyes. "*Gott* is *gut*. *Denki*. How's Rachel doing?" he asked hoarsely.

"She's been *wunderbar* throughout this."

Ben couldn't agree more.

"She's holding the new little *maedel*. I think she's about ready for some rest though. Do you want me to take him?" She nodded toward the bundle in his arms.

Unconsciously, Ben shifted his shoulders in protection of his son. Susannah smiled with understanding before ducking back into the bedroom.

Glancing down at the tiny figure in his arms, Ben caught his breath when he found his son looking back. He'd heard they couldn't see much at first, but still, the little one's intensity made him wonder. "Did you hear that? You have a little *schweschder*. Although I don't know how she could be littler than you." The miniature mouth opened in a yawn as the translucent eyelids drifted shut.

"That's right. Get your rest. Sounds like you're going to need it to keep up. Would you like to meet her?"

Ben returned to the bedroom. Rachel, propped up on the bed with a bundle duplicate to his in her arms, looked up. She smiled when she saw him. Her face revealed her weariness and remnants of her recent struggles, but to Ben, she'd never looked more lovely. Crossing to her, he carefully hitched a hip on the bed. Perusing his new daughter, he lowered their son so Rachel could see them side by side. Although still petite, and to his eye, even with only her face showing, beautiful like her *mamm,* it was obvious the little girl was bigger.

"You've got some catching up to do," he whispered to his son.

"Oh," Rachel sighed. "They're amazing."

Ben would've agreed, had he not been too choked up to do so.

He cleared the lump in his throat. "Have you thought of names?"

"We never talked about that, did we?"

"We didn't know who there'd be to name. We didn't know if we'd be naming a Fannie and Lavinia, or a Mervin and Iddo."

Smiling down at her new children, Rachel shook her head at his flippant choices. "Elijah and Amelia," she whispered.

Ben considered the two sleeping newborns. "Is that what you want?"

When Rachel looked up at him and nodded, he was lost in her dark brown eyes.

"Then that's who they'll be," he murmured. He straightened from the bed. "Now Eli and I will let you get some rest. We'll see you in a while."

Before he could leave the room, Mrs. Edigers stopped him, relieving him of the baby for what seemed an extended period of time as she reviewed the little one's condition. Her smile was tight as she handed the weightless bundle back. "He seems to be breathing all right, but he's so very small. Do you want to call…" She didn't finish the question but Ben knew what she was saying.

His heart clenched and his stomach twisted as he strove to find the proper response. Amish districts varied in their association with modern medicine. Theirs was slower to adapt in some areas, believing taking extraordinary medical measures to save a life conflicted with *Gott*'s will. But after an incident this past winter, when CPR administered by Hannah had saved the bishop during a heart attack and stents had put him on the road to recovery, some previous views were being reconsidered. Ben longed to do whatever was necessary to save his son, but although he'd subtly mentioned the topic around the community, no one had an answer for him on premature babies. When Mrs. Edigers simply nodded in understanding, Ben knew his confliction was evident on his face.

That's the way it continued the rest of the night. While Rachel slept, Ben sat holding his son, afraid he might never have another chance. He was shaken by the already fierce love he had for his children. Mrs. Edigers and Hannah came to check on them occasionally. Ben would sigh in relief any time Eli stretched or wiggled in his arms. When time ticked by and there was no movement, Ben would unwrap the baby to gently lay a finger on his chest and ensure by the shallow rise and fall of his tiny chest that his little one was still breathing.

Ben tipped his head to rest on the back of his chair. *Whatever happens, it's* Gott*'s will*, he reminded himself through the long hours. His mouth grew dry as he held his fragile son. Although he'd confessed privately to *Gott* and asked His forgiveness about wishing Rachel could be his wife when she had a relationship with his brother, he'd never confessed the sin to one of the district's ministers. Was it too late? Was this his punishment?

As fingers of light sifted through the window, he carefully rose from his seat, tucked an additional blanket around Eli against the coolness of the early fall morning and stepped out on the porch. Crossing to the railing, Ben turned so both of them faced the sun lifting in golden color on the eastern horizon. The calls of rousing birds, including the melancholy coo of a mourning dove, was a fitting accompaniment to the otherwise silence of the awakening morning. Lifting the bundle in his arms, Ben gently kissed the fine dark hairs on his son's miniature head.

After a few moments of quiet companionship, the squeak of the door announced they had company. Susannah stepped onto the porch. She paused a moment when she saw them before coming to join them at the rail.

At her questioning look, Ben's lips tipped in a rueful smile. "I just wanted to share a sunrise with him." With an understanding nod, Susannah stepped closer to peek into the blanketed bundle with a matching expression.

"How are Rachel and… Amelia doing?" It seemed so strange she had a name. It seemed so strange she was finally here. That they both were. He cuddled Eli more tightly. For now at least.

"They're doing well. They're both sleeping. It's been a tiring day, or should I say night, for them."

They watched as the shadows, cast by the rising sun and the big barn, shifted over the yard. When Ben cleared his throat, it seemed abnormally loud in the quiet of the morning. "I know whatever happens is *Gott's* will. But do you think in this case His will is affected by our…actions? Do you think we're being punished for something we did?" The last was spoken with a shaky exhale.

Susannah's gaze dropped to the child in his arms. "Is that what you're worried about?"

Ben dipped his head.

"You've confessed, *ja*?" At his nod, she continued, "If you've confessed to *Gott*, He forgives." She tipped her head in the direction of the rising sun. "See the sunrise, so far to the east you'd never reach it?" Placing a gentle hand on Ben's arm, she urged him to the side of the porch where they could look behind the house where the sky was just starting to lighten over the rolling Wisconsin countryside. "See the sky to the west? Immense distance. Immeasurable. In the *Biewel*, Psalms says as far as the east is from the west." Releasing the grip on his arm, she pointed from one to the other. "That's how far *Gott* separates us from our sins." She shook her head. "You are forgiven. What *Gott* wills in this has naught to do with you."

Ben's shoulders sagged as if the barn across the yard had been lifted from them.

"And however you and Rachel came to be man and wife, I know you'll be *wunderbar* parents to my *kinner*. To both of them. His *schweschder* is sleeping in her cradle. At their size, it's big enough for two. Shall we put them in together? They've been companions for some time. Maybe the contact will do them both *gut*."

"*Ja*. We'll be right in." Ben lingered with Eli a moment longer on the porch, absorbing the awakening morning with a peace that'd been elusive earlier. Reentering the house to join Eli with his sister, Ben affirmed the important bond of siblings. He'd found peace with *Gott*. Now he needed to make peace with his *bruder* if he ever saw him again.

Chapter Fourteen

Rachel watched as Ben laid first Eli, then Amelia, into one cradle. They each had their own, but somehow she knew the twins liked to be together at times. They'd seemed to be getting bigger daily in the week since they'd been born, but they'd both fit in a single cradle for a bit yet. Eli still appeared as delicate as gossamer, but when he could stay awake long enough, she could tell that for him, he was eating like a draft horse after a day in the field. There was no sign of jaundice in either child. When she had a chance to sleep, Rachel slept easier than she had in months.

She was amazed at how adept she and Ben were getting after only a week of handling the *boppeli*, often with both little ones at a time. She was also amazed at how she could function on what little sleep she was getting since the two arrived. Her gaze followed Ben as he sank down with a tired sigh into his chair. He was something else that amazed her. Although always attentive to her personally, after the way he'd seemed detached when she was with child, he certainly wasn't disinterested now. Any time they squeaked, he was on his feet to check them or carry them to her to be fed. She didn't know what other new *daeds* did, but between him and the hired girl, other than the lack of sleep, Rachel had never felt more pampered.

They should never have wondered about Miriam. A little older than the normal hired girl for that type of situation, she was a treasure. Having been the oldest girl of a large family, she set right to work on the household tasks and helped with the babes as needed when she arrived a few days after they did. Blond and blue-eyed like her older *brieder*, she also had the cheerful attitude, along with her siblings' sense of humor that made her good company. At first, Rachel worried Miriam would think the sleeping arrangements in their household were strange for a married couple, but the young woman hadn't said a word nor raised an eyebrow when Ben and Rachel went to their separate bedrooms at night.

Rachel was the one wondering about the arrangements. Her eyes would follow her husband when he'd say a quiet good-night at the end of the evening, drop a gentle kiss on the babes' downy heads and disappear into his room.

He never kissed *her* good-night.

Picking up her sewing, Rachel pursed her lips. She was surprised at how much she wanted him to. When would he? Would he, ever? When did the thought of a simple kiss on the forehead from her husband move her more than good-night kisses with his *bruder*? Kisses that had easily faded from her memory.

Rachel wrinkled her nose at the short length of thread she had on her needle. A glance at the spool on the end table reminded her she'd emptied it of blue thread before she'd fed the *boppeli*. Knowing the two others in the room would run the errand for her if she as much as murmured a word, she silently pushed to her feet.

They both looked up when she stood, Ben from his paper, Miriam from where she was darning socks in another chair across the room.

"I need to get some more thread."

Miriam instantly set her darning aside. "I can get it for you."

"*Nee*, I think I remember where I stored an extra spool of this color. If you keep this up, you two will spoil me. At the end of your time here, I won't want to let you go because I won't remember how to take care of my own household."

With a smile, Miriam picked up the darning again. "At the end of my time here, I might not want to go, if it means I'll have to take up housekeeping for Gideon. Of course, he might not have found us a place to live by then and I may head back to Ohio."

"Depends how motivated he is." Ben's dimple was evident as he lifted *The Budget*. "When he's motivated, I've seen him act pretty quickly."

"*Ja*, as much as I don't look forward to sweeping up behind Gideon and cooking for him while I'm here, I want to intrude on Samuel and Gail even less," Miriam lamented. "Maybe I'll have a talk with Gail and see if she can make it a little less appealing for Gideon to keep staying there. But I don't know if that's possible. From the very little I've seen, she looks to be a *gut* cook and housewife."

"Can't be as *gut* as mine," Ben murmured from behind his paper.

The quiet words warmed Rachel as she went into her bedroom and headed for the nightstand. Lighting the lamp upon it, she pulled open the single drawer. She smiled when she saw the blue thread, just as she remembered. Pulling it out, she went to shut the draw. As it was sliding closed, her gaze landed on something she'd forgotten all about. She went still at the sight.

Aaron's letter.

Pulling the drawer farther open, she stared at the simple envelope. Rachel blinked as she tried to remember when it had arrived. She couldn't even remember what it said. With a lengthy inhale, she set the spool on top of the nightstand and withdrew the envelope. Darting a look toward the door to ensure no one was watching, she turned it over and pulled out the letter. She quickly scanned the few penned words.

Dear Rachel, I have been thinking of you. I didn't mean to hurt you. I do care for you. Aaron.

Her breath came faster. Not because of the message but at the possibility that her husband had seen it. Ben never used to enter her room, but since the babes were born, he'd been in and out frequently. He'd brought the babes to her when she was in bed. Would he have had any reason to open this nearby stand? He'd never said anything indicating he'd seen it. But, Rachel gnawed her bottom lip, neither had she when it arrived. Should she have told him?

To do so now might change things. Negatively. And she was…happy. Really happy. In fact, Rachel blushed, the letter crackling as she tightened her fist around it, the only thing that would make her happier would be to have a real marriage with her husband.

Was she happier than she'd have been with Aaron? They'd had a lot of fun walking out, but when Rachel tried to visualize the day-to-day routine of marriage with her former beau, she couldn't see it working. Not like it was with Ben.

She stuffed the crumpled letter back into the envelope. With no return address, there was no way of responding to Aaron. It didn't matter. That part of her life was over. She was wife to Ben and mother to his *kinner*. A soft smile tilted her lips. There couldn't be a better husband or *daed* to the *boppeli*. Besides, she… cared for him. More than she'd ever thought she could.

Pinching the envelope between her fingers, she tore it, the sound strikingly loud in the quiet room. Rachel tore it again into quarters. Frowning at the multiple pieces, she tucked them back inside the drawer. She'd throw them away when Ben was out of the house. Closing the drawer on the shredded letter and that part of her past, she belatedly remembered to grab the thread as she blew out the lamp and headed for the door.

Rachel paused while still in the shadows of the room and peeped out at her husband. Now standing over the cradle, he was gazing down at the *boppeli*, a look of simple adoration on his face. Rachel's heart pounded as she watched. *Please,* Gott. *Help me know what to do so that someday he looks at me in the same manner.* Before she stepped through the doorway, Rachel pasted a smile on her face. They had their life now. It could be a *gut* life. The letter was in the past. As were any feelings she had for her husband's *bruder.*

Ben drew Sojourner to a halt in the growing line of black buggies parked in the pasture. He scrambled out in time to help Rachel and Miriam get down with the twins and the various desserts they'd brought to the first church Sunday since the babies were born. Being *hochmut* was wrong but Ben couldn't help thrusting his chest out a little in his *mutza* suit when all the other Amish women came bustling over to exclaim and coo over the two *boppeli.* Although it wasn't discussed when a woman was with child, it wasn't as if the community didn't know the babies were coming. Many had already seen them. It'd been a regular parade through their house with everyone visiting. *Gut* thing there were two, because they'd received more blankets of different types than it seemed the *kinder* could use in their lifetimes. The visits were *wunderbar* and most welcome. But he missed quiet evenings when, even though Miriam was there, it was like he and his wife had finally become a team.

"Oh, Ben, would you mind bringing in the church spread and bread loaves?" Rachel called over her shoulder.

When the women, all dressed similarly, left in a

flock like geese lifting off a pond with about the same noise level, Ben sighed. He was cut off from his wife and family. As Rachel would sit on the side with the women while he'd be with the men, he wouldn't have minded walking beside her and his *kin* to the big barn. With another deep sigh, he retrieved two loaves of homemade bread and the church spread from the buggy. Tucking the latter under his arm, he fell into step beside Samuel and Gideon Schrock as they trailed the women.

"'Bout like driving cattle to the barn," Gideon observed.

"Careful, I think these'll do more than kick you if you crowd them too much. Or they'll sure find a way to make you sorry you irritated them. I think cows are easier."

Ben chuckled at Samuel's comment. His previous coworker turned a jaundiced eye on him. "Sure, go ahead and laugh. I thought Malachi was bad, but you're setting an even worse standard for the rest of us, cosseting your wife the way I hear you're doing."

Recalling the rounded evidence under Gail's apron, Ben swung one of the loaves by its twist-tied wrapper, thumping Samuel on the chest with it. "Just you wait until…" His words fizzled out as he reddened slightly, embarrassed to mention the subject. He glanced at the two Schrock brothers. Although Gideon looked oblivious, Samuel wore an ear-splitting grin along with a faint blush under his black broad-brimmed hat.

"*Ja*," was all the usually loquacious Samuel said as they followed the chattering women.

During church, Ben's gaze kept drifting to the benches across the barn where his wife and Miriam held the *boppeli*. Things had been *gut* between him and Rachel lately. Really *gut*. Perhaps she was growing to care for him. He'd caught her looking at him when he was rocking the babes, a soft, approachable, yearning expression on her face. He'd thought he imagined it, or it was directed at the *boppeli* he held. Until he caught her sending it his way one night as he was heading for his bedroom, with no babies in the general area. Ben's pulse had galloped at the possibility the yearning expression was for him.

What might Rachel do if, when he was heading for bed, he dropped a good-night kiss on her forehead as well as the babies'? His pulse accelerated further. What would she say if they started a discussion about maybe just having…one bedroom?

Ben blinked several times at the loud voice that suddenly pierced his thoughts. Startled that someone might've caught on to what he was thinking, in church no less, he slumped on the backless bench as he realized the guest preacher was just getting fired up in his hour-long sermon. Flushing, Ben rubbed a hand over his bearded jaw, glad the covering concealed his blush at the prospect of finally perhaps being a normal husband to his wife.

His hand tightened on his chin as he considered the connection between his beard, the visiting minister and the members' meeting after church. They'd be starting the process of replacing one of the district's ministers. One had been chosen after Rachel's *daed*'s passing. Either the job had been too much for the one selected or the draw of a widow with a large farm in Jamesport, Missouri, had been too tempting. For whatever reason, the man had moved to Missouri to marry the widow, leaving the district short a minister again. One of the requirements for a man when he was baptized into the church was the willingness to serve in the lifelong role of minister if selected. It was a job few aspired to. For the first time in a selection process, Ben was eligible to be nominated to fill the role.

His hand crept up to cover his mouth as his eyes grew wide. He shifted his attention from the visiting preacher, obviously comfortable with the job, to John Stoltzfus who had preached the first sermon of the day, who obviously was not. Ben felt much more in accord with John, a *gut* man whom he and Rachel had confessed to last winter.

But if he was selected, he couldn't say no. Dropping his hand, Ben's gaze shifted around the interior of the big barn, where the members of their growing community sat on the backless benches, men on one side, women on the other. His heart pounded at the possibility of standing in front of them and speaking for even a minute without notes, much less an hour.

Certainly he loved *Gott* and wanted to serve Him, but the thought of serving in that capacity made the hands now clamped on his thighs sweat. How could he do such a thing? He couldn't even tell his wife that he loved her. Ben pressed his lips together as he recalled the story in the Old Testament. Moses had felt incapable of a job and *Gott* had used him to lead His people out of bondage in Egypt.

Surely if he was chosen, *Gott* would provide what he needed. Hadn't He already? Ben's attention rested on Rachel. *Gott* had given him Rachel. A blessing more than he could ever have hoped or imagined. She was gently rocking one of the *boppeli* in her arms. He didn't know which one for sure, but it was probably Eli because already his son was the more vocal of the two. Not crying, just letting one know he was there.

Ben slid the palms of his perspiring hands along his pants. If he could tell the whole district of his love for *Gott*, surely he could tell his wife of his love for her? The prospect made him dizzy with fear. Doing so would leave him exposed. What if she didn't feel the same? Would she pity him? Ben swallowed against the bitter taste in his mouth as his stomach churned. Better to have the whole community pity his efforts as a preacher than to have his wife pity him for declaring unrequited love. Better to be silent and appear a fool than speak and remove all doubt. But was he a fool for not telling her how he felt? For not having the courage to take the steps to make their marriage better?

He wouldn't remember the words now droned by this guest minister, but Ben remembered the ones of the speaker for the fire department training. *You can be comfortable, or you can be courageous. But never both at the same time.* At the time, Ben assumed the man was speaking of physical courage. Which for Ben was easier to address than courage of any other sort.

But the man's words were fitting for other types of courage, as well.

Surprisingly, considering their tenseness at the outset of their marriage, he and Rachel had grown comfortable with each other. They were still living contentedly in the same house, unlike the young couple at their wedding who'd started out marriage in the same manner with a *boppeli* on the way. But was he still comfortable with…comfortable? Or could he summon the courage to make the marriage into what he yearned for? More than friends. True partners. There were no guarantees she'd ever feel the same way if he said the words first. But it was time to have the courage to do so.

Ben leaned forward on the hard bench as he considered his wife's down-bent head. He would do so at the next opportunity. It wouldn't be tonight. She and the babies would be tired tonight after their first public outing. But maybe tomorrow? They were making their marriage work. They'd developed a respect, a partnership with each other.

The chasm was Aaron. Ben's lips firmed in a mirthless smile as he recalled it was the biblical Aaron who had spoken for his reluctant brother, Moses. It was time Ben spoke his heart. It'd been months since Aaron had left. Surely Rachel was over him by now?

His eyes prickled with emotion as he watched Rachel lift the bundle in her arms to kiss the *boppeli* she held. Would he have ever gotten over Rachel? Widening his eyes keep any hint of sentiment at bay, he forced himself to focus on the preacher's closing words. He didn't want to let his mind wander any more. Because he knew the answer was no. Ben just hoped Rachel's sentiment wasn't the same regarding his brother.

Chapter Fifteen

Rachel stared in shock at the man on the other side of the screen door. Under the flat-brimmed straw hat, he had her husband's dark hair and blue eyes. But no dimples were in sight. Even if the action would reveal he had them, this man was far, far from smiling.

"I'd heard I'd find you here." His gaze touched on where Eli was tucked in her arms, before shifting to Miriam who'd come up behind her carrying Amelia. His jaw clenched under the shadow of his hat. Rachel didn't know if it meant he hadn't heard about the *boppeli* as well, or that he had.

"Aaron." She couldn't say the obvious. That it was a surprise to see him. The look on her face must advise that. The look that jolted from shock to joy to yearning to—as she watched him stare at her *boppeli*— guilt.

"I thought you'd wait for me."

"I did." She had. For weeks. Watched and hoped, even prayed for his return. Rachel swallowed as she shifted uncomfortably. All the while pregnant with his *bruder*'s children.

Through the screen door, Aaron's unsmiling attention remained on the bundle in her arm. "Apparently not for very long."

His cynical words stabbed Rachel like the tines of a pitchfork. Aaron had perhaps not even cleared the county line and she'd been in his *bruder*'s arms. For comfort in her distress at her intended's departure, but still. Remorse soured her stomach. Eli started to fret. Rachel couldn't blame him. The soft cradle of her arms had stiffened into a tense, unyielding berth.

Things couldn't be changed, whether feelings had or not. She had to make Aaron understand that what'd happened with her and Ben hadn't been intentional. That she hadn't set out to betray him. That *they* hadn't set out to betray him.

"I… We …" She didn't know how to start.

"Yah, I got that part."

Aaron's set face indicated any explanation would have a difficult time finding a receptive ear. Still, Rachel had to try. She turned to see Miriam, although she'd put Amelia in her nearby cradle, was still a few steps behind her. Closing the distance between them, she gently transferred Eli to her. The young woman tenderly cuddled the baby, but Rachel could tell from Miriam's fierce expression that she'd be willing to throw the interloper off the porch should Rachel request it. And kick him down the drive, as well. Happily.

"I'm going to step outside." At Miriam's sharp look, Rachel continued, "It'll be all right. Aaron and I have a long history. Seeing each other again is a bit of a… shock to us both. I won't be far. Call if you or the *boppeli* need me."

Miriam nodded, but the protective look in her eyes told Rachel they'd be watched out the window and the hired girl wouldn't hesitate to dash out the door if needed. Warmed by the young woman's support and loyalty when she was clenching her own hands to keep them from trembling, Rachel repeated, "It'll be all right."

At least she hoped so. She turned to where Aaron remained, stone-faced, at the door. He wouldn't do anything to harm her physically. At least not the Aaron she'd once known. But his being here was an emotional calamity. Years of having been his sweetheart, of thinking he was *Gott*'s chosen one for her, tugged at dormant longings, vying against the renewed and deepened guilt that flooded her. Was he staying long? Had he come back for her? What would Ben do if he knew he was here? Trepidation regarding the Raber brothers' relationship in the short- and long-term weighed her steps as she opened the door and crossed the porch with Aaron falling in behind her.

He didn't say a word as he followed her to the self-sustaining swing Ben had built for her by the garden. She sank onto it, as, achingly aware of Aaron's presence a step behind her, she didn't know if her shaky legs could carry her any farther. The swing's chains squeaked and the wooden seat shifted under her, much like Rachel's world right now. She looked out at the mostly cleared garden. Some of the remaining vines were dead, just as her feelings for this man needed to be. She strove to prune the rustling dormant longings before they could take root.

Aaron stood stiffly beside the swing.

"How long have you been back?"

"About the length of time it took to stop at your, well, what used to be your home, and then get here. For some foolish reason, I wanted to see you first."

Exhaling a tense sigh, Rachel tipped her head toward where an older car was parked in the driveway. "Are you staying, or returning to the *Englisch*?"

Aaron's lips twisted. "I *was* planning on staying. At least when I thought I had someone to stay for. Now, I don't know anymore."

Flinching, Rachel bowed her head. Regardless of what she felt or wanted—her sentiments were still blunted by shock—Aaron's folks would want him to stay. Aaron's *bruder* would want… What would Ben want? Either way, the thought Aaron would leave the community for good because of what they'd done was unbearable.

"We didn't intend for this to happen." Pressing her hands together on her lap, she lifted her head.

"Regardless of what you intended, it did happen. And now it can't be changed, can it?" Aaron's chest rose and fell under the force of his emotions. "I wonder, did you ever really care for me?"

Just as he said, it couldn't be changed. When Rachel couldn't do anything more than stare mutely at him with crumpled features, Aaron turned in disgust.

"I think I'll go see my *bruder*." The last word was spat out like an unripe persimmon.

He stalked to the car. The engine roared to life. Rachel cringed at the spit of gravel as the vehicle spun out. When it charged down the lane, she burst into tears.

She cried enough to water the garden for a summer during a drought. She cried for Aaron. This wasn't the Aaron she'd known. She couldn't imagine being the recipient of the kind of betrayal she and Ben had inflicted on him. No wonder he was shocked and agitated.

She cried for herself. All she'd ever wanted was to be a wife to the man she loved and a *gut* mother to his children. She knew whose wife she was and would be as long as he lived, but she was so confused over whose wife she'd been meant to be. Forgotten romantic girlish feelings for Aaron seeped into the small patches of her mind that weren't absorbed with motherhood and homemaking. Patches that'd grown feelings for Ben. Could they ever regain their burgeoning happiness now that Aaron had returned?

She cried for the two brothers whom she'd unwittingly come between. She'd never forgive herself if she shattered what used to be a close relationship permanently.

Ben's fingers itched to urge Sojourner into a faster speed. He couldn't wait to get home and share his good news with Rachel. Things had been going so well for Schrock Brothers' Furniture that Malachi had given them all a raise. Ben couldn't have picked a better time to receive such news, with two new babies to support.

His smile felt like it stretched from one buggy wheel to the other. Maybe they could save enough for their own farm with room for a bigger garden sooner than they'd thought. Sojy must've felt his excitement, because her gait quickened.

He blew out a breath. The raise would also be a good lead-in for other information he planned to share. That he loved her. Maybe admit he'd always loved her? *Nee,* that might be a little much. But it was time to tell her. Perhaps after supper, he could take her outside where it was private—on the opposite side of the house from the cattle, his lips twisted wryly—and tell her that he loved her. He was finally ready to say it. He hoped she was ready to hear it.

An oncoming vehicle was rapidly approaching on the narrow country road. Ben reluctantly checked Sojy as he guided her closer to the shoulder. The driver reduced his speed. At least he was courteous enough not to fly by and hog the road. Not recognizing the car, Ben idly glanced over as it passed. Sojy half reared and the buggy jolted toward the ditch at his involuntary jerk on the reins when he saw the driver.

Instantly soothing the offended horse, Ben craned his neck to look back down the road. His mouth went dry at the sight of the car's glowing brake lights. When it started to back up, he forced a hard swallow as his heart started to pound.

This wasn't a reunion to have in the middle of the road. Peering ahead, Ben saw the entrance to an alfalfa field. With tense hands, he directed Sojy to it, driving her far enough into the stubbled vegetation that the driver of the car, should he choose, could pull into the field entrance.

The driver hadn't hesitated. Ben heard the vehicle pull in behind him as he set the buggy's brake. His chest rose and fell as if he'd been the one racing down the road. As he stiffly climbed down from the seat, Ben didn't know what to expect as a greeting. A hug? A punch to the jaw? Both were abnormal to Plain folk. Amish didn't believe in overt display of affection. They didn't believe in physical violence either. But this was far from a normal situation.

There weren't many houses down this road and therefore few reasons to be down it. As he didn't recall his brother being a close friend of Jethro, Ben knew there was only one explanation for Aaron to have come from that direction. He'd been to the house to see Rachel. He'd found out where she lived and he'd tracked her down. If he'd wanted to see Ben, he would've known to find him at work.

But he hadn't.

Crossing his arms over his chest, Ben clenched his teeth. He didn't care to have his *bruder*, or any man, hunting down his wife behind his back.

What'd been Rachel's response? Had she been anticipating Aaron's arrival? Had there been more letters since he'd found the one in the drawer?

Aaron was driving a car. Did that mean he didn't plan to stay? Had he come back to get Rachel to go with him this time?

The possibility of losing his family had Ben going

rigid as he watched his brother slowly climb out of the car and shut the door.

"So you finally have something faster than what I drive." Ben wanted to grab the words back as soon as they escaped his mouth. In the vibrating silence, he'd striven for some weak joke to break the tension. Not to competitively increase it. But he couldn't stop himself.

It was going to be the fist to the mouth. Aaron was capable of throwing one. Ben almost welcomed it. Despite Aaron's flat-brimmed straw hat, perhaps he'd been with the *Englisch* so long he'd forgotten that he was Amish, or had been. Ben watched warily as his older *bruder*'s hands clenched. When Aaron spoke, Ben would've rather had the physical blow.

"I should've known you'd go after her the moment my back was turned."

Ben's mouth was dry. There was no way he was going to mention that Rachel had sought him out first.

"You shouldn't have left her without a word. She needed comfort."

Aaron's grimace migrated to a smirk. "Is that what you want to call it?"

Anger warred with guilt as both barreled through Ben. "You left all of us. You know, I've thought of you as many things throughout the years, but I never thought you were selfish. It was selfish, Aaron, to leave as you did, without telling anyone you were going. Where you were going. If you'd ever be back. Without reaching out to tell *Daed* and *Mamm* wherever you were, that you were safe. Makes me wonder why I thought so much of you when we were growing up. I should've been a better judge of character." Ben's gut twisted even as he spewed the angry words. More of them that he wanted to take back. He'd have climbed back into the buggy to stop the tirade if his knees weren't so shaky.

Aaron's face was pale under the brim of his hat. "I wondered what kind of reception I'd get. I didn't figure on red-carpet treatment, but I certainly didn't expect my own *bruder*," his lips curled at the word, "to betray me and steal my girl. Looks like the exhaust from my bus hadn't even cleared town when you two got together. Talk about being stabbed in the back. I should've shaken loose of you years ago if this is the thanks I get for letting you trail behind me."

"Well, don't worry about it now. Because—" Ben's gaze drifted behind Aaron to dwell on the car "—even if you think fit to return to the community, I'll figure out some way to steer clear of you."

"That's funny. Because I was, until I discovered what I was returning home to." Pivoting, Aaron strode to the car and jerked the door open. Sojourner flung up her head when the engine revved and dirt flew as the car wheeled out of the field road.

Ben sagged against the buggy's wheel. What had he done? What had come over him? He squeezed his eyes shut, his face contorted. Well, that was obvious. He was afraid. Afraid that somehow he'd lose what he was discovering he loved more than he could imagine, Rachel and the *boppeli*. Would they go with Aaron? He didn't think so, didn't think Rachel would agree to be shunned, which she would if she went. But even if she stayed physically, would she be emotionally distant again, realizing she'd married the wrong brother?

How would he face his parents, knowing his brother had left for reasons of his own before, but this time Ben was the one to drive him away?

Perhaps permanently.

Panting, he stayed by the wheel a moment with his hand pressed against his stomach, reluctant to clean out the buggy if he got sick while in it. When he finally climbed onto the seat, his movements were as slow and stiff as an old *grossdaddi*. He felt like he'd aged fifty years in the past fifteen minutes. Listlessly, he guided Sojy back onto the road. Where just a half mile back, he'd been so excited to reach home, now he dreaded what he'd find there.

It was as he'd feared. Aaron had obviously been to the house. Rachel came out on the porch as he drove up the lane. Her face was pale and drawn, except for her eyes, which were red from an obviously long bout of tears. Ben lingered as long as possible taking care of Sojy and the other livestock. Trying to think of what to say. Determining it was better to be silent. Only a fool would bleat his love to a woman who loved another.

Rachel's eyes misted anew when he entered the house. How was he to respond to that? To a wife who wept when he walked in because he wasn't his brother coming home to her? To a wife who was trapped for a lifetime with him when she obviously wanted someone else?

Not even the presence of Miriam could keep the meal from being stilted, although the hired girl tried a few topics of conversation before surrendering to the tense silence around the table. Ben would've been surprised if any of them took a bite, only stirring their food around the plates. He didn't linger after supper, heading straight to his room, a solitary room that would now be endlessly his.

Chapter Sixteen

The ticking of the clock outside his bedroom marked the seconds, minutes and hours that crept by. Sleep was impossible. Ben's heart was still hammering, his stomach still churning from his conversation with Aaron and the lack of a needed one with Rachel. The only moments that'd brought peace were the ones when he held the *boppeli*. Obviously alert to his tension, they'd initially squirmed, their blue eyes seeking his face. As they'd relaxed, he had as well, the rigidity seeping from him as they eventually fell asleep in his arms.

Thinking of them, he alerted to the occasional squeaks he knew were coming from the cradles now in Rachel's room. The babies were waking. Knowing he wouldn't be sleeping, and needing their comfort again, he slipped from bed and quietly dressed. After lighting a lamp by his cushion chair, he tiptoed into Rachel's room and headed for the cradles while casting a glance toward her motionless figure on the bed.

The babies were stirring, but their *mamm* was not.

Not surprising, when he'd heard her up with them two hours earlier. Although she had Miriam to help care for the house and *boppeli*, the two little ones required a lot of work. The amount of tears Rachel had obviously cried today would've also physically exhausted her. Ben quietly and carefully scooped up Amelia and Eli and carried them out of the room.

No stranger to diaper duties, he had the twins changed before they became fully awake. Glad they kept formula on hand for such occasions, Ben prepared a bottle for each and with some negotiating, settled down to feed them. It took a bit of coaxing, as the twins preferred their *mamm*, but as they grew hungrier, they latched on to the bottles.

While watching them eat, Ben again felt his tension ebb as his heart filled.

"You two will have a bond that can never be parted." Ben sighed. "You'll play together. You'll work together. You'll learn from each other. You'll probably argue at times. I imagine Eli will tug on your hair, Amelia, if it's not the other way around." The backs of Ben's eyes prickled at the thought of the two wee ones in his arms having discord in their lives that couldn't be repaired. The possibility broke his heart.

"But you'll love each other. You'll learn and understand the other's strengths and weaknesses. We all have weaknesses." Ben bit his lip as he gazed at his children, who studied him solemnly in return. "You need to stand up for each other. You're family."

Their little faces grew blurry as Ben blinked back tears. He couldn't leave things this way with Aaron.

Pride and fear shouldn't get between family. Closing his eyes, he grimaced as his awful words this afternoon echoed in his head. If he had driven Aaron away, Ben didn't know how he'd forgive himself.

When he opened his eyes, he found the babies regarding him with concern. Their mirrored expressions raised a misty smile. "Being silent in this case would be more than appearing a fool. It would mean being one. I need to go talk to him, don't I? Apologize. For a lot of things. Should I tell him I always I—" Ben had to clear his throat to get the word out. "Always loved your *mamm*? I suppose that's something a child wants to hear. Or at least know that their *daed* loves their *mamm*. It's something she probably wants to know, as well. But I don't know if I can tell her, now that the man she really loves is back. See, we can't change things, but I don't want to rush her, like I feel I did to…" Ben smiled "…have the surprise of your arrival. I want to give her time. I wouldn't feel right to be a couple when she's thinking of someone else."

Amelia's little brows furrowed as she sucked at the bottle harder.

"*Ach*, please don't think me a coward for not telling her. It's enough that you two know now. By the time you can tell her, maybe we'll have worked something out. In the meantime, just know that I'm here for you and her, and I cherish all three of you more than you can ever imagine."

Eli's eyelids were getting heavy. Ben jiggled him gently to wake him enough to eat a bit more. "Anyway, regarding Aaron, I feel I cheated my *bruder*. Always wanted and then had a chance to take something that was his. I can see why he feels upset and betrayed. This life with your *mamm* should've been his. You should've been his." Ben's arms tightened around the babes. "But I thank *Gott* every day that you're mine. Already I can't imagine living without you."

Removing the finished bottles and shifting Eli to his lap, he lifted Amelia to his shoulder to gently coax a burp. "But I can't imagine existing with this discord between Aaron and me. I must apologize. I hope he'll forgive me." Achieving success with Amelia, he switched the babes' positions. "Even if he doesn't, at least I'll know I've tried to set things right."

Balancing both *boppeli* on his lap, he watched their eyes drift shut as he carefully swaddled them. "Thanks for the talk. You're both *gut* listeners. I'll talk to Aaron as soon as possible. With your *mamm*, we'll give her some more time. I'm trusting you two to keep what I said a secret." He rose from his chair. Bending first one arm, then the other, he kissed both their brows and quietly slipped into his sleeping wife's bedroom to return his children to their cradles.

Ben left the farm following chores early the next morning, glad it was a Saturday and he could put the onerous task behind him. With a parting glance at the house, his lips twitched, knowing the babes wouldn't tell Rachel that it was he, and not Miriam, who'd gotten up with them in the middle of the night. Knowing they wouldn't share his other admissions either. His smile faded as he turned Sojy at the end of the lane.

Now he had to keep his vow. He was guessing Aaron, if he hadn't already departed again, would be staying at their folks' farm. If not, maybe his *daed* would know where to find him. Even though he dreaded doing so.

Several pensive miles later, Ben sighed in relief at the sight of yesterday's car parked in front of his family farm's big white barn. His chest tightened when Aaron came to the barn door, a pitchfork in his hand, as Ben drew Sojy to a stop next to the vehicle. The two brothers watched each other warily as Ben set the brake and stepped down from the buggy.

When his feet hit the ground, Ben remained rooted for a moment. "Where's *Daed*?" It seemed a safe place to start. He hadn't decided if he wanted a witness to what he needed to say.

"He and *Mamm* went into town." Aaron gave a studiously negligent shrug. "They said they had errands, but I imagine they wanted to share the news about the prodigal son returning."

Glancing over at the car, Ben shifted his feet. "And has he?"

The admission was slow in coming. "Probably."

"Where's the rest of the family?" Ben tried to peer into the quiet depths of the barn. "Our two younger *brieder* aren't helping you?"

"I told them I had it. After being stared at, tiptoed around and asked how I was doing for the past sixteen hours, I was ready for a little alone time."

"I guess that's something I didn't ask yesterday." Needing something to do with his hands, Ben scratched the back of his neck. "How *are* you doing?"

"I've been better."

Ben nodded toward the shadowy barn behind Aaron's stiff figure. "You still want alone time, or do you want some help?"

"I remember how to muck a stall, if that's what you're asking."

"I learned how to muck out one pretty well too, because someone did a *gut* job of teaching me."

For the first time, a shadow of a smile touched Aaron's face. "He should've taught you to respect your elders."

Ben was surprised he didn't collapse to the ground in a heap with the relief that swept through him. "You're not that much older."

"Old enough that you're still an irritating little *bruder*." Aaron gestured with his head. "Come on. There's work enough for two. Or maybe I'll just let you take over. You seem to be *gut* at that."

Already moving toward the barn door, Ben hesitated at his words. Aaron's face was now in the barn's shadows. He couldn't see his *bruder*'s expression. With a heavy thickness in his throat, he stepped into the barn. Following Aaron to the wooden wall where various tools hung by hooks and nails, he removed a pitchfork.

"About…that." Resting the pitchfork on the ground, tines down, Ben curled his hands around the wooden handle. "I'm sorry for what I said yesterday. I'm sorry for a lot of things. I can't imagine what you must have felt coming back to find…the situation you did." Ben blew out a breath through pursed lips. When Aaron didn't respond, only met his eyes with a steady gaze and set expression, Ben continued, "I want you to know that none of this was Rachel's fault. We didn't mean for what happened...to happen. We were both upset when you left. I let things go too far. Then when she told me—" he swallowed hard "—about the *boppeli*, and we didn't know if or when you were coming back, we had to do something."

Still no reaction from his *bruder*. Looking away from the man's obviously clenched jaw, Ben shifted his attention to the line of stalls on the far side of the barn, where the brown heads of his *daed*'s Standard-breds were watching them curiously. "It wouldn't have mattered, but for a while I wondered if it was..."

"We never did that. Rachel and I. Don't think that of her."

Ben reluctantly returned his gaze to Aaron. "*Ja*, I know that now."

Aaron pivoted to stride a few steps and stab the pitchfork into a bale of straw lying in front of an empty stall. Dust and small bits of yellow chaff flew into the air and Ben tightened his hands on his own pitchfork handle when Aaron unexpectedly kicked the bale. He blinked in surprise when his *bruder* heaved a heavy sigh and turned to sink down upon it.

"That was part of the problem."

"What?" Ben cocked his head at the unexpected response.

"I didn't ever think of her...that way." Aaron rested his chin on fisted hands propped up by his elbows on his knees. "Rachel is a *wunderbar* girl. Fun. An easy companion. I don't think there's a better girl in the district. But as time went, I began to think of her more as a *schweschder* than a girlfriend. I still love her…but not in that way. Surely there's something more in a married relationship than that?" He regarded Ben as if his *bruder* might have an answer.

Ben thought of how much he loved his wife. Deeply, in so many ways, but none of them sisterly. Aaron was right to wonder.

"I didn't know what to do. Everyone had expectations for us. Her *mamm*. Our parents. The whole community. The thought of marrying her and having her as a wife forever…" He shook his head. "But I didn't want to hurt her, or embarrass her publicly by breaking up right before everyone expected a wedding."

"Disappearing instead wasn't a promising alternative." Ben's jaw tightened as he recalled the pain Rachel went through.

Aaron ducked his head. "I know. I was a coward. I don't care for conflict or the thought of hurting someone. It's pretty sad when you're glad to be kicked by a horse. Probably too bad I didn't get kicked in the head. I was relieved when I broke my arm and my baptism was delayed. There was so much pressure to be baptized and then married. I still wasn't sure what I wanted. And even if we did marry, I needed a way to support her. But I hurt her anyway. I hurt both of you." His gaze met Ben's wide eyes. "For that I'm sorry."

Ben didn't know if he'd be able to stay upright without the support of the pitchfork.

Aaron snorted. "I actually came back to be baptized. Marry Rachel. Here I came to be noble and go through with it all. You wouldn't even let me do that. Just like things got before I'd left, you'd already done it for me. I think that's what upset me so. The shock of how things had changed and all the self-debating I went through before finally determining to do the honorable thing and live up to everyone's expectations." Pushing to his feet, he stepped toward Ben.

"Do you still love her?" Ben watched his *bruder* approach. The answer made all the difference, but he couldn't make the question more than a whisper.

"*Ja*. But not in the way you do." Aaron clamped his hand on Ben's shoulder. "Maybe it was prophetic of me to think of her as a sister, because that's what she is now. My sister-in-law."

"I couldn't leave things the way they ended yesterday. Our relationship means too much to me."

Aaron squeezed his shoulder. "Me too."

"I'm afraid she still loves you."

Aaron winced. "We'll work around that."

Tension seeped from Ben. With Aaron willingly yielding the field, somehow, someway, he and Rachel would work it out. He couldn't suppress the silly grin that slipped onto his face. "Maybe she just needs to get to know you better. You'd only shown her your charming side. And I know from experience, it's very limited."

Aaron released Ben's shoulder with a brotherly shove. Ben didn't budge. "Why waste charm on a little *bruder*? They're stuck with you anyway." His eyes narrowed on Ben as he smiled crookedly. "Maybe along with mucking out a stall, I should've coached you on how to be charming to women. But, as you've somehow managed to be married anyway, I guess I'll have to take my charm and find another woman to practice it on."

"You won't find a better one."

"I can tell you believe that. I'm glad for you." Aaron observed Ben solemnly. "I'm glad for Rachel, as well. Loving her like a sister, I want the best for her. And I know she won't find a better man than the one she has."

Ben glanced away. He couldn't respond for the lump in his throat. When he looked back to his brother, Aaron was smiling ruefully.

Aaron sighed exaggeratingly. "I guess, since I'm back, hopefully there's someone worthy out there I can scare up." Aaron turned to jerk the pitchfork from the straw bale. "In the meantime, I'll show you that, even though it's been awhile, I can still outwork my little *bruder*."

"I don't know." Shifting his pitchfork to one hand, Ben strode over to a half-filled wheelbarrow. "I had a *gut* teacher."

"I don't suppose you need a car," Aaron mused as he entered the empty stall behind him.

"No more than you do," Ben replied, pushing the wheelbarrow within his *bruder*'s reach.

"Maybe I can find some young fool entering his *rumspringa*. They think they know everything then."

The two brothers set to work. Ben didn't know what Aaron's thoughts were, but his, now that he'd worked up the courage to resolve the relationship from his past, were on how to bolster his courage even more to resolve the vital one of his future.

Chapter Seventeen

Only exhaustion had freed Rachel from her thoughts and allowed her to sleep last night. When Ben didn't come in after chores, her anxiety, already high, ratcheted up another degree. She wanted to talk with him. She *needed* to talk with him. She'd intended to this morning, but he'd left instead—to where, she didn't know. By the time his rig finally pulled into the lane later in the morning, she'd almost worn a path in linoleum pacing to the window. Aaron's return had fractured the relationship she and Ben had worked so hard to create. Would they be able to mend it again?

Her heart thudded when Ben stepped into the kitchen. Its cadence, which marginally calmed when his gaze—touching first on her, then on Amelia in her arms—accelerated again when a smile tipped his lips. Relieved, confused, Rachel could do no more than return a mute stare.

In the silence that pulsed throughout the tidy room, Ben finally spoke. "I saw Isaiah Zook this morning.

He's planning to move some more steers over here. I need to finally get that bunk fixed."

Rachel rested a hip against the counter. Was he expecting her to balk at the news? It wasn't the conversation she wanted, needed, but after yesterday, at least they were talking. But this was Ben's choice of topic after that emotional upheaval? She glanced at the nearby open door, where Miriam was currently emptying the manual washing machine. The conversation she wanted didn't need an audience, even a sympathetic one. She'd have to find a more solitary time and place to initiate it.

At her hesitant nod, Ben continued, "I'll be working on it for the rest of the morning. Call me when lunch is ready?"

Once more, Rachel nodded. Ben opened his mouth to speak, only to close it when his gaze also lit on where Miriam was visible doing laundry. But his hesitant smile lifted even more, until there was a slight promise that the dimple Rachel had grown to treasure might put in an appearance. What did it mean? She was left to wonder as he turned and went out the door.

And wonder she did. Through feeding the twins and putting them in their cradles. Through preparing a casserole while Miriam took the laundry to hang on the clothesline. Through washing up utensils. While doing so, Rachel glanced out the kitchen window at the loud rattle being generated from the farmyard. Ben had emptied the pen in order to work. The steers, now shut in the pasture along with Billy and the other bulls, were roughhousing with each other. Some were knocked against the metal gate that kept them from the pen where Ben was repairing the feed bunk. She furrowed her brow as the gate lifted upon the pressure of one of the many broad black-and-white heads that crowded against it. The rusty gate dropped back down with a squeak, followed by a bang.

Frowning, Rachel's attention moved from the cattle to the man currently sawing a board at the opposite side of the bare dirt pen. She envied him the physical task, knowing busy hands calmed the mind. She'd known he'd wanted to fix it for a while, but events—his injury, the arrival of the *boppeli*—had forestalled it. Maybe the bunk needed mending right at this moment. Or maybe it was just an excuse to get out of the house. And away from her and a needed conversation?

But that's not what his parting smile had said. Although not actually speaking, Rachel snorted—that was Ben's way—his smile had said…hope. Hope for them to find a way through the shock of Aaron's return? Hope and a way the three of them could reside harmoniously together going forward in the community?

Rachel knew her heartache of yesterday wasn't because she wanted to be with Aaron. *Ja*, she cared for him and hoped that he could find happiness somehow. But she'd realized her shock and grief at his return had been for the impact to her and Ben's growing relationship. She'd become…happy with Ben. Very happy. The thought of continuing to build a life with him and their children made her want to crow like an overzealous rooster.

Did he have any inkling of how she felt? Rachel's

fingers clenched on the sink as Ben paused sawing for a lingering look toward the house. She'd been one who'd needed to be told she was appreciated in order to feel worthy. Just because Ben wasn't one for saying the words didn't mean he never wanted to hear them. Did he know her feelings for Aaron had faded away? That it'd been an annual blooming in its time and not a perennial that would grow stronger every year, like her feelings for Ben?

How could he know, if she hadn't told him?

Rachel discarded the possibility of talking to him in the evening. By the time the *boppeli* were put to bed—with the knowledge they would wake again in a few hours—both she and Ben would be tired. Too tired for this type of discussion. Besides, he didn't seem to welcome deep conversations. Facing a reluctant communicator in a quiet room with only the ticking of the wall clock could get awkward. Much better to talk with him when his hands were busy and there were other distractions. And if the conversation didn't go well— Rachel drew in a shaky breath at the possibility—it would be easier to be outside and return to the house on some premise than have the discussion later that night and need to retreat silently to her bedroom after a stilted talk.

Scanning the kitchen, she looked for some excuse to go outside. As Miriam stepped back inside with an empty laundry basket, Rachel's gaze landed on a pitcher drying on the dish rack.

"I'm taking a glass of lemonade out to Ben. I'll be back shortly. Call me if the twins wake up." Snagging the pitcher and hastily making the lemonade, Rachel poured a glass and headed for the door.

Crossing the porch, she steadied herself with a few deep breaths. She was going to tell her husband she cared for him. Surely brides did that all the time. Although most do it before they're married. And probably definitely before they have two children. Rachel grimaced as lemonade sloshed out of the glass over her trembling hand. At this rate, she'd be fortunate to have anything in the glass by the time she reached him. Focusing on Ben, bent over the end of the bunk as he hammered in a board, she started across the driveway, the gravel barely noticeable under the summer-toughened soles of her feet.

In the months they'd lived there, she'd never been all the way across the gravel to the strip of grass along the pen fence. Except for when Ben, severely injured, had been lying under the bunk. She was relieved that now, like then, the lot was empty. Otherwise, she didn't know if she'd be able to get close enough to hand Ben the glass, much less stay and talk.

How should she start this vital conversation? Rachel searched for words to say after *would you like some lemonade?* Should she make small talk? Ask about the cattle, as they were right there in their domain? Her lips twitched. That'd surprise Ben and throw him off balance. Maybe that's what he needed. Also, it would show him she was interested in what he was interested in. Hopefully easing from that into what she was interested in. Whom she cared for. Whom she loved.

Looking toward the pasture gate to get some conversation inspiration from the black-and-white beasts, Rachel stumbled to a halt, sloshing lemonade. While the other cattle had drifted away from the gate to graze in the pasture, over the top white rails she could see the big black back of the bull, Billy. She'd grown used to seeing him standing by the secured gate, broodingly watching the steers when they were in the pen. But something was wrong. Was he in the pasture or in the pen? For a moment, she couldn't tell. Her frantic gaze finally located the gate, sagging low to the ground next to the deserted post used to secure it.

Billy was loose in the pen.

His attention was fixed on Ben, still bent over his task and unaware of the present danger. The mostly black head was lowered and visible between the white rails. Chills ran up Rachel's spine at the bull's large, protruding eyes. As he pawed the bare dirt, clods of it flew up to dust the black sleekness of his arched back.

Her gaze darted back to her unsuspecting husband. Rachel opened her mouth to scream. To her horror, no sound resonated in warning. Her breath was locked in her chest. Her feet frozen on the gravel of the driveway. As she watched the bull's stealthy progress across the pen, unbidden, a thought prickled into her mind.

A widow would be free to marry again.

And no one would be surprised to see a man marry his deceased *bruder*'s young widow and take responsibility for his *kinder*.

Rachel clenched her hand, the ridged design of the glass cutting into her white-knuckled fingers. For a moment, she stared at it blankly. A second later, lemonade splashed over the gravel as her arm cocked. Breaking free of her rigid stupor, she lunged forward. Finding her voice, Rachel yelled at the top of her lungs. Still a few feet from the fence, she launched the glass into the pen. It fell beside one large cloven hoof. The bull didn't turn his broad head.

But when Rachel smacked into the fence and scrambled up it, she had his attention. Climbing up until the top rail pressed against her hips, Rachel leaned over it, waving her hands above her head while shrieking for all she was worth. Billy spun to face this new challenge. As Rachel sucked in a breath for another scream, her heart stuttered at the bull's rumbling huffs. She couldn't risk a glance away to confirm Ben had been alerted to the danger.

With a mighty bellow, Billy charged.

Rachel's piercing scream was squelched when hands grabbed about her waist and jerked her backward off the rails. Breathless from surprise and the tumble to the ground, she flinched when the fence cracked as Billy hit it. The post leaned, but held. Dirt flew as the bull nimbly spun to peer through the rails with his bulging eyes. Rachel's heartbeat hammered in her ears as he banged his head against what now seemed a flimsy barrier. With a final snort, Billy pivoted and arrogantly trotted away.

All the energy vaporized from Rachel. Her head flopped back against the moving pillow that cradled it.

"Are you all right?" The question rumbled as much from Ben's chest beneath her ear as from his frantic tone behind her head.

For a moment, Rachel's rapid panting prevented an answer. She realized, as her head was bobbing up and down in its position on Ben, he was breathing briskly, as well. Knowing her head was nodding in an accidental affirmation to his question struck her as funny. Was this shock? She began to giggle. Feeling his racing heartbeat under her ear and knowing he was safely there with her, that the bull hadn't hurt him, overwhelmed her with emotion. A few sobs joined the giggles until she was crying in earnest.

Twisting, she pressed her cheek against his chest, curling her fingers into his shirt as she wet it with her tears. Carefully holding her, Ben struggled to sit up. "Rachel! Rachel! Did he hurt you?"

Shaking her head, she sniffed loudly. "*Nee*," she confirmed nasally.

"What is it then?" Urgent concern punctuated his words.

"I'm just so glad he didn't hurt you." She continued to shake her head. "I don't know what I'd do without you. I love you so much."

Ben's heart rate under her ear picked up even as he went motionless. Rachel stilled, as well. Drawing a few shuddering breaths, she lifted her gaze to meet his stunned blue eyes. Dazedly shifting into a seated position on the grass, he pulled Rachel into his lap, positioning her so they still faced each other.

"When? How?" His face tightened fractionally. "Is it because of the *boppeli*?"

"*Ja*," she admitted. "It's because of the *boppeli*."

The dismay on his face would've been imperceptive,

except that she knew it so well. Lifting her hand, she laid it against his cheek. "If it weren't for the *boppeli*, I might've missed you. And I can't bear the thought of that."

Ben's eyes glowed. Turning his head slightly, he kissed the palm of her hand.

Miriam came out on the porch. With a concerned frown at the sight of them on the ground, she hastened down the steps. "Is everything all right?"

Glancing at each other, they grinned. Rachel felt his dimple crease under her hand. She'd been scrutinizing the *boppeli*, hoping at least one might have their *daed*'s dimples. "*Ja*. Everything is all right. Everything is really *gut,* in fact."

Regarding them oddly, Miriam shook her head and returned to the house.

Rachel brought her hand down. "She probably thinks we're nuts."

"We are. Or at least I am. I'm nuts about you. And maybe both of us together. We didn't go about this marriage in the normal way. *Boppeli* first, then marriage. Followed lastly by a clumsy courtship." Ben cradled her in his arms. Rachel felt his kiss against her hair. "Any regrets about the way things worked out?"

Did she? Knowing now how it ended. How it always should've ended. How she was so very, very glad it ended. Safe, secure, thrilled to be in his arms, she nodded. "*Ja*. One."

She felt his indrawn sigh surround her as he prepared himself for her response. Dear, quiet, always supportive Ben, whose expressions weren't always verbal, but were strongly communicated nonetheless. "What is it?"

"That I didn't walk out with you first and only."

Ben kissed her. For their first, it was one worth waiting for. And, as Rachel melted into his arms, she definitely knew it wouldn't be their only.

Moments later, Ben rested his cheek against hers. "That's *gut*," he murmured. "Because for me, it's always been you. And only you."

Epilogue

"Are you sure she doesn't mind?" Rachel was glad her voice didn't reflect her jitters.

Ben's hand was a reassuring presence on her elbow. Even though she didn't turn, she knew his dimples were in appearance. "I'm sure. The cows aren't just standing outside the barn door at night because they want some food. By that time of day, they want to be milked."

Rachel flushed, recalling how she felt when the twins hadn't nursed in a while. Tentatively, she reached toward the large black-and-white figure a short arm's length away and drew in a shuddering breath. Touching the cow with trembling fingers, Rachel squeaked and jumped back when the skin tightened and lifted beneath her hand. Ben's hand at her waist steadied her, but she could hear his chuckle over the cow's ensuing *moo* that echoed through the Lapps' milking parlor.

Maybe it was his presence in her life that steadied her. She couldn't imagine hers without it. Or without month-old Eli and Amelia, currently inside the Lapps' house, being doted upon by *grossmammi* Susannah and Gail and Hannah's mother, Willa Lapp, while she and Ben were in the barn, borrowing the dairy farmer's most gentle cow to help Rachel face her fear.

She was so glad the bull, Billy, was gone. Isaiah had sold him quickly after the last incident, proclaiming he'd rather have his friends alive than the best milking herd in the county.

"It's okay. Blossom is just asking where the rest of the girls are. She's not used to having the place to herself." Taking Rachel's hand under his own, he gently placed it against the cow's side again. Rachel's fingers curled slightly into the warm hide, marveling at the live tension pulsing under her palm in the Holstein's large belly.

"Are you sure you want to try to milk her today, or are you *gut* and is this enough for now?"

Rachel smiled at his words. Her apprehensive body's rigidity evaporated as she leaned back against his sturdy chest. This was enough. Ben was enough. He was much, much more than enough. For now and always. Rotating her hand, she braided her fingers with his. His arms tightened around her as he rested his chin against her hair.

While *Gott* had always known Ben was her chosen one, she'd had more of a journey to make the discovery. Lifting their entwined grasp from the cow's side, Rachel pressed the back of his hand against her cheek. How could she not have seen before that he was the one? It was right there in front of her in, well, black-and-white.

Whatever her fears, now and in the future, she knew she could face them with this man by her side.

She closed her eyes with a heartfelt sigh. "*Ja*. I'm *gut*. I'm very, very *gut*."

* * * * *

WE HOPE YOU ENJOYED
THIS BOOK FROM

LOVE INSPIRED

INSPIRATIONAL ROMANCE

Uplifting stories of faith, forgiveness and hope.

Fall in love with stories where faith helps
guide you through life's challenges, and discover
the promise of a new beginning.

6 NEW BOOKS AVAILABLE EVERY MONTH!

LIHALO2021

HARLEQUIN
PLUS

Announcing a **BRAND-NEW** multimedia subscription service for romance fans like you!

Read, Watch and Play.

Experience the easiest way to get the romance content you crave.

Start your **FREE 7 DAY TRIAL** at <u>www.harlequinplus.com/freetrial</u>.

LOVE INSPIRED

Stories to uplift and inspire

Fall in love with Love Inspired—
inspirational and uplifting stories of faith
and hope. Find strength and comfort in
the bonds of friendship and community.
Revel in the warmth of possibility and the
promise of new beginnings.

Sign up for the Love Inspired newsletter
at **LoveInspired.com** to be the first
to find out about upcoming titles,
special promotions and exclusive content.

Jason stared at the woman in the doorway of the principal's office. "*You're* A. Green?"

Just looking at her sent shock waves through him. What had happened to his late brother's wife?

She was still gorgeous, no doubt. But she was much thinner than she'd been when he'd last seen her, her strong cheekbones standing out above full lips, still pretty although now without benefit of lipstick. She wore a business suit, the blouse underneath buttoned up to her chin.

Her eyes still had that vulnerable look in them, though, the one that had sucked him into making a mistake, doing what he shouldn't have done. Making a phone call with disastrous results.

She recovered before he did. "Come in. You'll want to sit down," she said. "I'm sorry about Ricky running into you and your dog."

He followed her into her office.

He waited for her to sit behind her desk before easing himself into a chair. He wasn't supposed to lift anything above fifty pounds and he wasn't supposed to twist, and the way his back felt right now, after doing both, proved his orthopedic doctor was right.

Beside him, Titan whined and moved closer, and Jason put a hand on the big dog. "Lie down," he ordered, but gently. Titan had saved him from a bad fall.

"I didn't realize the two of you knew each other," the secretary said. "Can I get you both some coffee?"

"We're fine," Ashley said, and even though Jason had been about to decline the offer, he looked a question at her. Was she too hostile to even give a man a beverage?

The older woman backed out of the office. The door clicked shut.

Leaving Ashley and Jason alone.

"The website didn't have a picture—" he began.

"You always went by Jason in the family—" she said at the same time.

They both laughed awkwardly.

"You really didn't know it was me who'd be interviewing you?" she asked, her voice skeptical.

"No. Your website's kind of…limited."

If he'd known the job would involve working with his late half brother's wife, he'd never have applied. Too many bad memories, and while he'd been fortunate to come out of the combat zone with fewer mental health issues than some vets, he had to watch his frame of mind, take care about the kind of environment he lived in. That was one reason he'd liked the looks of this job, high in the Colorado Rocky Mountains. He needed to get out of the risky neighborhood where he was living.

Ashley presented a different kind of risk.

Being constantly reminded of his brilliant, successful younger brother, so much more suave and popular and talented than Jason was, at least on the outside…being reminded of the difficulties of his home life after his mom had married Christopher's dad…no. He'd escaped all that, and no way was he going back.

His own feelings for his brother's wife notwithstanding. He'd felt sorry for her, had tried to help, but she'd spurned his help and pushed him away.

Getting involved with her was a mistake he wouldn't make again.

Don't miss
The Veteran's Holiday Home *by Lee Tobin McClain,*
available October 2022
wherever Love Inspired books and ebooks are sold.

LoveInspired.com

LIEXP0822

IF YOU ENJOYED THIS BOOK, DON'T MISS NEW EXTENDED-LENGTH NOVELS FROM LOVE INSPIRED!

In addition to the Love Inspired books you know and love, we're excited to introduce even more uplifting stories in a longer format, with more inspiring fresh starts and page-turning thrills!

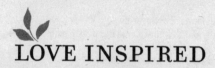

LOVE INSPIRED

Stories to uplift and inspire.

Fall in love with Love Inspired—inspirational and uplifting stories of faith and hope. Find strength and comfort in the bonds of friendship and community. Revel in the warmth of possibility, and the promise of new beginnings.

LOOK FOR THESE LOVE INSPIRED TITLES ONLINE AND IN THE BOOK DEPARTMENT OF YOUR FAVORITE RETAILER!

LITRADE0622